MAKE *it* SWEET

OTHER TITLES BY
KRISTEN CALLIHAN

Dear Enemy

MAKE *it* SWEET

KRISTEN CALLIHAN

Ⓜ Montlake

Published by Montlake, Seattle

www.apub.com

Amazon, the Amazon logo, and Montlake are trademarks of Amazon.com, Inc., or its affiliates.

ISBN-13: 9781542016889
ISBN-10: 1542016886

ne Teagle Johnson

States of America

For the ones who find themselves in need of a little extra comfort and care.

Prologue

Lucian

I was five years old when I told my parents I wanted to fly. My parents, I'd come to learn, would do anything within reason to make me happy. They took my plea at face value and arranged for us to go on a small plane ride.

"Well," my dad asked me as we sat in the back seat of that loud vibrating plane. "How does it feel to fly?"

It was nice and all, but I was just sitting there. The plane was flying, not me. Perplexed, they let the matter drop. But I didn't. I yearned to fly. Deep within my bones, I needed it, though I couldn't say exactly why. Problem was I didn't know how to achieve that goal.

Two years later, my dad signed me up for hockey lessons on a whim. I laced on a pair of skates and learned. I got stronger, better, faster.

That was when I figured it out. It wasn't in the air that I'd be able to fly. It was on the ice.

Ice.

I loved the ice. To me, the ice was a mistress: cruel, cold, beautiful, brutal, essential. I knew her intimately—her crisp scent, her relentless chill, the various sounds she made, the smooth support she provided as I twisted and glided over her body.

I loved her from the first skate. She set me free, gave me purpose.

When I was on the ice, I was flying. Not that floating, disconnected flying, but speed so slick and fast you were no longer flesh and bone but something else: a god.

I loved flying over ice so much I might have taken a different path, become a speed skater, maybe. And sometimes, on off days, I'd go out there and do just that—skate faster and faster around the ice.

But simply skating didn't provide the challenge I needed. Hockey did that.

God, I loved hockey. Every damn thing about it. The clap of my stick against the ice, the resonance of connecting with the puck. The game spoke to me, whispering in my ear even when I was asleep—my body humming, as though I was still on the ice.

I saw the patterns, the plays. I made them happen, coaxed them out. If skating was flying, good hockey was a dance. I had five dance partners. When we all worked together? It was fucking poetry. A true thing of beauty.

There was nothing like taking the puck down the ice, working your way through traffic, and then, with a little flick, sending the biscuit sailing right into the basket. Instant hard-on. Every. Time.

Hockey defined me. Center. Captain. Two-time Stanley Cup winner—the first time as one of the youngest team captains to have his name engraved on that big beautiful monstrosity of a cup. Winner of the Calder, the Art Ross . . . I could go on.

The point being hockey was my life.

And life was damn good. My team was a well-oiled machine, not a chiseler or plug among us to drag everyone down. We were in the playoffs, making another run for the cup. It was ours to win.

The guys knew it. There was something in the air—a crackle of electricity that tickled the skin, got in the joints, and made them twitchy. We'd felt this way before. And we'd won.

Brommy was particularly jovial as we put on our gear. His big hand clamped down on my head and mussed my hair vigorously. "Got a nice head of lettuce growing there, Ozzy. You need some dressing for that?"

In the early days, everyone had called me Ozzy in reference to my last name, Osmond. Then it was shortened to Oz—as in *The Wonderful Wizard of Oz*. As in I got possession of the puck, and magic happened.

I ignored the white lights that flickered before my eyes and the way Brommy's rough treatment of my head made the room swirl—momentarily—and slapped his head in return. "Not all of us style our flow, Goldilocks. But then, you need all the beauty help you can get."

A couple of the guys snorted in good humor. Brommy grinned wide, displaying his grille and the lack of his right lateral incisor. If I'd had a tooth knocked out, I would have had the surgery and gotten that shit fixed. But Brommy liked showing it off. The massive left guard thought it made him look more intimidating.

He also loved to tell women that he'd caught a biscuit in his bracket. The bad idiom made him laugh every time. Women fell for his goofball act, so I wasn't going to argue with his methods.

"We can't all be pretty as you, Cap." He reached for the medal of Saint Sebastian that he wore around his neck, kissed it twice, and then tucked it back under his gear. I couldn't fault him for the ritual; I taped my sticks. Anyone else did it and . . . well, I wasn't willing to let anyone else do it. Or touch them before a game. Not an option.

"Please. Linz is the pretty one." Which was why we called him Ugly. Go figure.

"Linz doesn't have a gorgeous girl promising to love him forever." Brommy nudged me with a grin.

I fought my own. "This is true."

Cassandra, my fiancée, was gorgeous. She loved hockey and had the same taste as I did in everything. We never fought. Being with her was easy. She took care of everything so I didn't have to worry about anything other than playing the game. Her words. But I appreciated them.

3

I hadn't planned on getting married. But Cassandra was so low maintenance that when she asked if we were ever going to make it official, I figured, Why not? It wasn't as though I'd find anyone more easygoing. Cassandra was the cherry on top of my perfect sundae life.

The guys traded more insults. I taped sticks with Jorgen, listened to Mario's pregame anthem of "Under Pressure," and stayed the hell out of the way of our goalie, Hap. You messed with him before a game, and you might as well have dug your own grave.

Mentally, I was ready. Physically, my skills had been honed to perfection. But behind it all was a new whisper, the barest hint of sound that I didn't want to hear. I'd been ignoring that nagging voice since my last concussion. It sounded a lot like my doctor. I hated that guy.

I knew I wasn't supposed to hate the people who wanted only to help me. But I did. Because what the fuck did he know? I knew my body better than anyone. My life was perfect. Nothing, and no one, was going to change that.

So I pushed that insidious little voice back into the shadows, where it belonged.

I'd always been good at pushing away things that didn't matter. *Focus on the prize. Focus on the game.* That was it. *Keep the mind clear and the body strong.*

I kept that focus when the game started. I kept it with every play.

It wasn't until I was on the attack and the puck got caught up in the boards that I heard that voice again. For the first time in my life, I felt true fear. It lit me up. Hyperawareness prickled over my skin. A flicker of time. Barely two seconds between life as I knew it and disaster.

I'd heard that things slowed down in your worst moments. It didn't for me.

One second, I fought for the puck, my shoulder snug against the boards to protect me. The next? The first hit sent me spinning around. The second hit, a defender coming in at full speed—a six-foot-six, 220-pound wall of muscle—slammed into me.

My head banged against the glass. A bomb went off in my head. And that whisper? It was a full-on scream, saying only one thing: *Game over.*

Lights out.

Emma

Life was good. Was I allowed to say that? Sometimes I wasn't sure I should. As though by acknowledging that I was happy and everything I'd ever wanted was slowly falling into place, I might jinx it. But damn it; life *was* good.

After years of struggling to make it as an actress—God, that one desperate commercial role I took as the girl with diarrhea; try mentioning that one in casual date conversation and see how it goes—I'd finally landed a starring role in a hit TV series. *Dark Castle*. Fans were mad for it. And with that role came instant fame.

How fondly I remembered the first cast meeting. Most of us had been fresh-faced nobodies, so eager and excited to be there. Our director, Jess, had looked around, her eyes serious but also holding a glimmer of, well, I didn't want to call it *pride*, because she didn't know us from Adam at that point, but *warm understanding*, maybe, and she warned us.

"Take this time before we air and use it to go out. Do all the things you enjoy. Because after the world sees this show, your lives won't be the same. Privacy will be a thing of the past. Every time you set foot in public, someone will notice."

My costar, Macon Saint, snorted at that. "Good thing I'm a hermit."

The man was utterly gorgeous in a barbaric sort of way—which was likely why he'd been cast as the Warrior King, Arasmus—but the remote coldness in his eyes made me believe him.

Then he'd fallen in love. And the great grump Macon Saint had transformed. He smiled at everyone now and laughed regularly, as though he just couldn't contain his happiness. It was both endearing and annoying.

Annoying because I had no idea what that sort of giddy "I'm over the moon for my partner who gives it to me on the regular, and it is spectacular" kind of relationship felt like. I wanted to know. Believe me; I did. But thus far, it had eluded me.

Jess had been right: our lives changed dramatically. Privacy was fleeting, something I achieved with a bit of preplanning and a bit of luck. I could still go out occasionally, but there was no guarantee that I'd be left alone or someone wouldn't take my picture.

On the flip side, I was adored by fans, and cute kids often asked for my picture, which was a little weird given the content of *Dark Castle*, but I had to assume they were more into the whole Princess Anya aspect of my role than the sex and beheadings.

Not so cute were the creepers who liked to stand a hair too close while asking for a nice selfie. I'd learned to put my hand on shoulders first, effectively positioning the fan far enough away to prevent "accidental" groping.

My life changed in other ways. I met Greg, a superhot and easygoing football player who also happened to adore me—his words. Greg was supportive but didn't hover or complain about my grueling work schedule. His schedule was as bad as mine, with him on the road fairly often during the season. But we made it work.

By the end of my third year on *Dark Castle*, I felt content, comfortable in my role. Princess Anya was incredibly popular. People would always ask either Saint or me when his character, Arasmus, and Anya would marry. We hoped to give them the answer during the season finale. Chances looked good. They'd reached the citadel, and he'd finally proposed.

All that was left was for Anya to accept and for the wedding to happen. The somewhat unnerving thing about working on *Dark Castle* was the fact that the producers and writers hid both the premiere and final episodes from their actors out of some ultraparanoid need for secrecy, despite the fact that we all had signed nondisclosure agreements.

"You ready for this?" Saint asked me as we settled around the table with scripts in hand.

"As I'll ever be, lover boy."

He snorted with good humor. Despite Saint's gruff nature, I truly enjoyed working with him. He was never selfish and never tried to take over a scene. All my costars were great. The work was challenging, but we all rose to it and got along like family. Well, a family that did their best to destroy each other on-screen.

Once everyone was ready, we started to read through our parts. It wasn't until we neared the end that the blood began to drain from my face, and my fingers grew ice cold. Because it was becoming increasingly clear that Anya was about to die.

I sat there, numbly saying my lines, all too aware of my costars' looks of pity, letting the script wind down to the final moment where Anya got her head chopped off with an ax by her and Arasmus's greatest enemy.

But it wasn't until I left the room to sit alone in a trailer that I would no longer occupy next season that it fully hit me. I was out of a job. My happy space was no more. My dream role was gone.

Heartsick and struggling to keep fear of the unknown at bay, I went home. I kept a temporary rental apartment in the small Icelandic town where we filmed. Greg was with me since his season had ended, and training camp had not yet begun.

I looked forward to a long soak in the apartment's tiny sitting tub and then a good snuggle with Greg, who would let me cry on his shoulder and tell me everything was going to be okay.

Only that wasn't meant to be. So lost in my own sorrow was I that the noises from within the apartment didn't truly register until I was practically on top of them. And by *them*, I meant Greg and the young waitress who'd served us dinner two nights ago.

It was a strange thing, really, seeing my boyfriend's naked ass thrusting between widespread thighs. Was that what he looked like when he was on top of me? Because I had to say he appeared rather ridiculous, pumping away like an unhinged bunny. Then again, I'd never liked that particular method of his; I'd rarely orgasmed when pounded like a piece of meat. His partner, however, didn't seem to have that problem. Either she was faking it, or she loved it. But her rather enthusiastic squeaks of delight cut short as she caught sight of me, and all the color drained from her face.

Sadly, it took Greg a bit longer to realize she'd frozen beneath him; Greg always was a bit of a selfish lover. When he finally noticed, he was as smooth as ever, observing me from over his sweaty shoulder without making a move to get off the woman.

Silence fell like a hammer. Or maybe an ax. Why not? An ax could sever more than one thing today. Greg swallowed twice, his gaze darting over me, like he couldn't quite believe I was there. In my own home.

His voice was somewhat shaky when he finally spoke. "You're early."

So many things to say. Scream, maybe? Cry? But I was numb. Completely numb. So I said the only thing I could. "Funny, I think I arrived just in time."

And like that, the carefully constructed life I was so proud of crumbled to dust.

CHAPTER ONE

Lucian

One truth I'd learned in life: the tender care of a woman who loved you was the best refuge when your soul was broken. Of course, I hadn't thought the woman I'd run to would be my grandmother. Yes, she loved me. And yes, her place, Rosemont, was an excellent refuge. But the sad truth was there was nothing left for me anywhere else. My fiancée was gone, my career was gone, and I was broken.

Which meant I was at Rosemont. And, apparently, at my grandmother's beck and call. There was no such thing as privacy when you lived with her. *Meddling* wasn't her middle name, but it should have been.

Her droll, musical voice managed to rise above the sound of my hammering. "They have this wonderful new invention called a *nail gun*, Titou. Or so I'm told."

Suppressing a sigh, I set my hammer down and turned to find her standing at the base of my ladder, hands on wide hips, a fond but slightly reproachful smile on her thin red lips.

"I like my hammer."

A glint lit up her glass-green eyes. "A man should not grow so fond of his tool that he closes out the rest of the world."

I swear to God. This was my life now—having to grit my teeth through sexual quips told by my unrepentant grandmother.

"Did you need something, Mamie?"

Failing to get a rise out of me, she sighed, and her shoulders sagged. She was wearing one of her silk caftans, and when her hands flipped up in annoyance, she looked like a small head stuck atop a fluttering orange-and-blue curtain.

I bit back a grin; otherwise, she'd ferret out why I was smiling and would be in a huff for the rest of the day.

"Do you remember Cynthia Maron?"

"Can't say as I do."

"She is a very dear friend to me. You met her once when you were five."

It was typical Mamie, ever a social butterfly, to have perfect recall of everyone she met. I didn't bother pointing out that not everyone had that talent. "All right."

I also didn't see where she was going with this, but I knew she'd get there eventually.

"Cynthia has a granddaughter. Emma." Mamie tutted under her breath. "Poor dear has had a time of it lately and is in need of relaxation."

"She's coming here, isn't she?" This wasn't my house. Mamie could invite whomever she wanted to visit. But damn it—I'd come here to get away from everything. That included guests.

"But of course," Mamie huffed. "What else would I be talking about?"

It was petty of me to complain.

Rosemont had always been a haven for those who needed it. The massive Spanish revival estate, complete with multiple guesthouses, lay near the base of the Santa Ynez Mountains in Montecito. Bathed in the golden California sunlight, the extensive grounds, redolent with the heady fragrance of roses and fresh lemons, overlooked the Pacific Ocean. To be at Rosemont was to be surrounded by grace and beauty.

For me, it had always been a refuge. A place to heal. Over the years, others, invited by Mamie, found that same healing.

"It was just a question," I muttered, instantly feeling like the angry fourteen-year-old boy I'd been when I first came to live here.

She made another annoyed tut but then waved my churlishness aside with a swat of her hand. "She's arriving today. I thought we could have coffee and cakes at around four."

Instantly, I knew where this was going. But I played ignorant. Partly because dread prickled down my back and partly because it would annoy my grandmother. Ah, the games we played. The realization that it was the only type of game I *could* play anymore sank my mood faster than a stone plummeting into a cold, dark well.

"All right." I stepped down from the ladder. "Do you want me to stop working while you have your party?"

A string of muffled French curses followed before a sharp pinch to my side nearly made me yelp.

Mamie's eyes narrowed to frost-green slits. "Oh, you test me these days, Titou."

I knew I did. Regret thickened in my throat. I was shit to be around. Mamie was the only one who could stand me anymore. I knew all this. That I couldn't seem to pull out of it was the problem. My entire life had *gone to shit*. Most days, it was all I could do not to scream and rage until my voice gave out.

Not talking unless absolutely necessary seemed the best and safest solution.

I couldn't even give my grandmother an apology. It was stuck there, a big-ass lump at the center of my chest.

Again she sighed. She peered at me with those cool-green eyes that were the exact shade of my own. People often said that looking into them was like gazing into a mirror—they were so reflective. Those eyes could cut a person to shreds with one look. The saying wasn't exactly wrong; I felt flayed just now.

Her cool knobby fingers caressed my cheek for a brief moment, and I fought the urge to flinch. I didn't like people touching me now. At all.

Her hand drifted down, and she visibly regrouped. "Now then. I expect you to join us."

"No."

Perfectly plucked brows lifted high. "No?"

I felt all of two years old. And just as damn petulant. Rubbing a hand over my face, I tried again. "I'll only end up accidentally insulting your guest or messing it up in some equally embarrassing way for you."

This wasn't a lie. I'd lost all my ability to charm; it had leaked out of me and never returned. Some days I wondered about that, about how I'd changed so much, so quickly that I no longer felt right in my own skin.

"I believe our guest will be able to handle the likes of you," Mamie said dryly.

Don't fall for it.

"And why is that?"

I fell for it. Damn it.

Her smile was nothing short of smug and victorious. "She is Emma Maron. You know of her, yes?"

Emma Maron. The name danced around my sorely abused brain. I knew that name. But how? Emma . . . an image of wide-set, big doe eyes the color of indigo ink and a plush, pouty mouth filled my mind's eye. Oval face surrounded by white hair with electric-blue tips.

Recognition slammed into me like a blindside hit. Princess Anya. Emma Maron was one of the stars on *Dark Castle*. The delicately beautiful but brutally fierce Princess Anya, who led armies alongside her lover, Arasmus, the Warrior King. Okay, I was a fan. Of the show. In which there were at least four main story lines. Even so, I couldn't believe it took me so long to place her name. Then again, my brain was crap these days.

"You've invited an actress here?"

"I've been told famous people prefer to lick their wounds in a private setting," Mamie deadpanned.

Point to Mamie.

"Why does she need to lick her wounds?" I felt compelled to ask. "She's a star of the most popular cable show running."

"Not anymore, the poor dear. Apparently, she's been cut. Some evil wizard removes her head with an ax at the end of the season."

"No shit?" Frankly, I was shocked. Anya was insanely popular. The season finale had yet to air, but I was guessing there'd be an uproar about it.

"Language, Titou."

"Apologies, Mamie." The woman had a fouler mouth than me when she got pissed off, but she was still my grandmother.

"Hmm." She eyed me for a second. "I said too much. That bit of information is strictly confidential. She could get into trouble if word got out."

"Who would I tell?" I made a gesture toward the estate grounds, devoid of people, that currently encompassed my social life.

"Yes, true. And you see now why this is the perfect place for her. We have total privacy here."

"If she's in need of privacy, then it's even more reason for me to stay out of her way."

The last thing I could handle was interacting with pretty blonde actresses.

"Pish." She waved a hand.

"Mamie," I began, tired now. All the time, so fucking tired. "The answer is no. I'm not socializing. I'll stay out of your hair and lay off the hammering while you're eating, all right?"

We stared each other down. A bee buzzed past, vibrated in my ear. I didn't flinch. Whatever Mamie saw in my expression had her relenting with a soft shake of her head. "Very well. I shall host alone. Although what I could possibly say to entertain a young woman, I'm certain I don't know."

My grandmother was the most colorful and lively person I'd ever met. And that was saying something, given my profession. Pain lanced my heart. My *former* profession.

I leaned down and gave Mamie a kiss on the cheek. "I'm sure you'll think of something."

She hummed—a long, drawn-out sound that said I'd stated the obvious—then gave me one of her imploring looks. "We'll need treats to accompany the coffee . . ."

Mamie could manipulate with the best of them, but she was also transparent as hell about it. My lips twitched. "I'll take care of it."

I put my foot back on the ladder tread, when she made her final attack.

"Oh, and you must pick Emma up at the airport."

And there it was. I knew without a doubt that my meddling grandmother was matchmaking. We both knew. The difference being Mamie actually thought she had a good chance of succeeding. How wrong she was. She could plunk down the most perfect woman in the world, and it wouldn't matter. Not anymore.

"Mamie . . ."

"Her flight gets in at ten—"

"No."

"So you'll need to get going fairly soon."

"Mamie—"

Green fire flashed in her eyes. "Do not try my patience, Lucian. I have already promised Emma that someone would pick her up. You will go."

When my grandmother spoke in that manner, you listened. No exceptions.

"All right, Mamie. I'll go."

I sure as hell didn't miss the glint of satisfaction in her eyes. "Good. She's in Oxnard."

"Oxnard," I all but shouted. "Why the hell didn't she fly into Santa Barbara?"

She gave another one of her Gallic shrugs. "There is some sort of union strike, and the airline diverted flights."

"Great." Oxnard was an hour away, and that was if traffic behaved. Which it never did.

"You are a hero, *mon ange.*"

Yeah. Right. A hero.

I didn't say a word but simply packed up my tools. *Let her think she won.* I'd pick Princess Emma up at the airport. I'd be as polite as I was capable of, and then I'd stay the hell away. And my grandmother would just have to live with the disappointment.

Emma

I noticed the guy in baggage claim immediately. Mainly because he was gorgeous. With swagger. There were different types of gorgeous. The flawless pretty-boy, take-a-picture-and-hang-it-on-your-wall-to-admire gorgeous.

And then there was the rough-and-tumble, oozing-sexual-energy, make-your-knees-weak-and-your-insides-flutter gorgeous—with swagger. This guy had swagger to spare.

Swagger in the loose-hipped, confident stride as he headed my way. I watched him approach, unable to pretend I didn't notice him. How could I not? He was at least six feet four, with wide shoulders, narrow hips, flat abs, and thick thighs. Inky hair that contrasted with olive-toned skin fell in a messy tumble over his forehead.

He was still too far away for me to discern the color of his eyes other than that they were pale and staring back at me from under stern dark brows.

Oh my.

Another wave of attraction swept through me, so strong that I nearly pressed my hand against my belly to brace myself. But I caught it just in time and shook it off. Because no matter how hot the guy was, no matter how very sexy the swagger, any occasion in which someone approached me these days was cause for caution. From the moment I'd decided to major in theater, I'd been chasing fame, needing its protection and power so I could land the roles I'd wanted. Now that I had achieved it, I found myself struggling with its constraints; no longer could I go out on my own without risking uncomfortable encounters with press or a fan who didn't understand personal boundaries. The first times it had happened, I'd been terrified. Now, I was simply guarded.

For a flickering moment, I regretted the lack of a protection detail, which I had been traveling with since *Dark Castle* became a hit, but it was too late to do anything about that now. I was on my own, and he was definitely headed my way.

Maybe he needed directions or something. In which case, he'd be out of luck. Like a thousand other passengers, I wasn't supposed to be here. My flight from Iceland via San Francisco was supposed to land in Santa Barbara. We'd been diverted to Oxnard, and the place was a veritable zoo.

Because of the change in arrival, I'd been told that my driver would pick me up but might be a little late. So I'd tucked myself near a bank of chairs and kept my eyes peeled for someone in a uniform carrying a sign with MARIA written on it. Maria was my code name when I traveled. Not very imaginative, but it did the job.

From behind the safety of my white Jackie O. glasses, I watched Mr. Swagger draw near.

He didn't attempt to charm with a smile or even a pleasant expression. In truth, he appeared slightly annoyed, those severely straight brows knitting together, his firm mouth tight at the corners. It didn't dampen the effect of his hotness. At all, damn it.

If anything, I was in serious danger of tittering like a teen with a crush as he stalked up to me, stopping far enough away to be polite but close enough that I could take in the details.

His hair wasn't black but a dark, rich brown. Blunt features that were strongly carved in the way an old master sculptor would admire. Midway down the high bridge of his nose was a bump, as though his nose had been broken at some point. There wasn't a hint of softness in that face, except for his mouth, which was generous and could have been plush if he ever stopped pressing it in a grim line.

The true showstoppers, however, were his eyes. Oh hell, his eyes. I gaped. I couldn't help it; they were stunning. Deep set under the angry slashes of his brows and framed by long thick lashes, his eyes were an eerie icy green.

When it came to my looks, I had been a late bloomer. In high school, because of my too-big eyes and sharp, thin face, boys had called me *mouse* or *rabbit*. I had hated it and had been uncomfortable with men for a long time. But time and acting had changed everything.

I was around gorgeous, charming men all the time. They went hand in hand with the profession. Attractiveness was simply another commodity. Even so, I had been wide eyed and gawky around men at first. But I'd never felt weak at the knees with just one look. None of them had ever struck me senseless the way this man did with his scowling eyes.

I wasn't even sure my sudden breathless state was attraction or crumbling nerves; it wasn't every day an insanely gorgeous guy with swagger walked up and gave you a look like he'd rather be anywhere else on earth. I frankly had no idea what he was about. I was tempted to glance over my shoulder and make sure there wasn't a camera crew filming this to put on some national let's-fuck-with-the-celebrity show.

There was something oddly familiar about him, as though I'd seen him many times before. But that couldn't be right. I'd remember a guy who looked like this. I'd have made a note of it in my mental diary and underlined it twice.

And then it got so much worse. Because he spoke. And sweet hot cream, the man had a voice. I felt that voice in the back of my throat, behind my knees.

"You're Emma Maron."

I let that rich rubble of a voice roll over me, soaking in the sheer enjoyment of listening to it, before what he said truly registered. He knew who I was.

A fan.

Disappointment tweaked. Fans were definitely out of the potential dating pool. It would be too weird and . . . why the hell was I even thinking of dating? I wasn't here to meet someone. I was here for a relaxing getaway, to read some books, maybe sleep all day, lick my wounds in private. And all this man had done was ask a question.

One that he was waiting for me to answer. Apparently, with little patience, given that he was squinting at me like I was an unfortunate problem to solve. Which made no sense; he'd come up to me.

He shifted his weight, long thick thigh muscles moving beneath well-worn jeans. I pushed down a flush of heat and focused. Maybe the guy was embarrassed. That had to be it.

I gave him my public smile. Polite. Friendly, but not too friendly. "Yes, I'm Emma."

His nod was perfunctory, and he started to pull out his phone. "I—"

Oh hell. He wanted a picture. It happened all the time now, and usually, I was happy to comply. Except I had just gotten off a thirteen-hour flight and was gritty and tired. Even my hair hurt. More importantly, it would attract attention. Attention I couldn't handle on my own if people crowded me. Having lived through that sort of experience once before, I was terrified of it happening again.

"I'm afraid I don't pose for selfies outside of controlled functions," I cut in before his request could make things more awkward. "But I'm happy to sign something if you have a pen?"

My words froze him, his hand still in the act of tugging the phone from his jeans pocket. But then he blinked, a ghost of a bemused smile haunting the corner of his well-shaped lips. "You think I want an autograph?"

Sharp prickles of utter horror exploded along my skin.

"I . . . ah . . ." *Shit.* "No?"

"No." He pulled his phone out and flicked it on. "I'm here to pick you up. For Amalie Osmond." Not quite hiding that tiny smug smile, he handed me the phone. "Just wanted to show you the confirmation email."

Oh, God, please let the ground swallow me up and take me away. "I . . . I'm so sorry. I assumed . . ."

"I gathered as much."

I might have imagined the glint of amusement in those frost-green eyes; the rest of his strong features remained granite. Which served to fluster me even more.

"It's just . . . when people approach me these days, it's usually for the purpose of an autograph or picture."

"I get it." The corners of his lips twitched. Once. "It happens."

I could safely say this particular scenario had never happened. For the first time in years, I felt like the gawky, shy kid I'd been for so long and fought so hard to get past. I had a choice here. Either succumb to embarrassment and retreat or brazen it out and play a little. I sucked it up and forced what I hoped was a breezy smile. "You have no idea."

Oddly, he grunted, as if struggling to refrain from commenting. An awkward pause pulsed between us, then a thought occurred to me, and I stood up straighter. "Wait. You didn't use the right name."

His brows lifted in an imperious way that I was certain had worked to get his way multiple times before. Not today, Mr. Swagger. I returned the look with equal measure.

His brow lowered a fraction, and his mouth definitely twitched. "So . . . you're not Emma Maron?"

Har.

My gaze narrowed. "There is a specific code name my drivers use when picking me up."

Clearly, he didn't like being called *my driver*. But how else was I supposed to explain? Technically, he was my ride. Or maybe not. "It's a simple security procedure."

The hardness around his eyes softened. "You're right. Security is important." His gaze turned inward as he scratched the back of his neck, obviously flustered. "Shit . . . I don't remember any . . . ah! Right." Wintergreen eyes pinned me with a triumphant look. "Maria."

Relief flooded through me. I didn't want this guy to be a potential stalker or killer or whatever. Truth was I didn't want to have to worry about any of those things. Yes, I loved acting and loved that I had made it this far, but there were times—such as every moment I was out in the real world—that I wanted nothing more than to shed that skin and just be plain old me, who no one knew or noticed.

Now that he'd passed my test, he turned his attention to the baggage carousel, the stern scowl firmly back in place. "You have bags?"

"I'm going to assume that was a rhetorical question."

He lifted a brow, that deadpan expression not cracking.

Tough crowd.

"Okay . . ." I exhaled. "Um, I'm sorry, but what is your name?"

Mr. Broody blinked, as though he'd shocked himself by forgetting to give it to me. "It's . . . Lucian."

"Are you sure about that?" Okay, I couldn't help myself. He was so serious; seeing him crack around the edges sent an odd little thrill through me.

Lucian's dark brows snapped together. "You think I don't know what my own name is?"

"You hesitated."

Lucian grunted, setting his big hands on his narrow hips.

"And I don't know . . . you don't look like a Lucian."

"Really."

It was kind of fun needling him. He fell for it so easily.

"Lucian wears white linen and loafers. Offers you a mint julep before selling you an antique chifforobe."

"He sounds like a hoot. Tell me—what should my name be, then?"

"You're more of a Brick. Surly ex–star athlete with a big chip on his shoulder who hides from the world and drinks away his pain."

He blinked again, his head jerking just the slightest bit, as though I'd landed a direct hit.

Then again, maybe I'd imagined that, because he merely gave me another bland look, and that lovely hot-cream voice rolled out in the same insolent drawl. "As much as I'd love to hear more of this *Cat on a Hot Tin Roof* revival you've got planned, Maggie, the bags are coming out."

Flames licked over my cheeks. God, he had my number. When nervous, I tended to fall back on imagining the world as a play or movie. It had been a while since I'd watched the movie version of *Cat on a Hot Tin Roof*, but truly, Lucian had that sullen yet oh-so-hot Paul Newman thing going on. How could a girl be blamed for getting sidetracked?

"Right." Suppressing a sigh, I headed for the carousel, and he fell into step beside me, his steady gait easily matching my more rapid one. Clearly, I wasn't going to outdistance him, so I slowed, my heels clicking on the shiny linoleum.

"Which ones are yours?"

"Oh, I can grab . . ." His steady stare had my words trailing off with a sigh. "The aluminum Fendi ones with the red straps."

Without a word, Lucian—and really, he was far too big and gruff to be a Lucian—turned and began hauling my bags off the conveyor belt. When he set the last of them down, he shot me another look.

"These *all* of your bags?" he said, as though I'd brought a trousseau. There were only four.

"Unless I'm suffering from sudden amnesia, yes, those are all of them."

"Hmm."

Two grunts and a *hmm*. Lovely.

"I like to be prepared," I felt compelled to say.

He gave me a sly, sidelong glance. "Didn't have a pen handy, though."

"A pen?"

"For that autograph I wanted."

Argh.

"If you're going to ask for an autograph, Brick, you should approach with pen in hand."

"I'll keep that in mind."

Well, this was going to be a fun drive.

CHAPTER TWO

Lucian

It figured Emma Maron would be more beautiful in person, more potent. Though her hair was now a honey gold instead of white and blue, I'd recognized her immediately and felt a tug of hot attraction. A year ago, I'd have been laying on the charm from word one, already plotting to woo her into my bed. I would have been pleased as punch that Mamie put her in my path. Well, I would have done all that if I hadn't been engaged back then. The fact that I'd plain forgotten I had been engaged at all was unsettling.

This woman was a walking distraction. I didn't do well with distractions lately. Especially ones with smiles of spun sugar and the confidence of a first-class sniper—God knew her verbal hits had perfect aim. That combination shouldn't have been sexy. But it was.

I felt a twitch along my whole body as I opened the passenger door of my pickup truck and waited for her to get in. For a brief second, she'd paused and glanced at me with those wide indigo-blue eyes, as if she was waiting for me to take her hand and physically help her up into the truck. And the twinges within me became a full-fledged body clench.

I didn't want to touch her. It felt dangerous. Like some awkward boy, I feared physical contact with this woman, as though it might mess with me so badly that I'd spew even more dumbass replies in the face of her bubbly effusiveness.

But then she merely flashed me a quick breathtaking smile and hopped in with surprising ease. I shut the door with a sigh of relief. But it was short lived. The drive was over an hour. An hour stuck in close quarters with the world's favorite barbarian princess.

Not that she looked like she had the strength to hurt a ladybug. Of course, on *Dark Castle* she possessed magic and could melt the faces off poor unfortunate souls. Fiction or not, it made a man tread lightly.

Rolling a crick out of my neck, I got into the truck. And was hit by her scent. Five seconds in the damn vehicle, and the entire thing was imbued with the fragrance of her, rich and sweet, poached pears in crème anglaise. *No, do not think of pastry cream. Or licking it.*

My response to her was unnerving as hell. For a year I hadn't felt a glimmer of sexual need or attraction. Hadn't even missed it—which was cause for concern as well. But I'd been resigned to my apathetic state. As effectively as sticking a plug into a socket, Emma Maron had shocked my system into wakefulness. And I didn't like it.

"So how far is it to the house?" she asked as I started the truck.

Too long. Forever.

"About an hour."

I didn't miss the little wrinkle of alarm that knitted her brow. But she quickly smoothed it out and sat back. We made it all the way outside of the airport before she broke the silence. "This will be fun."

The dry sarcasm had an unfamiliar urge to smile rising up within. I swallowed it down. "Oh, definitely."

"What word did you use before?" Her plush mouth curved on a sly smile. "A *hoot*, was it?"

"A hoot and a holler," I deadpanned, making her laugh. Jesus, her laugh. Husky and easy. A bedroom laugh. I shifted in my seat and concentrated on the road.

But I couldn't stop myself from glancing her way. Mistake.

God, she was gorgeous. Pure and cleanly beautiful. From the rounded crests of her cheeks to the delicate sweep of her jaw, she had the kind of face sculptors memorialized in marble and the rest of us gazed upon for centuries to come.

Of course she was beautiful. She was an actress. Meant to be idolized on the screen. Emma Maron, a.k.a. Princess Anya, future queen and conqueror on *Dark Castle*. The guys and I used to watch the show while traveling between games. Anya was a favorite. Particularly since . . .

I'd seen her breasts. It hit me like a puck to the helmet, and my ears began to ring. I'd seen those perfect creamy handfuls with sweet pink tips that pointed upward, defying gravity and begging to be sucked. I had watched her on her hands and knees, perky tits bouncing as Arasmus slammed into her from behind.

I actually blushed. Me. The guy who'd had dozens of women throw themselves at him every night since high school. I'd had sex so many times and in so many ways it had become a blur. Nothing shamed me or made me uncomfortable. Yet I started to get hot under the collar, my cheeks burning. After nearly a year of being disinterested in all things sexual, my dick decided to make its presence known and start rising. Now, of all times. Now, when I was stuck in a damn truck less than three feet from a woman, I finally got a hard-on. Lovely.

I felt like a damn lecher.

"At least it's a beautiful drive," she said, breaking through heated thoughts of creamy breasts with cotton candy nipples.

"Hmm" was all I was capable of saying.

But she was right. We'd be hugging the coast for a while, and although some people here stopped paying attention to the Pacific, I doubted Emma Maron would. Which was good. She'd concentrate on the scenery, and I'd concentrate on driving. Instead of her. Not that she made it easy. She didn't take my silence as a hint.

"No offense—"

"Which means you're about to offend me," I cut in dryly.

"But you don't seem like the chauffeur type," she finished in an amused tone.

"I thought I was the sullen ex-jock who liked to drink away his pain." Though I was only throwing her earlier observation back at her, something low and uncomfortable twisted in my gut; she'd hit far too close to the bone with that one. I didn't drink. But the rest?

Her gentle huff distracted me. "Well, I hardly imagine good ol' Brick offering to pick anyone up at the airport. Especially if it's an hour away."

She had me there. My hands fisted the wheel a bit tighter. "Amalie is my grandmother."

"Ah." There was a world of understanding in that one syllable. She glanced out the window before speaking. "I've never met her."

"And yet you're here to visit?"

Her smile tipped wryly. "Weird, right?"

"I'm not going to judge."

She snorted at that, but it was without rancor. I flicked a glance her way, and our gazes snagged. We shared a small smile, as if to say we were both full of shit. But then she shrugged.

"I was . . . going through a rough time and called my own grand-mother. She told me of this wonderful estate called Rosemont and the utterly charming friend of hers who owned it." Emma sent me a shy look before forging on. "She said it was the perfect place to hide away and come back to myself."

At that, she hunched her shoulders, as if bracing for my scorn. She wouldn't get that from me. The fact that she'd made herself vulnerable to possible ridicule from a perfect stranger sent a surge of unexpected pro-tectiveness through me, and I gave her something of myself in return.

"My parents were killed in a car accident when I was fourteen." I waved off her immediate words of sympathy. "Amalie became both grandmother and mother to me. Her second husband, Frank, had just bought Rosemont. So that is where we lived during the school year. It's a nice place to . . ."

Heal. Mourn.

I gripped the wheel and took a moment to push away memories of being that lost, angry kid. But it was no use. They came anyway. "I wouldn't go so far as to say it's some sort of magical place . . ." *Sure, that's why you ran to it as soon as you could.* "But it's beautiful and private. And Amalie will most definitely take care of you."

That thought in particular made me both happy and uncomfortable. Emma should have someone looking after her. But why did it have to be here, where I couldn't escape? As it was, I'd talked more to this woman in a few minutes than I had to anyone in months.

Thankfully, Emma just nodded and looked thoughtfully out the window at the mountain range streaking past.

"I've been helping her fix up the property," I felt compelled to say, though why, I had no idea. She didn't need to know. And still my mouth wouldn't shut up. "Mostly the guesthouses. They've been falling into disrepair over the years. Yours has been renovated, though."

Shut up, Oz, you hoser.

"I never doubted it," she murmured.

Blissful silence fell. For about ten seconds.

"So you're a contractor?"

Part of me wanted to laugh. Part of me wanted to howl into the void. This was what I'd become. A man who used to have adoring fans, crowds of them hanging out after a game in hopes of getting an autograph. A man who the hockey world had expected to earn his team another Stanley Cup victory. Now nothing more than some guy working for his grandmother and chauffeuring a famous actress who didn't have a clue who he was.

Not that I'd expected her to be a huge hockey fan. But there wasn't even a glimmer of recognition. I'd had international campaigns for an energy drink, a watch company, sports cars, and health bars. Hell, she presumably lived in Los Angeles at least some of the year. A fifty-foot billboard of me holding my stick while wearing nothing more than tight red boxer briefs and a smile hung over both Sunset *and* Los Feliz.

I thought of that asinine billboard, copies of which dotted cites around the world, remembering how the guys used to comment about Lucky Luc flaunting his sack of jewels, and cringed.

Maybe it was better that she didn't recognize me. Maybe that was why when she'd asked me my name, I'd said Lucian. Aside from my parents, no one called me Lucian. I had always been called Oz or Luc.

At my side, nosy little Emma made a sound, the tiniest of "Hello? Earth to Lucian" prompts, reminding me that I hadn't answered her. Was I a contractor?

"Something like that."

I snapped on the radio. Truth was I had absolutely no desire for her to recognize me. That would lead to questions and the inevitable truth that I could no longer do the one thing I loved most in life.

Stomach like lead, I drove in grim silence. And for once, Emma didn't push for polite chitchat. The Pacific opened up before us in an endless blue expanse. Sunlight sparkled off the water, throwing up glints of gold that flared and shimmered. I reached for my sunglasses and put them on as Emma oohed and aahed.

"Most of the year, I live in LA," she said with a faint smile. "But it never gets old, seeing this ocean."

I'd once thought the same. The pickup snaked along the road, where dusty-brown-and-green-tinged mountains looked like ancient dinosaur feet stepping into the sea. At least that was what I'd said once as a kid to Mamie. The memory did little to ease the tight bands across the back of my neck and over my forehead.

Breathing steadily, I gave her a quick "It's beautiful" and kept driving. Despite the growing headache, I couldn't deny the beauty so affecting Emma Maron. The California coastline was awe inspiring, humbling. The ocean crashed and frothed against the granite cliffs and swirled in eddies around small bits of golden beaches.

Like Emma, I'd come back to California to let the land soak into my battered soul. To find peace. But I didn't feel it. Peace eluded me. The pain in my head increased, digging in with fingers that touched the back of my eyes. And with the pain came the nausea, thick and greasy. Hell and shit-fuck. I hadn't been hit with a migraine for weeks. Why now?

But I knew. The doctor told me I might experience headaches under sudden stress. It was her. Without even trying, she'd yanked me right out of my nice, safe cocoon of numbness, and I didn't want to be woken up.

I cracked the window, refusing to give in to it. Next to me, Emma lightly sang along to Fiona Apple. I doubted she was even aware of doing it, but I didn't mind. Her voice was soft and sweet. A nice distraction.

The sun rose higher, the glare intensifying. My headache swelled with it. A fine sweat broke out over my skin; light reflected off the ocean, and the road merged into one big glittering blur.

A migraine hadn't hit me while driving before. Humiliation warred with common sense. The road wasn't any place to fuck around in the name of male pride. I had to stop. I had to tell her I wasn't fit to drive. I let out a slow breath, preparing to confess to Emma.

But she spoke first. "Do you mind if we pull into that overlook coming up? It's just so beautiful, and I want to take a picture for my Instagram account."

I wasn't about to complain and gave her a short nod that made my weak-ass brain slosh around in the pain soup that had invaded my skull. Lights burst in response. I ground my teeth and tried to breathe through it.

The whole situation pissed me off; I'd skated with torn muscles, split lips, a busted-up nose. I held on to my stick with broken fingers taped up for one-quarter of a season. But I couldn't handle this. This one thing had brought me down.

After turning into the semicircular dirt-and-gravel overlook, I put the truck in park as soon as possible and practically stumbled out. Emma didn't notice, hopping down on light feet and all but racing to the edge.

The sea here was aqua where it met the froth of waves at the shore. A little ways down the coast, surfers bobbed on their boards, waiting for a good wave. Emma tilted her head back and drew in a deep breath of sea-scented air. Sunlight touched the golden strands of her hair and turned her skin the color of a perfect brioche. For a sharp second, I forgot all about my throbbing head. I forgot how to fucking breathe.

She was stunning. She had to be cold in the white sundress she had on; the air was brisk and damp in the wind. But she didn't show it. Instead, she spread her arms wide, as though embracing the world, and the sunlight turned the white cotton of her skirt translucent, revealing the lines of her sweet little body in a silhouette.

I had no business noticing these things, especially not with her. Yet I couldn't seem to help myself; Emma Maron was impossible to ignore. Not just because of her beauty but in the way that she soaked up joy, as though simply breathing was a gift. Maybe it was, but it didn't feel like it at the moment.

With an inward curse, I looked toward the water and followed her lead, sucking down deep breaths and willing the migraine to subside. But it gave me a big "Fuck you" and surged with such force that I swallowed down a gag.

"This is glorious, isn't it?" Emma said.

"Yep."

"I spent months filming in Iceland, which has utterly gorgeous landscapes," Emma babbled in the background of my hell-pain. "Some of them downright eerie, like a moonscape, but I'm still awed by the Pacific. Makes me want to drop to my knees and give thanks or something."

I wanted to drop to my knees too. But not to any ocean god. Maybe the pain gods, if I thought for a moment they'd leave me alone.

I didn't notice her approaching until she was at my side. Even then she was mostly a blur of color and warmly scented skin. But I heard her clearly.

"Listen, Lucian, I wanted to ask you . . ." She stopped, huffing out a half laugh like she was struggling to find the right words. "This is kind of embarrassing . . ."

I'm an expert at embarrassment these days, honey.

My vision cleared enough to find her smiling weakly and wringing her hands—God, please don't let her recognize me now.

"It's just that I'm feeling a tad carsick . . . I get that way after long flights and having to be in a car so soon."

She had to be messing with me. She had to know I was fading fast, and this was her solution. Sharpening my gaze, I looked her over with a critical eye. She was a bit green around the gills, her throat working, as though she couldn't properly swallow.

"You're sick?" was my clever reply.

She went greener, a light sweat breaking out over her smooth skin. "It's stupid . . ."

"It's not stupid. It happens."

The lines of her lovely face grew strained. "I thought pulling over might help, but . . ." She forced her gaze to mine. "Would you mind terribly if I drove for a while?"

Her thin fingers clenched together. God, we were a pair.

Given that I wasn't fit to drive, and she was offering . . .

"Okay," I managed to say. "Sure, if that's what you need."

Her pleased expression did funny things to the center of my chest. "Thank you so much."

31

"Keys are in the ignition," I told her with a weak-ass nod, then headed for the passenger seat.

"Great. Just one second." She walked toward another parked pickup at the edge of the overlook. An old man sat in a battered lawn chair next to the flatbed, selling bottled water out of a cooler.

Emma bought a few, loaded them in her arms, and headed back to me. I might have imagined the pep in her step, because she met my gaze, and it was as if a wave of sickliness washed over her. But she braved it with a deep shaking breath and then handed me the icy bottles.

"I find this helps me too. Help yourself if you're thirsty."

Water *would* help. A lot. I eyed the frosty bottles in my lap and then the woman walking around the front of the truck. Had she done this for me? I couldn't tell. Which was annoying. Unnerving.

Bemused, I opened a bottle for her and one for me, then tucked the rest of the bottles in the big storage compartment between the seats. Emma slid into the driver's seat and promptly went about adjusting everything to her liking.

Was it weird that I found that sexy too? Probably. But I was too wiped out to care. Tipping my seat just enough to release a bit of pressure on my lower back, I grabbed my bottle and drank deeply. And then nearly wept in relief as that cold water washed down my throat.

"You know where to go?" I asked her, even though she obviously knew which direction we were headed, and I could tell her when to turn off.

Her answering tone said as much, but she simply said, "We're headed for Montecito, right?"

"Right."

Emma turned out onto the road with calm efficiency. As soon as we were underway, she opened the windows a little to let in the breeze, then turned on the air conditioner. With a quick glance my way, she explained, "Also helps with nausea, you know?"

Yes, I knew.

I grunted and, under the cover of my sunglasses, closed my eyes. I drank my water and let the fresh air ease me. Emma softly hummed a tune, and it took me a minute to figure out it was "Maria" from *The Sound of Music*.

For some reason it made me want to laugh. Not at her or the song but because it seemed so her. I drank more water instead, as she drove with smooth ease.

"You're a good driver," I found myself saying.

A small smirk played about her lips. "You doubted me?"

"Didn't say that. I figured you had to be at the very least proficient if you asked to drive."

"I could have been deluded," she countered sweetly. "Full of my own self-importance yet dangerously incompetent."

"Met many people like that, have you?"

The corners of her eyes crinkled. "A few."

"Hmm."

She passed a slower car. "Truth is I love driving. Especially on scenic roads. Back in Iceland, a couple of us rented sports cars on our day off and drove in tandem through the countryside." She appeared lost in thought, a melancholy look on her face.

"Princess Anya made that show."

Her jolt of surprise was visible and swift.

Shit.

Then she turned my way with a wide grin. "You watch *Dark Castle*?"

Double shit.

"It's a good show. I watched it . . ." On the road between games. "Sometimes."

Smug was a good look on Emma Maron. Although I was beginning to think every look on Emma was good.

"So you liked Anya, huh?"

Anya. Not her. Anya was a character on a show. A character I'd seen naked and—fucking hell. Double, triple fucking hell.

I pulled my leg up a little higher to hide my thickening cock. But I couldn't stop picturing her naked tits. Damn it. I was the absolute worst letch.

"Liked her better with her head intact," I muttered, earning a lilting laugh from Emma.

"Yeah, me too." She said it with a smile, but it soon faded, and I knew I'd hit a nerve. "I guess Amalie told you."

"I've been sworn to secrecy. Not that I have anyone I could actually tell."

That seemed to appease her. But then her slim shoulders slumped. "It'll be out eventually. In one spectacular finale."

The finale aired in six months. "Did you know? That you were, ah . . ."

"Getting the ax," she supplied with a waggle of her brows.

A chuckle left me. "Yeah, that."

The show was notorious about hiding plot twists not only from their fans but their actors as well.

"No," she said soberly. "Not until I read the script during the read through."

I knew that voice, the bitter pain laced with confusion, as if she was wondering, Did this fuckstorm that happened to me actually happen? I knew it too well.

They killed her off without warning. In front of her peers.

"That's some shit, Em."

She was silent for a beat before answering. "It sure is, Lucian."

CHAPTER THREE

Emma

After months of being in Iceland, driving in California was like stepping into another world. Sun, sea, mountains. Many coastlines had the same features. But even though I lived in California only part of the year, there was something that felt like home about the quality of light here, golden and warm; the endless stream of cars; the surfers bobbing like corks in the water before they caught a wave.

I glanced at the water, and a lump rose in my throat. Being here reminded me that LA waited, and with it, all my fears and doubts. If I didn't find another role soon, I was screwed. Problem was we weren't allowed to tell casting directors Anya was dead. Not until the finale aired. Which left me in a tough spot of pretending all was well. So here I was, supposedly taking a break after a rigorous filming schedule. All part of the plan, according to Dan, my agent, and Carrie, my manager. Let the world think it was life as usual for me.

It was, of course, a lie. Being let go from *Dark Castle* had sent cracks through my fragile world. I had to believe Dan and Carrie when they told me not to worry, that offers for new parts would come pouring in. Only unlike some of my costars, I hadn't been offered any parts in the show's off-season. I'd already begun to worry about being typecast.

Death of a career in Hollywood came swift as the ax that beheaded Anya. If word got out that no one wanted me, then no one would risk offering me anything. It was like some horrible self-fulfilling prophecy of doom.

Hands cold and clammy on the steering wheel, I turned my attention back to driving and the man slumped in the seat next to me. The aviators he wore covered his eyes, but the steady rise and fall of his wide chest made it clear he'd fallen asleep. I stole another glance and smiled a little. Even in sleep his generous mouth was pinched and turned down at the corners, like he didn't want to give in to peace.

My smile faded. Stubbornness aside, there was something heartbreaking about him being unable to fully relax in sleep. Was he in pain? Was that it? I wanted to reach out, smooth my hand over the strong line of his jaw, now shaded with stubble. But he wasn't mine, and I would come off as a creeper.

So I drove. Soon enough, we were veering away from being directly next to the water. The highway became lined with turnoffs, industrial parks, and malls. I knew we were going to Montecito but didn't know the exact location. When we neared an exit, I turned off and pulled into a fast-food restaurant.

Lucian stirred. It was clear by the way he jerked and then sat up straight that he hadn't realized he'd dozed off. I suppressed a smile, knowing he was probably disgruntled by the fact. The poor guy had more than his fair share of pride. Just as clear was the fact that he'd been suffering a migraine earlier.

I knew the signs—the way he'd tried to shade his eyes from the light, the need for air, and the paling of his tanned skin. He'd been suffering but hadn't been able to admit it. I hadn't missed that he'd been suspicious about my sudden car sickness—and for good reason—but I was nothing if not an excellent actress. And if my act got him to rest and allowed me to drive us safely to our destination, then so be it. Not that I thought he'd risk it, but he had been struggling and obviously loathed to confess he couldn't drive.

So then, problem solved.

Now, however, he looked around at the parking lot in confusion. "What's wrong? You hungry?"

That he immediately worried about my comfort was cute. I put the pickup in park. It was a nice vehicle, well kept and clean. Given that he was renovating Amalie's estate, I knew he didn't drive it for show but for utility.

"Nothing's wrong. I thought since we were close to Montecito, I'd let you drive us the rest of the way."

The other thing I knew instinctively? He wouldn't want his grandmother seeing us pull in with me at the wheel. A truth that stretched between us like sticky toffee, pulling and clinging. It made me nervous, and when I was nervous, I talked too much.

"That is if you're feeling . . ." Shit. "Ah, I mean if it's all right with you."

The engine ticked as he stared at me, obviously hearing my slip.

Lucian grimaced but hid it by rubbing his big hand over his face. The rasp of his stubble sounded in the silence. "I'll drive."

But neither of us moved. We continued to stare each other down and then, as if by silent agreement, turned to open our respective doors and exit the truck. I walked around the front of the truck, only to halt when I met Lucian midway.

He was tall enough that he had to dip his chin to meet my gaze. Lord, but he was a big beautiful man. Wintergreen eyes stared at me with such intensity my skin flushed with heat. I couldn't move or think under that stare.

"Were you really carsick?"

That hot-cream voice compelled me to tell the truth. I had to fight against it, and those damn eyes. I blinked up at him, all sweet innocence.

"Lucian, are you accusing me of lying?"

"Yep."

Well then.

His granite expression didn't change, but something glinted in his frosty gaze that told me he wasn't angry so much as wanting to know the truth. Two could play it that way.

"Tell me, Brick. Would you have admitted you had a migraine if I asked?"

Firm lips twitched; the glint grew amused. "Eventually."

"Hmm."

His dark brows winged up at that. "Hmm? That's your answer?"

I shrugged. "Why not? You use it often enough."

The twitching corners of his mouth threatened to bloom into a full-fledged *half* smile. But he got it under control just in time. "Just so we understand each other."

"I guess we do." That should not have filled me with bubbles of anticipation. But it did. With a businesslike nod, I moved to pass him, but he halted me in my tracks by ducking down.

Though his lips didn't touch my ear, I felt them there like a hot stroke to my skin. I nearly shivered when his voice rumbled out in a dark whisper. "Thank you, Emma, for saving me from my masculine pride."

I couldn't have hidden my answering smile if I'd tried; it fell over me like sunshine, warming me from the crests of my cheeks to the tips of my tingling toes. "You're welcome, Lucian."

He grunted—oh, how I loved the way this man grunted—and then took the driver's seat.

We didn't speak as he pulled out, but he turned the radio back on and appeared relaxed behind the wheel. I swore I caught a hint of vanilla emanating from him. Not the cakey sweetness of a scented candle but the dark floral note of true vanilla. I couldn't imagine a guy like Lucian splashing on cologne, but it was so enticing I was tempted to lean in and give him a sniff.

That would go over like a lead balloon. The man was already cagey enough without me sticking my nose in his collar.

"Are we close?" I asked to distract myself.

"Yes." He shot me a sidelong glance. "I apologize for falling asleep."

"I have migraines from time to time. Sleep is the best thing for it."

"Hmm."

"You're going to make me smile every time you hum, you know."

Oh, but he drew so close to a smile just then. "And this is bad why?"

Did he know he was flirting? Did I?

It wasn't smart, regardless. I would be here only for a while, and sleeping with the grandson of Granny Cynthia's best friend was not only idiotic—it was asking for hurt. I didn't do well with casual. And somehow I knew that Lucian wasn't the type to stick. More likely, it would end with him avoiding me and me feeling like a fool.

Lost in thought, I almost missed when we turned off the highway, driving onto an extremely narrow road that wound through the countryside. I was suddenly glad I wasn't driving this leg of the trip. It wouldn't have done us any good if I got us lost while Lucian slept. I caught glimpses of the sparkling blue ocean through the trees. Here and there were rooftops of massive homes hidden behind gates. A lush and sunny Eden.

Lucian pulled up to a pair of wrought iron gates attached to an endless stretch of white stucco walls covered in wisteria and bougainvillea. A wrought iron arch spanned the gates, and the name Rosemont, done in gold letters, graced the middle.

"Welcome to Rosemont," Lucian said without fanfare.

Under the shade of olive trees we drove up to the estate. We were going slow enough that I put down the window and let in the fresh air.

"God, I swear I smell lemons," I said, taking a deep breath.

"You do. The estate has many different citrus trees."

"Lemons remind me of happiness."

"Happiness," Lucian repeated, as though baffled.

"I don't know how else to explain it." I shrugged with a small laugh. "I smell lemons, and I feel happy. Hopeful."

He grunted.

The road opened up to a circular driveway. The main house lay in graceful repose. Part italianate villa, part hacienda, and all California. Climbing red and pink roses undulated over cream stucco and wound around wrought iron railings.

"It's utterly stunning," I said, gaping.

"Yes, it is." For once there was a softness in Lucian's voice, but he didn't look at the house. He parked, then looked at his phone. His mouth pinched as he read. "Mamie had to run an errand, but she'll be back in about an hour."

"Mamie?"

"Amalie. I call her Mamie. My term for *grandmother*."

"That is so sweet."

"You're trying to piss me off, aren't you?"

"It's so easy. At least make me work for it."

Lucian's gaze tangled with mine, and my breath caught, heat simmering low in my belly as I thought about all the ways he could do just that. Maybe he thought the same, because those wintergreen eyes weren't cold in the least. But then he blinked, and any hint of sensual teasing left him.

Without another word, he got out and started unloading my bags. I followed, but he shrugged off any attempt to help him with them. Honestly, it was a little impressive the way he handled four big suitcases without any apparent effort.

"You're in the Cyrano," he said, taking a winding garden path crowded with draping palms, lemon trees, and climbing bougainvillea.

"As in Cyrano de Bergerac?"

"That's the one. Mamie likes to name the guesthouses after notable names in French literature. The Dumas is almost ready. Then I'm working on the Baudelaire."

"Cyrano is one of my favorite characters."

"It only extends to the name. Not the decor." He stopped at a bungalow house that looked like a miniature of the big house. "Don't expect busts of big-nosed men or anything."

"Now I'm highly disappointed."

"You'll live." Lucian led me inside. I loved the arched doorways, cloud-white stucco walls, and dark wooden beams. A set of tall french doors let in the golden California light.

"Bedroom is there." He pointed toward a door off to the side of the cozy living room. "Bathroom is en suite. You'll find towels and fresh linens there. Kitchen is fully stocked. And . . . what else?" Lucian scratched the back of his neck while surveying the little bungalow with a critical eye. "Oh, there's a list of numbers for Amalie and the main house on the dining table."

"It's lovely, Lucian. Thank you."

He grunted. As expected. I fought a smile. The man practically vibrated with the need to retreat. I suspected being stuck with a stranger for over an hour and suffering through a migraine had pushed him to his limit.

I set my purse down on a cute Spanish-style armchair. "Jet lag is getting to me. I think I'll take a nap."

"I'll get out of your hair. Just ring the house if you need anything. Sal will help you if Mamie doesn't answer."

I didn't bother asking who Sal was. Lucian was already backing out of the house like it was on fire. I wanted to smile. "See you later, Lucian."

He blinked, long lashes tangling with the long strands of his mahogany hair. "Have a nice nap, Emma."

With that, he was gone. And the house felt oddly empty.

After helping myself to a glass of lemonade I found in the fridge, I headed to the bedroom and crawled onto the tall, big bed to call my friend Tate.

"You get in safe?" she asked without preamble. I'd cried enough times over the phone for her to be protective and worried about me.

"Yeah. Flight was fine. The estate is beautiful. I'm going to look around in a bit. Drive here was . . . interesting." As soon as I said the words, I wanted to take them back. I didn't want to talk about Lucian, but the imprint of him was on me, as fresh as if he'd actually run his hands over my body, and I couldn't keep it contained.

As feared, Tate's voice perked up. "Interesting how?"

I could lie or prevaricate, but I'd already opened my big mouth about him. "Where to start? I thought my driver was a fan trying to hit me up for a selfie." Over her cackles, I told her the rest, grimacing at the memory. "He's actually Amalie's grandson."

"He's hot, isn't he?"

"I never said that."

"Which is how I know he is."

Wrinkling my nose, I took a sip of lemonade. It was surprisingly good and fresh. "Okay, he is. But he's completely guarded—"

"I don't blame him, Miss No-Pictures."

"You can't see me, but I'm giving you the finger."

"I'm kidding. Hey, it happens. You get in that self-protect mode, and everyone is viewed as a potential threat." Tate was also an actress and starred on a long-running, highly popular cable sitcom. Her tone turned teasing. "Although I've never had it happen with a hot guy I'd be in close proximity to for the entirety of my vacation."

"God. I feel like such a moron. He was clearly torn between wanting to laugh his ass off at me and running out of the airport."

"Take it as a challenge. Once you show him the real you, he'll be unable to resist."

I already had been myself. And I certainly didn't want to make a challenge out of Lucian—or any man.

"Doesn't really matter," I said with forced levity. "Men are not on my vacation to-do list."

"Men should always be on the to-do list, Ems. At the very least, they should be doing you, especially on vacation."

"I have no interest starting something. I'm still recovering from Greg." Just saying his name caused my insides to clench uncomfortably. After I caught him, he'd been on the next plane home to LA. It had taken me a month to wrap things up in Iceland. And then I'd had nowhere to go, because Greg and I shared a house in Los Angeles, and like hell was I going to go back to it while he was there.

I needed to find a new place to live. I needed to get my life back in order. The desire to just hunker down and stay here wasn't at all like me. I usually strode through life, determined to take it by the coattails and make it my own. But from the moment my grandmother told me about Rosemont, I'd grabbed on to the idea like a lifeline, something inside me insisting that was where I needed to be. Maybe it was foolish. But I was here now, and even though my interactions with gruff and far-too-hot Lucian Osmond had me jittery and anticipating our next collision, I felt good.

"Greg was a shit-burger," Tate said, pulling back into the conversation. "But don't write off all men because of it."

"You know me better than that." I frowned and plucked at my sundress. "It's not that. It's . . . this guy"—for reasons I didn't want to examine, I couldn't voice Lucian's name just yet—"all but screams *back off*. I've never met someone with more walls around him." And yet, he had flirted. I hadn't imagined that. He'd flirted, but he didn't like that he had. "And there's no escaping him here. Can you imagine the awkwardness of the day after? No thank you. I'm going to sit back and enjoy my solitude."

"Solitude sucks, Em."

I bit back a smile. "Spoken like an extrovert."

"Says the introvert."

We both chuckled.

"Well then," she said. "Do what you have to do to feel better, and then come back home. I miss you."

"Miss you too."

I hung up with a sad smile. I did miss Tate. But I didn't want to go back home. Truth was I didn't have a home now. It was unsettling, and I snuggled down into the bed, wrapping my arms around that empty ache that took up residence in my chest.

———

Turned out I needed a nap. With the windows cracked to let in the sweet wisteria-scented breeze, and while curled up on a plush bed with silky blankets, I slept without tossing or turning, without care. It was glorious. I woke feeling rested and alert.

After taking a long hot shower and taking time to dry my hair, I walked back to the living room and found an envelope had been pushed through the mail slot.

It was an invite to coffee and cakes at four. On cream vellum paper with actual calligraphy writing. A vibrant rainbow-hued butterfly, edged in raised gold, graced the bottom corner of the note, right beside the signature scrawled with a flourish: **AMALIE**.

It was so wonderfully old world and beautiful. I pinned the note on the small corkboard hanging by the back door in my kitchen and got ready. And then dithered. Did I arrive early? Just on time? Never late—that would be rude.

Twenty minutes to four, I decided to quit stalling and just go. Outside, the air was crisp but not cold. I followed the winding path made from moss-edged slate to the big house. The invitation had instructed me to head toward the north terrace, wherever that was.

When the path turned, I followed it toward a gate that had been left open.

With every step forward, the flutters of anticipation in my belly grew in size and strength. It unnerved me. I met new people every day. As an actress, I was thrust into constant social situations. But I knew that wasn't why my body felt tight and warm or why my heart beat just a little faster. It was him. I wanted to see him again and wondered if I would.

That Lucian of the grunts and *hmm*s had gotten under my skin in less than two hours was more than unnerving. It was downright alarming. Especially since I knew he'd do his best to ignore me like the plague. It was written in every line of his big, beautiful, tense body.

"So get over it. You're an actress. Just play it cool," I muttered under my breath.

"Talking to yourself?" drawled an unfamiliar voice behind me. "You'll fit in just right."

The shock of finding I wasn't alone had my heart lurching into my throat. I spun around to find a tall Hispanic man with an incredible Elvis pompadour smiling at me. There was no malice in the expression. He seemed happily amused.

"Hello there." He held out a perfectly manicured hand. Long red nails glinted in the dappled sunlight. "I'm Salvador. Everyone calls me Sal."

I took his hand and shook it. "Hello, Sal. I'm Emma."

"Oh, I know who you are." He smiled wide. I found myself crushing on his crimson lipstick. "I put the invitation in your mailbox."

"Right. Lucian said I should contact you if I needed anything." Mentioning his name brought forth a fizzy anticipation that needed to be ground down into dust. Then again, wouldn't it be better to know if he lived on the property or just worked here and went home to . . . God, was he married? Involved with someone? He'd flirted, but plenty of asshats who were in relationships did that. No, I wouldn't think about dickhead Greg. Still, there was a lot I didn't know about Lucian. And damn if I didn't want to.

I bit the bottom of my lip, trying to figure out how to ask the questions burning in me without coming off as utterly nosy. "Do you . . . ah . . . I was going to ask . . ." About Lucian, which was none of my business. Chagrined by my nosiness, I filled in the blank with the first thing to come to mind. "What is that fantastic lip color you're wearing?"

With a wink, he nudged me. "Velvet Ribbon. Very hard to come by. However, I have an extra tube, if you're interested."

"You're serious?"

He nodded and extended his arm to gesture toward the open gate. "Of course. We're neighbors for the time being."

When I stepped inside, Sal hooked my elbow with his and led me along. "I live in the big house with Amalie. I'm her assistant and stylist."

Sal spoke of her with a kind of awed respect and deep fondness, and I felt as though I should know who Amalie was, aside from being Granny Cynthia's friend. The only people I knew of who had stylists were either famous or involved with someone famous. I glanced at Sal's impeccably tailored black slacks and gold silk Versace shirt, which I knew cost more than most people's monthly rent. His style was Miami meets Nashville, but it worked for him.

"Amalie has been wanting to meet you for some time," Sal continued.

"I admit I don't know much about her." We passed a fountain with a statue of a naked man holding a trident. "Granny said she was lovely and had just the place to relax for a while."

"Your granny was correct on both counts." Sal guided me through the arched center portico and into a courtyard with another fountain in the center. This one of Aphrodite rising from the waves.

Sal took me down a side path to a wide lawn. Here, the main house spread its wings into two sprawling sections. I gazed around, catching glimpses of the interior through several sets of french doors.

Before the house lay the pool, surrounded by formal gardens that were cleanly trimmed. On the other side of the lawn, a separate path started at the foot of a massive eucalyptus tree and wound upward into the hillside, where there was another bungalow.

"It truly is an estate," I blurted out.

"Rosemont is one of a kind," Sal said. "It's gorgeous, isn't it?"

We both stared at the deep-blue ocean touched with pinpoints of golden sunlight far below. Then Sal exhaled a happy sigh and gestured to a table set up under a large portico that ran the length of the house. The round table and four chairs looked as though they'd been plucked from a society wedding—shimmery-pink tablecloth, a full set of old and grass-green china, crystal glasses, low bouquets of plump blush-colored peonies. There was even a crystal candelabrum.

"Wow."

"We like a little drama with our parties," Sal said.

"This is a party?" No, I was not going to look around for *him*.

"Honey, every meal should be a party—don't you think?"

"Yes, Sal, I do."

"Have a seat. Amalie wanted to greet you but received a phone call from France." Sal gave me a slanted smile. "Relatives. Can't ignore them."

"That's all right." Good Lord, there was a delicate crystal butterfly set at each plate. Tucked in between the wings of one of the butterflies was a little card with my name scrawled upon it. Who was this woman?

The rest of the butterflies were without names, so I took my seat. There were three others open. And no, I was still not going to wonder about *him*.

That's right, Em. Just let it go.

As soon as I sat, Sal fussed over me. "Do you want anything to drink? White wine? Champagne? Club soda?"

"Thank you, but I'll wait for Amalie."

"I'll tell her you're here." In a ripple of gold silk, Sal glided back to the main house.

I was now a ball of twitchy nerves. For years, I'd struggled to make it in the acting world, putting up with a lot of shit that still made my skin crawl, although I'd turned away from things I just couldn't make myself do. Many times, I'd reflect upon my life, and it seemed unreal, made of glass or spun sugar.

My fingers twitched within the folds of my skirt as fear and nerves swirled inside me. I didn't want to think about failure. Or loss. But it was hard, sitting here on this wild and lonely stretch of earth, not to feel like maybe this was my charmed life's last gasp.

"Ah, there you are," exclaimed a husky but very feminine voice.

A statuesque brunette woman who could be anywhere from age fifty to seventy strode toward me with a wide smile on her vividly pink lips. Dressed in a bubblegum-pink silk pantsuit and silver rhinestone slippers, which should have looked ridiculous but somehow came off as retro chic, she was stunningly beautiful. And her eyes were the exact shade of Lucian's. But whereas his were mostly cold and standoffish, hers sparkled with sly cunning and wry humor.

I liked her instantly. "Hello."

I stood to greet her, and she enveloped me in a warm hug and a cloud of Chanel N°5 before kissing me on each cheek.

"It is so very good to meet you, my dear." She stepped back, holding on to my wrists, and surveyed me with bright eyes. "You look like your grandmother."

"So I've been told. Thank you, Mrs. Osmond, for letting me stay here."

"Call me Amalie. And you are very welcome." She gestured to our seats and then took one. "In truth, you are doing me a favor as well. This house needs a breath of fresh air. Sal and I were becoming quite bored."

No mention of Lucian. But I wouldn't—couldn't—ask. This was his grandmother. And something told me if I showed the slightest interest in his whereabouts, she'd be all over that—either to warn me off him or matchmake.

"This place is utterly gorgeous," I told her.

"Isn't it?" She looked around with a happy sigh. "It belonged to my second husband, Frank. Venture capitalist. Which meant a lot of money but far too much stress. Poor dear's heart gave out on him three years ago."

"I'm sorry."

"I am too. He was a nice man. Not the love of my life but a good companion."

I tried to think about marrying someone only for companionship and was horrified to realize I'd been living with a man who I tolerated as a person but whose looks were what attracted me the most. At least Amalie had settled for someone she liked. I'd been taken in by a handsome face and a similarly famous background. I had become *that* person. And I didn't like it.

Never again. I wasn't going to fall for a man just because I admired the way his ass filled out his jeans. There had to be more. A connection past the physical. Which definitely meant not lusting over a pair of jade-green eyes under stern brows.

Amalie gazed out over the extensive ground. "It's really too much property for one woman. Ridiculous, really. But there's something about Rosemont that sinks into one's bones and soothes the heart. Besides, there is plenty of room for guests." She laughed at the obvious understatement, and I smiled.

"So, my dear"—she placed her cool hand on top of mine—"you stay for as long as you wish. Let yourself heal."

The kindness sent an unexpected wave of emotion rolling over me, and I found myself blinking rapidly. "You shouldn't tempt me like that. What if I never left?" Because right then and there, I wanted to stay forever. Hide away like a child.

She smiled, wide and knowing. "Something tells me you never stay knocked down for long."

Before I could answer, Sal came out of the house, rolling a food cart laden with silver-domed trays and coffee service. I jumped up to help him, and he tried to shoo me off. "I'm fine."

"Yes, but let me help anyway," I said.

He shot a grin at Amalie. "Don't you love her already, Ama?"

Amalie's eyes, so unnervingly like Lucian's, beamed. "Yes, I believe I do."

Heat rushed to my cheeks. I didn't do well with compliments, which was unfortunate given that people loved to fawn over famous actresses. Not that Amalie and Sal were fawning. They genuinely seemed pleased to meet the real me. But insecurities were hard to shake.

"I could end up being a screeching harpy," I felt compelled to say.

Amalie laughed. "Goodness, but I hope you show a bit of temper now and then. I suspect you might need it soon enough."

With that, she took a phone with a brilliant rhinestone-covered case and tapped out a message before slipping it back into her pocket. "Now then, where were we?"

Amalie seemed entirely too pleased with herself. I didn't have to wonder why; a few moments later, her grumpy grandson strode around the corner with a harried expression, as if called to an emergency. When he saw his grandmother sitting with a pleasant smile, his steps slowed, and those wintergreen eyes narrowed in annoyance. And I knew he'd been tricked somehow.

But he didn't turn on his heel and leave. He visibly braced himself and strode forward, the glint in his eyes promising retribution.

CHAPTER FOUR

Lucian

I knew better. I really did. When Mamie texted that she needed me and to hurry, I did just that, dropping the project I was in the middle of and coming to her aid. I knew it was time for her to have coffee and cakes with Emma. But all I could think was what if Emma had gotten hurt, tripped, or—fuck—fell off the side of the hill.

Ridiculous. I was such a sucker.

All made apparent when I practically ran onto the terrace and found my grandmother, Sal, and Emma sitting in obvious safety and contentment. Emma glanced at me and then away, as if embarrassed. She probably was—for me. Because it was clear to everyone there that my sly grandmother had tricked me.

There was the rub; I could make it obvious, turn back around, and leave, but it would send a message to Emma that I didn't want to be anywhere near her. And I just couldn't do that. I could try to avoid her, but I couldn't be rude.

It felt downright painful to approach the table. The woman had somehow flipped a switch in my body, making me aware of every inch of her. She breathed, and I noticed, damn it.

"Mamie," I said to my wily grandmother. "You texted."

She was without repentance. "Ah, yes. It is time for coffee. Have a seat."

My back teeth met with a click, the joints of my jaw aching as I bit back my annoyance and took the empty seat across from Emma; Mamie was crafty enough not to put me next to her, where I could pretend she wasn't there, but right where I could see her. And fucking *want*.

For her part, Emma's gaze darted around, as if assessing the scene and figuring out how to act accordingly. I didn't blame her; it was always awkward to be pulled into someone else's meddling schemes.

My grandmother was evil. I'd always known this. Hell, it used to amuse me when she turned those evil powers on others, which was probably why I was suffering through this coffee time from hell right now. Karma. It was a bitch.

I glanced at the path that would take me away from here. Not much chance of that now.

Mamie turned her eagle eyes on me. "Titou, your cup."

Suppressing a sigh, I handed her the fragile china coffee cup that was too small for my hand and would shatter with one wrong move.

Indigo-blue eyes settled on me, golden arched brows rising delicately. "Titou? Is that your nickname? You don't look like a Titou."

Sal snickered, choking on a mouthful of coffee, and Emma—damn it, even her name was cute—grimaced, as if it just occurred to her that maybe she'd been rude.

Mamie trilled out a kind and gentle laugh. "In a roundabout way, it means *little boy*."

Emma's eyes widened as her gaze flicked to my body. A flame ignited in my chest. I ignored it. But I couldn't ignore the slight husk in her voice. "*Little* boy?"

Hell.

Mamie smiled indulgently. "Well, he was little at the time."

"Must have been when he was two," Sal said sotto voce.

I cut him a glare, and he winked at me before blowing a kiss.

"Two?" Mamie shook her head before sipping her coffee. "*Non.* My Titou was small for quite some time. It wasn't until he started playing—" She cut herself off so quickly she nearly choked, her papery skin going pale.

Inside me, everything clenched and rolled. I was almost used to the sensation, it happened so often now. *Almost* didn't make it remotely better.

A small wrinkle pulled between Emma's brows, as she caught on that something was off.

But Mamie rallied quickly and pulled a wide, tight smile. "Playing, running, and so on must have given him an appetite for growing. And speaking of appetites, let us eat. Emma, darling, you simply must try one of these."

Mamie liked a wide selection of treats, so there were assorted macarons, a plate of butter cookies half dipped in bittersweet ganache, candied-orange-and-cardamom cakes, and, my personal favorite, a paris-brest with praline cream and raspberries.

Emma hesitated, looking at various trays dotted over the table. Her eyes glazed over, rosebud lips parting with a soft exhalation. Yearning and lust all rolled up into one. Like that, I was turned on.

Jesus. Would this coffee ever end?

"Oh, I don't . . ." Emma stalled, clearly at war with the desire for sweets. I got it. During the season and in training, we were hounded about what we put into our bodies. Fitness was everything, and trainers had particular ideas about how to achieve it. I was under no illusions: Hollywood had a shitty and exacting standard, especially for women.

Mamie put her hand on Emma's slim wrist. "I used to be a model; did you know this?"

"Really?" Emma shook her head slightly. "I'm not surprised. You're beautiful."

Mamie always had been and was not the least bit humble about it, but she was good at acting the part. "How sweet you are."

"Only stating a fact."

From one stunning woman to another, I supposed.

"This was in the sixties and seventies." Mamie selected a cardamom cake and gently placed it on the center of her plate like it was art. "Everyone had to be as thin as a stick. One was expected to live off water and cigarettes," Mamie said with some asperity, but there was a teasing note as well.

Exaggeration was part of her lexicon. It threw some people off because they never knew when she was being serious. Those people never got a second invite.

Emma, however, grinned. "I haven't tried the cigarette diet. I'm not certain my lungs could take it."

"Most certainly not. Keep them pink and healthy, darling."

"I'll try."

I didn't want to think about anything pink or healthy on Emma. With a grunt, I reached for a vanilla-cherry macaron. Emma noticed— seemed she was as aware of me as I was of her—and then looked quickly away. Like me, she was trying to ignore the problem. Somehow, that only made it worse.

"But what is life without food?" Mamie continued with a shrug. "Not one I want to live in. So . . ." She slapped her hand down on the table. "This is what you do. Pick one thing to try, and you savor it. Eat your treat slowly, letting the flavors play over your tongue. And tomorrow?" Her shrug was insouciant. "If you feel you absolutely must do something, go for an extralong run up the hill. Or perhaps simply imagine doing it, and go on about your day, which is what I would do."

Emma laughed. And every hair on my body lifted. Jesus, her laugh got to me every time I heard it. A bedroom laugh. The kind you expected to hear after a good long morning of lazy fucking, when everything was languid and warm, and you laughed for the simple fun of it.

I swallowed down a mouthful of macaron, and it nearly got stuck. I didn't know why that particular analogy came to mind; I certainly never had mornings like that. I never relaxed enough with anyone to get there.

But the image remained. I saw her in the sunlight, golden hair spread over my rumpled pillow, her lips swollen and soft. Rubbing a hand over my face, I tried to get it together. I was *not* doing this. Sal's gaze clashed with mine, and he looked about two seconds away from laughing his ass off. Yep. He knew exactly how badly I was affected.

"Imagine it, huh?" Emma said, still smiling.

I knew she was talking about exercising, but my randy newfound sex drive heard it differently and kept on imagining us in bed. *Hell.*

Mamie shrugged again. "As with life, food is meant to be enjoyed. Never go to war with it, for we rarely win."

Emma's smile held the brilliance of the sun.

I turned away and focused on Mamie. She was encouraging Emma to pick a pastry. For the first time in, well, ever, a tangle of nerves besieged my gut. I'd had people eat my food for years. I didn't care one way or another what they thought of it. Baking and cooking were hobbies I did for myself—no one else. And yet here I was, wanting to impress this woman with what I had made.

Emma bit the inside of her cheek, pulling a little dimple in. She might as well have been a kid with that excited expression. "Mmm. I don't know. They all look so good." She tore her gaze away from the treats and looked around at the rest of us. "What do you suggest?"

Sal started in on the cookies. Mamie began to offer cake.

"The brest." It came out of my mouth in a growled command. Shit.

Emma's eyes widened. "I'm sorry? Breasts?"

Sal snickered.

Shifting in my seat, I fought the urge to get up and flee.

Do not, under any circumstances, think of her bare breasts, asshole. Yeah, too late.

"The paris-brest." With a jerk of my head, I nodded toward the pastry shaped like a wheel. "It's a dessert named in honor of a bicycle race at the turn of the nineteenth century."

"Ah." She flushed pink. It was cute. "Right. The *brest*."

"It is most delicious," Mamie said, doing an excellent job of hiding her amusement. "A pâte à choux pastry—you know, like you have in an éclair. Filled with praline cream and topped with fresh raspberries."

"Oh, yes please."

Before Mamie could reach for the serving knife, I did. I couldn't help my-damn-self. If Emma was going to eat something I'd created, I was going to serve her.

Even if watching her eat would eventually kill me.

She gripped the sides of the table, as though trying to hold back from prematurely reaching for her plate. Greedy girl.

My dick approved. Far too much.

Calmly as I could, I served her a slice, adding some raspberries, and then served Sal so I'd have something to do with my hands. They felt too big and unwieldy as it was, made clumsy by a five-foot-six slip of a woman.

All my efforts to ignore Emma were a sham. The second she lifted the spoon, I sucked in a breath, watching her pink lips part, and caught a glimpse of her tongue. The whipped-cream confection slipped into her mouth, and she moaned.

The sound coiled around my cock, palmed my balls with hot hands. I nearly moaned too. I knew the taste in her mouth, how smooth that cream was on her tongue. That was my cream. I made it. My hands gave her that pleasure, whether she knew it or not. Her moans were because of me.

The rush of it washed over me, and I was a little dizzy.

She slid another dollop in her mouth. Slowly. Savoring it. Her lids dipped down. Lashes fluttered as she sighed.

Sweet holy hell.

Silence fell over the table, and Emma stopped, looking around self-consciously. She licked away a lingering golden pastry crumb from the corner of her mouth—she was definitely going to kill me. "Sorry. It's just really good."

Satisfaction washed over me, as clean and cool as fresh ice. I wanted to take that spoon from her hand and feed her myself. Make her moan again and again. Shit.

Grunting, I helped myself to a cardamom cake. If I ate a piece of the brest now, I'd probably come in my pants.

"Where did you buy these?" Emma asked Mamie.

"Oh, I didn't buy these," Mamie said. "They're homemade."

"Really?" Emma popped a raspberry into her mouth. "You're a wonderful baker."

I shot Mamie a quick warning look, so she merely sipped her coffee and hummed vaguely. Yeah, I was a chickenshit for not wanting Emma to know she was eating my food. But there it was; I'd become . . . shy about it.

Sal watched us the whole time, obviously finding my discomfort funny as hell. But instead of pushing me under the bus, he threw me a lifeline—probably because he lived on the grounds and didn't want to have to sleep with one eye open.

"Mamie is multitalented." He set his empty coffee cup down and reached for a champagne flute. "She's the one who first taught me how to sew."

"This is true," Mamie said. "He was this cute little boy who used to find his way into my dressing room to play with my gowns while his father was here for work."

"Papi is Amalie's business manager," Sal explained.

"One day," Mamie said, "Salvador accidentally ripped a Halston."

"Ugh," wailed Sal, covering his face with his hands. "It was a vintage gold lamé evening gown."

I had no idea what that was, but I guessed by Emma's expression of pained sympathy she did.

Mamie laughed fondly. "He was so upset about it I taught him how to mend the tear."

"Never looked back." Sal grinned. "She gave me the Halston for my sixteenth birthday."

Emma rested her chin on her hand. "And did you wear it?"

"Sadly, I wasn't quite ready to brave that. By the time I was, I couldn't get the damn thing past my thighs. It's still hanging in my closet, though. You'll have to pry it from my cold, dead hands."

Emma laughed again. And I stuffed another macaron in my mouth. I'd probably leave the table with a food headache, but it was either cram my face with sweets or stare at Emma like a moony-eyed fool.

"I was happy to have someone with whom to share my love of fashion," Mamie said. "Alas, my Titou was not interested."

"How would you know, Mamie?" I took another macaron. "You never offered."

"Well, now I just might." She slapped my arm playfully.

The corner of my mouth curled. "Too late. I am offended and no longer interested."

"Petulant boy." Mamie chuckled before wrinkling her nose at me.

Emma watched us with keen eyes. "You two are very close," she said when our gazes snagged.

"Even before my parents passed, we were close."

If Mamie was surprised I'd told Emma about my parents, she didn't show it but gave me a fond, misty-eyed look of affection. I might have softened over that look. But then I remembered her meddling. I shot Mamie a sidelong glance. "She used to read me bedtime stories when I was little."

Mamie became very interested in the clunky cocktail rings on her fingers. Had she honestly thought I'd forget her little ruse to get me here?

I turned my attention back to Emma. "My favorite was *The Boy Who Cried Wolf*."

Emma's lips twitched, a light entering her eyes, and I found myself responding to it as though that lightness spilled into my chest, expanding the hollow cavern. I fought a smile, fought it hard, because all I wanted to do was grin wide and laugh with her.

"Scared me straight," I said blandly. "Never misled another poor soul again."

"Oh, all right," Mamie snapped with humor. "Consider me chastised. Now, shut up and eat your cake. There's a good boy, eh?"

A chuckle escaped me before I could rein it in. But it felt good. It felt better when I caught sight of Emma, her lips parting as if in wonder, blue eyes sparkling. And then she smiled at me, as if I'd made her day simply by laughing.

The smile speared me, dead center, and for a second, I didn't know how to breathe. The only other time I'd felt this way was while flying over the ice, weaving through defenders, and, with a sweet little flick of the wrist, sending the biscuit into the basket.

Grief and loss crashed into me, cold and dark. It knocked the laughter right out of me, and I found myself lurching to my feet, rattling the dishes in my haste. Blood rushed in my ears; my throat was sore and tight. My voice sounded as from a great distance when I mumbled a lame "Excuse me. I need to get to work."

And then I got the hell out of there, knowing they were all staring, knowing I'd made a fool out of myself. I just couldn't find the strength to care at the moment. One thing was certain; I needed to stay far away from Emma Maron.

———

Mamie hunted me down an hour later. It wasn't hard to find me; I was in the kitchen. With hockey out of my life, the kitchen had become my refuge, the one area that still felt familiar and pure. Here, I was in total control. Here, I was still king.

I didn't look up from my task of reaming a Meyer lemon. There was a certain satisfaction to be had in annihilating fruit.

"What are you making?" she asked, coming up alongside the long marble countertop. Given that Mamie's father, my great-grandfather, had trained me, she knew exactly how much baking meant to me and how much I had needed to get back to it. The day I'd arrived back at Rosemont, beaten and defeated, she'd all but shoved me into the kitchen and told me to get to work. I'd been cooking for her and Sal ever since.

"Tarte au citron."

Mamie glanced at the twelve small tart pans I had prepped. "Petite tartlets. Delicious."

I grunted. I'd make the tarts and then start on the dough I planned to proof overnight in the fridge. I'd been experimenting with breakfast rolls, and the method seemed to work well. Then again, dough was a fickle mistress. What worked one day might not work another.

Even so, I would prefer to work with dough right now, take some of this . . . energy out on it. But the tarts . . . well, they had to be done.

"I apologize for leaving so abruptly." It hurt to say, but some things always did.

Mamie tutted lightly and without censure. "I understand. Though perhaps our guest might not."

Our guest. My gut flipped uncomfortably. I was six feet four and 220 pounds of bone and muscle. Men feared facing off with me. And yet I'd run away from a five-foot-six woman I could lift with one arm like my ass was on fire.

What must she think of me? I grabbed another lemon, sliced it open, and crushed it over the sieve with my bare hand. Bright, fresh citrus invaded my senses. She liked the scent of lemons. Said they reminded her of happiness.

The kitchen was warm with the heat from the ovens, where I was baking baguettes. On the stove, tonight's dinner simmered away, releasing the fragrant mix of wine-roasted vegetables and thyme. Ordinarily, I found pleasure in these things, but not today.

"You think I ought to apologize to her; is that it?" I ground out.

Mamie stared at me for a long moment, then sighed. "Only if you want to. Insincere apologies are worthless."

"I'll do it," I said, concentrating on my lemons. "But I don't want to."

She laughed and set her cool hand on my arm. "Ah, Titou, your blunt honesty is a beautiful thing. Never change."

"Hmm."

"Leave it be for now. Perhaps later . . ."

"Mamie." I set the lemon down and turned her way. "You need to quit with the matchmaking."

"Matchmaking?"

I gave her a long look. "I mean it. I'm not ready for a relationship."

The thought of opening myself up to anyone, much less someone who might own my heart and therefore crush it, turned my stomach.

Fact was I'd kept away from women since Cassandra had waltzed out less than a month after I'd quit the game. She'd made it crystal clear that my position on the ice was what she valued. Then again, I'd been in such a dark place at the time—I had to take some blame as well; I wasn't exactly easy to be around anymore. I'd been bitter when she left, but I didn't miss her, which was fairly telling. I'd become *that* person, shallowly wanting someone for how easy they made my life, not for who they were on the inside.

"Who said anything about a relationship?" Mamie countered, as though that wasn't exactly what she'd been scheming. "I simply think you could use some companionship your own age."

"Sal is my age," I pointed out just to annoy her.

"And if you actually spent any time with him, maybe I wouldn't worry so much."

"We spend enough time together. He tells me what he wants to eat, and I tell him not to leave his shoes by the pool." The amount of times I'd tripped over his fucking purple clogs . . . I was liable to chuck one at his head if it happened again.

"Oh, yes, highly in-depth conversation right there." She scoffed, then wiped at the counter, as though trying to clean it; my workspace was *immaculate*. "Emma is different."

No kidding.

"Perhaps you can relate to her."

"Relate to her?"

"Yes, relate." Mamie huffed. "She, too, has lost her way a bit."

"Mamie . . ." I rubbed my face with a tired hand. "I haven't lost my way a *bit*. I'm . . ." Broken. My throat closed up, and I grabbed a carton of eggs and a bowl. "I'm not the man I used to be. He's just . . . gone. And what's in his place isn't anything a woman with a lick of sense would want."

The egg tapped against the side of the bowl, and I cracked it open with care, concentrating on separating the pale whites from the deeply golden yolk. "Headaches, frustration, rage, apathy. I try to control these things, but they're there all the same. Don't push her in my direction. She deserves better than anything I could ever offer, Mamie."

I didn't see my grandmother move, but suddenly her frail arms wrapped around my waist, and she hugged me from behind, resting her head on my back. "Titou. Mon ange."

I closed my eyes, feeling horrifyingly close to crying. I did *not* cry. I hadn't even when they told me that was it for hockey. But I had to make her see. "I lost everything that meant anything to me."

Mamie gave me a surprisingly strong and fierce squeeze. "You are *here*. Alive." She drew back and glared at me with angry eyes. "It might feel like nothing right now. But you are alive. And that is all that matters."

That was the rub. I could have stayed in the sport I loved with my whole heart. And risked dying. I chose life, but it didn't feel that way. Training camp began in a few weeks. That knowledge sat like a black hole in my chest.

I blew out a breath and cracked open another egg. "I'm here," I agreed. "And that's going to have to be enough for now."

She hummed, the sound uncomfortably similar to my own non-committal noises. "I won't push you anymore, Titou. Only keep in mind that there is a young woman here who is alone and uncertain about life too."

As if I could forget.

Chapter Five

Emma

After Lucian's abrupt departure—make that after he up and fled the table—I'd spent the rest of the time making awkward conversation with Amalie and Sal.

Neither of them had made excuses for Lucian, and I hadn't expected them to. Obviously there was something personal going on with him. It wasn't my place to fix it—or him. But that didn't stop me from wanting to know him. Which was disturbing.

I took a long walk on the trails that wove through the gardens facing the sea. By the time I finished, the sun was sinking in a liquid ball of fire behind an indigo sea. I watched it set, arms wrapped around myself for warmth, then headed back to my house.

I had told Amalie that I planned to stay in for dinner, and when I returned, I found a casserole dish on my stove with a bottle of red wine and a crusty baguette accompanying it. The casserole turned out to be a meltingly good coq au vin that I savored in front of the fire while dipping chunks of bread into the rich, dark sauce and sipping luscious cabernet.

One thing was certain. I was going to be spoiled with food here. I almost missed the little white box in my fridge, noticing it only when I went to put away my leftovers. Curious, I pulled the box out and untied the red ribbon holding it closed.

Inside was a golden-yellow tart, its custard so smooth and glossy it shone in the kitchen light like a little sun. A tiny whipped-cream heart sat in the center of the tart with a single rosemary leaf spearing the delicate center.

Delighted, I took the tart out and set it on a plate. It was almost too pretty to eat, and my diet certainly didn't need more sweets in it, but I remembered the rich caramel-and-cream delight of the afternoon's treats and couldn't resist.

The custard cleanly parted for my spoon, the crust crumbling just a little. Closing my eyes, I pushed the spoon past my lips and groaned. Tart-sweet lemon, bright as the dawn, played with delicate cream and a butter-rich crust. Perfectly balanced, it slid over my tongue like a kiss, played along the sides in an elusive tease, prompting me to take another bite.

I lovered over the countertop, I ate that tart with my eyes closed, bite after luscious bite. Letting it fill my senses.

It wasn't normal, getting emotional about dessert, but I found myself tearing up. It tasted oddly like hope, that tart. Like maybe every-thing would be okay if things like this existed in the world.

Someone put all their skill and care into something that wasn't meant to last but was to be enjoyed in the moment. In return, I felt cared for too.

My spoon hit the empty plate, and I opened my eyes with a whim-per. I refused to lick the plate. But then caved and swiped my finger across it to catch a last bit of custard. Sucking on my finger, I put the plate in the sink, then grabbed the thick wrap sweater I'd left on the chair.

I needed air after a treat like that. Still emotional but also content, I stepped out onto the balcony that jutted out from my bedroom. From my vantage point, I could clearly see the pool directly below.

With the pool lights on, it glowed a deep turquoise in the darkness. Wisps of steam rising from the water made it clear the pool was heated, and I thought briefly about going down for a swim. But I was too sated to move.

The view was enchanting. Lanterns marked the paths winding through the gardens. Édith Piaf drifted out, mournful and bittersweet, into the balmy night. Resting my arms on the balcony rail, I listened to "La Vie en Rose," and it almost felt as though I was in a classic movie. I could see the screenplay now:

EXT. OLD CALIFORNIA ESTATE—NIGHT
Young woman stares wistfully out into the night. A sweater hangs around her shoulders, warding off the chill.

I was so caught up in the fantasy I almost missed the movement in the shadows by the pool. A man stepped into the light and stared at the water. Dressed in jeans and a long-sleeved shirt of some dark color, he had his back to me. But I recognized his height and the breadth of those strong shoulders instantly. Lucian.

He set down a toolbox by the pool ladder and took out a screwdriver to tighten the bolts around the base. With that done, he set the toolbox aside and stood to stretch his muscles before lowering his arms.

While I stared at him, *he* stared at the water, as though it might give him an answer. To what, I had no idea, but a trickle of concern crept along my back. Because he seemed lost. I could be entirely wrong about that, but it was part of my craft to study body language. His was fairly screaming defeat.

Standing a bit straighter, I wondered if I should call out to him. But what to say? I hadn't a clue. *I should leave him to his privacy.* I was about to do just that.

Then he moved.

All thought flew from my mind when he pulled the shirt from over his head, revealing the elegant sweep of his back, the hard-packed muscles rippling under smooth skin. Arms, chiseled like a god's, reached down and . . .

"Oh, sweet baby Jesus," I murmured fervently.

He pushed his jeans off and bared an ass that was, frankly, spectacular. Those tight globes flexed as he kicked the jeans away with one long leg.

Turn away. Get out of here.

I shouldn't look. I coveted my privacy, and I was blatantly watching Lucian strip naked. He deserved his privacy too. But I couldn't blink. I couldn't move. He was . . . glorious. My fingers gripped the railing, holding on tight.

The light of the pool gave his skin an unworldly greenish cast. He rolled his shoulders . . . *unf* . . . and then dove in. The water rippled outward in his wake. I actually shivered with lust as I tracked him along the bottom of the pool, a pale arrow of flesh darting through the turquoise glow.

Silently, he surfaced on the far side of the pool, then neatly turned to do laps. Perfect form. Long strong arms. Clean, steady strokes.

Édith Piaf kept singing as Lucian set a steady but brutal pace. He went at it lap after lap. I grew fairly dizzy with rude thoughts about his stamina. The night was cool, but my flesh was hot. God, that water looked so good. I could practically feel it running over my fevered skin.

My heart thudded against my ribs in time to the beat of his arms slicing through the water with a chuff, chuff, chuff. I didn't blink. I fooled myself into thinking I had to keep watching over him. Make sure he was okay.

The thinnest of excuses. But there was something about the way he attacked the water, the way his body moved, that could not be ignored.

"Non, Je Ne Regrette Rien" began to play when he finally stopped, resting his arms at the closer end of the pool. He floated there, for a few seconds, catching his breath maybe. Water dripped from his hair into his face.

I should go. I need to go.

In a moment.

Music swelled over the night, proud, hopeful, bittersweet.

I felt it all around me. All around him. And, in that moment, I ached for Lucian. I didn't know why he hurt, or what drove him. But I wanted to put my arms around those broad shoulders and hold on.

Then he planted his big hands on the side of the pool and, with an effortless push, thrust himself up and out of the water.

"Sweet mercy . . ." My knees went weak, and I gripped the rail to keep from falling over. *Oh, Édith, I don't regret anything either.*

His body was a Bernini sculpture come to life—Triton looking down on mere mortals. Water sluiced over rippling planes of muscles, trickled down dips and cut grooves, heading straight toward . . .

His dick. Even from far away, it was impressive. Long and thick with a wide head and plump balls. My lips parted, heat flushing my cheeks, and my nipples tightened.

Lucian ran his hands through his dripping hair, pushing the shining dark mass back from his clean, strong face. Not pretty or model handsome. He was too blunt for that, all hard lines and aggression. But beautiful just the same.

And bleak. My happy bits cooled off. His expression was utterly bleak. Cold as ice. I could wax poetic about his looks all night, but it wouldn't change the fact that this man was ultimately a stranger. One who was remote and closed off as a frozen wall. I grew up with men who wore that expression. I'd run from those men. And today, he'd all but run from me. I needed to remember that and keep my distance.

Slowly, I backed away. Down below, Lucian moved around, whether to gather his clothes or swim again, I didn't know. I didn't look. I shouldn't have looked to begin with, shouldn't have let myself get caught up in the fantasy of him.

CHAPTER SIX

Emma

My little house had a kitchen, but I was beginning to wonder if I'd ever need to use it. I woke from a surprisingly restful sleep, given that it was haunted by images of a certain naked man swimming endless laps, to find the sun shining and my spirits high. When someone knocked on the door, I wrapped myself up in a robe and answered to find Sal carrying a big wicker picnic basket.

"Breakfast," he announced with cheer.

"You didn't have to do that," I said, taking the basket from him.

"Girl, do not, under any circumstances, say no to the house kitchen." He wagged his brows. "Trust me; you will be missing out."

Given the delicious aroma of fresh bread wafting up through the lid, I didn't doubt his word. "Would you like to share some? I can make coffee."

"Sure. But there's coffee in the basket. The house doesn't approve of drip brew."

"Wow." No wonder it weighed a ton.

I let him in, and together we emptied out the contents onto the kitchen counter. Along with French press coffee and fresh rich cream, there was a pot of thick honey yogurt, a plate of glistening fruits—melon, honeydew, and cherries—a small jar of strawberry jam, and sweetly scented rolls.

"Pain aux raisins," Sal informed me. "Amalie's favorite."

"They smell delicious." I leaned in a little, lowering my voice. "Don't tell her, but I hate raisins. So you can have at them."

"Oh, I won't tell Amalie a thing," Sal promised solemnly. "But the house has a way of finding out what you like."

"You say that like the house is its own entity."

"When it comes to the kitchen, it might as well be."

I laughed and started to set our goodies onto the silver tray provided. "Does she have a temperamental chef?"

"Very temperamental. But you needn't worry about him. If your paths happen to cross, I'm certain he'll be a big pussycat around you."

"No thanks. I deal with enough egos in my profession."

Sal clearly struggled with a grin, but he merely picked up the tray, and I grabbed the silver coffee carafe and pretty porcelain cups.

We took our breakfast out onto the terrace and set it on the little café table. Part of me wanted to avoid this spot with its perfect view of the pool, but that was cowardly. Besides, he wasn't out there now. I tried not to feel disappointed. Or guilty.

"So . . ." Sal took a bite of melon. "What are your plans for today?"

"To do absolutely nothing."

"Good plan."

I tasted the yogurt and nearly moaned. Jesus, everything here was spectacular. Rich and creamy with just a hint of honey, it melted on my tongue and woke my taste buds up. A sip of coffee with hints of chocolate and caramel had me sighing in appreciation. "On second thought, I definitely need to fit in some exercise, or soon I won't fit my clothes."

"Blame Amalie's new chef. I've put on ten pounds this month alone." He patted what appeared to be a small potbelly hiding under a billowing silk blouse with a vivid-blue-and-purple pattern.

"Is that Pucci?" I asked, then resumed devouring my yogurt.

"You know your fashion."

"Alice, one of the costume designers, would talk nonstop about fashion." My good humor flitted away on the breeze as I realized I had no idea when I'd ever see her again.

Sal must have noticed, because he looked me over with kind eyes. "You miss the show when the season comes to the end, don't you?"

He didn't know I was never going back. I wanted to tell him, but I couldn't. That didn't mean I couldn't admit to some things.

"Yes. Every season, I never think it will be hard . . ." My eyes misted, and I blinked fiercely. "It's ridiculous, really. An actor's life is moving from role to role. We do our job, go home . . . but we all have such great chemistry that I . . . really do miss them when the season is over."

"Just because all good things must come to an end doesn't mean we aren't allowed to mourn them."

"You're right." Lord knew I was in mourning.

"Besides, you'll be back on set next year." Sal spooned some fruit onto my plate. "Here, try the melons. They are fabulous."

The melons were, in fact, fabulous.

After Sal left, insisting on taking the plates and basket back to the main kitchen for me, I curled up on the deep little love seat by the empty fireplace and tried to read. But my mind kept wandering, distracted by thoughts of thick thighs and tight abs.

I didn't know what the hell was the matter with me. I'd seen naked men before. Hell, Saint had the body of a god, and we did endless scenes together half-naked without me even blinking. He was just scenery as far as I was concerned. Greg the asshole had a spectacular body as well, one I appreciated just fine—well, before I found out it was inhabited by a cheating dickhead.

But this hot, pulsing memory of Lucian naked disturbed the hell out of me. I wanted to touch him. I wanted to run my tongue up the neat valley between his abs to collect those drops of water, put my mouth on his tight nipple and flick it, make him groan and shudder.

"Oh, for crying out loud," I exclaimed, tossing my Kindle aside and getting up. Reading was a lost cause. I needed air.

Since I couldn't get the image of Lucian out of my head, I would exorcise it by facing the scene of the crime; I would go swimming. Maybe a cool dunk in water would wash away my sin of voyeurism.

Deciding to ignore the bikinis I'd brought, I put on a conservative pale-blue retro one-piece that I could swim in without worrying about anything riding up or slipping. I was well aware of the hypocrisy of not wanting to flaunt my body to any potential observers when I was guilty of gawking the night before. But I wasn't trying to get attention. I wanted to swim.

Sure you do, Em. Keep telling yourself that's all you want.

I told my inner voice to shut the hell up and slipped a yellow sundress over my head. Slathered in sunscreen and floppy hat firmly in place, I grabbed my pool bag and headed out.

The grounds surrounding the main house were empty. In the distance, I heard the sound of a lawn mower or maybe hedge clippers, so there were people around somewhere. Sal had told me he planned to spend the day shopping for fabrics down in Santa Barbara. I had no idea what Amalie was up to, but I didn't want to push myself on her. As for *him*, he said he was renovating the other guesthouses. I'd spied two of them tucked along the other side of the property, far more remote than mine. So maybe he was there.

It didn't matter. I wasn't here for Lucian either. Even so, nerves jumped and punched around in my belly as I neared the pool. The heels of my slingback sandals clicked along the terra-cotta pavers. The pool lay still and deep blue in the sunshine. And though I was here to swim, I edged past it, as though Lucian might pop out of its depths and glare at me. Which was ridiculous, given that the water was crystal clear—without a hot man in sight.

At the far end of the pool was a pool house with italianate columns that held up a wisteria-covered terrace. The glass french doors to the pool house were open. I couldn't help but peek in. The lovely living room was done up in French country style, with dusky-robin's-egg-blue walls, sisal rugs, faded-yellow linen couches, and pretty alabaster lamps with blue shades dotted here and there.

A kitchenette was on one side, and behind a pair of open blue damask drapes, a white iron bed was tucked in the alcove on the other end. Several artworks were on the floor, propped up against the wall. A box filled with small vases and various decorative knickknacks sat beside them.

Someone was either still putting things up or taking them away. Then I noticed the pair of faded jeans lying in a lump by the end of the bed, well-worn work boots tossed next to them.

Blood rushed to my fingertips and then back to my cheeks. I knew those jeans.

It was his room. Shit, shit, *shit*.

Heart pounding, I spun around to make a run for it, and almost plowed into a wide chest. Double shit-sticks. Heat burned my cheeks as I grimaced, wishing myself away from this spot. But it was not to be.

The deep grumpy rumble of his voice cut through the thick silence. "Help you with something, Em?"

Swallowing down my dignity, I tilted my chin—because he was that damn tall—and faced him.

A shiver ran through me at the coldness in his pale-green eyes. He inspected me, as though he'd found a rat in his room.

I licked my dry lips and attempted to speak. The words escaped in a high crackling question. "No?"

Glacial eyes narrowed. "You don't know? Is this something we need to discuss? Your propensity for responding to questions with an uncertain *no*?"

Ugh. This man was not going to turn me into a wimp. I lifted my chin, which unfortunately thrust my boobs out, not that he appeared to notice. "I was about to go for a swim."

God, that sounded ridiculous.

His brow quirked, as though he agreed. "Pool's back that way, Em."

Em. I liked the way he said my name; so much feeling in one syllable. But not the smug humor in his eyes. "I am aware."

"So what? You decided to snoop in here first?"

If I wasn't the color of a tomato by now, it was a close thing. *No matter. Act it out.* "No, I didn't decide to *snoop*. I wandered around the pool, saw the open door and—"

"Snooped."

I growled. At least, it sounded like a little growl. Lucian did a double take, but his passive, unimpressed expression remained.

"Snooping implies I was going through your things. A quick glance inside a room is more of a . . ." My voice trailed off as I struggled for the right word.

With a dubious grunt, he crossed his beefy arms in front of his chest and gave me a look that clearly stated he knew I was full of shit but enjoyed me trying to talk my way out of it.

Damn it. I let out a breath. "All right. I apologize for *snooping*. It wasn't my intention. It's just a very pretty room." *Too pretty for you,* I added on silently.

Weirdly, I was fairly certain he heard the unvoiced criticism. His lips twitched, drawing my attention. They were pale against the dark scruff of his unshaven jaw and chin. Pale and wide. A mobile mouth, Tate would have called it. The kind of lips that were expressive, kissable.

Except when they pressed flat. With a jolt I realized I'd been staring.

"You done?"

I flinched at the plainly put question. God, was I? I wanted to look at them again. Which was horrible considering he was annoyed and grumpy and obviously wanted me gone.

Just play it cool. "With what?"

Yes, very smooth, Em. Very smooth.

He sighed, slow and long, as though dealing with a moron. Admittedly, I felt a bit like one at this point.

"Done looking around?" He sounded pleasant, as though he might soon offer tea.

Damn it, I played a badass princess. One who never got flustered. *Reach for that remote dignity, Em.* "Yes, I am done."

"No request for a tour?"

Oh, now that was cute.

"No, thank you. I've seen enough."

Oddly, he didn't move. I'd have to skirt around him to get out. Not that I would subject myself to that humiliation. I lifted my brows, letting the question rise in my eyes. Was he going to get out of my way or what?

He didn't. He stared, hard, uncompromising. But then his gaze lowered, just a fraction of a second, down my body. I felt it in my toes. As though irritated at the slip, he grunted and went back to glaring at me, but he appeared more annoyed at himself now than at me.

Even so, I wasn't exactly feeling very charitable at the moment. "Are *you* done?"

"Done?"

I smiled sweetly. "Staring."

He paused a beat, those absurdly long lashes sweeping when he blinked. Then it was as if a light went off in his head, and a slow, easy smile spread over his face. It transformed him. From brooding brute to beautiful man.

The ice melted from his gaze, turning those green eyes to translucent sea glass. That gaze drew me in, impossible to look away from, even though a prickle of warning danced up my spine—because there was that evil smile to consider.

Then he spoke in a deep, honey-laden drawl. "What's the acceptable time limit? How long did you stare last night?"

Oh, no, no, no.

The blood rushed from my face in hot prickles of horror. A strangled sound escaped my lips.

Lucian leaned in, close enough that I caught a whiff of bitter chocolate and sweet oranges. Why did he have to smell like dessert? He sounded even better—hot cream and honey. "Did you like what you saw?" The question rippled over my skin, sank into my bones, a soft caress that dared me to answer *yes.*

Before I could, he went on, that smooth voice sharpened with cynicism. "Or are you just a perpetual snoop?"

My eyes snapped open. I hadn't realized I'd closed them. Or that he'd drifted so near. I could reach out and touch him if I wanted. Rub my palms over the firm planes of his chest . . . then I registered what he'd said. The disdain, the snark.

A clean rush of anger surged forward. Because one other thing became perfectly clear. "You knew I was there from the start."

He didn't flinch. "Yeah, I knew."

I didn't want to find that titillating or hot. But I did. Damn it.

But I was an actress. I could fake it.

"Well, then I guess I have to ask, Did you really expect me to turn away from a show so freely offered?" When he blinked in surprise, I tutted in reproach. "Who would suspect you were an exhibitionist. Tell me—did it get you off knowing I was watching? Or would anyone looking on do the trick?"

Lucian huffed out a laugh, as though he couldn't believe my audacity but kind of liked it. His lids lowered as his gaze slid back to my mouth. And everything went hazy, the air between us too heavy. The rumble of his voice rippled along my skin, licked up my trembling thighs.

"Do you really want me to answer that, Em? Knowing you might not like my reply?"

Oh, the arrogance. I sucked in a breath, ready to tell him off. His eyes glinted with hot sparks, as though he wanted me to lay into him, like it would be the excuse he needed to do the same.

But it wasn't violence I pictured. It was sex. Frantic, sweaty, angry . . .

A lilting, amused voice broke through my unraveling thoughts. "How wonderful it is to see you two getting along so well."

As if zapped by a prod, we both snapped straight and turned as one toward the voice.

Looking like a dark-haired, witchy Endora, Amalie stood in the open doorway with a small curl of a smile on her thin hot-pink lips. "Do stop panting all over our guest, Titou."

When he growled low in his throat, she smiled wider. "My, but you are stirred up. Perhaps you both could use a little cooling off in the pool."

With that, she twirled around and sauntered away, leaving us to exchange one more long unsettled look before Lucian stalked off. As soon as he was gone, my shoulders sagged, and I took a shaky breath. The man was too potent. And Amalie was right; I definitely needed a long swim to cool off.

CHAPTER SEVEN

Lucian

What did they say about the best-laid plans? I'd blown my plan to keep away from Emma all to hell. Worse, Mamie had caught us . . . discussing . . . and thought she knew something that she really didn't. She'd be relentless now.

I gathered my dough and kneaded it, pushing through with the balls of my hands, then gathering the cool, springing mass back with my fingers, over and over. It was hypnotic. Necessary.

Back when hockey was my life, I'd taken my frustrations out on the ice. Even if it had been only to lace up my skates and get out there on my own. I could spend hours on the ice, just flying.

Unable to help myself, I closed my eyes and remembered. I could almost feel the frosty air on my face, the subtle glide of my skates. I could nearly hear the clap of my stick on the ice, the way it felt to hit the puck.

My chest clenched. Hard.

Fuck.

Opening my eyes, I went back to kneading, picking up the dough to slap it hard onto the counter. I'd chosen a nice sourdough sandwich bread to make, knowing the dough would require a lot of kneading to get the gluten going.

This was my therapy now. Baking and, to a lesser extent, cooking. The precision and concentration needed to create something truly exceptional crowded my brain and didn't leave room for all the other dark and twisted thoughts. For a while, at least.

But I couldn't chase Emma Maron out of my head. Which was a problem. It was my own fault for continuing to engage with her. But what was I supposed to do when I walked into my temporary home and found a fairy princess gazing around with wide blue eyes? I had to get her out of my space. I thought she'd scare easily and run.

Instead she'd called my bluff and left me hard and aching for her. She'd wanted to know if it mattered who saw me naked. As if there was any doubt.

I'd caught sight of her on the little balcony the moment I'd walked up to the pool. It had been a mild shock but not enough to stop me. Knowing she was watching had been a bit of titillation, a small thrill in my otherwise staid life. I even played it up, getting out of the pool in a way I knew would let her see everything. It hadn't turned me on, exactly. My heart had been too heavy with old memories last night. But it had been something different, something outside the simmering rage and frustration I usually carried.

When I'd looked up to find her gone, I'd been weirdly disappointed. Foolish. Despite our heated exchange, I wasn't about to try anything with Emma. I just wanted to be alone.

Yeah, a regular Greta Garbo I was. I was also a liar.

The truth had barely crystalized in my head when Sal sauntered in, wearing a purple-and-blue silk caftan that was the same as the one Amalie wore today.

"You gotta stop dressing exactly like Mamie," I said by way of greeting. "It's doing my head in."

He stopped on the other side of the counter. "Don't tell me you have a problem with men who have fabulous taste in clothes."

"Please. Who brought you that overpriced banana-yellow drapey dress you just had to have when we were hanging out in Paris five years ago? If it was fabulous is debatable."

Sal's look of disgust almost made me smile. "Only you would refer to a gorgeous Tadashi Shoji couture gown as an *overpriced banana-yellow drapey dress*. Really, Luc, the disrespect."

"It draped and was yellow."

"Ugh." Sal sighed dramatically, then eyed me. "I am *not* dressing like Amalie."

"Yes, you are. To a T, as Amalie would say." I glanced at him before going back to my dough. "You're even wearing the same shade of lipstick she has on today."

Sal peered at himself in the reflection of a hanging copper pot and then frowned. "Shit. You're right. We're merging."

"I can't handle two Mamies right now. One is more than enough."

His laugh was self-deprecating, because we both knew the power of Mamie; without even trying she had a way of enfolding you into her world. "Fine. I'll leave the Pucci to Amalie. But I'm not giving up my Dolce or Chanel."

"Aside from Chanel, I don't know what any of those things are."

"But you do know Chanel."

"Doesn't everyone?" I didn't bother mentioning that Cassandra loved all things Chanel—not Amalie's particular perfume, thank Christ—but I'd been on the receiving end of enough bills to know the fashion house and fear it. Cassandra liked to shop. A lot.

It was a relief to realize I didn't miss her. Not even the idea of her. I slapped the dough on the counter with a satisfying thwap and then looked at Sal. I'd known him half my life by this point, yet while I was becoming a shadow of who I'd once been, he'd come into his own.

My fingers sank into the smooth, springing mass of dough. "You know and like yourself exactly as you are, Sallie. That's a rare thing."

As soon as the words were out, I felt exposed. Raw. Biting back a grimace, I focused on my task. But I felt his quiet pity along my skin. It invaded my lungs like the sour stink of scorched milk.

But when I glanced up, I found his eyes were filled with understanding and a solemn affection that made me realize we were more like brothers than either of us had ever acknowledged.

"Luc, did it ever occur to you that I found that confidence, in part, because of you?"

Shocked, I shook my head woodenly.

Sal smiled faintly. "It meant something to this queer boy that a big brute of a hockey player accepted him without question. It meant something that you were ready to throw down if someone so much as looked at me the wrong way."

I swallowed thickly. "Some people are assholes. I couldn't stand by and let anyone shit on you."

"I know. That's my point, Luc. None of us live in a vacuum. Sometimes we have to accept the support of others."

Hell.

I stared at the counter, not knowing what to say.

The moment stretched, then broke so cleanly it was as if nothing had been said. Sal went back to humming and watching me work the dough.

"Did you need anything?" I asked, knowing that he and Amalie had decided to tag team me on the topic of Emma.

Proving me right, Sal shrugged, then straightened the sleeves of his caftan. "Thought you might like to know how breakfast went this morning."

The breakfast Sal had with Emma. Against my will, my heart rate kicked up.

"I don't."

Sal gave that lie the respect it deserved. "Your girl didn't like the pain aux raisins."

"She's not my . . . she didn't like the rolls?" It shouldn't have upset me. Taste was subjective; people liked different things. But . . . she didn't like them.

Sal snagged a gouda-and-rosemary cracker from a tray I had cooling. "She doesn't like raisins. But she devoured the yogurt with a passion that was near orgasmic."

My lower abs went hot and tight in response. I suddenly resented Sal for being the one who got to see that. It was my own damn fault; I'd sent him off with the breakfast basket instead of delivering it myself.

I concentrated on my dough and the nonorgasmic information Sal had given me. "So no raisins."

What then? Croissant? *Pain aux chocolat? Chaussons aux pommes?*

"She loved the fruit as well," Sal said, cutting into my thoughts. He smirked, munching on the cracker. "Though you can hardly take credit for that."

Watch me, buddy.

I'd picked that fruit, cleaned it, sliced it at just the right thickness. That was my fruit. Every bite she'd put in her mouth, every moan of pleasure she'd made, had been because of me. And fuck, that turned me on so badly my hands shook.

She liked fruit. I'd try the chaussons aux pommes, then. I'd be shocked if the woman didn't enjoy apple turnovers.

"Plotting your next form of culinary seduction, are we?" Sal stole another cracker.

"Stop eating those. They're for lunch."

"Oh, and what are we having them with?"

"Sliced apples and pears, lavender honey, and cheeses. Tomato soup—" I caught sight of Sal's smug face and glared. "You know what? Get your own lunch."

"Somebody is grumpy."

"Hmm."

"Maybe you should go for a swim."

"Maybe you should go—"

"Temper, temper, big guy." Sal grabbed a pear this time. "We both know you're snarly because you're horny."

"It's like you don't even value your life."

"Amalie would kill you if you harmed one hair on my beautiful head, so I think I'm safe."

"Don't count on it."

Sal rolled his eyes, not in the least intimidated. "Give it up. You're all marshmallow on the inside, Oz. No one who bakes the way you do could possess anything other than a sweet heart."

With a snarl of disgust, I slapped the dough onto the counter and counted silently to ten. This place was supposed to be a refuge from stress. So far, I had a grandmother trying to matchmake, an actress driving me to exhibitionism, and a fashion stylist getting on my last nerve.

Sal tossed the pear from hand to hand like it was a ball. "Why are you denying that you want her?"

I grabbed the pear out of midair and set it on the counter. "Do you see me denying it?"

That got him. He paused, nonplussed. "Well, hell. Then what's the problem?"

So many things.

"That woman is the type you keep." Forever. "I'm not in the market for that. And trust me; she's not in the market for what I have to offer either."

"So you're just going to stay in here the whole time, beating your dough?"

"Har." The kitchen suddenly felt too small. I rolled my stiff shoulders, but they wouldn't ease. Fuck it. "You want to get out of here? Grab a drink?"

Sal's perfectly plucked brows arched. "It's almost lunch."

I untied my apron and hung it on the hook by the pantry. "Amalie and Emma can figure out how to serve themselves."

Just the thought of Little Miss Snoop invading my kitchen wafted over my skin like the blast of an oven opening. I rolled my shoulders again. "You coming?"

CHAPTER EIGHT

Lucian

Lesson learned: never underestimate Sal. He was as slick as his Elvis pompadour.

We were on the path to the front of the house when we ran into Emma. She'd finished up her swim—something I'd been doing my best *not* to think about—and was on her way back to her bungalow. But did that stop Sal from calling her over to us? Not even a little. He did it with a barely concealed glee.

Nor did it stop him from inviting her to lunch with us. The man damn well knew I'd been trying to get away from her. But I wasn't about to be rude and protest. So when her deep-blue gaze flicked to mine, doubtful that I wanted her to come, I felt compelled to suck it up and insist that she join us.

So here we were, at my favorite burger-and-shake shack overlooking the pale sandy beach and the brilliant-blue ocean beyond. Surrounded by beachgoers and surfers, Emma stood out like a mini sun, drawing covetous or curious looks. She seemed oblivious. I didn't know if any of them actually recognized her; she wore big white sunglasses and a floppy white hat trimmed in yellow daisies. It should have looked ridiculous, but like Sal, she had style that just worked for her.

Sal, however, I could ignore with ease. It was damn near impossible to ignore Emma. I felt the whole of her along the whole of me, as though she was constantly running her slim hand over my skin. It was unnerving as hell.

My skin prickled when she set her tray on the table and sat down next to me to gaze at the ocean with a satisfied sigh.

"I've missed Southern California."

"When's the last time you were here?" I found myself asking.

"Eight months ago." Her plush mouth tilted wryly. "Not that long, I know. But it feels that way." I couldn't see her eyes behind the glasses, but I felt her gaze all the same. "What about you? Are you originally from California?"

Discussing my old life was a bit of a touchy subject. But she obviously had no idea who I was, and knowing where I lived wouldn't change that. "I grew up in Evanston, Illinois. My dad, Amalie's son, was a curator for the Art Institute of Chicago. He met my mom his first year there; she specialized in painting restorations."

"Wow."

"Yep." I'd grown up around art and beauty, my parents fully expecting me to follow in their academic footsteps. And yet they hadn't so much as blinked when it had become apparent that hockey was going to be my life. They'd encouraged it because I'd found my passion.

"I've lived here and there. I've been in Washington, DC, for the last couple of years."

"That's quite a change."

I knew where this was headed. Why did I leave? What did I do there? I headed it off best I could. "It was time. Amalie needed help." *Big fat hulking lie right there, Oz.* I needed Amalie way more than she needed me.

I was twenty-eight years old, and I had run to my grandmother to lick my wounds.

Thankfully, Sal finally got his order and joined us.

"Burgers and beer." He plunked down his tray. "To think we left behind tomato soup and an artisanal cheese board."

"You didn't have to come." I gave him a long speaking look.

Which he ignored. "And miss all this?"

All this was encompassed by waving his hand between me and Emma and then, very weakly, toward the food. Subtlety was not Sal's style.

Emma frowned, apparently not noticing the outright war of glares going on between Sal and me. "We left lunch behind? Now I feel bad. Everything I've eaten at Rosemont is so delicious I hate to think of any of it going to waste."

And wasn't that insanely gratifying. I had the urge to toss our burgers into the trash and haul her back home so I could feed her.

I grunted and took a sip of my bottled beer. "Amalie will eat it."

Emma appeared slightly mollified. But the small furrow between her delicate brows remained. "I heard the chef was temperamental."

Sal choked on his burger. I wasn't taking bets on who told Emma that little bit of information.

I shot him a side-eye before answering. "He can be."

"Have you met him?"

Now would be the time to clear things up. Only she might not want to eat my food once she found out. I wasn't exactly her favorite person.

"I live on the estate. Of course I have."

"What's he like?" Definitely building castles in her head.

"Temperamental."

Her mouth snapped shut before she glared—yes, I felt that glare through her owlish sunglasses. "You're annoying."

I saluted her with my beer. She scowled and tossed a balled-up napkin my way. It fell short of my plate by a foot, and I chuckled.

Shaking her head as though I was nothing more than a minor annoyance, Emma picked up a fry and poked at her pile of ketchup. "For some reason, I have a hard time picturing Amalie putting up with difficult staff."

This was true. It surprised me that Emma understood that much about my grandmother. Then again, maybe it shouldn't. Emma was far too observant.

I affected a bored shrug. "She has a soft spot for him."

"Oh, are they . . ." Her face lit up as she smiled. "You know, into each other?"

Sal choked so hard on his burger that little bits escaped. Much to his mortification. "I'm going to have nightmares," he muttered, wiping the table frantically with his napkin. Only I knew he wasn't talking about the mess.

"Not everything is about sex, Snoopy."

"I don't think everything is—what did you call me?" She whipped off her glasses. Sparks of outrage shot from her eyes. It was a good look for her. "Did you really just call me Snoopy?"

I grinned, feeling lighter than I had all morning. "Nosy Parker work better for you?"

"Not even a little, Magic Mike."

"Mike danced. He didn't swim."

The pert nose of Princess Anya lifted a touch. "He put on a certain type of show. That's the point."

"A type you apparently like to watch."

Her cheeks pinkened as she bristled. I started to chuckle again but then caught sight of Sal, who had his phone up and pointed our way. "What the hell are you doing?"

I'd forgotten all about him. Which, admittedly, was easy to do around Emma.

"Filming this for Amalie. She'll be so pleased."

"Sal!" Emma hissed, horrified.

He took pity on her and set the phone facedown on the table. "I kid. I'm not going to send anything to Amalie. That would be a gross violation of privacy."

I snorted, and he gave me a beatific smile. "I'll just save it for later when I want to annoy Oz."

"You don't need a video for that, Sal."

Sal flipped me off, his hot-pink nail like an exclamation point, but then he laughed and sat back to drink his shake. "He's quick, Emma. Very quick."

I knew he was teasing. But it hit far too close to home, when the guys would call me His Quickness.

Quick feet, fast hands.

I could hear them in my head. My guys.

His Quickness is on it. You slapping on those ruby slippers and taking us to Emerald City, Oz?

Stupid stuff. Shit we said to get pumped, to take the pressure off. I missed every damn second.

"You've got him grunting again, Sal," Emma said, misinterpreting my sudden change of mood. It elevated slightly, along with my heart rate, when she reached over and patted my forearm. "Don't worry, honey pie; you'll be all right."

"Honey pie?" My voice sounded far too rough.

She shrugged an elegant shoulder. "Something my granny used to say when she thought I was being petulant. 'Don't worry, honey pie; the world will keep turning.'"

"Did it piss you off when she said it? Or did you believe her?"

Emma grinned wide, displaying that dazzling smile fans and press alike adored. "A bit of both."

God, I wanted to return that smile. I wanted a lot of things. It was one thing to like the way she looked. It was something else to like *her*. And I did. I liked her a lot.

"You two are so cute," Sal said.

Emma's smile dropped. "And you are a horrible tease. Stop tormenting Lucian."

"He needs more tormenting of that type, if you ask me." He pushed back from the table. "I'm getting a Diet Coke to chase this shake down. Anyone want anything?"

When we both shook our heads, he left, and silence fell between Emma and me.

"Why does he call you Oz?" she asked out of the blue.

I'd been hoping she'd missed that. But Emma missed very little. "My last name is Osmond. Some people call me Oz." I copped a smug smile. "Are you going to tell me I don't look like a funny little wizard now?"

She laughed. "To be fair, there's nothing little about you."

My lower gut heated. "Not a damn thing, honey pie."

"Certainly not your ego."

"It isn't ego when it's true."

Emma rolled her eyes and picked up her water to take a drink. Her gaze went to Sal standing in line. "You get the feeling that Sal and Amalie are trying to throw us together?"

"Caught on to that, did you?"

Her nose wrinkled. "They aren't exactly subtle about it."

She didn't sound annoyed—more like embarrassed. I wasn't sure how to feel about that, so I didn't bother dwelling.

"No." I took a sip of beer. "They aren't."

Emma rested a forearm on the table and leaned close, bringing her light, sweet scent with her. "Don't worry. I'll stay out of your way."

And then it hit me. She was looking out for my comfort. She would end up leaving if she thought I wanted it. The truth was right there on her expressive face.

"Don't." The word tripped free without my permission.

What the hell, Oz?

A frown of confusion formed between her brows. "What?"

You can still fix this. Backtrack, moron. Backtrack.

"Don't stay out of my way."

Idiot.

Surprise smoothed out her features as her indigo gaze darted over my face, trying to read me. I didn't know how she could, when I couldn't even figure myself out.

"It's ridiculous," I blurted. "Trying to avoid each other just because they're bored and have watched too many episodes of *The Bachelor*."

Amusement lit her eyes. "Don't you mean *The Bachelorette?*"

I hid my smile by taking another sip. "I said what I meant."

"You got it wrong. I'm definitely the prize."

Yes, you are.

"Whatever you say, Snoopy."

She laughed, a glorious sound that danced right over my heart and tugged the breath right out of my lungs. A man could be persuaded to do foolish things to hear that laugh again and again.

Apparently, I wasn't the only one affected. Heads turned our way, and that was when it happened.

Emma

I liked Lucian. This was worrisome, because despite his teasing and quick wit, he was as closed off a man as I'd met in a long time. But he made me laugh, even when he was pretending to be a grump. *Pretending* because it was clear he'd been enjoying himself.

Not so much by his manner, but in the crinkles around his jade eyes when he suppressed a laugh and the way his wide shoulders relaxed the more we sparred. I knew he even enjoyed Sal needling him; theirs was a strange friendship, in that neither one seemed to want to admit to it.

Lucian because he clearly didn't want to admit to being happy about anything. Sal was more of a mystery, but I had to wonder if, despite his flamboyant outer shell, he was actually a bit shy.

Or maybe I was full of it and imagining things that weren't there.

I wasn't imagining the way Lucian looked at me now, though. That stern brow eased, his eyes widening just a little, as though shocked, as his lips parted. He appeared . . . awed. At the sound of my laughter, apparently.

That awe floored me. My insides swooped with a funny sort of flutter I hadn't felt in ages. Not since I was sixteen, when soulful artist and high school crush Michael Benton had smiled at me. Even that moment hadn't been followed by a hard kick to my sternum as my heart began to beat faster.

This was what happened when liking someone mixed with attraction. Unwanted but strong and pure. I didn't know how to hide it or shove it away. I could only stare back at Lucian with equal awe. I'd vowed to keep away from shallow attraction, but what was I to do with this? With him?

My laughter had caught people's attention. I knew this on an instinctual level, honed after fame graced me with her light. And though it was a sign that my career was a success, public attention could also be a pain in the ass when I wanted to be left alone.

I braced myself as a few young men walked toward the table. Funny thing was Lucian did, too, even though they were in his periphery. His awareness of the situation surprised me, but then again, maybe who I was never left his mind.

I didn't like that idea. Fame was a weird phenomenon. You chased it, but once you had it, you never felt secure or safe. Paranoia about who was in your life for what reasons, fear that you'd never be good enough, popular enough. I clenched my fists in my lap and hated myself for worrying about any of it.

But fame also had a funny way of making you a fool. Something that became glaringly obvious when the trio of young men walked past me without a glance and beelined straight to . . . Lucian.

And he knew. His entire body was tensed, as if expecting an impact. I could only sit there and gape as he was surrounded by what were clearly adoring fans.

"Oz! I can't believe it's you."

Oz. They called him Oz like Sal had. Who the hell was he?

Lucian tried valiantly to adopt an easy expression, but I knew him enough now to tell that his smile was fake as hell. "Hey, guys."

"Oh man, this is totally cool," said the blond. "Whatcha doing here, Oz?"

"Having lunch."

They all laughed the unsteady laugh of those who knew they'd stated the obvious but were too enthralled by fame to show any real embarrassment.

"Tough break about the Cup."

"They haven't been the same without you."

"You're not really quitting forever, are you?"

The questions peppered Lucian like pellets, and his expression grew more remote with each hit. Sal hustled over, looking more than a bit panicked. The boys didn't notice; they were too busy gazing upon their idol.

"That hit, man. God, it looked bad."

"Had to have hurt like a bitch. Do you remember it?"

Lucian stood abruptly. Woodenly, as though every inch of him was frozen inside. I had no idea what they were talking about, but clearly everyone else did. I stood as well, unable to sit there when Lucian was on the brink of bolting.

"I've got to get going, guys." His voice was a thread pulled too tight.

"Aw, man."

"Can we get a selfie?"

For a second, I thought he might snap. But he smiled—more of a grimace—and bit out a terse "Sure."

Without being asked, Sal stepped in and took the phone, as though well versed in doing so. I stood there, numb and confused. The young guys posed for a few photos with Lucian "Oz," and more people started to hover, the crowd murmuring with greater intensity. How the hell did everyone know him? Why didn't I?

His face had been familiar, though, when I'd first seen it. But I hadn't been able to place him. And then he'd opened his mouth, all gruff and snappish, and he'd simply become Lucian—hot but closed-off man who liked to take late-night naked swims and make me laugh despite myself.

The second the photos were taken, Lucian said goodbye to the guys with a finality that was polite but firm. He grabbed his tray without looking my way, dumped it, and began to stalk off, as though in a trance, leaving Sal and me to hustle after him or be left behind.

"What the hell?" I hissed to Sal as we followed. Ahead of us, Lucian strode with purpose, his big body stiff as a log.

Sal's expression was taut with unhappiness. "It's his story to tell. Just know . . . he's going to be difficult for a while."

Difficult? The man already was.

Lucian unlocked his truck but didn't acknowledge us before he got in. The pickup was a four door, but I wasn't about to force Sal into the back seat so I could ask questions. I hopped in the back seat, hoping to catch Lucian's eye in the rearview mirror. But he never glanced my way.

Many times, he'd been silent, broody, sarcastic, but he had yet to ignore me until now. It shocked me how much it bothered me. It was as though I'd become fully awake and alive under his attention, only to dim when it was taken away. No one should have that power over me. Except it didn't feel like oppression. It felt right and real in a way that scared me.

Worse, though, was my concern because he was hurting. The encounter had shaken him.

The drive back was tense and silent. I took the time to breathe deep and easy. It was something I'd learned to do while on the set to keep myself grounded. *Dark Castle* was a good working environment, but tempers and egos still flared now and then. God, but I already missed it. Or maybe I missed the safety of a steady job. Frankly, the show had a reputation for its sex scenes, and I was more than happy to never do another nude love scene again. Saint had been a perfect gentleman, but it still made for an uncomfortable afternoon of filming.

Those thoughts distracted me long enough for Lucian to reach the estate and turn into the drive that snaked around to the side of the house. Without preamble, he put the truck in park and got out.

Sal and I exchanged a look, and then I braced my shoulders and followed. It wasn't easy catching up to him. The man had long legs and was hell bent and determined to outpace me. But I was an expert at speed walking—as my ass could attest.

Lucian didn't break stride or look my way. But he knew I was there. "Not now, Em."

I hopped over a paver, my pace just shy of making me pant. "If not now, when?"

"How about never?"

"Yeah, that's not going to work."

He snorted with feeling. "You're operating under the misconception that I owe you anything. I don't."

Definitely touchy.

"And I didn't owe you anything when you asked about *Dark Castle*. But I told you how I felt anyway."

"That's on you."

We rounded a corner, heading toward the tennis court. I had no idea where he was going; maybe he simply thought he could wear me out and pull away.

"You're right." I stopped on the trail, my arms falling to my sides as I caught my breath. To hell with it. I didn't need to be chasing a man who didn't want to be bothered.

Weirdly, as if compelled, Lucian came to a halt and half turned my way to glare at me from over his wide shoulder. His body remained tense and poised to take flight once more.

"We owe each other nothing," I said, raising my voice enough to be clear over the ten feet that separated us. "But no one lives in a complete void. Your grandmother and Sal walk on eggshells around you."

Oh, but that got him. Red suffused his neck, and he stalked back my way, coming within touching distance. "You know nothing about them. Or me."

Yeah, that hurt. It shouldn't have, but it did.

"I know enough. They worry about you. They love you."

Lucian's nostrils flared. "I mean it, Emma. I do not do well with guilt trips."

"If you feel guilty, that's on you."

He turned his head and scowled. But he didn't go.

That he was listening, despite his anger and despite the fact that I didn't have any real right to lecture him, had me softening my tone. "All right, I'm nosy. A snoop. Fine. I admit it. But tell me you wouldn't be asking questions if the tables were turned."

Lucian's jaw bunched, and I knew he was grinding his teeth. Stubborn ass.

"Who the hell are you?" I blurted out.

At that, he laughed, but it was without humor. "I'm Brick, remember? The sullen ex–star athlete, washed up and hiding away in the big house."

"Fine. Be a dick." I turned to go, when he spoke again, sharp and broken, like shards of glass.

"You were so close to the truth, Em." Eyes of frosted sea glass met mine. "The world knows me as Luc Osmond. Oz, the great and powerful. One of the best hockey centers to dominate the ice, or so I was told."

A glimmer of recognition flickered to life. Of his spectacular body clad in scant boxer briefs, his face smiling down at me while I drove through LA traffic. "You have a billboard."

He winced. "Of all the things you had to remember . . ."

"It's an impressive billboard."

He didn't take the bait and smile but merely shrugged, the tiniest lifting of one shoulder. God, how had I not recognized him? He had ads. Lots of them. His face had brooded at me in magazines, ads for watches, colognes. I was fairly certain I'd seen him play once by way of reading next to Greg while he watched a game.

"You played for Washington."

"Yeah."

But something happened. What had those guys said? Something about a bad hit.

"Were you hurt?"

He didn't look injured. He moved like silk and steel.

Lucian huffed out a breath. A world of emotion inhabited that brief sound. A world of regret and despair. "You could say that." He swallowed thickly, his throat working hard, and stared off again. The strong lines of his profile were strained. "Concussion syndrome. One too many knocks to the head."

Blood drained from my head to pool at the base of my spine. It hadn't been his health on the line; it had been his life. The thought of this proud, intelligent, loyal man no longer being here . . . it made my insides scream in horror and my arms ache to hold him.

Which was more than foolish. We were barely acquaintances. He didn't want me poking around in his life.

"So here I am," he went on in a dead voice. "Out of the game and fixing up my grandmother's estate." That blazing gaze swung my way,

97

angry and hurt. It sliced through my tender skin. "Is that enough for you? Or do you want a rundown of my symptoms too?"

"No." I swallowed past the lump in my throat.

"You sure?" He stepped closer, eyes wild. "You don't want to hear about the short temper? The memory lapses? Headaches? Well, hell, you know all about those, don't you? I can't even pick a woman up at the airport without having a spell."

"Lucian . . ."

"Call me Oz. The old man behind the curtain, pretending to be something he's not."

Now he was feeling sorry for himself. He had good reason. But it didn't help him. Not one bit.

"No. You told me to call you Lucian."

"Because I was hiding," he bit out. "So you wouldn't know what a damn wreck I am."

"You are *not* a wreck."

If anything, he got more agitated, his skin darkening with displeasure and frustration. "Do not pity me."

"Don't you yell at me," I snapped back. "I'll pity you all I want."

"What?" He gaped in outrage. "You actually admit that you feel sorry for me?"

We were nearly nose to nose, both of us shouting like children. Didn't stop me, though. "Why not, when you're acting pitiful, stalking off to sulk, or lashing out at anyone who dares to care?"

An irate growl escaped him, like he just might blow. With a jerky, harsh movement, he raised his hand. And that was when it happened. I flinched. Violently.

We both froze.

I took in the entire scene with an acute awareness that bordered on painful. The move horrified me because I didn't want that to be my first instinct when a man raised his hand. But it was there all the same, hanging in the air like a neon sign. Worse in hindsight, because I could clearly see by the angle of his arm—now frozen in shock—that he had been about to run his hand through his hair in frustration.

He'd seen my reaction. There was no escaping that.

He finally broke the taut silence. "You thought I was going to hit you."

Not a question. We both knew it.

I hated that I'd flinched, that I was ashamed of my reaction. I hated that a vital piece of me had been altered. It was another thing taken from me without my permission. But I couldn't change it; I *had* flinched, and now I had to own it.

I lifted my chin, because I was also not going to apologize. "You're a big guy who's in my face arguing with me. And you're right—I don't know you from Adam. So yes, I'm going to be wary."

When Lucian spoke, his voice was soft and carefully modulated.

"If it makes you more comfortable, I'll stay out of your way for the rest of your visit. Regardless, I want you to feel safe, so can I explain something?"

When I nodded, he continued.

"I've been in a lot of fights. On the ice. And once off it. But all of them were against guys who could hold their own. This scar"—he pointed to a faint line under his left brow—"was from a left hook I didn't see coming. I returned the favor and broke the guy's nose. I'm telling you this because I won't lie and say I'm a stranger to violence."

He didn't blink, didn't hesitate to meet my eyes. "But you? You could slap me, punch me, kick me in the nuts, call me names, disparage Mamie, whom I love more than anyone on Earth, and I still wouldn't ever raise a hand to you. Because I don't hit women or anyone weaker than me. Ever."

He stopped there, his concerned gaze darting over my face. "I apologize that my behavior made you feel unsafe. It wasn't my intention. If you believe anything about me, believe I will always be the guy who stands with you, never against you."

As if that settled everything, he moved to go.

"I wouldn't do those things," I said. When he quirked a brow in confusion, I clarified. "I wouldn't hit you or disparage Amalie. I'm not abusive either."

His expression turned baffled, as though he didn't know what to make of me. "Okay." That was it.

But then he paused, as if something else occurred to him. "Just so we're clear, if you do hurt Mamie or try to take advantage of her, I won't hit, but I will escort your butt off this property for good."

Then he gave me his back once more and stalked off.

"Jerk," I snapped.

"I heard that," he called, still walking.

"Good," I cried back, lifting my voice so he'd hear me loud and clear. "Because I never said I wouldn't call you names."

His snort was the only reply. He was almost out of sight, about to take the stairs that led to the beach.

"Lucian!"

I hadn't expected him to stop, but he did.

"I'm sorry too," I said to the stiff wall of his back. "For saying you were acting pitiful."

He didn't move, but I knew he was listening keenly.

"You're not. I don't pity you. You just piss me off."

I couldn't hear him, but I saw the way his chin ducked down, his head angled slightly to the side, and I knew he'd snorted. In humor or annoyance was another question altogether. "Good to know, Snoopy."

This time, I was the one who turned around and walked away. It didn't feel good, precisely, but was a slight victory nonetheless.

CHAPTER NINE

Emma

I spent the rest of the day and much of the next morning hanging out in my bungalow. It was nice not having to go anywhere or do anything. I was determined to remain relaxed.

Well, as relaxed as I could be with a certain hot, annoying ex–hockey player stuck on my mind. God, but I had to repress the urge to google him. I itched to watch him play. But I knew it would be a mistake; I wouldn't be able to function properly around the man if I saw him all bulked up and badass in hockey gear. I wasn't a fan, but I knew I would be if I saw Lucian play.

I was quite proud of myself for resisting the temptation. I did not, however, resist the temptation of all the lovely meals the kitchen kept sending my way. Breakfast included delicate palm-size apple turnovers, something I would ordinarily pass on, given that the ones I'd had in the past had been too sweet and cloying. But I knew from experience that the food here should not be ignored.

The first bite of turnover was my undoing. The pastry was not heavy or greasy but light and flakey, golden layers that shattered at the first bite, then melted on the tongue. The filling consisted of sliced

apples cooked until just tender, their tartly sweet juice a perfect comple-
ment to the richness of the crust. Heaven.

Frankly, I wasn't sure what I'd do when I left here. Probably go
into withdrawal. For the first time, I truly envied Amalie having such
an incredible chef. Pastries could be bought at a bakery. Sure, these
were the best I'd had, but I could get something close to it if I wanted.
Except it wouldn't be the same. Here, I was pampered with an exacting
attention to detail that left me feeling utterly cared for.

The fact that the raisin rolls were not included made me think that
yes, Sal had blabbed, and yes, the house had listened and tried another
approach to please me. Perhaps I should have been embarrassed or upset
that Sal told the chef, but I couldn't find it in myself to be, not when
the results were so delicious. I was definitely going to send a thank-you
note to the kitchen as soon as I found something to write on.

Now that breakfast was over, I found myself itching to do something. Anything. Loneliness hit me in an unexpected wave. The stink
of it was I couldn't call any of my friends; they were all dying to know
about the finale, and I couldn't tell them. I might have hung out with
some of my costars, but I was still smarting. Basic pride pushed me to
hide away and lick my wounds.

With that depressing thought, I washed the dishes and tucked them
back into the basket. A knock on the door had me hurrying over with it;
the house was nothing if not efficient in breakfast delivery and pickup.

Basket in hand, I opened the door. And found Lucian standing
there, looking freshly showered and impossibly large on my sunny
stoop.

He was here. He was *here*.

He eyed the basket. "Going on a picnic?"

"You know this is the food-delivery basket." I was ridiculously glad
to see him but determined not to show it like some panting puppy.
Damn it, but the man was unfairly potent, smoldering with swagger.

"I don't have food delivered to me. That's only for guests." He seemed to find this amusing. I found it a tragedy.

"You are missing out, then."

Lucian's mouth quirked. "If it's so good, why are you here, ready to thrust it out the door?"

I was fairly certain he was messing with me. But I took it in stride because I liked when he did. "It's empty, honey pie. I thought you were here to pick it up."

"I'm supposed to be busing your dishes now?"

"You're trying to piss me off, aren't you?" I said, tossing back the words he'd used on me during our first meeting.

He grinned wide, the gesture so quick and stunningly beautiful on him it made my breath hitch. "It's so easy," he answered, just as I had. "At least make me work for it."

"Don't worry; I will."

That shut him up in a hurry. His nostrils flared, all that smiling lightness sliding into something darker, something with promise. Heat coiled around my thighs, as an insistent thud strummed between them.

As though he'd physically felt my reaction, he blinked and swallowed hard. But then his expression returned to basic neutral, which was to say typical stern-and-intense Lucian, and he cleared his throat. "I was actually here to ask if you wanted to go on a hike."

Flabbergasted, I gaped at him like a fish flipped out of water. It was the absolute last thing I'd expected him to say. And judging by the darkening color along his neck, he knew it.

Shifting his weight, he peered at me from under his brows. "I made you uncomfortable, didn't I? Shit."

"No." I lifted a hand to forestall any potential leaving on his part. "Not at all. You just surprised me."

That was an understatement. We hadn't parted on the best of terms, and he'd been extremely clear about wanting to be left alone. I'd been committed to trying to do just that. But he was here, and I had missed him. Barely a day, and I had missed the sound of his voice, the pleasure of talking to him.

He ducked his head and shook it wryly. "Surprised myself."

"Did you?" I said, barely repressing a laugh. Because I wanted to. I wanted to freaking spread my arms and laugh with unfettered giddiness.

He looked back up at me from under his thick lashes. "I figured you might be bored. And yesterday, I was . . ." Wincing, he clasped the back of his neck, which did lovely things to his ropy forearms. "An asshole."

"You were," I said solemnly—the effect ruined by the smile breaking loose. "But then I wasn't exactly a peach either."

He didn't smile, but his eyes glinted with amusement. We stared at each other, sharing a look that said we both understood perfectly how ridiculous we'd been. Then Lucian inclined his head toward the outdoors. "Well? Do you want to go?"

I was still recovering from the shock of him actually inviting me to do something with him, but I shook it off. Because wherever he was, I wanted to be, which should have terrified me, but it weirdly made me feel stronger. Nothing in my life was certain right now, not my career, not my living arrangements, and certainly not my love life. But when Lucian and I were together, I felt wholly myself, not the "everything is perfect; keep moving along" front I projected to the world.

"Sure. Let me just get dressed. Don't move!" I shoved the food basket into his arms, then paused, flushing. "Sorry. Come in. I'll just . . ." I tripped over a slipper I'd left on the floor. "Yeah . . ."

His chuckle followed me into the bedroom, where I dressed with the giddy excitement of a preteen. I didn't know how I'd get through the day without either making a bigger fool of myself, strangling him, or jumping him. None of those options particularly appealed to me—well, the last one did, but I couldn't act on that. Didn't matter; I was going.

Lucian

Was I making a mistake inviting Emma on a hike? Probably. But I found I didn't care. I'd been a raging dick yesterday. I'd let things get to me, let the grief for what I'd lost take over. Problem was, when I grieved, I raged. The doctors had warned me that it might be difficult to handle things, that my personality might be a little different.

A little. Right. All my life, I had been laid back—always the one to go with the flow, forget the nonsense. I was almost a stranger to myself now. My skin didn't fit right over my bones. There were times it felt as though a swarm of hornets attacked my head, buzzing and stinging.

And I lashed out.

It shamed me to the core when I remembered Emma's pretty face going pale, her entire body recoiling, as though expecting a strike. She had been afraid of me. For one horrible second, she'd thought I would hurt her. It had made me sick to my stomach, but it was only when I'd finally settled down in the darkness of my room that I'd felt the full weight of that remorse.

I could no more keep away from her now than I could stop breathing. She needed more than just a tersely uttered apology. She needed reassurance, care.

I wasn't sure if taking her for a hike in the mountains was enough, but she appeared happy as I parked the truck at a lot near the base of the trail.

"I have a pack," I told her, grabbing it. "I can carry whatever you need."

"What do you have in there?" She rose up on her toes, trying to peek into it, which brought her far too close for comfort. My lids lowered as I caught a whiff of her sweet scent. I swore I detected a hint of apples. What had she thought of chaussons aux pommes? She clearly appreciated my food, but I was greedy; I wanted the particulars. And yet I couldn't bring myself to ask.

I held the pack up, out of her reach, teasing her because it made her face light up in a way that I was quickly becoming addicted to. "Easy there, Snoopy. I've got all the essentials."

Her indigo eyes narrowed. "Do you have sunscreen?"

"Of course I—hell. No, I don't."

Emma huffed, shaking her head at my egregious error as she dug out a bottle from her bag-like purse. "They never do," she muttered. "Would it kill you men to take care of your skin?"

"Hey, I wash my face." I did it every time I shaved, which was every damn day with the rate my beard grew out.

Emma scoffed and kept muttering. "And those pesky little things like skin cancer, premature wrinkles, and age spots mean nothing, I guess."

"Well, no, I mean, I hadn't thought . . ."

I trailed off. Because Emma began to slather lotion over her face and along the smooth golden skin of her bare arms and neck. She wore a tight white workout tank with dark-blue stretchy pants, highlighting every glorious dip and curve of her body.

Her body. It was insanely cute, though she probably wouldn't want to hear that. The top of her head barely reached my shoulder. She wasn't delicate, but compared to me, she damn well looked it. Nicely rounded arms, perky breasts that would perfectly fit in my palms, a short waist leading into a fantastic ass that bounced whenever she walked, and curvy thighs and legs.

I knew the shit standards Hollywood pushed on their actresses, keeping them this side of too thin. Emma was slim and fit, but nothing short of starvation was getting rid of that ass and those thighs, thank the Lord.

My hands itched to palm her sweet butt. But I did not want to get slapped and was a grown man who knew better. I dragged my eyes up. Concentrating on her face hardly helped. She had the kind of lips that always looked freshly kissed, rosy, and lush, the top lip slightly larger than her bottom lip. Anytime I looked at her mouth for too long, I wanted to kiss it. Hell, anytime I thought of her mouth, I wanted to kiss it.

Fuck. This was a bad idea.

I glanced away, squinting into the sunlight that Emma declared was slowly ruining my skin.

"Here." She thrust the sunscreen under my nose, snapping my attention back to her. "Put some on."

I wasn't about to argue. I slathered on the lotion as best I could. It was cool, at least, and didn't stink. There was that. All the stuff Cassandra used stank of dead flowers or fake fruits.

Emma made another noise of annoyance and stepped in front of me. Despite her obvious disgust in my apparently inadequate skin-care regimen, her eyes were fond as she peered up at me.

"You have streaks of it everywhere," she admonished before frowning. "You're too tall."

You're just right

"You'll have to blame my parents on that one, Em."

The corners of her lips curled.

"Bend down, will you?" She was already reaching up for me.

Rendered a deer in headlights, I did as she asked, my face slack, my gaze stuck on hers. With gentle but deft movements, she ran the pads of her fingers over my skin, along the bridge of my nose, down the sides of my cheeks. Biting back a groan, I lowered my lids and breathed deeply. They were simple touches, nothing more than her smearing sunscreen on me. And it felt so good I wanted to purr or whimper. Something. Anything to get her to keep doing it.

But she stopped, done with her task. Leaving me to straighten and get my shit together.

"There." She put on her sunglasses. "Now we're ready."

Yep, I wanted to kiss her. "Great. My skin feels safer already."

"I am immune to your sarcasm, honey pie."

I'd had nicknames foisted on me my entire life. Some were awful, some funny. What I hadn't felt until now was pleasure from hearing one. Emma calling me *honey pie* sent a ping of pleasure straight into my chest every time. But it was tempered with disappointment today.

Because she'd stopped calling me Brick when she teased. I knew it was a result of my self-pitying rant yesterday that I was a washed-up athlete. Her consideration chafed. It shouldn't have, but it did. I wanted her to feel free and easy with me. But I'd smashed the foundation of our budding . . . whatever it was. I could blame only myself. I would rebuild it, though. It had become imperative to me in ways I didn't really want to examine.

Heading out, we set a steady pace. Emma was in good shape, and I had to slow my usual stride only by a little. The path moved upward through sweet-smelling grass and rustling trees. We didn't speak but kept walking in easy silence. I liked that about Emma; sure, she would give me shit without hesitation, but it was never cruel, and she didn't feel the need to fill silences when she didn't have anything to say.

We reached a stream fed by water meandering down the mountain. The stream was a low trickle right now, but Emma slowed to admire it. With a sunny smile, she glanced my way. "Thank you for inviting me here. I needed this."

I was beginning to realize I'd take her anywhere she wanted. Whatever she needed, I'd do my best to provide. It was unsettling as hell, but some things weren't worth fighting against.

Mamie had it right; I was here. So was Emma. And the fact was I wanted to be around her, whether it was a smart idea or not. She took me outside myself, to a place where every thought wasn't mired in rage or regret. I was under no illusions that Emma Maron could fix me; no one could do that. But I enjoyed the moments I had within her orbit, and that was more than I'd had before she fell into my life. Even when I'd been playing, I'd never had this level of connection with a person.

I managed a mumbled "Welcome," but she was off again, and I followed. We didn't speak again until an hour later when we reached a clearing that overlooked the valley. A fine sheen of sweat glittered on Emma's skin as she raised her face to the sun and let the breeze wash over her.

I did the same and pulled off my shirt to fully feel it. The sound of Emma's barely concealed gurgle of surprise nearly brought a smile to my mouth, but I kept my eyes closed and my expression neutral. I hadn't thought much about it when I'd stripped my shirt. But she liked what she saw. I'd known this when I'd confronted her after she watched me swim naked. It had been written all over her expressive face then.

I felt her gaze like a hot brand now, appreciating me. I may have milked it a little, flexing my pecs and abs before stretching my arms out overhead.

"Careful," came her bland voice. "You might tweak a nerve stretching like that."

I let my arms drop and gave her a baleful look. "You calling me an old man, Snoopy?"

"I'm calling you a show-off, honey pie," she countered, then paid me back in full by bending over to touch her toes, that perfect peach of an ass aimed my way.

Hell.

She bounced just enough to make my dick perk up. Cursing, I turned to put my shirt on and then dug into the pack as she huffed out a light laugh.

"You're an evil woman, Em." I handed her a bottle of water.

She grinned. "You had it coming, Lucian."

"Yes, I did." I found myself smiling, despite the ache of desire in my lower gut. I liked Emma, but I *loved* the way she teased. It reminded me of the camaraderie I'd had with my guys, but better. I'd never wanted to haul any of my teammates onto my lap and devour their mouths. The mix of needful lust and fun was strangely intoxicating.

I pulled out another water and drank deep before offering her an energy bar. We found a wide, smooth boulder to sit on in the shade and drank the rest of our water. Emma drew her knees close to her chest and rested her arms on them. Her profile softened with contentment.

Which meant I had to ruin it.

"I'm sorry for scaring you yesterday."

Emma stiffened, and I silently cursed myself for saying anything. But then she tilted her head my way. Her calm blue eyes moved over my face, as though assessing. I held myself still, pretending I didn't itch to hop off the damn rock.

"You didn't scare me," she said softly, carefully. "Not really."

But I had. I'd been there. I'd seen her fear. "I'm . . . loud when I lose my temper," I said, feeling like an asshole. I shouldn't have lost my temper with this woman at all. "I used to be . . ." Better. Whole. "Calmer. Anyway, it was unforgivable and I—"

Her hand landed on my forearm, warm and steady.

"Lucian. Don't. You have no reason to apologize. We were arguing. It happens."

"But—"

"My dad hit."

Whatever I had planned to say came to a screeching halt, a red mist moving over my gaze. She'd been hit. My fists curled. I wanted . . . fuck. I wanted to hug her. Hold her.

Her nose wrinkled as she traced along the seam of her pants. "It was his favorite method of discipline, if you can call it that." She grimaced, glancing away. "Sometimes, I flinch, even though logic tells me there's no real threat."

I swallowed twice before I could find my voice. "Understandable. Fear is mostly reactionary."

If you ask, I'll hold you. I won't let go until you feel safe again. Ask me, Em.

110

With a frown, Emma shrugged, as if she could push it all away. "It's embarrassing. I'm not that weak and frightened girl anymore."

No, she was strong, resilient, beautiful. And yet she was embarrassed. It was fundamentally wrong.

"You think being physically abused is a sign of weakness?"

Emma ducked her head, the sunlight glinting on her hair like a halo. "I . . . no. I don't know. I guess a part of me always wonders, If I'd been stronger, bigger, would it have happened?"

I understood. Far too well. What-ifs plagued my life. I let her worries sink in and thought about them before answering with measured words. "I have this buddy. He's a big guy, six-five, solid muscle. No one with any sense wants to mess with him." My thumb flicked a bit of gravel from the edge of the rock. "He had a girlfriend. They'd been together since high school."

A frown wrinkled between Emma's brows. "And he hit her?"

"No. She hit him."

Her eyes went wide. "What?"

I shrugged. "She'd get into these rages without provocation. She'd scream and rant, throw shit at his head, slap his face, claw his skin. He'd just take it, simply shut down, and let her rail."

The memory sank like a stone in my gut. The deadness in Hal's eyes, how he'd held himself stiff and apart from everyone.

"It was one of those things you wouldn't believe until you witnessed it," I said to Emma. "Then you wondered why he stayed. Took him years to leave her. She was all he knew, and she'd somehow convinced him it was all his fault."

"God." The empathy in Emma's voice wrapped its soft hands around my heart. I leaned a hair closer to her.

"Point is. This was a big guy, strong and powerful. One good swat from him, and she'd be out for the count. But he wasn't about to raise his hand to her or to any woman. Because he knew his strength and wielded it responsibly."

My gaze met Emma's deep-blue one. "Of course, there are men who hit, and they get off on using their strength to hurt others. But at the most basic level, abuse isn't about the physically strong versus the weak. It's a mindfuck, designed to break down your dignity and confidence."

Her gaze moved over my face as we stared at each other. And I got the impression that she was working things out in her head. Slowly, like the tide coming in, her expression opened up, and she gave me the smallest of smiles. It rushed into all the dark corners of my heart, and I had to mentally brace myself.

"You're right," she said.

I cleared my throat and gave her a solemn nod. "I usually am."

It took her a second; then she huffed out a breath. "Oh my God, you're terrible." She sounded amused, though, as she nudged me with her shoulder.

I nudged her back; it was either that or haul her onto my lap. "That's no secret, honeybee."

"Honeybee?" she repeated, a warning in her voice.

I bit back a grin. "If I'm going to be a honey pie, makes sense you'd be the bee."

The sweep of her brows lowered ominously. "Why? Because I'm after your honey?" She scoffed long and loud, and I had to laugh. If anyone was after honey here, it was me.

"Bees make honey, Em." I nudged her again, hard enough to rock her and make her squeak with a laugh. "And you seem intent upon making me sweet."

CHAPTER TEN

Emma

Make Lucian Osmond sweet? I suspected he always was; he simply didn't know it.

I was in a ridiculously good mood on the drive back to Rosemont. Though prone to long periods of silence, and sometimes gruff, Lucian was good company. I didn't mind the silences; I tended to daydream and get caught up in my own worlds anyway. And the gruffness, the grumbles, and the huffs were kind of adorable. Not that I'd tell him that. Or maybe I should; he'd probably end up doing it more.

Thing was, I didn't know what was going on between us. I liked him. Lord knew I wanted him. And if he didn't know that, at the very least, he knew I found him attractive. I wasn't completely oblivious. I'd seen him looking as well. Never leering or too lingering. But he seemed to like what he saw as well.

When he let his guard down, he flirted. But it was clear he resisted it. Which was smart. Both of our professional lives were up in the air, he was clearly working through a lot of stress, and I . . . technically, I'd just broken up with my live-in boyfriend. Who I hadn't thought of for days. Greg was just one in a line of disappointments. Either I had completely crap taste or crap judgment. Regardless, it was for the best to stay clear of relationships for a while. *Focus on becoming a better me and all that, and stick to simple friendship with Lucian.*

Then I caught a glimpse of his big body in the driver's seat next to me, a ratty Captain America T-shirt stretched tight across his wide shoulders but hanging loose over his flat belly. He wore cargo shorts that just reached his knees.

Were men's knees supposed to be sexy? Their calves? One sight of Lucian's bony knee, delineated muscled thigh, and hard calf, lightly dusted with dark curling hair, made me want to reach out and stroke his leg, creep my hand under those shorts to cup what I knew would be firm and meaty and . . . damn.

Keeping my hands to myself and my mind out of his pants was going to be difficult. Which was weird; I loved men and sex, but I'd never been preoccupied by either. Until him.

I put down the window as we turned onto Rosemont's drive. "I'm starving. What do you think they'll have for lunch?"

"I don't know. I was going to make myself a sandwich." Lucian glanced over, a glint in his pale-jade eyes. "You're wrinkling your nose. Disrespecting the humble sandwich, Em? Or have you been spoiled by the elaborate meals from the kitchen?"

"I was not wrinkling my nose at your sandwich." I *might* have been. The lift of his brow said he read me like a book. I huffed a laugh. "Okay, fine. The house kitchen is spoiling me rotten. I should end it now and tell them not to send me any more meals."

"Don't go overboard," he murmured, eyes back on the road. "You'll offend Amalie. She's very proud of her kitchen."

"It was an empty threat. I'm hooked well and good."

The corners of his eyes crinkled. "If it's difficult for you to fix your own meals, I'll make you a sandwich."

"Hey. I'm not a princess. I can make my own sandwich—thank you very much." Though the idea of Lucian making one for me had its merits. Spending more time with him, chief among them.

114

He tossed me a challenging look. "Can you really?"

"You don't have to look so dubious. All right . . . I admit I am a horrible cook. Everything comes out bland or dry. But I can slap peanut butter on bread."

His expression told me all I needed to know about his thoughts on my sandwich-making abilities. "Don't worry, honeybee; there will be lunch ready for you. Meals are one thing you can count on at Rosemont."

"Snoopy, honeybee . . . I'm not certain I like that you have so many names to tease me." Lie. I loved it. But he didn't need to know that.

Lucian, however, got that gleam back in his eyes, even though he kept them on the road. "Put Brick back into the rotation, and we'll be even."

My heart skipped a beat. He'd noticed I'd stopped using it. I felt awful for having called him something that hit too close to the bone for him. And yet here he was challenging me to use it again. Maybe there was power in embracing what could be perceived as a weakness and making it your own. Or maybe men were strange beasts, and I'd never fully understand them.

Either way, I shrugged, as if unaffected. "How about brick head? Seems accurate half the time."

Lucian chuckled and pulled into his parking spot under the shade of a towering eucalyptus. "Sounds about right."

His humor ebbed as he caught sight of the two SUVs parked in the lot.

"Looks like Amalie has company."

Lucian grunted, then got out, still eyeing the vehicles. He waited for me to round the pickup and come alongside him before heading toward the path that led to the grounds and my bungalow. Silence fell as we walked, and I could feel the tension radiating off him.

However he was before, I didn't know, but this version of Lucian Osmond did not like unexpected guests. If I had to guess, he would disappear until they were long gone.

Then again, I'd been assuming the guests were Amalie's. But as we rounded the corner that took us to the terrace of the big house, Lucian's step faltered. A low and vicious "Motherfuck" tore from him as he spotted the people having drinks at one of the tables.

There was an undercurrent of pure panic in his tone, and I felt compelled to brush my arm with his just once, my finger trailing over his curled fist. He jerked his gaze my way, pale eyes pained, panicked, and a little surprised. But he'd felt my touch, and his pinky twined with mine for a brief moment of acknowledgement.

"Friends of yours?" I murmured.

"You could say that." Lucian moved just enough to put space between us.

One of the men stood and shouted a jovial "Oy! Ozzy!"

Visibly bracing himself, Lucian trudged forward. I could, in theory, retreat to my bungalow. But it would be rude. More importantly, I'd be abandoning Lucian to face whatever this was.

Maybe he doesn't want you around to witness it, my inner voice hissed. But it was too late. We were already at the table.

There were three guests, all of them around our age. The one who'd shouted stood and spread his massive arms wide in clear happiness. A big bear of a man, he was taller than Lucian by an inch but likely outweighed him by a good twenty pounds. Shaggy sandy hair with a thick beard that framed a smile broken up by a missing right lateral incisor—the man lumbered over to a stone-faced Lucian and gathered him up in what looked like a bone-bending hug.

"Oz," he said, practically picking Lucian up. "You dick. No word in months, and all this time, you've been hiding away in paradise."

Lucian let out a strained ghost of a laugh. "So you decided to invade it, huh?"

"Didn't leave me much choice, did you?" The man's smile was still in place when he let Lucian go, but it was strained now. And I knew he was unsure of his welcome. A pang went through me, because it was clear this man thought the world of Lucian.

His blue eyes glanced over at me and paused. "Hello . . ." I was treated to another tilted but charming smile. "And you are . . . holy shit." His booming voice cracked. "You're Emma Maron, aren't you?"

Instant spotlight on me. I felt it every time. My smile automatically wanted to go into public-relations mode. I resisted the urge. This was Lucian's friend. "Yes."

Lucian grunted, then inclined his head. "Emma, this lummox is Axel Bromwell. We call him Brommy."

"We hockey players love our nicknames." Brommy extended a bear paw for me to shake. But he lifted my hand and kissed the air over my knuckles. "Princess Anya. It is a pleasure."

"Emma, please." It was awkward enough with Lucian stiff at my side.

"Jesus, Brom, cut it out," Lucian grumped. "She's not her character."

Brommy rolled his eyes. "I know that. You stored your stick up your ass, didn't you?" He didn't appear to be bothered by this notion, though, and took my hand to link our arms. "Sorry about that, Emma. Momentarily starstruck is all. I'm okay now."

I snickered, and he winked, eyes bright. "But feel free to pull out a whip if I misbehave again."

Princess Anya *had* been handy with a whip.

Behind me Lucian growled an unintelligible curse. Ignoring him, Brommy led me to the table, where two other newcomers waited. I noticed the man immediately. How could I not? He was a slightly washed-out version of Lucian—same basic bone structure, though his nose was slimmer, more elegant, and his face a bit narrower.

His hair wasn't the rich, bittersweet-chocolate tinged with cherry highlights but was medium brown. He had green eyes under straight brows, but whereas Lucian's and Amalie's were stunningly pale like frosted-over jade, his were a warmer grape green. Beautiful in their own right and calculating.

The worst of it was he noticed my study of him and liked it. I had the idea that he assumed I was interested. I wasn't. The man was gorgeous, but I didn't feel a glimmer of attraction. It didn't stop him from rising and kissing my hand as Brommy had done. But where Brommy made me want to laugh, this guy had me wanting to snatch my hand back as soon as possible.

"Hello, lovely," he said. "I'm Anton."

"Are you Lucian's brother?"

Behind me Lucian made a noise that I interpreted as "As if."

Anton's smile was sly. "First cousin. I got the good genes."

"Hmm." My attention moved on to the woman who stood and was practically hopping from foot to foot with impatience. She was probably a few years younger than me and cute as hell.

She, too, had brown hair, although hers curled in a bouncy halo around the oval of her face. And those grape-green eyes.

"Tina," she blurted out, shoving Anton to the side. Either she was strong as hell, or he was used to her pushing him out of the way. Probably both. "Anton's sister and Luc's cousin. And oh my God, I'm going to be a dork like Brommy, because I just love, love, love *Dark Castle*, and I can't believe Mamie didn't warn us you were here. I'd have worn something cuter, gotten my nails done, something, anything, to mark this momentous occasion—"

"Breathe, Tiny," Lucian cut in, amused.

She immediately let out an expansive breath and wrinkled her nose. "Shit. I am such a goober."

Laughing, I shook her hand. "No, you're wonderful."

Tina grinned at that. "I'll calm down in a second, I promise."

"Good, I wouldn't want to get my whip."

Lucian grunted—the one I knew meant "Lord help me." I shot him a side-look, but his expression remained bland. He stood fairly close, just to the right of me, but it was as though his entire body leaned toward the pool house. He wanted to escape. Badly. But he was rooted to the spot.

I felt for him. Especially when everyone took their seats, and Tina pulled out one for me, leaving an empty one next to mine for Lucian. He hesitated. These were his cousins and good friend; he might have had a chance to run off, but then Amalie came out of the house, crimson silk caftan flowing, a beaming smile on her face. And I knew Lucian's chances of retreat were gone.

He obviously did too. With a sigh, he plopped down in the chair.

"Ah, good, you two are back." Amalie grinned, her red mouth wide as she sat at the head of the table, a queen at court. "We can have lunch."

This being Rosemont, no sooner had she announced this than the waitstaff arrived carrying plates. It wasn't lost on me—or, I suspect, Lucian—that they had exactly the right amount of meals to serve all of us.

Curiosity had me wanting to see this whole strange reunion play out, but I was starving, and when the plate was set before me, bearing a personal-size quiche with a side salad of baby greens, my stomach actually rumbled.

From under his unfairly long lashes, Lucian shot me a look, the corners of his mouth twitching. He'd heard.

"I told you I was hungry," I muttered to him.

Those expressive lips twitched again. "We'll have to work harder at keeping you fed, bee."

He said it so low, barely moving his mouth, that I was certain only I could hear it. But Anton was watching too closely, and his gaze darted between us. "So, Luc, you're dating the princess. Nice move."

My eyes narrowed.

Lucian sat back in a lazy sprawl of limbs that belied the tight warning in his voice. "*Emma* is a guest of Mamie's, Ant. Remember that, will you?"

By the way Anton scowled, I doubted he liked his nickname, but before he could respond, Amalie nodded with an elegant wave of her hand.

"This is true. You boys keep Emma out of your squabbles."

Which all but guaranteed I'd be the center of them.

I turned toward a still wide-eyed Tina. "They fight often, do they?"

Tina appeared amused but resigned. "Since they were kids. Doesn't help that they both play center."

"Both *played*," Anton corrected, like an ass. "I am not retired. Thank Christ."

His declaration fell like a lead ball onto the table. And my heart ached for Lucian. Even Anton seemed to realize how horrible he'd been. He grimaced, his face twisting with genuine remorse. "Shit, sorry, Luc."

Lucian might as well have been made from granite. "No problem."

Brommy, who had been given two quiches, leaned in and caught my eye. "Ant is just salty because we kick his ass during every playoff. Isn't that right, Ant-Man?"

Anton smirked. "Kicked your ass last year, didn't I, Bromide?"

"That's because we didn't have—shit. Sorry, Oz." He ducked his head and shoveled a hunk of quiche in his mouth.

They didn't have Lucian playing for them. He must have missed the last bit of the season.

Lucian suddenly snorted. "Well, this is fun."

Brommy lifted his head and winked. "Just like old times."

Lucian chuffed out a weak laugh and started to eat. I relaxed enough to do the same. The food was, as expected, delicious.

"What is in this quiche?" I asked, trying to hide my moan.

"Sun-dried tomatoes and gouda," Amalie said.

"You cooking today, Mamie?" Anton asked with a sly look.

"It is a small thing to heat an oven, no?" The frost in her gaze dared him to say otherwise, and I smiled around my mouthful of food.

"So," Tina said to me. "I know you can't give details, but are we going to love the finale?" Her green eyes gleamed with excitement. "I cannot wait."

Under the table, Lucian's foot touched the side of mine. Support. In the smallest of ways, and yet it felt like everything.

"Well," I began diplomatically. "People will certainly be talking about it; that I can guarantee."

"Oh, I knew it!" She leaned close. "You have to tell me—what's it like working with Macon Saint? He's gorgeous. That body. God."

"Hey," Brommy cut in. "Hot-bodied men right here."

"Oh, are there?" Tina squinted, peering around. "I'm having trouble locating them."

"Lean in a little, sweets, and I'll give you a guided tour."

After making a face at Brommy, she turned back to me. "Tell me all about Saint."

"Yes," Lucian said, finally meeting my eyes. His were piercing and slightly evil just then. "Is he as dreamy in real life?"

Tina chucked her napkin at him.

I gave him a bland smile. "Yes, he is."

That wiped the amusement from Lucian's face.

"He's wonderful," I told Tina truthfully. "A gentleman with a very dry sense of humor. He's extremely generous as an actor and never hogs the scene. We've become very close over the years."

Lucian grunted.

I kept my gaze on Tina. "He's also engaged."

Brommy laughed. "The hot ones go quick, Tiny."

"You're finally admitting you are not hot?" she countered with sauce.

"We both know that would be a lie. I've had offers, but I'm smart enough not to get caught."

Tina made a *sure* sign with her hand while rolling her eyes my way. I caught the look and grinned.

Anton watched our interplay, then turned to Lucian. "Speaking of which, I saw Cass the other day. Seems she's hooked on to Cashon."

It was as if the air had been sucked from the space, which was impressive given that we were outside. Lucian went ruddy, his jaw bunching.

Amalie muttered something that sounded a lot like *imbécile* under her breath, then went into a litany of murmured French while glaring at Anton.

I knew I shouldn't ask; I knew it instinctively. And yet somehow my stupid mouth formed the words anyway. "Who is Cass?"

Eyes darted around, everyone looking at each other, as if to figure out who would say it. But Lucian, who kept his focus on his food, eating mechanically as though he barely tasted it, answered as blandly as toast. "My ex-fiancée."

And it hit me: Lucian had lost a lot more than his profession.

CHAPTER ELEVEN

Lucian

"You up for company?" Brommy didn't wait for my answer but took the empty seat next to me on the small patio that overlooked the ocean.

It was impressive that he'd ferreted me out, given the size of the estate, but Brommy had a knack for such things. I dug my hand in the small cooler at my side and pulled out a bottle of beer for him.

"Thanks." A snick rang out as he opened it.

The sun had all but disappeared behind the ocean, leaving only a brilliant gold sliver. In a blink, that was gone, too, and the sky deepened to a soft smoky blue that reminded me of Emma's eyes. Which was hokey as hell but still true.

Brommy sat back with an expansive sigh, tilting his head up to look at the stars that were starting to shine in the velvet twilight. A breeze rolled over us.

"Man, I love this weather," he said.

"It's great. If you ignore the droughts, rampant wildfires, mudslides, and earthquakes."

He chuckled. "Still beats the shitacular humidity of DC."

"We weren't there for the weather, Brom."

That shut him up, and I felt like a dick for saying it. Brommy didn't say anything for a bit—just drank his beer and stared out into the night. When he finally spoke, his usual jovial tone was subdued.

"Ant is an asshole."

"He can't help himself around me." I took a drink. "We've always brought out the worst in each other. Both of us playing hockey only made it worse."

But he'd won that particular competition, hadn't he? I might have been the better player, but he still laced up his skates.

"That shit he said about Cass—"

"I honestly don't give a shit," I cut in, then glanced over at a doubtful Brommy. "I'm serious. You know what the strongest emotion I feel is when I think of Cassandra? Relief."

"Man . . ." He shook his head with dark amusement.

"It's horrible, isn't it? I was going to marry that woman, and I was too complacent to even notice that I didn't love her. Hell, I barely liked her."

Sometimes, I still couldn't believe how close I'd come to making what would have been one of the biggest mistakes in my life. Worse, I'd let Cassandra—she'd never wanted me to call her Cass—believe I loved her. It was a shit thing to do to anyone.

"A sweet smile and a nice set of tits make many a man blind."

"I'd like to think I'm better than that."

"So do we all, my friend." He raised his bottle in a wry salute. Then finished off his beer. "Don't feel too badly about not seeing it. She's a pro. Total puck bunny."

"Don't let Tina hear you. We're not supposed to use that term, remember?"

As Tina would say, it was sexist and crude. She wasn't wrong. Then again, neither was Brommy; there were women who made it a mission to land a hockey player. Given that most of us loved the attention they gave us, it wasn't exactly an uneven exchange. Just not one I was interested in devoting my life to.

Brommy's snort was eloquent, but then he sobered. "I missed you, man."

A lump the size of my fist rose in my throat. I missed him too. So much that sometimes I found myself turning to make a joke only to realize he wasn't there. None of my guys were. All that I had left were ghosts.

I wanted to apologize for not calling him, for ignoring his calls and texts. But how to tell him that anything to do with hockey, including him, was too much for me? If I got too close to the game, I felt like an addict in withdrawal, my fingers shaking, my heart racing with an insistent need to get back onto the ice.

I couldn't tell him that it had to be all or nothing when it came to hockey. In the dark, next to my best friend, I could only look down at my fisted hands resting on my thighs.

He spoke slowly, carefully. "I'm not going to pretend I know how it feels, Oz. I just . . . hell. I don't know what I'm saying other than I'm here if you need it."

The lump grew, pressing against the roof of my mouth. I swallowed convulsively. "I should have called."

"You don't have to do anything you don't want."

"I've been feeling sorry for myself."

"The shit you are," Brommy said with heat. He looked two seconds away from kicking my ass.

I had to smile at that, but it didn't last. "Yeah, Brom, I am. No, let me say this." If I didn't now, I might not ever. "Thing is, every athlete has to face the day when their body can't do the job required of their sport. I knew that going in—though I never wanted to think about it."

Brommy grunted in broad agreement. We all knew. We just didn't want to dwell.

"Nothing lasts forever. I know that. But this thing with my head?" Unable to help myself, I ran an unsteady hand through my hair, feeling the sea mist in the tangled mass. "It's getting better. I'm healing."

"That's a good thing," Brommy said quietly.

"Yeah, it is. But you're not getting it. Aside from my head, my body is in perfect condition. I'm in the prime of my life, Brom. I fucking owned the game. And this one thing took it from me. I wake up thinking I'm on the ice."

I leaned forward, my insides twisting, and clenched my hands together. "I almost wish I'd blown my knee or something tangible. At least that way, I wouldn't—" I blew out a breath. "I don't know what I'm saying. Other than I cannot stand the fact that the only thing holding me back is my head."

Brommy didn't speak when I finished, perhaps knowing I needed a minute. From the house came the sound of a woman's laugh, drifting on the night breeze. My lower gut clenched when I realized it was Emma. I wanted to be with her, soaking up her laughter, teasing her into making me laugh too. I turned my head to the side, as though I could block it all out.

"It's shit, Oz," Brommy said. "Fucking sucks. But maybe you're looking at it the wrong way."

I shot him a glare, and he held up a massive hand.

"Hear me out. You say it would have been better if you blew out a knee." He nodded slowly. "No way to play well with a busted-up knee, sure. But what made you great, what made you a legend, is your hockey sense."

He leaned forward, pinning me down with a hard stare. "Your brain, Oz, is what makes you, you."

I ducked my head, unable to hold it up, and closed my eyes. "I know."

"I know you do, man. But I'm going to say it anyway. A man might limp around on a busted-ass knee, but he's still himself. You scramble that brain, and it's lights out."

In the darkness, my throat worked. I wanted to speak but couldn't.

"Frankly," he said. "I admire the hell out of you. Because we both know there are some dumb fucks still at it who really shouldn't be. You got out with your head intact. Literally."

The tone of his voice took all the remaining fight out of me. He cared. A lot. And that wasn't a small thing. I knew now, more than ever, the value of that sort of unwavering friendship and support.

"I'm sorry. For being an asshole."

He huffed out a laugh. "Hell, I'm used to that."

I gave him a dry look but pushed on. "I mean it. I've become . . . withdrawn, short fused."

"Become?" His sandy brows rose high, and he laughed again. "I hate to break it to you, Oz, but you always were."

"The fuck I was."

"The fuck you weren't," he countered. "You'd get in those moods, pulling into yourself, shutting everyone out, acting like a grumpy son of a bitch. Do you not remember every damn playoff season?"

Blinking, I stared at him. He was serious. "I was fun."

"Yeah, you were. You were also a competitive asshole who'd get wound too tight under extreme pressure."

Poleaxed, I slumped back in my chair. "Well, hell."

I'd forgotten the exhaustion, the stress. I'd hated that part. Hated it. How the hell had I forgotten that?

"Don't freak." He slapped my shoulder with his paw. "We never fully see ourselves as we truly are. Yeah, you're a little more wound up now. What do you expect? Your brain is healing; you're grieving and stressed. Give it a rest, Oz."

"I take it back. I'm not sorry at all, asshole."

He laughed and grabbed another beer, then offered me one. Since I didn't plan on going anywhere for a while, I took it. We drank in silence, while all that he'd said rolled around in my head. I felt not lighter, but easier in a strange way.

"So," Brommy drawled, cutting into my thoughts. "Princess Anya, huh?"

"Don't call her that."

"Touchy. It's a sign of respect," he protested when I glared. "I love her in that role."

And that was part of the problem. I was all too aware of how much Brommy loved Emma as Anya. My memories of watching *Dark Castle* with him and the guys were crystal clear, and they weren't doing me any favors. Not when all the shit they'd said ran through my head. The way they'd groaned and said, "Look at those sweet tits bounce." How they'd cheered Arasmus for banging her hard and fast.

Hell. I'd never gone so far as to vocalize any of that the way Brommy and the others had, but I'd watched, turned on and enjoying the hell out of those scenes. I had objectified Emma, and it ate me up now when I thought about it. I'd let her down even before ever meeting her. She was funny, smart, sensitive, caring. And she'd been reduced to how she looked on screen.

It did me in to know my friends had seen her that way. And I knew fully fucking well what Anton had been picturing when he'd called her the *princess*. It made my blood heat faster than taking a cheap hit on the ice. I wanted to scrub their minds of Emma's nakedness. Which was wrong. She was proud of her work, as she should be.

"She's more than just a role," I told Brommy—told myself too. Because a reminder wouldn't hurt right now, when I wanted to punch my friend just for the knowledge he had.

He looked at me for a beat, then grinned wide. "Those sex scenes are messing with you, aren't they? Not that I blame you—"

"Brommy, I swear to God, if you so much as look at her the wrong way—"

He laughed, a full-bellied, slap-his-thigh release. "Shit. You're totally gone on her."

"Hell." I rubbed a hand over my face. "Would you shut up?"

"I can't. It's too good." He pointed a finger at me. "You're more protective of her than you ever were of Cassandra. You realize that, right?"

No. Yes.

"Fuck off."

"Go for it, man. She's sweet, funny, and doesn't seem to mind your grumpy ass."

"She's only here for a visit."

"And?"

"And nothing. I'm not messing around with Mamie's guest. If I want to get off, I'll . . ." *Use my hand as I have for nearly a year.* "Hit some club and find a one-night stand."

Brommy leveled me with a long amused stare. "You know I can always tell when you're full of shit."

I did know. Didn't stop me from returning his stare with a bland one. "Fuck off, Brommy."

"Fucking off," he promised, setting a hand to his heart. "But I'm going to enjoy the hell out of myself when you eventually topple."

I was glad someone would.

CHAPTER TWELVE

Emma

After the disastrous lunch, I went back to my bungalow and hid out. There were about a dozen emails to go through, none of them inspiring or able to lift the subdued mood that lay heavy on my shoulders. I almost jumped when the housephone rang, but it wasn't him.

Instead, Amalie invited me up to the house for dinner and cards. I didn't have it in me to decline; besides, if I stayed here, I'd brood. Like Lucian.

God, I wanted to hunt him down, see if he was all right, try to make him crack that small but delighted smile of his. All foolish thinking. He was a big boy; he'd lived his life just fine before I'd stumbled into it. He didn't need me, and it was the height of arrogance to assume I could make his life better in any shape or form.

What I absolutely refused to think about was the fact that maybe I needed him.

"No." I closed the door of my bungalow and marched toward the house. "You're just clinging to him because your life is uncertain, and you need a project."

I was not about to make Lucian a project.

Following the directions Amalie had given me, I found her and Tina in the kitchen. It was a gorgeous space, with lower cabinets of aged rich oak, Carrara marble counters, softly washed plaster walls, and dark-beamed ceilings. Tina sat on a stool at the massive center island while Amalie puttered around an eight-burner stove.

"Welcome," Amalie said, smiling over her shoulder. "Dinner is almost ready."

Whatever she'd cooked smelled fantastic. I took a seat next to Tina, who offered me wine.

"Where is Sal?" I asked. I had yet to see Amalie without Sal in tow.

"He's gone to LA for the week on a buying trip." Amalie winked. "Which really means he knew I was about to greet my other grandbabies and wanted us to settle in without him in the way."

"Would he be in the way?"

"Non." She waved a beringed hand. "But—"

"He doesn't get along with Anton," Tina cut in.

"I wonder why," I murmured, unable to help myself, but Tina laughed.

"We Osmonds can be a difficult bunch. Anton and Sal have been silently hating on each other for years because Ant once made the mistake of calling Sal *the help*."

It was a terrible thing to say, and I would have been livid.

"Oh, wow. Did Sal punch him out for that?" I was only half teasing.

"No." Tina beamed. "Luc did."

Mighty Lucian. Of course he did. I could picture it with ease and smiled. Damn it, I missed him. And it had only been a few hours. I took a sip of wine, annoyed with myself.

"We're going to eat out there." Tina nodded toward the open french doors, where there was a little terrace surrounded by lavender and rustling olive trees. "Want to help set up?"

"Sure."

While we set the table, Amalie brought out a cast-iron pan and set it in the center. Inside were roasted tomatoes covered in herbed breadcrumbs; it sizzled away and smelled divine. "There."

Tina brought out some french bread, and soon we were digging into our food.

"It's delicious, Amalie," I said. "Thank you."

She shrugged. "I am not so much for cooking anymore. But I used to make this dish for my children and grandchildren."

"It reminds me of my childhood," Tina said with a happy sigh.

Amalie took a small bite. "This was your favorite, no?"

"Yes. The boys loved coq au vin. But I always wanted this."

"I had coq au vin the other night," I put in, smiling at Amalie. "It was wonderful."

She gave me a vague shrug. "We love to eat well. Good for the heart."

Without warning, I thought of Lucian out there somewhere, and I wondered if he was heartsick. And though I liked to think my face wasn't easy to read, Amalie frowned, as though she knew I'd thought of him.

"I apologize for my grandson," she said.

Quickly, I shook my head. "There's nothing to apologize for. I would have left early too."

Lucian hadn't stomped away. No, he'd finished his meal in dogged silence and then simply stood and bid the women at the table a good day. Perfectly polite. Perfectly painful to watch.

Amalie's crimson lips curled in soft humor. "Non, I meant Anton. He was—"

"An asshole," Tina finished, earning a look of reproof from Amalie. "What? There's no better word, Mamie."

"Fine. An asshole, then." With her slight accent, the word took on a nice depth that had me grinning despite myself. Amalie tutted. "He means well most of the time."

"Anton knew exactly what he was doing." Tina scowled and spooned another tomato onto her plate. "And to bring that bitch up. He wanted to piss Luc off."

Curiosity bubbled up within me, but I fought it hard. If Lucian wanted me to hear about his ex, he would tell me.

"So what card game are we going to play?" I asked brightly.

Tina and Amalie thankfully got the message and moved the conversation away from Lucian. We cleared the table and settled down to play cards and drink more wine.

Amalie passed a deck of cards to Tina. "Shall you be staying here for summer, *ma fille?*"

Apparently, Tina had graduated from UCLA in the spring and was still finding her feet with what she wanted to do. I empathized. Tina shrugged in the way of all Osmonds, her glossy dark hair sliding over one slim shoulder. "I hadn't thought that far ahead, but if you're okay with it, then I will."

Amalie's repressive glare was tempered by a soft curl of her thin lips. "You never had to ask." She touched her granddaughter's cheek briefly.

Tina caught my eye, and her nose wrinkled wryly. "You're so together it probably seems ridiculous that I don't know what to do with my life. I know I want it to be exciting, filled with adventure. But I don't feel brave. Instead, my future feels like this big unknown void of . . . scary."

I was twenty-seven years old, and suddenly it felt ancient. In the face of her assumption that my life was secure and well ordered. "I'm an actress—I excel at showing the world what I want them to see. But my life isn't perfect." I made a decision then to trust Tina with the truth and told her about getting the ax.

Her mouth dropped open in horror. I smiled tightly. "Please don't tell anyone. I'll get in a world of trouble if the finale gets out."

She sat straighter. "Never. I am honored that you trusted me with this. And I think the producers were stupid as hell to drop you. Anya and Arasmus were my favorite part of the show!" She clasped my hand. "What will you do now?"

"I don't know. Find a new role." I glanced at both Tina and Amalie and cringed. "It's part of the business, but I can't help feeling a bit lost—or maybe just at a crossroads."

"That is life, my dear." Amalie poured more wine into my empty glass. "Life doesn't remain the same. It shifts and turns, and we must shift with it. Which isn't a bad thing. How boring would it be to never see any change?"

"I thought I liked change, but now? Not so much. Not when it comes in the face of failure."

Amalie sat back and regarded me with fond eyes. "Failure is simply opportunity in disguise. I do not know of a single success story that did not have its share of failures along the way. We try, we grow, sometimes we fail. You either crumble and stop living life, or you pick yourself up and use the experience to set a new course."

Her words bubbled through me, stirring something that felt a lot like hope.

Amalie's gaze turned inward. "To live is to adapt. We're constantly reinventing ourselves. Don't be afraid of failure or change, loves; it means you're alive."

Unwittingly, my thoughts moved to Lucian, and my heart clenched. Because I knew Amalie was thinking of him just then and worrying. I didn't want to worry about Lucian, too, but I did. He was hiding from life, even more than I was. From the glimpses he'd let me see of the real him, I knew that if any man needed to live life to the fullest, it was him. More unsettling was the fact that I wanted to be there when he did. Because Lucian living completely in the moment made me feel utterly alive as well.

For the rest of the evening, they delighted me with old stories and funny observations. Tina calmed down enough not to stare at me every few seconds and proceeded to beat me soundly in poker. And though I laughed and relaxed, Lucian was there, in the back of my mind, nudging along my spine.

Which was why, despite all my best intentions, I found myself putting on my bikini and heading for the pool in the dark of night.

———

I was no better than a teen sneaking out in hopes that my crush would hear me and show up. I knew this and berated myself for it, and still I toed off my sandals and undid my bathing wrap. My hands actually shook with nerves when I set my things on a lounger.

The pool house was dark, the french doors closed up tight. Maybe he was asleep. Maybe he'd left the property. But the pool light was on, producing a soft glow.

With as much grace as possible, I dove into the water. It was warm enough to soothe my skin, and despite my original mission, I started to swim, getting into the rhythm of the exercise.

On my fifth lap, as I reached the end of the pool, the sound of Édith Piaf caught my attention. *La Vie en Rose.* Heart skipping a beat, I stopped and turned around. Lucian stood at the other end, the wavering light of the pool casting shadows over his face. I shouldn't have been surprised; I'd wanted him to show up, after all. But a surge of adrenaline hit me like a drug, and my dreary night sparked with promise.

I was so gone on this man. It wasn't even funny.

His lips tilted in a small smile. "Thought you should get the full effect and listen to Édith while you swim."

"Shouldn't I be naked if I want the full effect of night swimming with Édith?" Yes, I was shameless.

His narrowed gaze said as much. But he didn't bolt. No, he stared me down with those stern eyes. "I'm certainly not going to stop you. But be forewarned, Brommy and Anton are out here somewhere."

Clever Lucian. Now, if I followed through with my teasing threat, I would be saying that I didn't mind anyone seeing me. If I didn't, I was making it clear that I wanted only him to see me that way.

Resting my elbows on the edge of the pool, I slowly treaded water with my legs. "Why don't you join me?"

"I'm not skinny-dipping with you, Snoopy." His smile was brief but wide. "Like I said, Brommy and Anton are out and about."

"And you don't want them seeing you naked," I said, as if this made perfect sense.

"I'm very shy."

"Sure you are." I kicked my foot, sending ripples his way. "But I meant regular swimming."

He was wearing a threadbare T-shirt of indeterminable color and athletic shorts that hung low and loose on his trim hips.

I eyed him up and down, enjoying the way he tried so hard not to fidget. "Stop dithering, and get in."

Lucian scowled. "Bossy." But he stripped off his shirt, which was every bit as hot as the last time he'd done it—more, really, because now I got to witness it up close and in full detail.

Quirking a straight brow at me as if to say "You asked for it," he dove in the deep end.

My belly tightened as he arrowed under the water, heading my way. He broke through the surface a few feet from me, wet and gorgeous and smiling with his eyes. If I wasn't already in water, I would have melted into a puddle of lust just looking at him.

Lucian combed his dripping hair back with his fingers as he treaded water before me. "Any reason you're swimming, Em?"

"Should there be?" I let go of the edge and headed his way.

Lucian immediately jerked back, keeping the distance equal between us. "Didn't take you for a night swimmer."

I moved forward again slowly. "You made it look so good; I thought I'd try."

It was too dark to tell, but I could have sworn he blushed. But then his eyes narrowed. "You're flirting."

"Am I?" I totally was. I couldn't help it; Lucian was kind of adorable when he reacted to my blatant attempts as though confused but intrigued. So often, he unbalanced me with his cool authority. It was satisfying to return the favor.

Competitor at heart, Lucian rallied. He planted his feet; he was tall enough to stand without dipping underwater. "You know you are." Lucian's gaze moved over me carefully, as though he was attempting to read my mind. "You're not trying to make me feel better about myself, are you?"

I paused, floating there, my heart squeezing tight. "I'm flirting with you because I enjoy it. I never know what you'll say, and it usually makes me laugh."

"Ah. I'm to play the role of jester."

"Are you deliberately trying to tick me off? Do you want me to go?"

His eyes glinted. "I don't want you to go."

"So you're trying to annoy me."

His chuckle was warm and sent little flutters of pleasure through my insides. "Just keeping you on your toes, Em."

That I could work with. I shot forward, ready to swim, and he darted aside like he thought I might jump him. I rolled my eyes, swimming around him in a lazy circle. "You're kind of twitchy tonight."

"Twitchy?" He apparently didn't like the sound of that.

"Mmm. Like you don't know whether or not to flee."

"You got that right. This line of conversation is tempting me to run right about now."

Funny.

I continued to circle, but he followed, keeping me in his sights.

"Is it because we've seen each other naked?" I asked.

Lucian jerked so hard he splashed himself. "Jesus, Em."

I fought a grin. "What? It's true. You told me you watched *Dark Castle*."

"Anya wasn't fully nude—"

"As good as. Aside from showing that little V of hair—"

"God . . . ," he moaned expansively.

"I was basically naked."

"You're trying to kill me. That's it, isn't it?"

The thick rasp of his voice had me smiling.

"Don't be such a prude."

"If you knew what was running through my mind, you'd never accuse me of being a prude."

My heart skipped another beat, and I found myself treading water again. "Do tell."

"Never you mind." Somehow, he'd drifted closer, edging me into a corner. "Now cut it out. There's a huge difference between seeing Princess Anya half-undressed on a TV screen and seeing you naked."

He seemed so thoroughly put out on my behalf about it that I could only stare at him in wonder.

"I fail to understand why."

Dark brows threatened to meet in the middle. "First off, that wasn't you. That was Anya, a character. She's make-believe. You're real."

The flutters in my belly soared up into the vicinity of my chest. "That's . . . sweet."

As though he hadn't heard me, Lucian continued on in lecture mode. "Secondly, I can't reach through a screen and touch those pretty breasts."

I bobbled, nearly going under. The flutters turned into a storm, and I had to grasp the edge of the pool to hang on. When I spoke, my voice had become far too breathy. "That implies there has to be touching involved to make it real."

Something had changed—he wasn't twitchy. He was resolved, closing in until there was barely a foot between us. Water glinted over the strong planes of his face, making those expressive, firm lips wet. I wanted to lick them, wrap myself around his strong, hard body, and hold on.

His eyes, pale as the glowing pool, pinned me to the spot. So much heat in them. Heat and need and a shadow of frustration, as though he didn't want to want me. His voice lowered, thick as hot cream. "Em, if you're naked in front of me, there's going to be touching."

Yes, please. Now would be good.

"Pretty presumptuous of you, honey pie."

Lucian, the rat bastard, smiled, those hot eyes intent on my face. "Who said it had to be you I'm touching?"

"What?" I could barely think. His nearness was making me light headed.

"I'm not above taking matters into my own hand, if that's the only option."

I pictured him handling all that . . . girth. The bottom dropped out of me.

"Oh, well played—"

Water rippled, and he was there, big body surrounding me, his mouth inches from mine. "To be clear," he murmured, "if you're naked in front of me, I'd rather touch you."

He was so close, vividly present. Deliciously beautiful. My lids lowered, my lips parting with the need to feel his. I wanted. *I wanted.*

Our legs brushed under the water, and a shiver danced up my thighs. Lucian grabbed the edge of the pool to brace himself, his arms bracketing me, which made it worse. Water droplets glinted on the dips and swells along his shoulders and arms, drawing my attention to the sheer strength of his body and how good it would feel to touch him.

He didn't say a word. He didn't have to; his proximity was enough to make my insides dip and my mouth dry.

I had to take control of the situation. "You want a peek, don't you?"

Over the quiet sounds of water lapping, I heard him swallow, surprise flickering in his gaze just before it lowered to my breasts. His voice dropped a register. "You gonna give me one?"

Lust punched through me, pure and hot. I loved sex—the dance leading up to it, the physicality of it, the release. But fame had changed sex for me. Men had started to expect a fantasy. They saw me as a virginal princess to be treated with reverence or a personal notch on their belt: *I bagged Anya.*

Lucian made it clear he didn't see Anya when he looked at me. That in itself made me want to show him more.

The water was cool, but inside I burned as my hand slowly rose to the edge of my bikini top. Lucian's gaze grew rapt, his lips parting on a shallow breath. God, that look. It had every inch of me drawing up tight. My breasts grew heavy, swelling with languid lust. I was utterly aware of him, of myself, as I traced the line of my bikini, flirting with the notion of pulling it to the side.

Lucian didn't blink, didn't move, but he seemed closer. My nipples stiffened, nudging against the thin fabric, begging to be seen by him. The tip of my finger hooked under the top, and I pulled it slowly to the side, feeling the drag.

Lucian grunted, low and protracted, as though the sound could make me go faster. The reaction in my body was a delicious clenching of my sex. I arched into that sound, my lids fluttering as I tugged the top farther over, stopping right at the edge of my nipple. And he jerked, the water sloshing.

"Em . . ." The plea came out in a thick rasp. "Baby . . ."

The muscles along his arms bunched as he gripped the lip of the pool, as though trying to hold himself back.

Oh, he wanted that peek. An ache built up inside me. My breasts had been seen by millions. But Lucian was right; that hadn't been me. Here, now, this was me. This was him wanting to see *me.*

The tip of my finger traced a path of heat along the curve of my breast, back and forth. And he watched, a man starved. Licking my lips, I stopped. It seemed we both held our breaths. And then, with the slightest of tugs, the top slipped over the beaded tip of my nipple.

Lucian groaned, the sound almost animal. I arched my back in response, pulled by his need, my bared breast coming closer to the wall of his chest. I wanted to feel his skin on mine.

But he didn't move. He gripped the edge tighter, his body working with heaving pants. "Fuck," he whispered. His pale gaze flicked to mine, a furrow knitting between his brows. "I want a taste. Please. *God.* Please, Em."

That he was undone nearly had me sliding under the water. But the need in his eyes made me whimper. Lids heavy with desire, I nodded, and he swallowed hard, his expression becoming fierce.

"Just a taste," he said, as if to hold himself to that. I whimpered, and his hot gaze snared with mine. Something passed over his expression—determination, reassurance, I couldn't tell; lust and need had scattered all rational thought. "Just a taste," he said again.

"Take it," I whispered, barely able to form the words.

Lucian let out a breath, his mouth moving closer. "Fuck. Em . . . lift that sweetness up for me."

My breath left in a swoosh, everything squeezing with a lovely tightness. With a shaking hand, I cupped my breast and lifted it out of the water. Offering myself to him.

On a groan, he ducked his head. The hot, wet flat of his tongue dragged over my cold flesh. I let out a cry, a bolt of pleasure punching to my core.

He made a sound of pure hunger, his lips gently kissing the tip before he sucked it deep . . .

"Last one in the pool is a dirty fool!" Tina's shout was followed closely by a massive splash as she launched herself into the water.

Lucian surged back, as though struck, then turned to block me as I hastily hauled my top back into place.

It was clear from the wide-eyed surprise on Tina's face that she hadn't noticed us. Just as clear from Brommy's slow stroll to the pool edge and the grin on his face that he *had*.

Whatever the case, the mood was effectively doused. I caught Lucian's eye, but his walls were up, and he shook his head with a nearly imperceptible motion. With an internal sigh, I swam over to a sheepish Tina and pretended nothing had happened.

I couldn't regret teasing Lucian to the point where he turned the tables on me. But I would definitely think twice about engaging that way again. Not when he apparently regretted his moment of weakness.

CHAPTER THIRTEEN

Lucian

After pulling back from the brink of falling on Emma in the pool like a man starved, I stayed away from her and hung out with Brommy. I managed it for two days. And I missed her.

It was irrational, annoying, nonsensical. You weren't supposed to miss someone you barely knew. You weren't supposed to crave the sight of them, the sound of their voice, the scent of their skin. Not like this. Holy hell, I'd had the sweet pink rose of her nipple in my mouth. I could still feel its shape on my tongue like some lust phantom designed to drive me out of my mind.

I put it down to being mentally weakened by months of sexual solitude.

My one concession was to bake. For her.

Baking had always been a private thing, something I'd learned at my great-grandfather's knee, but I had never sought to do more with it. But now? It had become both a challenge and intensely satisfying to come up with new ways to tempt and pleasure Emma. Feeding Emma somehow fed my soul as well.

She didn't know that the brioches in her breakfast basket had been formed by my hand. She didn't know the macarons—two each night, sent in a small box—were mine. But I did.

In moments of weakness, I'd close my eyes and try to imagine her soft lips parting over jewel-bright confections, pink tongue tasting the flavors of me—achieved by the strange alchemy of whipping egg whites, infusing creams, and straining ripe fruits, all melded together into an intense burst of flavor.

Had she preferred the inky-black chicory chocolate, the butter-rich caramel and burnt pear? Or did she moan for the juicy brightness of the grapefruit honey or blood orange and rose?

It was enough to make a man hard.

And aching for the sight of what he shouldn't have.

Which was why I kept doing it. Maybe I wanted to be found out. I could just tell the woman I was the one making her food, leaving little treats that no one else staying at Rosemont was getting. But there was something about Emma Maron that reverted me right back to the awkward, bumbling geek I'd been in middle school.

Mamie hadn't been exaggerating when she'd said I was small as a kid. Small and shy. When I wasn't on the ice, I was the guy most likely to hide away. Hockey had changed me into someone cocky, outgoing, fun loving. I liked that version of myself, but now that hockey was over, I realized that part of me was a role I'd been playing.

I wasn't sure who the real me was anymore, but I knew I wasn't prepared to march up to Emma's bungalow with cake in hand.

Keeping to myself as much as possible felt like the safer plan.

Because playing it safe is what got you so far in life.

I hadn't played it safe with the dessert I'd made Emma today, though. Already, I was regretting it. The choice was pure hubris. There was too much of me—*of us*—in it. But it was too late to take it back.

Emma

It was the pie that did it. And the kick of it was I didn't even see it coming. I should have. The signs were all there. But I hadn't been paying attention. I'd been thinking about a certain grumpy hot man who I wanted far too much for my own good.

A man who apparently was avoiding me. I hadn't seen him in two days. Once, I saw the back of him as he turned a corner, his stride—that freaking swagger that made me think of sex and sin—determined, as though he didn't want to be caught loitering.

It was my fault for pushing, flirting when he was obviously resisting. Then again, he was the one who'd taken it so far I still shivered when I thought about him drawing closer, his gaze on my mouth like he wanted to devour it. Devour me.

"Ugh." I flopped back on my sofa. "Stop thinking about him."

Perhaps I should leave. Find another place to hide out.

My insides twisted. I didn't want to leave.

Lunch arrived, breaking into my brooding thoughts. Yet another basket—this time brought around by a woman named Janet, who told me she was part of the house staff.

Was it worrisome that I was already salivating like Pavlov's dog? Probably. But it didn't stop the giddy anticipation welling up within me. I'd become inordinately excitable over daily meals.

The basket yielded a salad of baby greens and a canister of soup. An accompanying card written in a sharply slanting scrawl informed me that it was called avgolemono: a greek chicken-and-lemon soup. I had a choice of chilled chardonnay or iced tea to go with it.

And then I saw the dessert box. Delicious food aside, this was what made my day. These little treats that felt like they were made solely for me. Oh, I realized that everyone got the same desserts. But I let myself believe, if only for a little while, that they were for me alone.

Anticipation bubbled through my veins as I pulled the gold ribbon free. Inside was a caramel-colored tart about the size of my hand. Dark-golden custard had been piped in petal-thick ribbons to look like a flower. Just off to the side, as if touching down for a taste, was a tiny sugar honeybee.

My breath caught and held as my entire focus narrowed down to that bee. Forgoing a fork, I lifted the tart with my bare hands and took a large almost angry bite. And realized a few things. It wasn't a tart; it was a pie. And it wasn't caramel. It was honey.

Smooth floral notes of delicately sweet honey imbued the silky custard. Decadent but light, sweet yet rich. A honey pie, lovingly made. The tiny sugar bee, still perched on the edge of the flaky crust, mocked me.

That little bee nibbling on her honey pie.

A pulse of sheer heat lit up my sex, licked down my thighs, tweaked my nipples. I shoved another messy bite into my mouth, relishing the taste, wanting . . . him.

This was his work, made with his hands, his skill, his mind. My grumpy man with the ability to create sweetness in the most unexpected of ways.

Somehow, at the back of my mind, I'd known from the start. From the way he'd all but ordered me to try his brest. How he'd watched me eat it with that strange intent look upon his face. Pride. That was what it was. He was proud of his work.

I ate up my honey pie without pause, devouring it until it was nothing more than a sticky paste on my fingers, buttery crumbs on my lips. Moaning, I licked my skin clean like a cat might. I swore I felt claws prickling, aching to come out.

Because he had known, and I hadn't. Was it a joke to him? What had he said? The chef was temperamental. Oh, how he must have laughed on the inside at that.

With a growl, I washed my hands and headed for the door, half of me more turned on than I'd ever been in my life, the other half ready to tear into the most irritating man I'd ever met.

———

It took him over an hour to return, carrying in bags of groceries. I sat in the far corner of the big kitchen, comfortably perched on the counter and eating another honey pie—this one sadly without a cute bee. Apparently, that had been just for me.

He didn't notice me, which was what I'd intended, given that I knew the weasel would only pretend he was dropping the stuff off for the "chef" of the house if he saw me now.

God, but he looked good. Angry as I was, my eyes drank up the sight of him. Inky hair tousled and windblown, lush lips in that sullen pout. Dusky olive-toned skin smooth and dark against the white T-shirt he wore. The short sleeves of the shirt strained against his biceps, which bunched as he set down the heavy bags.

No one would ever doubt the man was an athlete; he moved with the assurance of someone who used his body like a machine—efficient, graceful, strong.

He turned to root through the refrigerator, and the tight globes of his spectacular bubble butt strained against worn jeans. Silently, he set a bottle of cream down, then reached up to the hanging pot rack for a saucier, exposing a sliver of toned abs as he did.

Sweet mercy, but I might truly orgasm watching this man work his kitchen. I didn't even know it was my kink. Maybe Lucian made it so. When he proceeded to separate an egg with an efficient snap of his wrist, I knew it was him. He was my kink. Damn it all.

"You do that so well." My voice cracked through the silence, and he practically jumped out of his skin, those frost eyes going wide and panicked. "Must have taken you years to learn your craft."

147

For a second, neither of us spoke. With words. Our eyes held an entire conversation.

Oh, I am so onto you, buddy.

Apparently so.

You should have told me.

Apparently so.

Nothing else to say?

Apparently not.

You are magnificent.

That one slipped out.

He sucked in a sharp breath, his nostrils flaring. And those panicked eyes went hot, focused.

"It was the honey pie, wasn't it?" His voice was a husky rasp in the quiet of the kitchen.

I pushed aside the remnants of the pie I'd been eating and licked my fingertips, enjoying the way he immediately zeroed in on that. A grunt rumbling from deep within his chest set off flickers of lust in mine. I ignored them.

"A bit too literal a choice." I hopped down. "But delicious."

Glaring, I made my way to the island. His expression grew wary, those broad shoulders stiffening, as though bracing for a fight. I grinned, wanting him off kilter. Lord knew he'd been doing the same to me for days.

"Hockey player"—I started counting off on my fingers—"carpenter, temperamental chef, baker, pastry maker . . ." I stopped before him, overwhelmed all over again by the sheer physicality of him. When I stood near Lucian Osmond, I *wanted*. "Maybe I should be calling you Renaissance man. Tell me, Brick, do you paint too?"

He rested a big long-fingered hand on the marble countertop. The muscles along his arm shifted as he leaned in a touch. "Yes, but only on pâtisseries."

Oh hell, he said it in French, with an accent that sounded like sultry sex. My breath hitched. And he noticed. His eyes narrowed, slowly lowering to my mouth, then easing back up to meet my gaze.

"You mad?" A challenge.

"That depends," I said, way too breathless. Damn it. "Was it a joke to you?"

"Honeybee, I never joke about pâtisseries."

God. Say it again. Say more. Breathe your words on my skin.

I swallowed hard. "Don't prevaricate with me, Lucian. Not now."

With a sigh, his shoulders slumped. "No, it wasn't a joke. I didn't say anything because . . ." He waved a hand, as if searching for the reason, then ended up lifting it in resignation. "It felt too personal. Like I was exposing too much of myself."

"I can see that." He was an artist. I'd felt his care and thoughtfulness in every bite he'd created. But more than that, it showed in the way his pastries looked, the way he presented them. "You are incredibly gifted, Lucian."

Faint praise. But I wanted to give it anyway.

As expected, he turned and busied himself by tossing the eggshell into a prep sink. "It's something I do to relax and keep busy."

I didn't want to think of Greg just then, but it wasn't until I'd started dating him that I got a true taste of a professional athlete's life. I thought it would be like mine, but acting had lots of periods of waiting around for takes and downtime between roles. Athletes were a different breed. Their lives were extremely structured, filled with days of training, practices, games, interviews, travel. There was little time for rest. Most pro athletes got off on it, the life itself giving them an adrenaline high.

How would it be to have it ripped away before you were ready? Not good.

My heart squeezed, and I suddenly wanted nothing more than to wrap my arms around him and just hug. If any man needed a hug, it was Lucian. But he wouldn't allow it. Wouldn't like it.

He shifted his weight, going twitchy in that way of his that meant he was gearing up to be defensive, to close himself off in his own protective world.

You can let me in. I won't hurt you.

"Did Amalie teach you?" I asked.

His chin snapped up—surprised, I would guess, at my shift away from the obvious subject. "Yes," he said after a moment, his voice gravelly. He cleared his throat. "Well, Amalie taught me to cook and bread making. You know, the recipes she learned as a child."

As he spoke, he busied himself by taking out a kitchen scale and flour. There was an ease about him now. "My great-grandfather, Jean Philipe, taught me pâtisserie making. He was a big name in France. His kitchens were filled with veritable armies of assistants, and it was always, '*Oui*, Chef.' But with me, he was simply *arrière-grand-père*, who wanted to teach me everything. When we kids summered in France, Anton and Tina would play outside, and I stayed in the kitchen."

A smile formed on my lips. "I admit I find it hard to picture."

The corners of his eyes creased in quiet humor. "Mamie wasn't exaggerating when she said I was small as a kid. Scrawny, really. And shy."

"You?" I teased. But I could see it. There was something about Lucian that would always be reserved.

He shot me a sidelong look, but his lips curled. "Yeah, me. A scrawny geek. Who wasn't stupid; if I was in the kitchen, I got fed. A lot. Plus . . ." He shrugged shoulders that were most definitely not scrawny. "I liked it. I always had trouble concentrating unless something took up all my focus. At home, I had the ice. In France, I had cooking, baking, pâtisseries. It relaxes me."

Personally, the precision and concentration needed to bake would drive me batty. But I understood.

We stood side by side, me far too aware of his warmth. He smelled of honey and sunshine. I wanted to burrow my face in all that goodness and soak it up.

"Will you stop now that I know?" I asked, worried.

His straight brows drew together. "Why would I do that?"

"I don't know." I shrugged, tracing the edge of the counter. "You said it was too personal, me knowing." I looked up and met his eyes. "I wondered if maybe you wouldn't want to make me anything anymore."

Lucian's stern expression belied the softness of his tone. "Honeybee, I'll make you anything you want."

The promise slid over me like hot caramel. Anything I wanted. I knew he would.

My fingers curled into a fist to keep from reaching out. "Surprise me."

His smile was wide and brilliant. Free. "You're on."

Chapter Fourteen

Emma

My favorite place on the estate became the kitchen. At least, when Lucian occupied it. Sunny and warm and filled with luscious scents like baking bread or rich chocolate, the space felt both safe and happy. It was a delight to curl up on the deep padded bench that ran along one wall and faced the kitchen island and stove, where Lucian worked.

Over the past few years, I'd been so busy with *Dark Castle* that I'd never truly gotten into cooking or baking shows. I reconsidered them now. Watching Lucian move about the kitchen, all firm confidence and loose-limbed grace, was pure porn for me. Heaven help me, but the way his ropy forearms moved as he briskly whipped up egg whites or heavy cream—because the man never used a blender for these things—would get me so hot and bothered I'd have to press my thighs together under the cover of the battered farm table.

And when he kneaded dough? Sweet baby Jesus. He did this little grunt every time he thrust the heels of his hands over the springy mass. A deep rumbling grunt as his whole taut body rocked toward the countertop. And then there was the pullback, when he'd breathe in, those wide shoulders of his rolling in a steady rhythm.

Grunt. Thrust. Breathe. Pull.

It was a wonder I didn't orgasm on the spot watching him.

"I can feel your eyes on me," Lucian deadpanned, not breaking rhythm.

I bet you can.

"It's mesmerizing."

He grunted again, this time one that I knew meant "Whatever floats your boat, Em."

I smiled. "I could film this and have an instant hit on my hands."

He glanced my way, all cool wintergreen annoyance—belied by the slight smile trying to pull at his lips. "Ex–hockey players baking?" He turned his attention back to the dough. "I guess there's a certain spectacle about it."

"You seriously underestimate your appeal here, Brick."

With a scoffing grunt, he neatly shaped the now-smooth dough into a ball and set it in a large bowl before covering it with a damp cloth. With that, he washed his hands and headed for the fridge.

"What's next?" I asked, leaning forward in anticipation.

"Piecrust for the tomato tarts we're having for dinner." His lips quirked. "You're welcome to help at any time."

"We both know it's better for everyone if I don't."

Lucian chuffed a half laugh. "No comment."

He kept trying to teach me, but so far, I'd been a complete disaster in the kitchen. If there was a cooking gene, I'd clearly missed out on it. As Lucian set a large hunk of butter on the counter and grabbed the flour, I smiled and read a few emails that popped up on my iPad.

Other than what I was calling *the pool incident*, we hadn't acknowledged the attraction between us. But it was there, growing and heating. And yet so was our friendship. I liked him, damn it. More than was safe. Attraction could ebb and flow, but truly liking another person meant it would hurt more to lose them.

Considering I didn't have Lucian in any long-term capacity, it worried me. Even so, I couldn't deny the contentment I felt in sharing his precious workspace. He outright chased everyone else out of his kitchen when he was in it. Only Amalie, and sometimes Tina, got away with a quick visit, but even they would be gently eased out the door after a minute or two.

"What's that grin all about?" came his darkly amused rumble.

The other thing about being in the kitchen with Lucian? He noticed everything I did, even when I thought all his concentration was on his food.

"Never you mind."

He hummed.

I clicked on my email and found one from my agent. My smile grew wobbly.

"Now you have to tell me about that one," Lucian said dryly.

I glanced up and found him looking at me with one dark eyebrow quirked in imperious impatience. I snorted. "Why is it that I'm called Snoopy, when you're nosy as hell?"

"I'm only nosy about you. You're snoopy with everyone."

My stomach fluttered at the confession that he only wanted to know more about me. I didn't show it, though, and rolled my eyes before reading a bit more of the email. "It's from my agent. A couple of casting directors have sent over scripts that might be promising."

"You're surprised?"

"I haven't been offered many roles since *Dark Castle*. So this is . . . unexpected. Good."

"Good." His brief smile was wide and beautiful, and it took my breath to see it. Then, as if it hit him that he was grinning with sunny feeling, he grunted and went back to cutting the butter for his crust. "What made you want to be an actress?"

I could have given him my canned, on-standby answer, but there should be honesty between us. "I wanted to be famous."

Lucian paused, his head jerking up.

I lowered my eyes, taking in my slim hands and wrists, which suddenly felt too fragile. "I was fourteen, and my dad was . . . in a mood. The Oscars were on, so my mom and I holed up in the den to watch. And there they were, all these women, wealthy, beautiful, and smiling."

I glanced up and caught Lucian's troubled gaze. My smile was one I'd used to reassure men for far too long, but it quickly slipped away under his calm quiet. Because with him, I didn't have to appease or pretend. I swallowed hard. "To me, that was power. And I thought if I could have that power, that level of wealth and fame, I'd be safe. I'd be free."

The preheating oven ticked in the resounding silence. Lucian's expression pinched, and I knew he wanted to comfort me. But I couldn't handle it in that moment.

"It wasn't until I actually tried acting that I realized how much I loved it. Acting is challenging, fun, a safe way to express my emotions. I'd always spun tales in my head. This way, I got to tell stories in another way."

Slowly, he nodded, a lock of inky hair falling over his brow. "You do it well, Emma."

Emma. Only he could make my name feel like a velvet glove sliding over my skin.

"Thank you." Success was a fickle thing; it could disappear at any moment. But under his regard, I wanted him to see me at my best. Which meant I had to get my head out of my ass, stop worrying so much, and get back into the game.

Strangely energized, I licked my lips and set my attention back on his vast marble-topped island. "You said you bake because it relaxes you, but is that the only reason?"

His head tilted, the corners of his lush lips curling. "We getting personal now?"

"I'd say so, given what I just told you."

The teasing look melted into seriousness. "You honor me with your secrets—you know that, right?"

Maybe it was getting a little too intense, because I had the sudden urge to cry or fling myself into his arms. "You going to do the same?"

He huffed, but it was self-deprecating. "It's the challenge. It takes precision, focus, and planning. And though baking is fairly rigid in terms of technique, creativity plays a big part in the ultimate goal." Lucian shrugged. "It may not seem much like hockey, but it involves both the mind and the body working as one and total dedication to the outcome."

"Do you ever think about doing it professionally?"

At that, he turned back to his work, a frown of concentration pulling at his brows. "No."

"Hmm. And yet your great-grandfather trained you. Did he want that for you?"

At this he smiled, a thin ghost of a gesture that haunted his handsome face. "Actually, he didn't. He wanted me to follow my dream of being a hockey player." The haunted smile grew sharp edges. "He said a person would never find true peace and happiness until they followed their passion and love. I suppose he ought to know. He loved being a chef."

The fact that Lucian referred to his great-grandfather in the past tense made it clear he was no longer with us. But I couldn't help asking, "Did he ever see you play professionally?"

Lucian's expression shut down. "Once. But he . . . well, I was never certain he really understood."

"I don't . . . what do you mean?"

Lucian let out a slow breath, as though pained. "Seven years ago, he was struck by a car when crossing the street in Paris." He swallowed thickly. "Jean Philipe survived, but his brain sustained a fair bit of damage. He wasn't the same man—confused me for my dad, lost words, memories, certain motor functions. He got worse over time. Amalie took care of him. Three years ago, he died of pneumonia."

"Oh, Lucian. I'm so sorry." I wanted to hug him so badly my hands shifted forward on the table, but every taut line of his body told me to back off.

"I am too." He blinked down at the marble countertop, spreading his big hands wide upon it. "I don't know if it was bad luck on my part or what, but I started getting concussions. Amalie was terrified. I placated her with assurances. Physical injuries were part of the life I led. But that last time, I lost consciousness. My brain became a liability. There are things about that time that I can't remember. Things that are fuzzy around the edges. But the horror of knowing that I could, if I wasn't careful, end up like my great-grandfather was crystal clear."

"So you quit."

"So I quit," he repeated before breathing out a humorless laugh. "I might not have. I didn't want to listen. It had taken waking up with Amalie, Ant, and Tina at my side and not knowing who they were for five minutes. It had been the fact that I kept asking them over and over again what had happened to me and not remembering that they'd answered me every time."

"Luc—"

"When my brain had calmed down enough to think more clearly," he pushed on, as though he had to get it all out in one swoop, "I hadn't been able to deny my family when they begged me to consider my health. Faced with the terror of losing myself certainly helped make the decision to retire a bit easier. But I resent it every day."

I saw that knowledge ripple over his big body and tighten it, as though he were internally hunkering down.

I didn't know what to say to ease that pain. Perhaps nothing would. Some things a person had to get past on their own. But I couldn't leave him alone in the dark with his thoughts; I feared everyone else had been doing just that—giving him space they thought he needed, while unknowingly abandoning him.

"What was his favorite dessert?"

Lucian blinked, as though coming out of a fog. His dark brows quirked over those icy eyes, and for a moment, I thought he might not answer, but he finally spoke, his voice a little rougher. "He was known for his innovation, but his favorite was always the classic: *gâteau Saint-Honoré*."

"Will you make it for me?"

He knew what I was doing. But he simply gave me a sly look. "You're constantly trying to taste my creams, aren't you, Emma?"

He was teasing, clearly wanting to make me blush and stammer. But I couldn't erase the image of licking cream off every delectable inch of him. God, I wanted that. So much so my mouth was in danger of watering.

I returned his look with equal measure. "Careful there, honey pie. One day, I just might call your bluff on all your thinly veiled cream innuendos."

To my surprise, he flushed a dusky pink across the high crests of his cheeks. But he held my gaze. "Maybe that's what I'm aiming for."

Those well-placed words hit me with a hot kick to the belly. But my response was lost among the sudden intrusion of Ant, Tina, Brommy, and Sal, all of whom invaded the kitchen looking for snacks, much to Lucian's irritation. He tried to chase them off, but they weren't having it, and we ended up sitting around the farmhouse table as a scowling, but not really pissed, Lucian whipped up a batch of madeleines just to "shut you all up."

They were delicious. But the quick, piercing looks he snuck my way every few minutes were what I craved more. Problem was whether I wanted to admit it to myself or not, Greg had knocked a huge dent in my confidence. I'd thought what we had was real, only to realize in the rudest of awakenings that I had been building castles in my head once more. I wanted something real, someone I could trust, and for all that I liked Lucian, I didn't know if he was the one to give me that.

———

Lucian

Brommy volunteered to help me install the new kitchenette cabinets in one of the small guesthouses. We'd been at it for a while when Emma tracked us down, breezing into the space like a summer sky. I drank in the sight of her.

Since finding me out, Emma had decided to park her cute butt in my kitchen and watch me cook or bake. Every day. While others would have been summarily chased out, I looked forward to her presence. Some days, I went as far as enlisting her to be my sous-chef. But Emma had terrible concentration and preferred chatting to proper measuring. The woman was destined to eat my creations, not help me make them.

Which was fine with me. I would never get tired of watching her taste my sweets. Tempted as I was to taste her in return, I'd managed to keep my hands to myself—barely. Apparently, I was a bit of a masochist when it came to Emma.

"I knew it," she said, smiling up at Brommy and me as we balanced a heavy upper cabinet between us. "I just had to follow the sounds of hanging, and I'd find you men."

Brommy choked on a laugh. "The sounds of *hammering*, if you please, Miss Emma. Walking in on banging is an entirely different matter."

"Why . . . ?" A little wrinkle worked between her brow for a second, then cleared with a deep flush. "Ah, yes, I can see how that would . . ." She gave up and laughed, her full-out-husky laugh that got to me every time.

It got to Brommy, too, who gaped at her with something akin to awe. But then he blinked, and the ends of his ears went red. Honestly, I'd never seen him reduced to a blushing bumbler by a woman before. It was impressive. Then again, so was Emma.

"Technically," I said, before Brommy could fall totally under her spell, "we're screwing." I held up my drill as evidence.

Her smile went wide. "You're terrible."

My arms were starting to tire, and I turned to secure the cabinet with the drill, then hopped down and grabbed a towel to wipe the dust from my brow. "You need something, Em?"

Her gaze darted to Brommy but then found mine again. Either I imagined it, or Emma Maron was nervous. "I wanted to talk to you, if you have a minute."

Brommy caught on quickly and hopped down as well. "I'm going to grab some more drinks." He took the cooler we had and then tipped an imaginary hat toward Emma. "Miss Emma."

A small smile tilted her lush mouth. "You can call me Princess, Brommy. I know you want to."

He grinned, and I scowled. Not that they noticed.

"See you in a bit, Princess."

"Brommy."

They nodded to each other like regal friends, and then he left, whistling a happy tune. Emma watched him walk away for a second, then swung her gaze back and caught me scowling. But her smile only grew. Right then, I would have given anything to know if she thought of that night in the pool, if she regretted how it ended. We'd never talked of it. But I hadn't forgotten. If anything, the memory was starting to take on painfully sharp edges.

Focus, Oz.

She wandered farther into the room, looking around at this and that. "I haven't said before, but you do good work."

"Hmm."

Emma paused at the sound, and amusement lit her eyes. "Do you enjoy construction?"

I shrugged. "It's something to do."

I was being closed off all over again, and I couldn't seem to stop myself. I knew she wanted to say something. That much was clear. And it was something she thought I wouldn't like. She hadn't yet asked me about Cassandra. I'd been expecting it but figured she was biding her time. Maybe that time was now. But I wasn't about to beg her to keep quiet or imply that I couldn't handle talking about my failure with Cassandra with her.

But she did none of those things. Instead, she leaned on the half-finished counter area and looked me over like I was prospective real estate. My body came to attention.

"I have a problem," she said.

Oh, the dirty possibilities of how I could solve her problems that went through my head. I shoved them back down into the gutter of my mind, where they belonged.

"Your family members are about to arrive, bound and determined to drive you up a tree?" I offered, stalling.

The corners of her eyes crinkled. "No, that's all you."

"Well, I hope you're not jealous. Spoiler alert—it's not as fun as it looks."

She shook her head wryly. "You'll miss them when they're gone, Brick."

The nickname pinged at my heart. "Ask them to leave, and let's see."

"Would you be serious?" She didn't sound too annoyed; there was a lilt in her voice. I wanted more of that.

"I was."

"Lucian."

"I like it better when you call me *honey pie*."

Huffing, she rolled her eyes but still couldn't hide that smile. "Dear sweet honey pie, would you shut it and listen?"

"Since you asked so nicely." Truth was I'd damn well do anything for this woman.

I think she knew as much, because her expression turned victorious. "I'm invited to a wedding in Malibu this weekend . . ."

Hell. I knew what was coming. My skin started to feel too tight, the air around me too thick.

"If you're looking for fashion advice, that's more Sal and Amalie's purview."

"I'll bear that in mind. Will you be my date?"

And there it was. Part of me wanted to do something mature like a fist pump because she'd asked me out. That part was drowned out by the ornery ass who did not, under any circumstances, want to be at any event that required conversing and interacting with others.

"Em . . ."

"Before you say no, the wedding will be very small and intimate. It's for my costar Macon Saint."

"And you thought it would be a good idea to bring me?"

I had no doubt she knew what I meant. I wasn't charming. I was barely social.

Emma shrugged, the strap of her pale-blue sundress slipping a little over the golden-hued curve of her shoulder. "I could go it alone. But I don't want to. A woman alone at a wedding is a target for ten million questions, none of them good. I'd rather have a wall of big snarly man mountain guarding over me."

She needs you. Say yes, you idiot.

"Brommy could do it."

Moron.

One of her brows arched delicately. "You want me to ask Brommy?"

My shoulders sagged in defeat. "No."

"Hmm."

"That's my line, Snoopy."

The gleam was back in her eyes. "It works so well I'm stealing it as my own."

God, she was cute. Perfect. I wanted to span her waist with my hands and set her on the cabinets so I could attend to her mouth properly. I held back and kept baiting. Like a moron.

"I'm surprised you didn't threaten to ask Anton."

Emma pretended to think that one out. "I could. He is very nice to look at." She smiled at my grunt. "But I have a suspicion he'd take it to mean I was interested."

"And you're not." I couldn't bring myself to frame it as a question. It was hard enough imagining. If she was, I'd . . . fuck if I knew. Go cry somewhere, probably.

But she wrinkled her nose. "Not even a little, honey pie."

The woman knew how to work me—I'd give her that. She was also observant as hell, and when my shoulders slumped in relief, her gaze narrowed. "We ever going to talk about it?"

No. Make that *hell no*. "Talk about what?"

The second I asked the question, I knew I was in for trouble. Emma wasn't the type to take my bullshit lying down.

Her lush lips slanted with dark amusement. "You licked my nipple, Lucian." I nearly choked on my own spit, my body coming to swift, heated alertness. Not that it stopped her from adding, "Maybe you go around licking women's nipples all the time, but I tend to give that privilege out to a select few."

Damn, but I felt privileged. Grateful, even. It remained the highlight of my erotic dreams ever since that night.

My voice grew hoarse and strained. "I don't do it all the time. It's been a while." Face flaming, I cleared my throat. "It was a momentary weakness due to . . ." *Desperately wanting you. I'd give anything to lick that sweet little nipple one more time.* "Pool shenanigans."

The light in her eyes told me she was struggling to either not laugh or not strangle me. Maybe both. "That's what you're going with?"

"Yes?" No. I didn't fucking know. The woman had me tied up in knots. I wanted her. She scared the hell out of me. I wanted to tell her what a bad bet I was. That we both knew she could do better. But I couldn't make my mouth form the words. And the moment to do so passed me by.

"Hmm" was all she said.

I stood there stoic and composed. And feeling like a fool. I should have turned and walked away, told her that it was best if we ignored each other for the duration of her stay. But that was not what I did. "This wedding-date thing important to you?"

Her brows lifted in surprise. But she didn't prevaricate, as I had done. "Yes."

And that was that. I could try to keep my hands to myself. I could try to tamp down my lust for this woman. But I could not see her disappointed.

"All right, honey. I'll be your wedding man mountain." I wiped my hands off on the rag, if only to keep myself from reaching for her. "But be forewarned. I'm not going to be charming or chatty or whatever. If someone tries to corner me and talk hockey, I'm bolting."

I felt like an ass as soon as I finished. But Emma just smiled, as if she'd expected me to say as much. "Ah, Brick, you say that because you haven't met Macon Saint."

Whatever that meant.

CHAPTER FIFTEEN

Lucian

"Tell me about this wedding and what to expect."

In deference to Emma's exceptional driving skills and my propensity to get a migraine when driving for more than an hour, she was behind the wheel, and I was comfortably slumped in the passenger seat.

Did I prefer to be the one driving? Actually, no. This way I had the perfect excuse to watch Emma as long as I wanted. It was a better view than the Pacific coast outside my window. By far.

Her pert nose wrinkled when she concentrated, which was cute as hell.

"Let's see. Saint, who you know as Arasmus, is a supremely private person. I don't think he'd be doing this if not for Delilah." Emma glanced my way, her eyes sapphire in the sunlight. "She was with us during filming last season and got close to the crew."

"And you too?" I tried to imagine being fine with watching my woman film love scenes with someone. And struggled. Not that Emma was my woman. And obviously it was all acting. Didn't change the fact that the man I was about to meet had had his hands on Emma's breasts. Had kissed her multiple times.

Maybe something of that showed, because she gave me one of those "You're fooling no one, but you amuse me" looks. "It actually helped, getting to know me. She could witness firsthand that there's absolutely no real spark between Saint and me."

"Never thought there was."

"Uh-huh. Neither did Delilah. Not really. But it can be hard trying to erase those final film images from your mind. Especially when they're meant to look hot." Emma's eyes lit with wry humor. "When you see the reality, how awkward it is, all the crew hovering about, it helps."

"Does it bother you? Doing those scenes?"

"The nudity? Yes and no. I felt safe and respected on the set. They keep it closed, with only a few key people on hand. But it was never a fully comfortable experience. And there's a certain creep factor with some fans that I don't enjoy."

My hackles raised so fast it was a miracle I didn't snarl. The thought of her being harassed made me want to tear things with my bare hands. "You haven't been . . . hurt or—"

"No," she assured gently, like she had to soothe me, when I should be the one comforting her. "Nothing like that. Nothing past the occasional leer and the foolish decision early on to read social media comments." She let out a short laugh. "Lesson learned there. For good."

I hated that she had seen ugliness. But I nodded in perfect under-standing and sympathy. "Never read the comments, Em."

She gave me a sideways look. "I bet you had worse."

"I don't know about worse. But I accepted that criticism was part of the life." I shrugged. "Hockey fans are pretty great. Listening to chucklehead sport commentators who thought they knew what went through my head when I played was more aggravating, to be honest."

"I bet." Emma turned off the highway and onto a smaller road that led to the sea. "At any rate, when I consider future roles, unless there's a really good character-development reason for it, I won't do nude scenes again."

My grunt earned a smile, which was what I intended. Emma pulled up to a residential gate, and we were buzzed into the property. Perhaps in deference to the wedding party, a valet met us in the drive. But Macon Saint opened the front door, his expression breaking into a fond smile upon seeing Emma.

"You made it." He gave her a bear hug, the kind I reserved for Tina, and then let her go to eye me in clear reservation.

The guy was about an inch taller than me and built like Brommy—bulky but all muscle. I could take him, though. I was quick, had a punch like a hammer and . . . well, hell, he was Emma's friend. Not an opponent on the ice. Didn't stop me from returning his stare with a deadpan expression.

But strangely, his reserve dropped, and he smiled. "Luc Osmond?"

"That's me."

"Holy shit, man." He offered his hand. "Huge fan."

I used to get off on things like this. Fandom. Knowing someone supported me and my team. Now I felt like an imposter. But I shook his hand back. "Likewise."

"Man, that game against Toronto—"

"Where's your lovely bride, Saint?" Emma cut in brightly, giving a good impression of someone who really didn't want to hear a couple of guys talk sports but was pretending to be clueless about it. I knew, however, she was trying to protect me.

It was a strange sensation, having someone read me so well. I wasn't sure if I liked it or if I was afraid I'd never get it back when she drifted out of my life. Either way, Saint got the message and stepped back to let us farther into the airy front hall of the house.

"In the kitchen, terrorizing her catering staff."

"I heard that," a southern drawl rang out. A second later, a curvy woman with light-brown hair and eyes the color of brûlée strolled up to us. She gave Saint a reproachful look that didn't dull the affection in her eyes. "I do not terrorize my staff."

He wrapped an arm around her waist and hauled her close. "Whatever you say, Tot."

The woman pursed her lips but turned her attention to Emma. "Hey! I'm so glad you're here."

They hugged before Emma introduced her to me. "Lucian, this is Delilah. Dee, this is Lucian Osmond."

"Luc Osmond," Saint said to Delilah with emphasis. "Hockey center for Washington."

Delilah slid him a look that said she had no idea why he had to put that part in, and I bit back a laugh.

I took her hand. "Nice to meet you both. Thank you for letting me attend your wedding."

"We're happy to have you." Delilah had that whole southern-hostess thing going on and gave me a wide polite smile. But it didn't meet her eyes. I had no idea what she saw in me, but clearly both she and Saint were protective of Emma. Since I was, too, I approved, even if the distrust was in my direction.

Delilah turned to Macon. "North is looking for you. I'll take Emma and Luc—" She glanced at me. "Or is it Lucian?"

"Luc is fine." I said it automatically, having been called Luc for most of my adult life. But I noticed Emma stiffen at my side—because she'd called me Lucian. I didn't look her way. Not now, with her protectors hovering in front of us.

"I'll take Luc and Emma to their room."

Room. She said *room*. I didn't imagine that.

No, no I didn't. Because I soon found myself being ushered into a well-appointed room overlooking the Pacific. Light poured in, slanting across the single king bed against the wall. Through a daze I heard Delilah and Emma talking, Delilah telling us to make ourselves comfortable. On the bed? The one fucking bed?

The door shut, and I blinked, suddenly alone with Emma. In our room.

Hell.

———

Emma

"I didn't think this thing properly through."

I set my bag down by the bed and turned to a scowling Lucian. "What's got your pants in a twist now?"

I absolutely knew what was upsetting him, and I kind of loved that he was a Grumpy Gus half the time, but I would never stop giving him shit about it.

His glare was green ice, but his expressive mouth quirked. "I didn't think about this being an overnight trip."

"Ah." *Wait for it.*

Lucian's gaze moved over the room. It was a very nice room—lovely, even—overlooking the ocean, with a generous en suite bathroom. "I definitely didn't think we'd be sharing a room."

There it was.

"I knew you were going to get fussy."

"Fussy," he repeated, as though the word was a snake.

"Fussy." I plopped onto the plush bed and kicked off my sandals. "To be fair, I didn't expect the whole 'one room to bind them' deal either."

He huffed in reluctant amusement, then crossed his beefy arms over his chest and quirked a brow as I continued.

"But unless we want to embarrass our hosts, which I don't, and go find a hotel somewhere, which will be less private, we're stuck with it. So we might as well be adults and suck it up."

"You're okay with this?" He stared down at the bed like it just might up and grab him.

"Are you going to try something on me without my permission?"

"No," he spat, clearly disgusted I'd even suggested it.

I fought a smile. "Do you think I'm going to try something on you without your permission?"

His eyes narrowed. "I get the point, Em."

I let my amusement show. "It's a king bed. And granted, you are a big guy, but there's plenty of room."

Lucian rolled his shoulders and went to set his bag by the far wall. "How very grown up of you."

"I like to think so."

"Hmm." The sidelong look he slanted toward me sent a bolt of heat and nerves straight through my lying soul. Because I *was* lying my ass off. The idea of sharing a bed with Lucian Osmond was daunting. I just might roll over in my sleep and cling to him like a monkey. I couldn't trust my base self not to touch him. In all honesty, I barely trusted myself not to reach for him when I was awake.

Truly, I hadn't thought this thing out very well either. But I was an actress. I could act like I was fine. But I didn't think I'd fooled Lucian. The man had a way of seeing right through me. It was damn inconvenient.

Against my will, my gaze slid over the rest of the bed for the briefest moment. It was a big white affair with fluffy pillows and a downy quilt. The temptation to grab Lucian by the hand and say, "To hell with it; just fuck me, please, I beg you" was so strong that my bones vibrated, my breasts growing heavy underneath my top.

Would he do it? Would he drop all his walls and blockades and give me relief from this relentless wanting? Or would he give me that look that said he thought I was ridiculous and then flee the room?

He was giving me a look now, cautious but considering. Exactly what he was considering, I didn't know. And that was the maddening part.

There were times when I felt as though I knew this man on a bone-deep level that defied how long we'd been in each other's lives. Something about Lucian made sense to me. I couldn't explain it further than that. And yet he'd told Delilah and Saint to call him Luc.

Embarrassment uncoiled in my belly. I didn't even know what name he liked to be called. It felt awful, strange. Reminding me that I didn't know this man who I'd be sharing a room with at all.

"Should I not call you Lucian?" I blurted out, all needy and uncertain.

A small wrinkle formed between stern brows. "I told you to call me that."

"You also told me to call you Oz. And for Dee and Saint to call you Luc."

"I know." One hand set on his narrow hips, he swiped the other hand over his mouth. "I sound addlepated."

"Addlepated," I repeated with a smile.

His answering grin was swift and brilliant, and it took a little of my breath with it. "A Mamie term."

"Ah."

His grin faded. "People have always either called me Oz or Luc. That's what I'm used to. But with you . . ." He paused, his lips parted and that frown returning, reluctant and annoyed. And he shrugged, more like a roll of his shoulder, as though he were trying to loosen the tension there. "You've called me Lucian from the start. It sounds right."

Warmth spread through me, slow like honey.

Our gazes collided and held as something simmered between us. Lucian's lids lowered in lazy perusal. Of me on the bed. I didn't miss the way his nostrils flared on a drawn-in breath, the way his dusky skin darkened. A pulse beat in my neck, steady, hard.

"Lucian . . ." It rolled over my tongue like cream.

Honey and cream. I wanted to pour both over those tight abs of his and just lick.

Perhaps he knew that, because he jerked straight. His jaw twitched, and those wintergreen eyes told me to behave. But I didn't want to. I wanted to tease and tempt him the way he tempted me.

One night sharing a bed with Lucian. I didn't think I'd survive it.

Chapter Sixteen

Lucian

That bed. That fucking bed. It would be the bane of my existence for the next twenty-four hours. That and the image of Emma sitting on the edge of it with a witchy smile that all but dared me to tumble her back and fuck her into the soft covers.

If she wanted to pretend there was absolutely no temptation in sharing a bed, fine. But I saw the faint flush in her cheeks as she looked up at me, the way her lips parted like an invitation to take a taste. And that made it worse. So much worse. If I thought for a second that she had no interest in me, I would grit my teeth and suffer through a night in bed with her without another thought.

But knowing she would be suffering too? That was another matter altogether. It felt like a physical imperative to ease her need and thus ease mine. And then what? When the sweat cooled, we'd still be the same people, me with a life going nowhere, while Emma's was open to countless possibilities.

Before, when I was a cocky son of a bitch, I wouldn't have cared about the after. I would have gone for what I wanted and damned the consequences. Now, everything felt too fragile, too real. There was a good chance I'd cling to Emma like a lifeline. And the humiliation of that prospect, when she would soon be moving on, was too much.

I had some pride left. I'd cling to that instead. And resist temptation.

Sure you will, Ozzy boy.

In an attempt to do right by Emma, I'd forgone my usual jeans and T-shirt and put on a fine-knit-collar top and wool slacks, the kind of thing I'd wear for interviews. I regretted the choice now. The collar, though unbuttoned at the top, still managed to choke me. And the slacks, while loose fit, felt clinging. Shit, everything clung and pulled. I needed air. Lots of it.

Emma still sat on the bed, one leg curled beneath her, the other hanging off the edge and slowly swinging like a pendulum. Every time her lower leg swayed, her toned thigh would bunch, then ease. The movement was hypnotic. I wanted to set my hand there and feel that firm golden flesh.

"What do you want to do now?" she asked. So very innocently. That leg kept swaying.

Devil woman.

"I need air." Without waiting for a response, I fled the fucking room.

Emma's soft laughter followed me. "Have fun exploring."

Yep. She knew. This was going to be hell.

It was quiet in the hallway, abandoned for the moment. I leaned against the wall and tried to level my breathing. Didn't help to kill the stiffness in my dick. It pushed out my pants in a bulge that even I thought looked obscene. Emma had to have seen it. And God, she was good at riling me up. I had absolutely no idea what she thought of it. I wanted to turn around and ask.

Hell, I wanted to turn around and show her. Beg her to give me some relief. I'd be good; I'd return the favor with interest. God, I wanted that. I just plain *wanted*.

No. That's not what we're doing this weekend. Behave, Oz.

Given that I now hated the voice in my head and still had a hard-on that would get me arrested for public indecency, I ran the heel of my hand down its rude length. Firmly. A grunt left me, and my abs clenched. I did it again, angling my body toward the wall, my free hand flat against the cool surface.

Damn it, I wanted to grind into something. No, I wanted her. Slick and snug. She'd wiggle so sweetly on my cock. I could picture it well, her riding my dick, those sweet little breasts bouncing for me.

"Fuck," I hissed, blood surging, and my hips gave an involuntary thrust. I was in very real danger of coming in my pants.

The horror of that was enough to quell my erection. Blowing out a breath, I straightened. My abs ached like they'd been punched. But at least I could walk normally now. And I headed downstairs, following the sounds of activity and the scent of food into a well-equipped kitchen. I was surprised to find the bride standing in the midst of half a dozen catering staff. Her hair was in disarray, skin flushed. She huffed out a sound of sheer despair and clutched her cell phone like she was trying to squeeze the life out of it. It was too late to back out—she spotted me.

"You need something, Luc?" she asked, polite but tight in a way that made it clear she was silently hoping I'd leave. I empathized.

I held up a hand. "Just wandering. Don't worry about me."

She smiled—thin, pained—then nodded before her shoulders slumped. The woman looked wrecked. Then I remembered she was a chef. Apparently quite a good one. Maybe she'd thought to cook for her wedding? The idea sounded like madness to me.

Before I could say a word, Macon Saint strode in, the big guy's expression drawn with worry. "What's wrong?" he said to Delilah, pulling her close before she could answer.

Delilah made a protracted wail and clutched him. "There's been an accident on the 101."

Saint paled. "Someone hurt? Who?"

"No," she said. "No injuries. Unless you count our wedding cake."

"Jesus, Tot. You scared the hell out of me. I thought it was something serious."

Delilah glared up at Saint. "This is serious!"

Saint cringed, and internally, I did too. Poor bastard walked right into that one. "I meant like death . . . shit, okay. It's serious."

Delilah squeezed the bridge of her nose and breathed hard. "My cake. Splattered all over the asphalt. How am I supposed to get a cake ready in time with all I have to do?"

"I can do it." Was that me who spoke?

They both turned my way. Yep, it was. Hell, I had surprised myself. But seeing Delilah frantic and in need of help that I could provide had kick-started a surge of adrenaline that I'd once only felt on the ice. Here was a challenge I could sink into, something I could do that was worthwhile—useful.

Saint immediately adopted a "Now I gotta deal with this fucking guy" expression. "That's nice of you—"

"He's not kidding," came Emma's voice at my elbow. I nearly jumped. The woman moved on cat feet.

Now that I noticed her, all other thoughts scattered. I couldn't concentrate past the warm edge of her arm brushing mine. It was hard enough to look at her without illicit thoughts flickering through my brain. What would she do if I leaned in and licked her?

"I'm serious," she said, breaking into my haze. "His pastries are the best I've ever tasted."

A flush of pride washed up my neck and over my face. At some point, hers had become the opinion I valued the most.

Delilah's brows lifted. "Seriously?"

I could do this. I *wanted* to do this.

"Well, I don't know about the best ever," I said. "But I do know how to make a cake. I promise I wouldn't do anything to ruin your day."

"He's being modest." Emma nudged me, as if to say, "Speak up, you dolt." But she didn't let me. "Saint, remember that week of filming we did in Lyon? And we went out that one night?"

Saint brightened. "Oh shit. That good?"

"Better. But I might be biased."

I had no idea what they were talking about, and Delilah clearly didn't either. But she was smiling, tentatively hopeful. Which was good. I didn't want to see this poor woman undone by a cake disaster. Besides, being tucked away in the kitchen instead of mingling with guests and struggling not to carry Emma away and do dirty things to her was more than fine by me.

Saint glanced down at his bride. "What do you think, Tot?"

Delilah pinned her eyes on me, suddenly 100 percent master chef. "What can you do?"

"Depends on what you want. What was the cake you had ordered?"

"A hazelnut sponge with vanilla-and-mango mousse. Vanilla buttercream with a fondant overlay and flowers."

Ideas flowed and pinged around my brain, kicking up that heady surge of excitement and challenge once more. This I knew. This I liked. "You're feeding what? Forty?"

"Forty-five. Fifty, to be safe."

"You want a traditional multitier with buttercream, then we're pushing it. Especially if you expect any sort of elaborate decoration."

"The cake feels cursed at this point." Delilah's scowl made me want to smile. It was as if she was personally offended by the bad luck, which I could understand.

"I could do croquembouche. That's relatively quick and a crowd-pleaser. There are endless possibilities of gâteau." My fingers twitched with the need to get started. "Do you have any favorite flavors? Food allergies?"

While I talked, Delilah began to smile.

"No food allergies. And you're hired."

"I'm doing it for free." I walked farther into the room, taking a look around. The kitchen was as good as what I had at home. Delilah was a professional chef, and I had no doubt she had the tools I needed. But I could always go to the store in a pinch. "What will it be?"

Delilah glanced at Saint, who shrugged. "Whatever you want, Tot."

"Can you do mango cream in the croquembouche?"

Mangoes must have been a thing with them, because Saint grinned.

"Of course. How about two croquembouches and perhaps *glace au beurre noisette* to accompany?"

"I think you are my hero," Delilah said with a relieved laugh.

"Dessert hero," Saint corrected, but he was smiling, too, in a reserved way that reminded me too much of myself. "Thanks, man. Seriously."

"It's not a problem."

"What was that last bit you mentioned?" Emma asked, looking a little glazed in the eyes. The woman really did love her desserts.

"Browned-butter ice cream. I'll be serving it more as a *semifreddo*, though, considering the time."

"Lord save me." She fanned herself.

I was supposed to be avoiding the temptation of Emma Maron. But I couldn't hide my pleasure in seeing her pant. Then a thought occurred to me. "You don't mind, do you? I'll be leaving you alone for a while."

Hell. I hadn't thought. I was here to run interference, not make dessert.

But Emma gaped, as though I was being ridiculous. "Are you joking? Delilah's right; you're a hero for doing this."

My ears felt hot. I shrugged and turned back to Delilah. "I'll need to go over what you have and run to the market."

"I'm not putting you out that much," Delilah said. "You make a list of whatever you need, and I'll send someone to get it. I'm moving some of my kitchen staff over to assist."

"All right, then. Let me at your kitchen, and I'll get started."

CHAPTER SEVENTEEN

Emma

"Dearest Emma," Dougal, my onetime set costumer, drawled, "I have to say I love your new man."

With that, he popped a cream puff into his mouth and moaned dramatically, placing a hand upon his chest.

I huffed out a laugh. It felt both weird and lovely to hear someone call Lucian *my man*. He wasn't, but it was nice to know the people I had worked with day in and day out approved of him. I was proud of Lucian. That much was certain. He'd come through today in a big way, creating not only two towers of croquembouche, swathed in glittering strands of angel-fine spun sugar, but also luscious ice creams paired with delicate butter cookies and mangoes cut to look like blooming lilies.

All of it without breaking a sweat. In truth, when he had sat down at my side just as the ceremony started, he'd appeared both pleased and relaxed.

"He's good, isn't he?" I said to Dougal and dipped my spoon into the ice cream.

"I'm going to assume you're talking about me," Lucian said at my ear, making me jump.

"For such a big man, you walk on cat feet," I grumped.

Chuckling at my obvious start of surprise, he took a seat. "Funny, I've thought the same of you."

"That I am surprisingly quiet on my feet for someone so big?"

He gave me a slanted look of reproach. "That you're good at sneaking up on me."

One long table that stretched the length of the house had been set up on Delilah and Saint's terrace. Tea lights and taper candles glittered upon the cream linen tablecloth. A webbing of string lights, fresh white flowers, and greenery had been erected overhead.

Now that dinner was over, people were up and mingling or devouring Lucian's desserts.

"You really did a great job," I told him truthfully.

"Hmm." He looked at my little bowl of ice cream. "You didn't try the croquembouche."

My nose wrinkled. "Don't tell Delilah, but I hate mangoes. Hate them."

Lucian looked at me for a moment while Dougal watched our interplay with great interest; then he grunted, stood, and walked away.

"Uh-oh," Dougal said with a laugh. "You've upset the chef."

Had I? He didn't seem the type to throw a fit if someone didn't like his food. But he had stalked off. I gave Dougal a helpless look, wondering if I should . . . well, I wasn't going to apologize, not for that. In fact, if he was off pouting, I just might leave him there.

But he returned before I could think any further, a plate of those pretty caramel-covered cream puffs that made up the croquembouche in his hand. My ire notched a bit higher as he sat down, straddling the chair in that way guys seemed to love doing, and faced me.

"I'm serious, Brick. I don't like them. And I'm not going to eat one just to placate your—"

"I know you don't like mangoes." A faint curl of humor danced on his lips.

"You know?" How? How did he know this?

"I've been feeding you this whole time, remember?" With his hot buttered voice, it sounded dirty, illicit.

"I remember." I sounded far too breathless.

He clearly noticed; that small private smile moved to his eyes. "You never eat the mango slices when I put them in any meals."

Understanding hit me, and I recalled that while I'd had breakfast fruit trays with mangoes, they'd stopped being included after the second time. Wide eyed, I silently gaped back at him.

Lucian's long clever fingers delicately picked up a cream puff. "Which is why I made some of these with vanilla-ginger cream."

Had I been gaping before? My mouth fell wide open. Behind me, I heard Dougal sigh, as if impressed. But I could only stare at Lucian, who looked smug but oddly shy as well.

"You did that for me?" I croaked.

His broad shoulder moved under his jacket. "That, and the combination of vanilla, ginger, and mango mirrored what Delilah and Saint had wanted in their original cake."

I could fall for this man. Fall hard. Maybe I already had, because my heart was too big, beating too fast. He gave me another small, barely there smile, his pale eyes gleaming with something soft and intent.

"Come now, honeybee," he murmured. "Try my cream."

I sputtered out a shocked laugh, and my face flamed, but as he'd commanded, I opened my mouth.

Lucian's nostrils flared. His hand shook a little as he lifted the cream puff and placed it on the edge of my lips. I opened my mouth wider, my tongue flicking out for that first sweet taste.

Rich, almost nutty caramel, the gentle crunch of pastry, a burst of smooth light cream with a hint of vanilla and ginger spice. Slowly, I chewed, my eyes locked with his, my body tight, and my mouth in heaven. He stayed with me, feeding me another bite, cream getting on his thumb.

My tongue slipped over the blunt end, and he grunted. Hard.

"Jesus," Dougal said, breaking the spell. "Do that in your room."

Caught out, we both turned his way. The big bald man with tiny round maroon glasses and a perfectly etched goatee was blushing so hard it turned his brown skin a deep rosewood. "Some of us are here without dates. No need to be taunting us with that prelude to kinky sex." Dougal fanned himself. "Gods below, I need a drink."

We watched him walk off, and my face flamed. I'd been two seconds away from sucking on Lucian's thumb and begging for more. Lucian, on the other hand, was unfazed and simply licked his damp thumb, giving me a wicked look.

"Jerk," I muttered, making him chuckle, a delicious rumbling sound that was pure male satisfaction.

Flirty Lucian was dangerous. And gorgeous. At some point between making dessert and the wedding, he'd changed into a finely cut smoke-gray suit with a pure-white shirt and a silver-blue tie. The combination of colors turned his skin bronze and his eyes like old sea glass.

He paused and lifted his dark, thick brows in inquiry. "Why are you looking at me like that?"

Because I want you.

I dragged a fingertip through an errant drop of cream on the plate and licked it up, enjoying the way he watched with intense interest. "Can't be helped, Brick. You really wear that suit."

If I didn't know any better, I'd think he was embarrassed by the praise. His voice came out in a rough rumble. "You seemed surprised."

I was not surprised in the least. The man could make a purple velour tracksuit look like a good idea. "I'm used to you in jeans. I wasn't sure you owned a suit."

He chuckled, as though quietly amused. "Honey, I have dozens of them. All handmade." He sat back, showing off the way his perfectly cut suit lined his long lean body. "I'm a hockey player, after all."

"I honestly don't see the connection."

"Hockey players wear suits or dress clothes on game day and during travel. As a sign of respect, team unity." He waved an idle hand. "To show we are, at least on the surface, gentlemen."

That was . . . insanely sexy. "And here I thought you were all about bloody battles on the ice."

Again came that dangerous, gorgeous smile. "We're that too. Though less so in recent years. We've been tempered."

"A veneer at best, huh?" God, that was sexy too. Though I supposed it shouldn't have been.

"With you, honeybee, I will always be a gentleman." He laughed softly, like he was imparting a secret. "Unless you don't want me to be."

I should have rolled my eyes at that, because he was clearly baiting me with that cheesy line, but he was also clearly relaxed and enjoying himself so much I couldn't help but smile.

"I'll let you know," I told him. "Until then, just sit there and look pretty for me, okay?"

He huffed out a breath, the smile still in his eyes, and shook his head slightly, as if to say, "What am I to do with this woman?" I was in complete agreement. I didn't know what to do around him either. Jumping on his lap and begging him to feed me more cream puffs felt like the best option.

"You look beautiful, by the way," he said, jolting me out of my lustful haze. His gaze roved over me, taking in the strapless periwinkle silk A-line dress I wore. But it wasn't what held his attention. His focus quickly returned to my face, as though that was what captivated him the most. "You probably hear that all the time."

I did. And being a woman, I'd been taught early on not to feel comfortable with praise. Which really was a mindfuck, because we were also taught to yearn for praise and acceptance. But all of that didn't stop me from feeling a warm swell of pleasure that Lucian found me beautiful.

His voice lowered, becoming more forceful. "When I first met you, it pissed me off that I noticed how beautiful you were."

"What?" The word came out in a garbled squawk.

Lucian's smile was wry and tight. "You're Amalie's guest. I have no right to look at you like that."

I had to disagree there. But he didn't give me a chance.

"Thing is, the more I get to know you, the more beautiful you are to me."

Oh. Hell.

My breath left in a gusty sigh, my heart swelling painfully within the confines of my chest.

"I like who you are, Em," he said, as though the confession was torn from him, and he didn't quite want it to be. But he didn't blink, didn't flinch as my lips parted with surprise. I swallowed thickly.

"I like who you are too."

At that, Lucian turned his head, giving me his fierce profile. He was clearly as uncomfortable with praise as I was. Too bad. He needed it. Needed to know that he had value. But we'd been spotted, and our delicate privacy was broken as Delilah walked over.

"Luc!" Delilah all but squealed with a beaming smile. "I need to give you a big ol' hug."

She was beautiful in her lace-and-silk sheath wedding gown, with orange blossoms in her hair. The only nod to color was the red of her lipstick and her high heels, the sight of which had made Saint smile so brilliantly and wide during the ceremony it had sent a pang through my heart to see it.

Now, she came up to Lucian, who immediately got to his feet and accepted her hug with grace.

Saint followed. While he wasn't grinning like Delilah, he seemed pleased and happier than I'd ever seen him. Marriage agreed with the man. As soon as Delilah finished hugging Lucian, Saint stuck out his hand and shook Lucian's. "Great work, man. Seriously."

"It was a pleasure to help," Lucian said, looking almost as uncomfortable with their praise as he had with mine.

Delilah pulled out a chair to sit, but Saint beat her to it, taking it for himself, then pulling her into his lap. She wrapped her arm around his shoulders and leaned into him with a sigh. "I'm beat."

Saint chuckled. "We haven't even gotten to the dancing you insisted on."

"Oh, we're dancing, Mister. Don't even think of trying to slink out of that." She eyed the plate of cream puffs Lucian had set on the table. "I just need a tiny rest first."

Lucian saw the direction of her stare and moved the plate over a little. "Want one?"

"Yes!" She grabbed a puff and took a huge moaning bite before feeding Saint the rest. "So good."

Delilah eyed Lucian. "You never baked professionally?"

"No. Just at home. Or for my teammates."

"His great-grandfather was Jean Philipe Osmond," I put in, hoping with Delilah's chef connections, she'd know who that was. "He taught Lucian."

Lucian slid me a look of reproach, but he didn't seem truly put out, more like surprised I was puffing him up. I arched my brow, as if to say, "What? You're being modest."

Delilah's eyes went wide. "No shit? Holy hell."

"I'm missing something," Saint said.

She turned and carefully wiped a tiny crumb from the corner of his mouth. "Jean Philipe Osmond was one of the greatest pastry chefs in the world. I have two of his cookbooks. They covered him for a semester in culinary school."

Saint's brows rose. Mine did as well.

I turned to Lucian. "You didn't tell me all that!"

He shrugged. "I said he was a big deal."

"You are the master of understatement—you know that?"

He flashed a quick grin that made my pulse stutter.

"Well, that helps explain it." Delilah peered at Lucian and then took another cream puff. "I don't know how much Emma told you about me, but I'm opening a restaurant in a few months. Just down the road."

"She told me. And that you are an exceptional chef."

Delilah gave me a happy look, but her attention was focused on Lucian. "I've been struggling to find a pastry chef."

It was clear where she was headed, and Lucian sat back, as though trying to physically distance himself from the whole idea. "I'm not a professional chef."

"You're as good as," she countered. "This is some of the best pastry work I've tasted, and I don't think you even broke a sweat."

"No, but . . ."

"Dessert plays a huge part on what I'm trying to say," she cut in. "I need someone who understands flavors and isn't afraid to stretch themselves creatively. A lot of professional pastry chefs I've met with are too rigid or worried about failing." Her golden eyes narrowed speculatively. "Somehow I don't think you'd be intimidated by critics."

Lucian shrugged. "People either like my food, or they don't. It's not my problem."

"Exactly," she cried out with a little laugh. "You're a brawler. I need that."

He made a sound of amusement, but beneath the cover of the table, I saw the way his fingers clenched, like he wanted to run for it. But he didn't. "I haven't ever thought about doing something like that."

"Babe," Saint murmured, picking up on Lucian's reluctance.

Delilah ignored him, her eyes wide and pleading. "I get it—this is a lot to pile on out of the blue. And a huge change in lifestyle for you. But would you consider looking over my menu plans and see if it stirs any creative interest for you?"

Lucian blinked, clearly surprised at her fervor. I wasn't. I'd spent time with Delilah and knew she was passionate about cooking and food. It wasn't a leap to see that she'd be excited to meet someone with the same sort of talent and passion for food. The funny thing was that Lucian didn't seem to understand how much of himself he revealed through his work. Delilah was right; he was a fighter. But he was also a thoughtful artist who evoked emotions through his food. His dishes were sensual in a way I didn't think he realized.

Under Delilah's unblinking puppy eyes, he relented with a quirk of his mouth, as though he wanted to keep resisting but didn't have the energy to fight her force of will. "All right. I'll give you my email, and you can send them over."

"Yes!" She did a little fist pump that had Saint chuckling and hauling her back against his wide chest. They looked so comfortable together, so much in love, that a small pang of envy pinched my heart. Delilah beamed up at him before giving me a happy, relaxed smile. "He's much better than Greg, Em. So much better."

A collective beat went around the table. Delilah clearly knew she'd spoken out of turn, her lips parting in distress. She was quick enough to understand that giving me a look of apology would be too obvious, but I knew she was sorry all the same. Saint, being more sensitive than most people knew, scooped his bride up and, in an impressive display of strength, stood and lifted her with him.

"If you'll excuse us," he said, holding her in his arms. "I have a few dances to claim."

They left us alone with the specter of Greg hanging over us like a big stink. I launched a preemptive strike. "I don't want to talk about it."

Lucian watched me with a predatory stillness, and I braced myself, wondering how he'd go about getting the information out of me.

"All right."

His simple acceptance made me feel small instead of relieved. But I held my tongue and fiddled with the rumpled edge of the tablecloth. People got cheated on all the time. It wasn't their shame; it was the cheater's. Even so, the memory of Greg between some stranger's thighs crawled along my skin and settled in my chest. Was I really so easy to leave?

"Somehow, I doubt it," Lucian said. And I realized that, much to my chagrin, I had asked the question out loud.

I ducked my head and plucked at a stray crumb that had fallen onto the blue puddle of my skirt. "Can we pretend I didn't say that?"

"All right."

"I'm just a little . . . raw."

Instinctively, I knew he'd understand that; Lucian was raw about a lot of things too. Silence stretched tight between us, taken up by the laughter of the party around us. Here, at the table, though, we were in our own bubble.

"I think about you." Lucian's rough but low proclamation had me lifting my head.

"About me?" But I knew. The force of his gaze told the tale, the way he seemed to strain toward me but sat absolutely still.

Lines of grim determination bracketed his lush mouth, as though he regretted speaking. But then he continued, the words tumbling over my skin in a hot wave. "Think about touching you again, tasting you. I go to sleep with your name on my tongue and your scent on my skin."

I couldn't breathe. Couldn't move, ensnared by the urgent pulse of his words.

"I wake up hard and aching, remembering how your sweet little nipple rose for me. Think about how I want to suck it again, fucking feast on you."

We stared at each other, heat and tension coiling between us like a living thing, tugging at my nipples, stealing my breath. His chest rose and fell in agitation, color washing over the sculpted crests of his cheeks.

I wanted. I wanted so badly.

He swallowed audibly. "You haunt me, Emma. Every damn thing about you does."

My fingers curled into a fist as blood rushed through my veins. "I think about you too. I've seen you bare but never got to touch. I want to."

Lucian grunted an agonized sound of want.

My words came out breathless. "I think about it at night, when I'm alone."

He closed his eyes, as though absorbing a hit. When they opened, the frosty green burned bright. "You don't know what that does to me, honey."

"Tell me."

A lock of his inky hair fell over his brow as he turned his head with a jerk, giving me his strong profile. "I feel owned. By you. And I like it."

I exhaled as my insides dipped.

But his expression hardened, the strong curve of his jaw bunching. "And I shouldn't, Em. I shouldn't."

Recoiling, I blinked hard, not expecting that. Pride shouted that I hold my tongue, but I asked the question anyway. "Why?"

"Because you deserve better than me." He grimaced but didn't shy away from holding my gaze. "You deserve everything."

"Lucian——"

But before I said another word, five of my former coworkers, drunk and cheerful, descended en masse.

"Emma love! There you are," Danny shouted, oblivious of the tension humming between Lucian and me.

Lucian held my gaze for a brief moment longer, remorse and wry acceptance darkening his eyes. Then he rose, stopping only to touch my shoulder with the very tips of his fingers. His softly murmured words drifted down amid the racket. "I'm sorry, Em."

It speared into my chest and left a hollow hole as he walked away, leaving me to deal with something far worse than talking about my cheating dickhead of an ex-boyfriend. I had to take a long slow walk down memory lane as my friends and costars decided that what I really needed was to be reminded of all that I'd lost.

Wonderful. Just wonderful.

CHAPTER EIGHTEEN

Emma

"You picked a good one, Emma." Delilah leaned back in the white wicker chair with a sigh, a glass of champagne in her hand. Fairy lights strung overhead gave the area a soft glow, but it was nothing compared to the luminous glow in her smile.

"I'd say you picked a good one." I lifted my glass in cheers.

She tipped her glass to that but wouldn't be dissuaded. "You don't want to talk about your new man? I would. He's gorgeous, talented, and clearly gone on you."

My mind tripped over that last bit. Delilah didn't know he wasn't truly my man; Lucian and I had decided it would be easier to keep that to ourselves.

And that hurt. Because I knew without doubt that I was "gone on" Lucian. I started falling the second I laid eyes on him. It was stupid, stupid, stupid. He thought he didn't deserve me and walked away, despite this overwhelming desire that simmered over anytime we got into each other's orbit. The feel of his mouth on my nipple had remained for days, haunting me with need and lust. But where the flesh was willing, the mind was not. Lucian wasn't going to give in. He'd made that perfectly clear.

Where did that leave me? Panting over him and making a fool out of myself. I had some pride. Some dignity.

I took a deeper drink of champagne and it fizzed down my throat, made me warm and sleepy. "Lucian and I aren't serious. We barely know each other."

Delilah took that partial lie with aplomb. "You brought him here. That's huge."

"It's stupid, Dee." With a sigh, I rolled my stiffening neck and blinked up at the lights. "He's reluctant to be in any relationship."

"But he came here with you—"

"As a favor." I grimaced. "And when the weekend is over, we'll go our separate ways, so to speak." It wasn't as though I could avoid him while staying with Amalie. I really needed to leave Rosemont and all its temptations. Getting back to real life as soon as possible was the smart, sane thing to do.

"I know I'm butting my nose in it," Delilah said slowly. "And I won't be offended if you tell me to piss off, but Greg didn't light you up the way Luc does with one look. And you might not see it, but that man comes alive when you're near."

"Too bad about one small detail . . ." I held my thumb and pointer finger a few centimeters apart. "He's emotionally walled up and unstable."

Delilah sighed, shaking her head. "It's hard for some people to put their trust in others. Even when they secretly want to."

"Are you talking about Saint?" I teased.

Her lips curled. "No. About myself. I resisted giving in to Macon tooth and nail. Because I was afraid of opening up to anyone, let alone someone who could truly hurt me if he wanted to."

"It's probably for the best in my case." A pain along my chest had me reaching up to rub it, but I resisted and let my hand fall to my lap. "I clearly make terrible decisions when it comes to love. Before Greg, there was Adam—a total fuckwit—who didn't cheat but constantly belittled.

Then there was Eric, a pompous dickbag who probably cheated but I never caught." My nose wrinkled. "The best I can say is that none of them gave me any STIs, and I'm probably better off on my own."

She chuckled and tipped back her glass to drain it, then set it on the table with a decisive click. "Being hopeful isn't bad decision-making. We give up hope, what's left?"

"Our vibrators."

We both laughed at that. And then she grabbed my hand. "I'm going to miss seeing you on set." Unaware of how deeply it cut to talk about it, probably because she was happily buzzed, Delilah smiled. "They were idiots to let you go."

My smile died. "Thank you. I'll miss you too."

"Don't tell anyone, but Macon is leaving the show."

"What?" I leaned in so we were close enough to speak in hushed tones. "Why?"

She shrugged. "He doesn't want to be typecast. Wants to move on to other things."

"Believe me—I empathize."

"Which is why this cut might hurt, but it will heal, and you'll be stronger."

"Yes," I said, not quite feeling it but wanting to. "I will."

A deep voice cut into our private conversation bubble. "What are you two whispering about?" Saint ambled up and smiled down at Delilah with deep affection.

She smirked at him. "If we wanted you to know, we wouldn't have been whispering."

He took that in stride and swooped down to kiss her. When he pulled back, she was flushed and grinning. "Love that sassy mouth, Tot."

Delilah's gaze grew hazy. "Take me to bed, hotshot."

"Or lose you forever?"

I rolled my eyes but couldn't keep from smiling too. "If you two are going to quote *Top Gun*, do it in the privacy of your own room."

Saint glanced at me and winked. "Good point. You mind if I steal my bride away, Em?"

"By all means. Steal, pillage, quote cheesy old movies to your hearts' content."

He chuckled and, with impressive grace, gathered Delilah in his arms.

She yelped but held on around his neck. "Beast."

"That's me." He nodded my way. "Night, Emma. Thanks for being here tonight."

"Thank you for inviting me. I'm so happy for you two. Now get out of my face before I gag on all the love."

Laughing, Saint walked off, and Dee waved bye over his shoulder. I waved back, smiling wide, but on the inside, my chest felt tight and cold. I envied her. Them. With a smallness that shocked me. I wanted love. I wanted affection and comfort. I wanted to know where my place was in the world and to know that I came first to someone.

What I needed to do was get my life in order. And that wasn't going to happen mooning over some man. But as I sat alone at a table, Lucian nowhere to be seen and my former castmates laughing and chatting it up in small groups, an overwhelming sense of depression filled me. Despite these current setbacks, I had a life others envied. I had my health, and I had friends. Yet I still felt utterly alone. And I had no idea how to fix that.

Lucian

I found her by the cliffs overlooking the sea. Rosemont was far enough up in the hills that the Pacific was a distant glimmer of blue. Here, it crashed violently against the shore, sending up mist and the scent of brine.

When I'd last seen Emma, she'd been surrounded by coworkers talking about their best moments on set. Then North, who was a stunt coordinator, and a couple of guys whose names I'd soon forgotten had pulled me away to talk hockey. It had been surprisingly pain-free to discuss the sport I'd loved and lost. Maybe because we'd discussed everything but me. But Emma had seemed happy, laughing in that glowing way of hers.

She didn't look happy now.

Illuminated only by the lights of the house and soft glowing lamps flickering in the twilight, she appeared ephemeral and small. I strolled closer, not wanting to startle. Something about the way she stood, as if she was struggling to hold herself up, made my chest clench. I hadn't thrown a punch in years, but for her, I'd fight the world.

But it occurred to me that my ill-advised confession and sloppy rejection of the very idea of us might have done this. If I could have kicked my own ass, I would have.

"You all right?" I asked, stopping next to her. Up by the house people had begun to pair up, couples laughing. But here, it was dark and lonely.

Dully, she nodded but then wrapped her arms across her chest. "Yes—no. Not really."

"Em." I slipped off my jacket and draped it over her shoulders. "Was it what I said—"

"No." Her reply cracked through the night. She sighed, as though trying to pull herself together, and spoke more softly. "No, it's not that. I've resigned myself to the idea that we're probably a huge mistake in the making."

That shouldn't have stung; I'd said as much multiple times. My chest still clenched, as though struck. Because it felt wrong, a betrayal of everything that was good and real in my life. But Emma was hurting, which meant I focused on her. "Then what's wrong?"

With another sigh, she tilted her head back and stared up at the sky. "I didn't think it would be this hard, being around them."

Them. Her former costars.

She laughed without humor, the sound weak and carried away in the wind. "It's stupid. Life goes on and all that."

"It's not stupid." I touched her arm, and she turned to stare up at me with dark eyes. "It hurts when what you valued in your life moves on without you."

She nodded, biting her lower lip. "I feel like a jerk, pouting over the loss of a role when you have it so much worse. It seems petulant."

I huffed out a ghost of a laugh. "You think that's what's going on in my mind? No, Emma. Not even a little bit."

Emma shook her head, but I didn't think she'd truly heard me. Dark thoughts had pulled her too deep. "The show was known for its wild directions, killing off people without remorse. But I can't help thinking, why me? Was it really for the good of the story, or did I do something wrong? Did I bore the audience?"

"People watched because of you," I said with a fierceness I hoped she heard. "Jesus, Em. You were its star. You shine. Nothing will change that."

Her gaze met mine, still a bit hazy, but she was listening. A small smile played on her lips. "It's pride. Ego, more like. Mine took a hit, and I wasn't prepared for the blow."

"We never are, bee."

Her smile turned warmer. "No, I guess we're not. But they keep coming, and I can't seem to get out from under it."

Hell. Now that? That was partially my fault. I'd confessed my want of her because I'd seen the way the mention of whoever the hell Greg was had hurt her. She'd flinched, the light draining from her pretty eyes. I couldn't see that and let her go on thinking she wasn't . . . everything. Then I'd fucked it up.

This woman turned me inside out, but she was precious and needed to know it.

Music drifted over the lawn. Nice and slow, a song about love and longing. Up by the house, couples danced under the string lights. I held out my hand. "Dance with me, Em."

She searched my face, as though not certain she'd heard me correctly. Did I ever want to publicly dance? No. But for her? With her? I held steady.

And when she slipped her hand into mine, something deep inside my chest clicked. Lock and key, she fit. I pulled her into the shelter of my arms, content to dance here in the semidarkness. She didn't appear to mind but melted against me with a sigh, her head resting on my chest, as though she could no longer hold it up.

That was fine; I could do the lifting for both of us. My free hand slid up her neck and into the warmth of her hair. And she sighed, the action moving through her body into mine. I closed my eyes and tilted my head just enough to feel the crown of her head beneath my cheek. "Everything is going to be okay."

Her broken whisper pierced my heart. "How do you know?"

"Because I believe in you."

Her body jolted before she sighed. "I believe in you too, Lucian."

God. Why did that hurt so much? I wanted to do right by this woman, show her the best of me, not just the broken edges. I didn't answer but simply held her.

We barely moved, just the slightest sway to give a nod to dancing. Emma let go of my hand and snuggled closer, her arms wrapping around my waist. A lump rose in my throat as I followed suit, winding my arm around her slim waist, holding her. Just holding her.

It wasn't a dance. It was a hug. Because she needed it. And while my mind picked up the particulars—the press of her breasts against my upper abs, the way her thighs touched mine, the warmth of her body—it didn't feel purely sexual. It felt like salvation. I hugged her, but she changed me from the inside out. It had been a lonely year, empty and cold, but here in the darkness, I felt whole. I hugged her because I needed it too.

It was almost too much, the exposed emotion. Like a raw wound being poked. But she felt too good to let go. And I was tired of resisting. Just plain tired of everything but her.

We swayed to Fiona Apple's husky voice singing "I Know," and when it ended, another song came on, a little more upbeat, but Emma stayed where she was.

"Thank you," she finally said, tilting her head back to meet my eyes.

Her face was light and shadows, eyes gleaming in the dark. I wanted to touch her cheek, see if it was as cool and smooth as it looked, but I couldn't seem to let go. Her gaze moved over my face, and I felt the exact moment she started thinking again. Her body tensed just enough to put a sliver of space between us. I wanted that space back, but I held still, kept my voice gentle.

"You okay?" I asked.

"What a question," she said with a small husk of a laugh.

I found myself smiling. "I know it's difficult assessing these feelings, Snoopy."

Her eyes narrowed. "Snoopy is a dog, you realize."

She said it as though slightly offended, like I'd never called her the name before. But it was all there in her face, the need to tease and be teased, to lighten the mood that had fallen over us. I got it. In truth, I needed it too.

"A cute dog."

"You're comparing me to a dog." Her brows rose like punctuation. "A dog."

God, she was cute.

"What do you have against dogs?"

"Not a thing." She rested her head on my chest again. "I just don't want to be called one."

Fighting a grin, I turned her, dancing now. "Stop fishing for compliments, Em. You don't need them."

"I don't?"

"Oh, come on, I told you that you're the most beautiful woman I've ever seen." I glanced down at her upturned face and lost my breath. "You're stunning."

"You still unhappy about that, Brick?"

My chin touched the top of her head. "Yes."

"Years I worried that men only wanted me for my looks. And now you come along, and you're pissed off I'm pretty." She sounded so aggrieved I wanted to chuckle.

"Stunning," I corrected, a smile blooming when she growled. My lips ghosted over the warm skin near her temple. "It's hard enough staying away from you."

A tremor went through her slim body, but she kept her tone bland. "And you think if I was unattractive, it would be easier?"

I paused, considering the question. "No, even then."

Her breath hitched, and I knew there would be more questions. Things that would change this moment of quiet perfection.

I put my hand on her head and guided her back to the spot on my chest that felt like it already belonged to her. "Stop thinking so much. Rest here for a while and just dance, little honeybee."

"It's a good thing you're so comfortable to lean on," she grumped without heat. "Otherwise, I'd protest this bit of manhandling."

I let my cheek rest on her head once more. "Don't worry; you can return the favor and order me around later."

Weirdly, I was counting on that.

CHAPTER NINETEEN

Emma

Avoidance could only go so far. Eventually, one had to give in. Lucian and I stayed at the wedding until the last of the guests began to amble to their rooms. And then we left too. To our room.

It had been all fun and games when I had teased him about our single room earlier. It didn't feel that way now. Not when he'd danced with me under the stars and told me he believed in me. No one had ever said that to me. Not like that, as though it came straight from their very core. Lucian believed in me. It changed everything. I wanted him. Him. No one else.

My fingertips were cold, my skin so tight that my movements felt unnatural as I dressed for bed in the ultraquiet of the bathroom. Given that I'd thought I would be alone tonight, my nightclothes consisted of a far-too-thin cotton nightshirt that reached the tops of my thighs and boy shorts underwear.

Honestly, I'd shown more in the pool. The man, like countless others, had seen me practically naked on television. Oh, the hubris in taunting him with that little nugget of information. It didn't feel particularly amusing anymore.

I dithered in the bathroom, rubbing lotion into my feet and legs, waiting for my damn nipples to go down. But my heart kept pounding against the fragile wall of my chest.

Realizing that if I stayed in the bathroom any longer, Lucian might start to wonder what the hell I was doing, I left that certain safety and stepped out into our room. His back was to me as he stared out of the set of glass doors that fronted the sea.

His buttered-toast voice rumbled along my anxious skin. "Wind is starting to pick up—" He turned and fell silent. Crystalline-green eyes ran over me, hot and slow and thorough. The sound of his swallowing, a subtle movement of his throat accompanied by a soft click, pinged in my chest, and my breath hitched.

Lucian closed his eyes tight for one thick moment, as though bracing himself. When he opened them, his eyes were clear and cool. A lie.

"I'll go wash up." He strode right past me, a man on a mission.

Good luck with that, Brick.

He hadn't been exaggerating about the wind, though. A gust blasted the windows and doors so hard they rattled. I hopped into bed, scurrying under the safety of the covers. At least that was what I told myself. That it was the weather I was hiding from. But when Lucian opened the bathroom door a few minutes later, the sound reverberated through me like a shot.

I couldn't help but stare at him as he quietly went around the room, turning off the lamps I'd ignored in my bid to get to the safety of the bed—which was seriously ironic given that the bed was the least safe place to be.

Like me, he was wearing a ratty T-shirt, one that molded to the planes and contours of his chest. But he'd switched out his suit pants for jeans. My lips quirked as he slowly made his way to the bed, leaving only the lamp on my side table on.

"Are you planning to sleep in those?" I asked.

Lucian froze in the act of pulling back his side of the covers, then straightened and squeezed the back of his neck. "I didn't pack anything else. I thought I'd be sleeping alone."

"I know." Guilt mixed with a weird protective tenderness for this man. Which was ridiculous, I supposed, given that he was more than capable of watching out for himself. "I didn't either."

He stood there, staring down at me with a helpless look, his jaw bunching. I sighed and leaned back against the plump pillows. "Just take them off. I won't be able to get comfortable knowing you're sleeping in your jeans."

Some of the old smarmy Lucian sparked in his eyes, and his smile went sideways. "That's a strange bit of logic, Snoopy."

"No, it isn't." I held up a finger to count my points. "The idea of sleeping under the covers in jeans sounds incredibly uncomfortable; ergo, me knowing you're in them makes me incredibly uncomfortable."

"I could sleep over the covers."

"Lucian. You're dithering."

"Dithering."

"Yes." *I should know.* I'd dithered like a master in the bathroom. "Just take them off, and get into the damn bed."

Again came that sideways smile, like he couldn't help himself. "There's that bossiness you've been hiding."

"Hiding?" I snorted, already feeling better. This I could do. "I never hide it. And I think you like my bossy ways just fine, Brick."

"I do." Holding my gaze, he unbuttoned his jeans and let them slide to the floor.

Mistake. *Huge* mistake, ordering him to take those off. God, his thighs. Could you call a man's thick ripped thighs beautiful? I pressed mine together, trying to suppress the desire to straddle one of those lightly furred, powerful thighs and ride it.

Didn't work, though.

He was wearing boxer briefs. Dove gray. Softly hugging all that hard . . .

Don't look. Don't . . . but the hem of the T-shirt only reached the top of his hips. The rest was lovingly displayed.

My eyes wrenched up to his amused ones. I grumbled and turned to flick off the lamp on my side.

Lucian's slow chuckle in the dark followed. The bed shifted as he got in, the covers rustling with his movements. Hyperaware, I could only burrow down and try to get comfortable.

"This is fun." His voice, dry with humor, sounded overloud in the darkened room.

I flipped around to face him, letting my eyes adjust. We'd left the curtains open enough that the room grew a dusky deep blue, and his eyes glimmered in the shadows, his inky hair a smudge on the white pillows.

"That wind is spooky as hell," I whispered. "We could tell ghost stories."

He hummed, as if contemplating the idea. God, but he was close. I was so attuned to him I could smell the soap on his skin and the faint mint of his toothpaste. I wanted to snuggle closer, put my mouth on his, and taste it. I clutched my pillow like a lifeline. I was not making the first move. A girl had some pride.

"Speaking of ghosts," he finally said in a low voice. "Who is Greg?"

I winced, my body tensing.

"I know you didn't want to talk about it before. And you can tell me to shut it now, if you want." Concern lined his hard face as his gaze moved over mine. "But the way your friends rallied around you makes me worry. Did this guy hurt you?"

Perhaps it was because I'd told him my dad hit, or maybe it was simply Lucian's nature to look out for people, but his concern about me ever being hurt warmed my fluttering insides.

"Not physically." I sighed. "Greg Summerland was my ex."

The bed jolted. "The quarterback?"

"Yes." I really hated that Greg was a hero to so many. I sincerely hoped Lucian wasn't a fan. But he sounded more surprised than awed. I supposed that made sense, since he was a pro athlete as well.

"When I was axed—literally—from the show, I went home to cry on his shoulder and found him screwing a nineteen-year-old girl on my living room floor."

"Ouch."

"It didn't look very comfortable on the knees."

"Em." His voice touched me like a caress. I didn't want sympathy. Not about stupid Greg and his wandering dick.

"What should I say? It was a blow. But I think I should have felt more than rage. He should have broken my heart. But it feels fairly intact."

Lucian thought it over before speaking. "Good point."

"I think so," I said with some cheek.

He started to smile, but then his expression clouded. "Greg is a star athlete."

"I am aware."

"I didn't realize you were familiar with the life."

"The life being all the craziness of rabid fans and the never-ending travel and practice schedules, you mean?"

"Yeah, that." He didn't sound very pleased.

"It isn't as though it was much different from my life."

He was silent for a second. "No, I guess not."

Lucian sounded so disgruntled I fought a smile. But my good humor crumpled. "I guess I thought he was above the whole skirt-chasing aspect that I'd heard so much about. At least, he claimed that wasn't him when we started going out."

"He left you with a bad impression of us, didn't he?"

"Us?" I asked.

"Pro athletes."

The flutters in my belly started up again, inexplicably strong. I curled into the feeling, half pressing myself to the bed. "Are you trying to tell me something, honey pie?"

He huffed a slight laugh but didn't smile. "Not all of us are like that, Em."

The flutters moved to my chest. "I know."

An adorable grunt was his reply. I was tempted to push and ask him why it mattered so much that I didn't swear off all athletes. But I didn't have the courage. Not when any possible rejection would level me. This man had hugged me close, held me up when I was low and feeling sorry for myself. He'd danced in the dark with me like it meant everything. I wanted it to mean everything, and that was my weakness.

He was quiet for a moment before speaking with clear reluctance. "You never asked about Cassandra."

"I figured that if you wanted to tell me about her, you would."

The corners of his eyes crinkled. "That your way of saying I should have minded my own business about Greg the moron?"

"Moron, huh?"

"If he screwed around on you, he was."

I laughed. "Yes, he was. And no, I'm not upset you asked."

His nod was perfunctory, as though he wasn't fully listening, and his gaze slid away. "When Cassandra found out I was retiring, she left. Put the ring on the front hall table and bolted."

Oh, Lucian.

My entire body squeezed with pain for him. "That moron."

A ghost of a smile touched his mouth, and he made a grunt of agreement. Less tense now, he turned his head back my way. "She wants to be an actress."

Oh, the irony.

"You say that like it's a four-letter word."

The corner of his mouth twitched. "I don't think it's a four-letter word. It's seven."

"Are you sure about that?"

"I can count the letters. I'm sure."

"I'm talking about the way you sneered at *actress* like it meant *dirt*. But it's good to know you can count up to seven."

"You make me crazy; you know that?"

"I'll take that as a compliment."

"I have no idea why you would." There was a surprising lightness in his voice. The idea that grumpy-ass Lucian Osmond was flirting with me again sent little bubbles of anticipation through my veins.

"At least I have an effect on you. That's much better than indifference."

He grunted, low and disgruntled. Silence fell in a curtain between us, growing thicker, more potent. I bit my lip, waiting, refusing to crack. And then:

"You think I'm indifferent to you?"

"We've already established that you aren't."

He grunted again. "Em . . ."

"Lucian."

I could practically feel him vibrating with annoyance and the struggle of whether to pursue the issue. He huffed out an aggrieved breath. "Completely crazy."

I ducked my head to hide my smile. "I know."

"You love it. Admit it."

"I'm hardly about to cop to that and lose my advantage, now am I?"

"Hell."

Grinning in victory, I snuggled down in the bed and tried to relax enough to sleep. Lucian apparently tried as well. The bedsheet rustled as adjustments for comfort were made. Once settled, we lay stiffly side by side, each of us too aware of the other to make the slightest of movements.

Outside, the wind howled and rattled against the glass, as if in protest of being kept out. Lucian cleared his throat and then stilled. My lips twitched as the pent-up nervousness I had been feeling all night came to the surface. A snicker rose in my throat. I struggled to keep it under control, but a titter came out in spite of my best efforts. The silence made it worse. I lost the war and giggled again.

"What is so funny?" he asked in the darkness. I could tell by his tone that he was trying not to smile.

I laughed again, trying in vain to stop.

"I don't know," I said between snorts and sputters.

"For Christ's sake," he exclaimed, sounding fully exasperated, which only made me laugh harder. I felt him turn toward me. "Are you going to tell me what is so funny?" He sounded strange in the dark room.

"Everything. This situation, your lack of sleepwear . . ." The giggles had me again.

"You're impossible," he said, trying to sound stern.

I bit my lip to keep from laughing, but a snort escaped. There was a quiet pause.

He snickered in the darkness. The sound of it set me off, and that set Lucian off, until we were laughing uncontrollably with the bed shaking under us.

"Oh stop; my sides hurt," I said, gasping for air. It was nerves. I knew that was what had set me off, but I couldn't get my laughter under control.

"You started it!"

I dropped my voice to imitate him. "I could sleep over the covers."

"Look who's talking. You should have seen your face."

The moon chose that moment to peek through the clouds, and its blue light poured through the window, illuminating the room. Lucian was looking down at me, eyes crossed, tongue sticking out in a truly terrible goofball expression.

"That's it . . ." I picked up my pillow and hit him with it.

He laughed in protest. "It's on, honey."

A soft pillow hit my face as he launched his retaliation.

I screeched in outrage, whacking him on the chest and diving under the sheets before he could get me.

He ripped the covers back, coming after me with a hearty laugh. I covered my head with my hands to protect myself, but he pulled them down, holding them securely with one large hand, and hit me soundly with his pillow.

I shrieked and tried to pull my hand from his viselike grip. Lucian only laughed harder as I struggled. I managed to get one hand free and dug my thumb into his ribs. He skirted away quickly, but I had found his weakness and went after him.

"Oh, no you don't!" I rolled halfway onto him and poked his sides mercilessly.

God, but he was adorable when he laughed like that, carefree and boyish. And sneaky. In a blink, he had me on my back.

I shrieked again, trying desperately to tickle him but having a hard time of it since my hands were trapped under me. My hand broke free, but he caught it and pulled it over my head. The action brought us face to face.

We went still, our chests heaving. Lucian's eyes searched mine, his breath fanning my face softly. Neither of us moved. I blinked back at him, utterly aware of the hard length of him pressed against my sex with only the barrier of our underwear preventing him from sliding in.

"We probably woke the whole house," I said in a strangled whisper.

His lids half mast, tension rode him so hard he trembled. And for a brief second, I thought he hadn't heard me at all. But then he swallowed audibly, and his voice came out hoarse and taut. "That's my cue to make a joke, but my mind is blank, Em, because I can't . . . I can't." He squeezed his eyes shut, then opened them wide. "I can't fight this anymore. I want you. I want you so fucking much."

My breath expelled in a rush. His gaze flicked to my mouth and then back to my eyes. Another tremor went through him. "Do you want this?"

Bad idea. The worst.

"Yes." It burst out of me. *"Yes."*

CHAPTER TWENTY

Lucian

Yes. That was all I needed to hear. I felt the word along my heated skin, tasted it on my tongue. One simple *yes*, and I trembled. Limned in moonlight, she gazed up at me, indigo eyes wide and wanting, lips parted and waiting.

A groan wrenched from deep within, and I dipped my head and took that mouth I'd been aching to claim. *Yes, yes, and yes.* Her lips moved against mine—soft, luscious, perfect. God, she was perfect. I kissed her, starved, desperate. She tasted of salvation—fresh, sweet water after burning for so long.

My hands slipped into her hair to hold on as I moved my mouth over hers. And she opened up to me, arching her back to press her breasts against my chest as she kissed me with a fervor that had my entire body clenching. Lust rushed through me so quick and hard my head spun.

I licked into her hot mouth, losing myself in her. Plush lips moved with mine. We found a rhythm, sweet and deep. I'd surge against the gorgeous give of her mouth, and she'd take me in. Each kiss sent a pulse of relief through me, as though I'd finally been given exactly what I needed. Each kiss made me frantic for more. Release and need. Release and need.

The covers rustled as I yanked them out of the way and hauled her closer. She fit against me like she was made to be there. I might have laughed at that simile before, but I hadn't yet had Emma Maron in my arms. Now, all I could think was "Where have you been all this time?"

I'd missed her before I'd even known her.

"Lucian," she whispered against my lips, her hands gripping my shoulders. "Lucian."

My name repeated like a prayer. God, but I wanted to grant her every wish.

"Em." I slid my thigh between her warm ones. Damp heat ground into my muscle as she clamped down and rolled her hips with a small helpless groan.

"That feel good, honey?" She was mostly shadows, and I itched to turn on a lamp so I could see her properly. But that would mean stopping, and I wasn't willing to let her go. I relied on touch, running my fingers along her arm, up to her neck, where sweat dewed on her skin. "You like riding my thigh?"

"Yes. Yes." That word again. Best word ever.

Her lips tickled mine as she panted, her sweet sex working in a little circle. I cupped her cheek and ate at her mouth as she took her pleasure. I'd been wanting to give it to her for so long. So fucking long. Her hands found my chest and slid down, mapping their way along my torso. It was nothing in the scheme of things, but that simple exploration, the way she whimpered and gasped into my mouth, sent licks of heat over my skin.

When her slim hand reached my cock and squeezed me through the barrier of my boxers, a groan tore from me. I shuddered, so close to coming from a furtive grope in the dark it would almost be funny if I weren't so worked up.

"Take it out," I rasped, flexing my thigh, knowing she'd feel it. I needed her hand on my bare skin. "Please."

Deftly she stole beneath the waistband and wrapped her fingers around my needy dick, giving it a firm tug. Then I was the one whimpering and gasping, fucking into the clasp of her hand because it felt so good. Sweet relief, hot pleasure. Alive. She made me feel alive.

My trembling hand found the curve of her waist, where her sleep shirt rumpled between us. The tips of my fingers slid underneath, finding silky skin. "Em." I kissed her. "Can I see you?"

Please. Please.

Emma suckled my lower lip, her hand busy stroking me, but she pulled away enough to catch my gaze. Her eyes were glassy, lips swollen and wet. "Take it off me. Take it off."

As though she couldn't breathe. I'd help her.

I tried to get the shirt up but then huffed out a laugh. "You're going to have to let go of my dick, honey."

She kissed me again, a greedy press of lips. "Don't want to."

I grinned, my chest filling with liquid light. "Believe me . . ." I kissed her soft mouth. "I'm torn up about it too." I found her neck, licked her slick skin. "You can have it back real soon."

"Oh, I will." She smiled, a wicked glint in her eye, and nudged closer, riding up my thigh, then let me go. I felt the loss immediately but didn't waste time in pulling the shirt off her. Moonlight colored the breasts I'd been trying so hard not to think of pale silver, nipples dusky shadows. They trembled, nearly touching the wall of my chest as she breathed, her arms around my neck, her gaze wide with anticipation.

"Christ, you're beautiful. So fucking beautiful, Em." She'd be beautiful in the pitch dark.

The curve of her bare breast filled my palm, and we both made a noise of pleasure. I tweaked the hard bead of her nipple, loving the way her lids fluttered as her lips parted. She arched into the touch, her head tilting to the side. I kissed my way along her neck, pinching that sweet nipple, tugging it.

Oh, but she liked that, whimpering and wiggling, lifting those sweet tits up higher in encouragement. I dipped down and dragged my tongue along one beaded tip. The sound she made was so dirty, hot, and greedy my dick pulsed. Holding that succulent breast plumped in the palm of my hand, I licked, sucked, and kissed it the way I'd been dying to.

"Lucian . . ."

She needed more, her hips grinding on my thigh with uncoordinated motions. My free hand moved to her ass—that spectacular ass—and gripped it.

I hauled her up close, my mouth finding hers. "Ride me, honey."

I worked her on my thigh, holding her ass as she rocked the slick heat of her sex up and down its length. Emma's breasts tickled my chest with every upward thrust, her lips feathering over mine. Our breath mingled, and I stole a kiss, messy and frantic. My cock throbbed for release, fucking ached for it. But watching her lids flutter, the way her gorgeous face strained with pleasure, made it worth the torture.

"I'm going to come if you . . ."—she gasped, nibbled my lower lip—"keep doing that."

"Good," I grunted, flexing my thigh, bouncing her. Oh, she *loved* that. "Come all over me, honey. Let me see you move."

Her head fell to my shoulder, her lips nuzzling my neck. She rocked and ground on my thigh, getting it hot and wet. But her clever hand slid down and found my needy dick once more. I made a noise that sounded a lot like pain, but it was unadulterated pleasure that had me pushing up into the clasp of her hand.

"Not without you," she said, jacking my length. Our mouths met, and the kiss became a wild thing. I kissed her until I couldn't breathe, then kissed her again. And she moved on me, her hand stroking and pulling.

Heat swarmed my skin, licked up my cock. My abs clenched as I groaned, curling myself around her with a shudder of pure lust. "I'm close."

"Are you?"

"Yeah."

Panting now, we worked each other, harder, faster. The air steamed, and she trembled. "Now, Lucian. Now."

"Fuck."

"Oh!" Her deep moan, the way she clenched all around me as her orgasm shuddered through her slim frame, set me off. I released with a shout, pulsing so hard my head went light.

For long moments we lay in a messy, slick tangle, struggling to catch our breaths. I closed my eyes and idly stroked her damp hair, my heart thundering in my chest. We hadn't even fucked, and yet I felt more replete than I had from any sex in my memory.

Emma snuggled closer, wrapping her arm around my waist as she traced a line along my back. "Wow."

Weakly, I smiled. "That's one word for it."

"You got another?" Her voice was husky and low. Pure sex. My cock twinged. Greedy bastard.

I ducked my head to peer down at her flushed face. "More? Again? Please?"

Her smile grew, the hand at my back smoothing with more purpose. "I like those words too."

I gave her a soft kiss and chuckled. But then paused as a horrible thought occurred. "Hell."

She kissed the corner of my mouth. "What?"

I sighed and caught her gaze with mine. "Tell me you have condoms."

Her expression of appalled disappointment might have been funny if I wasn't close to crying. At least my smaller head wanted to weep. All right, the bigger head wanted to weep too.

"Hell," she said.

Given that she was equally aggrieved, I found myself grinning. My fingers wrapped in the mass of her hair, gripping it as my mouth found hers. "We'll just have to do other things."

And I would. I'd do them to her all fucking night.

Emma

"I can't take it."

His tongue flicked my nipple, a sly tease. "You can."

Everything ached; my belly twisted in sweet knots of pleasure. Softly he kissed my nipple. So softly. Heat pulsed. I bit my lip, struggling to keep still, loving the taut desire pulling at my core. He held me there, cupping my breast with a firm hand, lapping at my nipple, and bestowing suckling kisses with the gentlest of touches in the intent to drive me out of my mind.

And I loved it. *I loved it.*

We'd run into the slight snag that neither of us had condoms. While I was certain there were some to be had in this house, I wasn't willing to go looking for some. Okay, my flesh was more than willing, but I couldn't bring myself to do it. Nor could I let Lucian go find some. My pride couldn't handle us begging like college kids in a frat house.

Besides, neither of us wanted to part for that long. We'd compromised, spending the night kissing and touching. No tongues below the waist, only hands. "When I finally get to taste you," Lucian had stated, "I want to be able to sink into you afterward. I need that, Em."

Well then.

I was good with hands. I thought so, anyway. Now? Now, he was slowly dismantling me. Kissing me for hours—slow, deep kisses until my lips were swollen and my body hummed. Hands exploring, teasing

213

my breasts, stroking my skin. I accustomed myself to the terrain of his body, mapping out the dips and swells of firm flesh, taut muscles, hot skin.

Every nerve heightened; every muscle ached. Covers pushed aside, we lay in a hot tangle of limbs and sweaty skin. Only the thin fabric of our underwear keeping us apart.

A necessary measure.

Except.

His hand slid under the band of my panties, the rough pads of his fingers finding my soaking sex. I groaned, then writhed, as he slowly circled my clit.

"God, you're lovely." Solemn green eyes watched me flush and pant as he petted and teased. "That sound you make. That little whimper. I'm going to hear it in my dreams, Em."

I whimpered again. The sight of his hand stretching my panties as he worked me sent an illicit shiver along my skin, and I clutched his shifting forearm, holding him there where I needed him.

"I know, honey." His lips brushed mine. "I know. I'm gonna be in here soon, Em."

"Not soon enough."

That earned me a chuckle.

I licked his upper lip, then nuzzled it. I loved his mouth. Loved the way he kissed, a little dirty, oh-so thorough. He worshipped with his mouth, devoured, and delivered. I kissed him deeper, needing it. Needing him.

Lucian's thick, long finger slid into me, and I groaned—a pained sound.

"That's it," he rasped, fingering me with agonizingly slow pushes. "Fuck, that's it."

I gasped, my head light, my thighs clamping around his hand, as though I could hold in the sensation.

"Spread your legs a little wider, honey. Let me in. Good girl." He cupped my neck with his free hand, his forehead pressed to mine. "One day soon, I'm going to work myself into this tight sweet honey box, fuck you for hours."

My thighs trembled, heat swarming me as my lower belly clenched. "Lucian." I wiggled my hips.

He added another finger, fucking them up into me at an angle that had me keening in pleasure. "Right here, Em. Right here is where I'm aching to be."

I wanted him there so badly. My body moved with him, rocking against his hand.

"Right here is where I'll worship." He kissed me gently, a simple meeting of mouths, as his thumb snaked out and found my clit. He pressed down, rougher now that I was worked up and at the edge. Just how I liked. White-hot head sparked and lit, and I came in a rushing wave that had me straining against him.

"Say my name." He rubbed my slippery sex, fingers deep inside me.

"Lucian." I sobbed. "Lucian."

His grip on my nape was warm, reassuring as he kissed me. "That's my girl," he said as I came down from my high, my body trembling. "My girl."

My focus came back as he slipped free from my panties. He lifted his hand to his mouth and, holding my eyes with his crystalline-green eyes, sucked his wet fingers clean.

A wicked smile curved his lush mouth as his voice rolled over me like warm honey. "Delicious."

I huffed out a weak laugh, falling into his damp chest. "Lucian Osmond, you wrecked me."

His arm wrapped around my shoulders as his lips touched the crown of my head. "Only fair. You've been wrecking me from the moment we met."

Chapter Twenty-One

Emma

I awoke to the rustling of the covers and a warm hand gently cupping my cheek. My eyes opened, and he was there, dark hair mussed, green eyes bright. He smiled, a slow breaking dawn over austere features, making them soft and open.

"Hey, Em."

"Honey pie."

The smile grew, reaching into my heart and tugging it. And then he leaned forward, his mouth moving over mine in a buttery kiss that melted my insides. It was gentle, reverent. A promise. I smiled against his lips, and he did, too, pulling back to meet my gaze once more, like he needed confirmation I was truly there.

Then, as though he couldn't help himself, he dipped his head again and kissed me with more boldness, sipping at my lower lip, nuzzling my upper one. My hand went to the strong curve of his neck to hold on, bring him closer. But he ended it too soon with a husky laugh. "I'm getting up and going to the store."

"The store?" It was the last thing I'd expected him to say.

Lucian quirked a brow, his expression laden with meaning. "Yes, the store. And then we're going home to put my purchase to good use."

Understanding fluttered through me. "Ah. Yes. Get your fine ass to the store, Brick."

He huffed out another laugh, kissed my lips quickly and perfunctorily, lingering only a little at the end. With a groan, he rolled out of bed.

I didn't know if I was supposed to ignore the massive erection he sported or be impressed by it. *No, ignore it,* I thought as he shot me a wry but completely unrepentant look and sauntered to the bathroom, the tight globes of his bubble butt moving like poetry.

Giddiness fuzzed through me. I'd fallen for men before. Had love affairs and long-term boyfriends. This should have been familiar territory. It wasn't. It was the difference between being an understudy in a play and landing the starring role. Everything was simply more.

And that should've scared me. But it didn't. At least not at first. Not when we were driving back to Rosemont, the wind in my hair, Lucian by my side. All I could feel was anticipation. Need. Lust. Happiness.

Happiness was such a fragile thing in my life. I'd find it, grab on to it with both hands, only to have it ebb away when I wasn't ready.

It wasn't until I pulled into the parking space at Rosemont that I realized something was wrong, that Lucian was no longer relaxed or smiling. He moved stiffly, his gaze sliding away from me.

"You okay?" I asked, nervous. Was he regretting letting down his walls?

He turned his head, his body tense. "Just tired."

Tired. God, that sounded like a line I'd use on Greg when I didn't want him to expect sex. My heart skipped a beat and then started a pained tattoo.

Lucian grabbed our bags and headed to the path. I followed, not knowing what to say.

We were almost upon the fork in the path where it split, one leading to my bungalow, the other toward Lucian's pool house. I tensed, feeling queasy with unease as I wondered which path he would take. But he didn't get that far before Sal appeared, strolling along without an apparent care.

Lucian stopped. "This mean Anton is gone?"

Sal scoffed, his hot-pink lips twisting. "No. It means that while I love my mami, I couldn't take another day with her blasting telenovelas at all hours."

"Maybe you should consider actually getting a place of your own," said Anton from behind me, making me jump in surprise.

Both Sal and Lucian turned his way with surprisingly similar scowls.

"Don't you have somewhere else to be?" Sal said. "Like hell?"

Anton smirked. "I'm too hot for hell. So it looks like you're stuck with me. At least until training camp—" He shut up with a grimace and glared at Sal, like it was his fault that Anton had slipped up.

Lucian stood stiff as a board, but his lips curled in dark humor. "Stop tiptoeing around me. It's annoying." With that, he strode off, leaving us all behind.

I didn't mind him walking away from his cousin, but it stung that he hadn't acknowledged me. Moreover, it pissed me off. Not looking at Sal or Anton, I pushed past and went after Lucian.

He was fast, even though his stride was steady. I didn't catch up to him until he was opening the door to the pool house.

"You left me behind."

He stilled and then cursed under his breath. But he didn't turn his head. "I'm sorry, Em. I didn't think."

"You didn't think," I repeated. And then felt like a complete fool. We'd had only one night together. One night of kissing like horny, desperate teens. Promises hadn't been made. Nothing concrete, at any rate. Maybe I'd read too much into it.

He opened the door wider and stepped in, leaving me to once again follow.

My irritation rose, prickling and tumbling about in my belly. Okay, maybe I *had* read more into last night than Lucian had. It *was* something, and I'd be damned if he just left it at this.

"What the hell is going on?"

In the act of dropping the bags on the floor, he ducked his head and took a long breath. "Nothing. It was a long night, and maybe we should rest . . ."

"Lucian."

He raised his head and met my eyes. His were bleary, his expression tight and hard.

I took a breath and let it out. "You have a choice right now. Shut me out, or let me in. I'm hoping you'll do the latter."

He blinked as if struck, and all at once, his stiff shoulders sagged. "I'm sorry," he rasped. "I can't . . . not right now . . ."

I braced myself as disappointment lashed over me.

He raised a hand in a half-helpless, half-frustrated gesture. "My head. It's my head, Em. I can't . . ."

Oh. *Oh.*

I took a step, but his snarl halted me.

He gripped the back of his neck tightly. "I don't think you fully understand the horror I feel over telling the woman I want more than anything that I can't perform because I have a fucking headache. It must be some cosmic joke, but I don't have it in me right now to laugh."

He looked so miserable, so disappointed, that my heart gave a big thump.

"I'm not laughing either," I said softly. Now that he'd admitted it, I could see the signs. Signs I had been too distracted by my own lusts and insecurities to notice. He was hurting again. Badly.

"Emma. Sweetheart. I don't want you to see me weak."

"Well, that's good. Because all I see is strength."

Lucian swallowed visibly, unable to form a reply. The stark lines of his face spoke of suffering, but he didn't relent—stubborn to the core.

With easy movements, I closed the door and then proceeded to pull the heavy drapes around the little house, blocking out the brilliant sunlight and plunging us into cool, dim quiet.

Lucian stood like a statue, watching me. I walked up to him, noticing the way his big body seemed to sway with exhaustion.

"Get into bed, baby."

A tremor went through his lips. "Baby?"

"As in honey, darling, dearest Lucian."

"You're going to make me blush."

Stalling. As though I wouldn't realize it. Foolish man.

"Good." I took his unresisting hand and guided him toward the bed. The man was neat; I'd give him that. The bed was made, the linens fresh. "Into bed with you."

He paused only for a moment, gaze moving between me and the bed. It finally seemed to seep through that thick stubborn wall of his that I wasn't going to relent, either, and he gave me a weak smile.

"Yes, ma'am."

With aching slowness, he stripped down to his boxer briefs and then crawled into the bed with a sigh that spoke volumes of pain. I covered him up, then caressed the stiff curve of his shoulder before heading to his bathroom to see if he had any medicine. I found far too many, including a prescription for migraines. It hit me again how much physical pain athletes had to deal with. That Lucian was all but weepy when his headaches hit told me how bad it was for him.

I gathered the rest of my supplies and went back to the bedroom. Lucian was already sprawled out, his arm clutching a pillow. "Lucian," I whispered, and he stirred, one jade eye peeking up at me. I held out a pill. "Take this."

With a grunt, he turned and raised up on one elbow to take the pill and the glass of iced tea I had for him.

"Drink it all," I said.

"Yes, ma'am—" He cut short as I stripped out of my sundress. Glass halfway to his mouth, he tracked my movements with a narrowed contemplative gaze. "You're beautiful."

Pleasure flowed over me. But I gave him a prim look. "Now is not the time for compliments. Drink your tea."

A tiny smile played around his lips, and he did as told, handing me the empty glass as soon as he was done. Far too conscious of being in my underwear and his eyes upon me, I grabbed the cool pack. "Where do you want this? Neck or forehead?"

Something moved through his eyes, an emotion I couldn't pin, and his throat worked on a swallow. When he spoke, his voice was rusty. "Neck. Please."

"All right, scoot over."

Watchful yet quiet, he made room for me, and when I lay back against the pillows, Lucian shocked me by curling into my body, resting his head on the tops of my breasts. When I placed the cool pack on the back of his iron-hard neck, he sighed in contentment and wrapped his arm more securely around my waist.

Smiling to myself, I ran my fingers through his thick hair. I'd felt it last night, but that had been frantic and fraught with desire. Soothing him, I could let myself enjoy the simple sensation of those silky strands. His hair was exceptionally thick, with a wave to it. I envied it; my hair would be a big unwieldy pouf at this point.

Lucian groaned, as if the sound had been wrenched from him. The tops of his shoulders went rock hard. Glancing down, I found his expression drawn and pinched.

"It's bad, isn't it?" I whispered.

"Yes." He breathed heavily through his nose, as though trying to manage the pain. I knew this level of migraine. It had teeth that dug in and wrenched you around like a rag doll. Getting out from under that type of pain was difficult and exhausting. But I knew one way.

"Lucian? Have you ever gotten a headache from sex?"

He stilled, a pulse of surprise going through his body and into mine. "Em . . . I really want to but . . ."

"No, I'm not asking for that."

"Okay." He sounded confused, his words heavy. "No, sex doesn't give me headaches. When I'm better, I'll be good to go. Promise."

I had to smile. "I'm sure you will be." Gently as possible, I detangled us and slid down to face him. His lids barely opened, and I stroked his cheek. "I want to try something to help make you feel good. Do you trust me?"

"I wouldn't be holding on to you if I didn't." His hand flexed on my waist, as if offering proof. "What are you thinking?"

"I want to give you an orgasm." His eyes opened wide at that, and I forged on. "It can help. It does for me when I'm suffering."

Lucian was bleary eyed, his movements slow, but the smile that flirted with his mouth made it clear he had all sorts of things to say. Then his gaze narrowed. "Are you telling me you get someone to make you come when you're having a migraine?"

My thumb eased over his drawn brows. "No. I make myself come. But I'd rather make you come now, if that's okay."

The smile broke free. "Sometimes, I wonder if I'm dreaming you."

The feeling was mutual.

I eased him back against the pillow. "No dream. Now, relax. Let me do this for you."

———

Lucian

She said it wasn't a dream. I wasn't so sure. She felt like one, her cool hands on my shoulders, guiding me onto my back as she rose above me, the nimbus of her hair like moonlight in the dim room. Her indigo eyes smiled as she caressed my neck. And I felt like crying.

It was the headache. They always made me weak willed and emotional. Not her. It couldn't have been.

I was excellent at lying to myself.

Her smooth palms slid over my chest, mapping it, as though she wanted to learn the shape of it by touch alone. Despite the pressure bearing down on my skull, threatening to crack it wide open, pleasure rippled along the trails her hands were mapping. She touched me as though I was an unexpected treasure she'd come upon, exploring with quiet delight.

A shudder went through me, and I rested my arms overhead, stretching out for her, silently begging for more.

Touch me everywhere. I'm yours.

She hummed under her breath, as though pleased, and bent down to kiss me. I was a man divided: head caving in on me, body swelling with soft pleasure. I didn't doubt her word that an orgasm would help. Emma wasn't the type to take advantage. But it caught me unaware just how good it felt to have her lips pressing softly along my skin. My tension melted, and I closed my eyes, letting my head fall to the side, sink into the pillow. Just feel.

Gentle hands, soft lips, and hot little breaths down my stomach. Pleasure, a thick syrup pouring over my limbs. My cock rose, growing heavy with desire. We were so new together, by all accounts, I should be panting madly, trying to take over. But I was slowly heating wax molding to her will.

Emma palmed me through my briefs, and I grunted. I wanted them off, no barriers between us. As if she heard the silent demand, she kissed my nipple and slowly eased the briefs down. I lifted my butt to help her. My dick slapped against my belly as it was freed. Emma made a noise of appreciation and then wrapped her clever fingers around me.

"Please," I whispered. My body was weak, but my need grew stronger, drowning out everything else. She complied, stroking, her lips on my lower abs, teasing along the V leading to my hips.

"Em . . ." My plea broke off into a groan as her hot mouth enveloped me. There were no more words. I let her have me, do as she willed, and I was thankful for it.

And it felt so good I could only lie there and take it, try not to thrust into her mouth like an animal. But she pulled free with a lewd pop and gazed up at me.

Panting lightly, I stared back at her, ready to promise her anything, when she kissed my pulsing tip. "Go ahead," she said. "Fuck my mouth."

I almost spilled right there. She sucked me deep once more, and a sound tore out of me that was part pained, part "Oh God, please don't ever stop." The woman was dismantling me in the best of ways.

Waves of heat licked up over my skin as I pumped gently into her mouth, keeping my moves light because I didn't want to hurt her, and because denying myself was outright torture. Apparently, I was into that.

She sucked me like I was dessert—all the while, her hand stroking steady circles on the tight, sensitive skin of my lower abs. It was that touch, the knowledge that she was doing this because she wanted to take care of me, that rushed me straight to the edge.

My trembling hand touched the crown of her head. "Em. Baby, I'm gonna . . ." I gasped as she did something truly inspired with her tongue. "I'm gonna . . ."

She pulled free with one last suck and surged up to kiss me, her hand wrapping around my aching dick and stroking it. Panting into her mouth, my kiss frantic and sloppy, I came with a shudder of pleasure. And all the tension, all the pain, dissolved like a sugar cube dropped into hot tea.

With a grunt, I fell back, a boneless heap of well-used man. Emma kissed my mouth lightly, then eased off the bed and got a cool washcloth. I closed my eyes and lay compliant as she carefully cleaned me. The tenderness of her touch threatened to shatter what was left of me, and I swallowed convulsively, unable to open my eyes.

Cassandra had fussed over me, sure, but she'd never really seen the true me in all my imperfect, humble glory. Deep down, I knew that. I liked that. It felt safe. Easy. Nothing about Emma felt safe or easy. She knew me in a way no one else did. And still she was here, caring for me.

The covers stirred as she got back into bed, resting her head close to mine. "Better?"

Was I better? My migraine had dissolved with the rest of me. But was I better? No. I was in true danger of losing my heart and soul entirely. As I drifted off to sleep, one thought held firm: the prospect of giving this woman the fractured pieces of me was terrifying.

CHAPTER TWENTY-TWO

Lucian

I woke weak but pain-free. Emma had effectively handled that. Part of me wondered if I had dreamed it. But as I was naked, my balls and abs tender with a satisfied ache, I knew it was real. She'd done that for me. Touched me with a greediness that had me coming far too soon. Touched me with a gentleness that wrapped itself around my heart and squeezed tight.

So tight it hurt. It was uncomfortable, this feeling—this exposure—like a scab picked too soon. Sprawled on my bed, I stared up at the ceiling, willing my body and brain to come back online and get a move on.

Emma wasn't next to me. I couldn't recall her getting up, but I'd been out of it, falling into the best sleep I'd had in ages. Sounds came from beyond the drawn curtains that separated my bedroom from the rest of the house. A little frisson of alarm went through me; she was in the kitchen. The woman was a right menace in the kitchen.

Grunting, I hauled myself upright and out of bed. It took a second for the room to settle, and then, with the gait of an old man, I walked to the bathroom. I might have retired because of concussion syndrome, but the truth was my body, like many of my teammates', had taken a beating over the years. Physical aches and pains liked to make themselves known when I woke up.

Right now, I felt the old twinges in my left knee, the zings of protest along my back and right shoulder. But these pains were good; they reminded me that I was alive. Stinking and sore, I took a hot shower, scrubbing away the remnants of the migraine. The sun was already low in the sky, a whole day lost to pain and sleep. Not the way I'd wanted to spend it.

While Emma's mouth had been a benediction, fucking glorious—a fever dream—I wanted to please her. Taste *her*. Take her. Not lie there helpless and needy. I'd make it up to her.

After toweling off, I slipped on a pair of shorts and padded out to the main room. My gait faltered at the sight of her standing in front of my stove. She hadn't yet seen me but hummed under her breath as she stirred a pot of what smelled like leftover tomato soup. Dressed in one of my T-shirts that ended midthigh, leaving the rest of her curvy legs bare, she took my breath, made my heartbeat wild and erratic.

I rubbed my chest, half convinced I was having an attack. But it was her. Just her. Heating up soup. This woman had the potential to turn my life on its head. Hell, she already was.

As if hearing my internal panic, she turned my way. A brilliant, happy smile speared me, dead center of my drum-tight chest. "Hey. You're up! I'm heating some soup." She chuckled, the sound tickling my skin. "And stating the obvious."

All that tightness melted like buttercream over warm cake. I struggled not to sigh like a besotted fool. But I probably failed, because her happy smile returned, wider now, like she was excited to see me. My body felt lanky—awkward, even—as I went to greet her, sliding my hand to the back of her slim neck before ducking down to kiss that pretty pink mouth.

She tasted like lemonade and Emma, a flavor I couldn't break down but that was fast becoming my favorite. She hummed with pleasure as I drew away with a last lingering nuzzle.

"I'm starved," I told her hoarsely. I was starved for her. And she knew it. Her face was far too expressive. On myself, I'd consider that a liability, but with Emma, I craved watching her, figuring out what she was thinking just by the way the delicate curves of her face moved.

But I was also weakened. So I sat down and let her serve me, knowing she took pleasure in doing that as well. I understood. Feeding people—pleasing them with food—was satisfying on a bone-deep level.

Delilah's offer flickered through my head, causing my pulse to kick up a little with anxious beats. At one time, I'd wondered if I should become chef de pâtissier like Jean Philipe. But that hadn't been his dream for me. He'd never truly gotten to see me play. What would he think of me now? Floundering without direction. He would have hated that.

Stomach quaking, I gave Emma what was probably a fake-ass smile as she set a bowl in front of me. "Thanks, Snoop."

She took a seat next to me and started to eat, her gaze darting to me with clear hesitation. "You okay?"

She claimed she saw strength when she looked at me, but I felt as though I'd only shown her weakness.

"I'm good." Another fake smile pulled at my lips. "Especially after your . . . what are we calling it? Remedy?"

"I was going to go with *blow job*," Emma countered with a cheeky smirk.

"I'm good with that." We ate in relative silence, and I let her fuss over me, getting me slices of bread, a glass of lemonade. Because it made her happy. And a happy Emma glowed with an inner light that I couldn't take my eyes off.

I waited until she'd cleared the dishes, watched her pert ass flex and move beneath the thin cover of my shirt as she bent to put the bowls in the dishwasher. When she came near again, I hooked my arm around the curve of her waist and hauled her onto my lap.

She came willingly, laughing a bit, as if startled. Her weight settled on my thighs, warm and grounding. My hands found the juicy globes of her ass, and I gave them an appreciative squeeze as I drew her closer. That I could touch her now was a gift. A dream.

Emma's hands settled on my chest. I felt that touch in the center of me.

"Hey," I whispered, smiling as I kissed her softly, lightly. A little hello. A small taste.

I felt her smile against mine. "Hey."

I kissed her again. An acknowledgement. "Thank you for taking care of me, Emma."

The concession was worth it, just to see the way her eyes lit with happiness.

Her hands tunneled into my hair. "You're welcome, Lucian."

I wanted to make love to this woman. Take my time, learn her secrets, what made her sigh, what made her cry out for mercy.

My mouth moved over the satin skin of her cheek to the curve of her neck. She shivered, tilting her head to give me access, her fingertips pushing deeper into my chest. She smelled good, sweet. The swells of her breasts brushed my chest, and my breath hitched, my hands gripping her ass harder.

Needy. She made me needy. Took me apart in ways I couldn't predict.

I loved it. Hated it. But I didn't stop kissing her, my tongue slipping out to taste her skin.

Emma shivered again, rocked into me, her fingers threading through my hair. "Lucian?"

"Hmm . . ." My lids lowered as I nuzzled the hollow of her throat.

"I want to ask you something, but I'm afraid you'll get upset."

Her words crusted over my skin, rendering me still. Then I breathed, pretended my pulse hadn't spiked. But she probably felt it, as close as she was.

More interested in kissing than talking, I trailed my lips back up to her jawline. "That sounds a lot like bait, honey."

"It is." She kissed my temple. The crest of my cheek. "But I'm also serious."

I had two options. Retreat or relent. Given that the latter would allow me to continue touching her, I relented.

"Ask, then." I nipped along the graceful line of her throat. "I'll take it out on your neck."

A sound of amusement hummed under her skin. "Fair enough. Your headaches. Are you seeing a doctor?"

I wasn't surprised. Not even disappointed—she cared enough to ask. I still felt exposed. Weak. I kept my tone neutral, my hands busy feeling her ripe curves.

"Yes, Em. I'm being monitored. I went for a checkup last week. My brain is healing. Actually, it's looking really good." My doctor had been both impressed and pleased with how well I'd healed. "The headaches are actually reducing in frequency. Migraines tend to come in times of stress; that's all."

Emma's swift expression of horror made me grimace.

"God, Luc—"

"I didn't mean you—"

"You got one when you met me. And again when we . . ." She flushed, pained, her gaze darting over my face. "Do I stress you?"

I held her firmly, my eyes never leaving hers. "Em, no. Okay? The word *stress* is misleading. Last night was something I've been wanting since I met you."

She softened a bit, but the worry remained, and I gave her a light squeeze.

"It was . . . I don't know how to explain." I blew out a breath. "It was emotional. Swift emotional highs and lows can throw me; that's all."

Emma looked as though she might argue, and I stopped her with a light kiss.

"I'm okay, Snoopy. I promise." I wanted to concentrate on other things now, like getting her into bed. But she held on to my head and met my gaze.

"I swear, Em. I'm not going to break if we—"

"I know. I'm just glad. Okay? I'm . . . very glad you're safe and well." The tender look in her eyes and the way her voice hitched wrapped itself around me, filled my head, and made it dizzy. If I hadn't been sitting down, I might have staggered. We'd known each other only for a short while. I wasn't supposed to feel this much this fast. Neither was she. Did she? I wasn't sure.

Uncertainty and vulnerability made me speak without thinking. "Eventually I will heal all the way. And then . . ." Shit. I hadn't meant to go there. It was too much information. Too much exposure.

Emma frowned. "And then?"

It was on the tip of my tongue to evade with a joke. But I wanted to tell her, test the waters maybe. Or maybe just have the words out in the open. Holding her gaze, I sat back in the chair, keeping my hands lightly on her hips. I told Emma something I hadn't uttered to anyone outside of conversations with my doctor, trainers, and former head coach. "I could wait it out, let myself heal, and go back."

"What? You . . . you'd do that?" She appeared horrified.

"Sometimes, I think about it. Hell, I dream about it. But I think about Jean Philipe, what my family went through, the shell of a man he'd become. I wouldn't do that to my family again."

I told myself this every day. But in the darkest corners of my soul, I was tempted. So fucking tempted.

The touch of Emma's hand upon my cheek pulled me back to the present. "Thank you," she whispered, her fingers brushing along my temple, as though she could somehow soothe my battered brain. "For taking care of this brain. I find I very much like it."

Right there, I was lost. I wasn't prepared. My life was a wreck, uncertain and unsteady. And she'd strolled in with her starlight smile, unrepentant, challenging me at every turn. Telling me I was still worth something. That I meant something. To her.

It scared the shit out of me. Because eventually she'd see that I was a man living a half life.

I gripped the tops of her smooth thighs, as if they could ground me, but I still felt as though the bottom was dropping out of my world. "Em—"

"Titou?" The sound of my grandmother's voice at the door, closely followed by a knock, had us both freezing in something close to horror. "Are you there?"

"Holy shit, it's Amalie." Emma's high-pitched whisper cut through the fraught silence, and she scrambled off my lap, practically dancing around in a panic. "What do we do?"

I gurgled down a laugh. "Hide?"

"Lucian! This is serious. I'm in your shirt." She gestured down her length, drawing my eyes to her bare legs. I'd had my hand on them for far too brief a time. "Shit. Where is my dress?"

She started for the bedroom, then glared at me over her shoulder as I laughed—I couldn't help it; she was adorable in her frazzled state. "And put a shirt on."

"Why don't you throw me the one you're wearing?"

She flipped me the finger instead.

"Titou? I know you're there."

"You think she can hear us breathing?" I whispered into Emma's ear as she hustled back into the room, wrenching her sundress over her pretty tits before thrusting a shirt at my bare chest.

Despite the quelling glare she gave me, she started to snicker. "God. How old are we?"

Ignoring the shirt, I snagged her about the waist and hauled her closer, brushing a kiss on the curve of her neck. "Why are you freaking out?"

"Because . . ." She lifted a helpless hand and waved it. "It's rude to Amalie for me to be . . ."

"Sucking off her grandson?"

"Oh my God." She punched my arm in horror even as her eyes sparked in amusement. "You are sick!"

"Titou!" Amalie sounded sharp now, annoyed that I hadn't answered.

I turned to do just that, when the door rattled and then began to open. I swung my gaze back to Emma. "You didn't lock it!"

Shit. My hair was sticking up wildly, I didn't have a shirt on, and Emma was still half-dressed. She rightfully smirked at the panic in my eyes. "Something wrong, honey pie?"

"She'll be relentless." I set Emma to the side as carefully as I could for someone rushing to get to the door before it could fully open, hopping over one of my shoes and skirting a chair. But it was too late. My grandmother waltzed into the house with an altogether fake look of surprise upon her face as she took in the scene.

"Well," she said expansively, "now I understand why you didn't answer sooner."

There I stood, full-on blushing in front of my grandmother. It was karma, payback for teasing Emma. I could sense Emma just to my right, her silence speaking volumes in my head. I knew if I turned and caught her gaze I'd see "Look who's laughing now, sucker" in her eyes.

My jaw ticced. "Mamie. You need something?"

Mamie's gaze moved from me to Emma and back again. "Oh, nothing really. Not anything serious enough to disturb you two right now." She clapped her hands together, the heavy rings on her fingers clinking. "Oh, but this is marvelous. I'd hoped this would—"

"We were just having lunch," I cut in.

I could all but feel Emma stiffen. And I winced internally. For all her protests, I didn't think she liked being relegated to *just lunch*.

Mamie's lip curled slyly, telling me exactly what she thought of my sad excuse. "Is that what you kids are calling it these days?"

God. Refusing to squirm, I narrowed my eyes at her. Mamie merely beamed.

"Well then," she said. "I shall leave you two to . . . eat." She gave us a queenly nod and then left us alone, quietly closing the door behind her with a definitive click.

For a long moment, neither of us spoke. Then Emma's musical voice, tinged with irony, drifted over the thick silence. "Just having lunch, eh?"

Wincing, I faced her. She stood by the table, hair mussed, lips still softly swollen from my kisses, her eyes glinting in either humor or irritation. It was a toss-up.

Hell. I needed to explain. "I—"

Emma burst out laughing. "God. That was awful. I felt like a fifteen-year-old caught in a boy's room."

A smile tugged at my mouth. "Creep into many boys' rooms, did you?"

"Sadly, no. I was a gawky homebody who didn't get a date until college. But I dreamed of it."

I couldn't imagine a time when I wouldn't want Emma. "If we'd met as teens, I would have invited you to my room. Or crawled into yours."

"No, you wouldn't have," she said with flippant assurance. "You wouldn't have even seen me."

"I would too. How can you say that?" I didn't know why I was arguing hypotheticals with her other than it was better than focusing on the rabid panic I'd felt when Amalie had found us together.

"You were one of the popular guys, weren't you?" She looked me over, as if seeing my younger self. "And probably hotter than you needed to be."

"Well, I don't know about *hot*, but okay, I was popular." I shifted my weight, rubbing the back of my neck. "It was hockey. And baseball."

"You played both?"

"I was a catcher. But baseball was secondary. I needed something to keep me in shape during off months."

"I'm surprised you had time for girls." She hadn't moved from her position by the chair. The light of the lamp she'd turned on in deference to my migraine cast a golden glow over her shoulder.

I found myself moving toward her, pulled by the need to touch that smooth skin, feel the soft curves of her body. "I had time for them. Probably too much."

When I reached her, she yielded, flowing into my arms with a sigh. Her hair held the scent of my shampoo, but her skin carried her own fragrance, warm and unique, addictive. I nuzzled her closer, drawing in a long breath. "I would have noticed you."

Her fingers trailed up my shoulders. "How can you be so sure?"

"Because I cannot conceive of a situation where I wouldn't." The words tumbled out, rushed in their honesty. I wasn't one for talking about feelings or *need*. I closed my eyes and swallowed hard, once again hit with the uncomfortable sensation of free-falling. Thing was, holding on to Emma only made it worse. The closer she got, the more I needed.

I'd lost too much to lose more.

"Amalie looked very satisfied," Emma said dryly.

I swallowed again, struggling to find my voice. "You know she's been after us to get together from the start." And damn it, I'd proved my canny grandmother right. She'd definitely crow over this. *I wouldn't be surprised if she started in on grandkids now.* "She was convinced we were the answer to all of our problems."

Emma snorted, but it was without rancor—just simple amusement. "She's a romantic. Some people think love fixes everything."

Love.

A wave of clammy cold washed along my back, and words spewed out of my runaway mouth. "Don't worry. I'll make it clear we're only messing around."

Emma pulled back, as if stung, a frown forming between her brows. "Messing around."

"Well, I won't put it like that. She's my grandmother. But I'll let her know it isn't serious."

The tiny line between her brows deepened. "Right. Not serious."

Fuck. This was going south and fast. But I couldn't seem to stop it. Or shut the hell up.

I rubbed my hands over her skin, trying to soothe her even as I panicked. "You've known from the beginning I wasn't looking for a relationship. I didn't plan this. I wasn't expecting . . . you."

"I wasn't expecting you either. I thought I'd go on vacation, read some scripts, and catch up on my sleep."

My hands couldn't settle. They kept moving over her satiny skin like it might be my last chance to feel her. And it just might. Because I couldn't keep my mouth shut. "That's the thing, Em. You're on vacation. How long are you even staying?"

Emma slid away. I felt the loss immediately, my body growing cold. I shoved my hands in my pockets to keep from reaching for her. Every selfish cell in my tightly wound body protested.

Still frowning, she leaned against the kitchen counter. "I don't know. A month, maybe. Amalie hasn't given me a deadline."

"You don't need one. Jesus, Em, I'm not trying to run you off. I'm trying to point out that it isn't serious for either of us."

"Again with *serious*. As if the very idea is horrific."

"Well . . ." *Shit. Shut it, Oz.*

Her glare became piercing. "Is this because I said the dreaded *L* word?"

"What? No." *Maybe. Fuck.*

"I only meant it in terms of romance and idealism," she went on, defensive and flushed.

"I know that. I'm not freaking out because you uttered lo—the *L* word."

She snorted loudly. "You can't even say it."

"Neither can you," I pointed out, then immediately flinched, knowing I sounded like a petulant ass. Her repressive look said she agreed.

"Shit. It's not that it's . . ." I ran a hand over my mouth, feeling the stubble of my evening beard growth. "Honestly, honey, I don't know what the fuck I'm saying. Other than you're leaving, I'm . . . I don't know anything about relationships—"

"You were engaged," she said with some asperity. "I think you know a little bit about the process."

"That's the worst part about it. When she left, I realized I didn't do shit in that relationship. She took care of everything like she was . . ." I lifted a hand, struggling. "A hostess, someone there to make sure I never suffered a moment of discomfort."

"Jesus."

"I'm not proud of it. I'm ashamed I didn't notice that's how it was until it was over."

Cassandra's voice flickered through my mind: *I thought you were more than hockey, Oz. I see now that you weren't.*

I didn't want to think about Cassandra. Not with Emma staring at me with hurt in her eyes. It was a blow to see her disappointment. But I couldn't lie to Emma. "I don't want a repeat of that."

"Good, because you wouldn't get that with me."

"Believe me, Snoop; I know. Thing is, I am pretty much a walking wreck right now. I make mistakes all the time."

God, it was as though I'd slapped her. Emma leaned away from me like she needed to put as much distance as she could between us. "You regret what we did."

"No! Fuck, no." I reached for her, but the hard look on her face made me hesitate. "I want you, Emma. More than I've wanted any woman. And that's the problem. If we have each other, it will be intense. And you might expect . . . forever."

Slowly she nodded, but it was as if she wasn't really there. Some part of her had retreated in a way I hadn't seen before. I hated it.

"You're right," she said. "Not about forever. I'm not sitting here waiting for you to profess your undying love or anything. But I did expect more than 'just messing around.'" She huffed out a flat, pained laugh. "I thought that we'd . . . I don't know, at least try for something real."

"Em . . ."

"But that's on me. I'm always building castles in the air, only to find out there's nothing solid to rely on."

Laid out in those stark terms, I couldn't disagree. Hell, it was what I'd been trying to articulate. Didn't stop the disappointment from eating at my gut. I was an idiot for talking about it. I should have taken her to bed and worried about the particulars later.

And because I was a guy, a greedy-ass moron who had just realized his mistake, I made an even bigger one. "We could still—"

"Fool around?" she supplied, lips pursing. "Screw each other, knowing it's not going anywhere."

"You say that like it's a bad thing." Shit. *Shut up, fuckwit.* But I didn't. "Sex doesn't have to mean everything."

Her expression soured. "But it will, Lucian. With you, it will." She lifted her chin, her body unyielding, and angled away from me. "I'm sorry if that makes you uncomfortable—"

"It doesn't." Christ, she was a gift. And I'd gone and thrown her away. I took a step toward her, a little desperate knowing that I was losing her.

But she was already backing up. "And it might be easy for you to keep emotion out of it—"

"That's the point, Em. I can't either. Not with you."

A sad smile played on her lush lips. "No, *that* is the point. You know this can be something more, and you don't want it."

I want it. I just don't deserve it. I'll break you. Like I'm broken.

"I don't want to hurt you."

Her smile twisted into something pained. "Don't worry. You stopped it before that could happen."

With an audible inhale, she ran her hand through her hair, as though gathering herself. "I'm going to go."

"No." I flexed my fingers, trying to figure out how to salvage something between us, trying not to reach for her. She'd been mine for such a short time. Not enough.

It's for the best. Do it for her.

"We can still hang out," I tried, cringing even as I said it. "Be . . ."

"Friends?" She shook her head, looking at me as though I was dull witted. "I'm afraid I can't be friends with someone I want to fuck."

"Hell, honey, you're killing me here."

But she didn't smile; her eyes were dull, that pretty mouth I hadn't tasted enough a flat line. "Somehow, I think you'll survive."

CHAPTER TWENTY-THREE

Emma

I didn't take Lucian's rejection well. One would think that the years of struggling to make it in the toughest business in the world would have rendered me immune to rejection. I'd been told *no* in so many ways, in such harsh terms, it should have been easy to hear one more.

But it was expected in acting. You took your knocks and kept going. You held your head up when they said you were too short, too fat, too flat chested, too young, too old. You told yourself that you put up with the shit because there was gold at the end of the rainbow. Some days that worked. Some days that didn't.

Rejection from Lucian, however, was an entirely different thing. It was a kick in the teeth, a punch to my chest. It hurt.

The worst of it was he'd been the responsible one in the room, the adult. I had forgotten all about where I was, who I was, who he was. None of that had mattered. I'd simply wanted him. But he was right; I was on vacation, and he was unwilling to even try out a relationship. Better to make that clear before all sorts of messy emotions got involved.

I couldn't do casual sex with him. I knew it as much as he did. So I'd lied and told him I wasn't hurt. Even as the cold ball of rejection and regret grew to epic proportions in my chest.

It grew in size and heaviness when I woke to find yet another breakfast basket on my doorstep. Lucian had gone all out this time, including my favorite fruits, perfectly ripe, sliced, and shaped into arrangements that looked like blooming flowers. Thick, creamy fresh yogurt with a golden-honey drizzle and toasted walnuts. Four different types of jams and, of course, the breads. An array of sweet and savory little breads for me to choose from.

I sent the basket back untouched. It was petty, but I had no appetite. Nor could I seem to make myself eat his food. I just couldn't. It hurt too much. It made me angry as well. I did not want his care in this way. Not if I couldn't have the rest of him.

See? Petty.

Not petty. Guarded. You have to protect yourself.

I snorted at that and made myself some coffee—not as good as *his*—choked it down, then went to talk to Amalie. I had to tell her I was leaving. I couldn't stay at Rosemont anymore.

Amalie texted that she was in the red living room. She'd helpfully included a map of the house, which made me smile. Rosemont's main house was huge, but with graceful proportions that made it seem, well, not cozy, exactly, but comfortable.

I made my way along the back terrace. Dappled sunlight glimmered beneath the teak arbors laced with purple wisteria that hung like grapes overhead. Each room that faced the back of the house had a massive set of glass doors, all thrown open to let in the fresh air.

Finally, I found Amalie in a beautiful room that might as well have been set in colonial Spain with its exposed timber beams, hand-painted Spanish tiles of blue and gold, and softly worn plaster walls. Amalie lounged on a large plush sofa covered in cream damask. Like a queen, she waved me in with a graceful roll of her wrist.

"Darling girl, I've been neglecting you, haven't I?"

"Not at all," I said, taking a seat next to her. On the square aged-oak coffee table was a silver tray set with breakfast for two. My stomach flipped sickly, clenching in protest even as my mouth watered. Damn that man; he'd trained my taste buds so well I feared I'd never be free of wanting another bite.

"Come." Amalie leaned forward and picked up a delicate pink coffee cup edged in gold. "We shall eat and chat." She paused, as if a thought occurred to her. "Unless you've already eaten?"

"I have," I lied. I was hungry and desperately wanted to eat, but I recognized Lucian's handiwork. Amalie's breakfast was slightly different than mine: fruits simply put in bowls—no flower shapes here—crusty rolls instead of a variety of sweet breads, and slices of both hard-boiled eggs and ham. The difference between her utilitarian breakfast and my extravagant one did funny things to my insides.

To my horror, a not-so-subtle rumble came from somewhere in the vicinity of my stomach. Cheeks warm, I ignored the sound and gave Amalie an apologetic smile.

"I'd love some coffee, though." God, that was weak. Damn my traitor appetite.

Thankfully, Amalie made no comment as she poured us each a cup and then settled back with a sigh. "So then, what is on your mind? Forgive me for saying so, but you appear upset." Her pale-green eyes, so uncomfortably similar to Lucian's, studied me. "Has something happened?"

"I—"

"Mamie," came a familiar deep voice from the hall. "I'm going to the store—"

Lucian strode into the room and halted upon seeing me, his words cutting off to dead silence. Pinned to the spot by his blank-faced stare, I could only look back, my heart fluttering in agitated beats. It was unfair how beautiful this man was to me. Not perfect, not flawless, but beautiful just the same.

Now I knew what he felt like against my skin, in my mouth. I knew the expression he made when he came, knew the sounds—those deep agonized groans of pleasure—he uttered. And he knew the same of me. He'd reduced me to a panting, needy mess solely with his mouth and hands.

The knowledge hung between us like smoke, thick and choking. We'd never do any of that again. It was over before it really began.

As if the exact thought filtered through his mind, Lucian's gaze deepened with what looked like regret—or perhaps an apology. Or maybe it was what I wanted to see. I didn't know anymore.

He swallowed thickly, his throat working; then he blinked, as if to pull himself out of a haze. "Hello."

There was no misunderstanding who he was talking to.

My lips felt numb and clumsy as I answered. "Hello."

Lovely. We'd been reduced to this.

He grunted, shifting his weight, a man deciding whether it was better to stay or flee the scene. He gutted it out, setting his hands low on his hips. "You didn't eat your breakfast."

My gaze narrowed, annoyance flaring through me. "No, I didn't."

Like hell I would give him an excuse. But I was far too aware of Amalie sitting next to me. And I sent Lucian a quick glare. How dare he rat me out in front of Amalie. He returned my look with one of sheer stubbornness, as though he could somehow will me to eat his food. Too bad. Those days were over.

He blinked again, and I had the strangest feeling that he was absorbing a blow. But then his expression turned to stone, and his attention went to his grandmother. "I got your note about wines. Do you need those for today?"

Amalie, who had remained thoughtfully quiet during our exchange, became animated once more. "Yes, my dearest. If you would be so kind." I had no idea what they were talking about, nor did I care. I wasn't going to go poking around in their lives anymore. "Tina has been asking to go out. Perhaps you could take her along?"

Lucian glanced at me, and that brief bit of attention lit over my skin. But he didn't linger. He focused on Amalie, the only outward sign that I was in the room betrayed by the hard line of his jaw. I'd become as much of an annoyance to him as he was to me.

"I'll take her." Again, he glanced at me, as though he wanted to say something. But he didn't. Not to me. "I'll be back in a couple of hours, then."

He hesitated, hovering at the threshold of the room, broad shoulders stiff. And an acute sense of sadness slapped me. For a brief time, I'd set eyes on this man, and it had made me feel alive to know I could tease him, that he'd give as good as he got. That I could ease the darkness in his eyes.

Now, he simply let his gaze skim over me, impersonal, withdrawn. "Emma."

"Lucian." It came out so stilted that I cringed inside. But I kept my expression neutral. Polite, even. And it sucked.

We exchanged the most awkward of nods, and he left, taking all the life out of the room. This was why I had to go. And this was why he had been right; it would have been worse if we'd gone further. *I should thank him for that.*

But I still couldn't bring myself to. Not yet.

Amalie waited a minute, perhaps to be sure Lucian was well out of hearing, before turning my way. I braced for her questions, but she simply sipped her coffee. "So then, what are your plans for the day?"

I sagged into the corner of the couch. "I've rented a car to drive into LA."

Her perfectly penciled black brows arched. "All the way to LA?"

"Yes. I need to start house hunting. I thought I'd take a look at some of the properties. Maybe spend the weekend there." I would rather check into a hotel for a few nights than know Lucian was nearby.

"Hmm." She sipped her coffee.

Oh, she was onto me. I refused to fidget.

"The sooner I'm settled into a new place, the sooner I can get out of your hair."

Amalie set her cup down with a gentle click. "My dear, you are not 'in my hair,' but one should never hide away from the important things in life. Getting your house in order is a wonderful idea."

It was a clear sign that I was a mess that I found myself oddly disappointed by her quick agreement. Disappointed and uncomfortable. She hadn't missed how awkward Lucian and I were in each other's presence. It was awful to think she might have thought I hurt him and wanted me to get as far away from her grandson as possible.

I stood on legs that weren't as steady as I'd like. "I'll see you in a few days."

On impulse, I leaned down and kissed her soft cheek, which smelled of Chanel N°5. "Thank you for everything, Amalie."

She petted my arm. "Ah, my dear girl, thank you for coming here. Do what you must. And we'll see you soon."

I made it all the way to the doors that led to the terrace, when her next words stopped me. "Just remember, it doesn't matter how far you go; you'll always be where your heart is."

The words hit like darts, and I closed my eyes briefly, my back to her. My heart was in my chest. Right where it belonged, damn it. I would repeat that until I believed it.

CHAPTER TWENTY-FOUR

Lucian

"You've stopped blinking," Brommy said, cutting into my thoughts. "And it's creepy."

We sat on loungers, drinking beers by the pool as the sun set. At some point, I'd stopped listening to Brommy's rambling conversation and, apparently, stopped blinking.

I turned my gaze from the water and cut him a glare. "Yeah, well, it's creepy that you've been looking at me long enough to tell."

He snorted, then took a pull of his beer. "Dude, I've been talking for ten minutes without a real response from you. At one point, I even asked if you preferred waxing to shaving."

I paused in the act of taking a drink. "Did I answer?"

"You grunted." He huffed and set his beer down on the flagstones. "What's up, Ozzy? You're in a worse mood than ever. No, scratch that. You're in a void. A weird-ass void, and it's freaking me out."

It was the real worry he tried and failed to hide that had me answering instead of grunting again. "I'm just off today."

Off. That was a nice way of putting it. Off. Not decimated.

Seeing Emma this morning had cut me to the quick. I'd thought I could handle it. That I'd be able to face her with the same detachment with which I faced most of my life now. What a joke.

I'd taken one look at her, and all the breath had left my lungs. I'd gone totally blank, not knowing what to say or do. She'd sat on that couch, every inch of her so unearthly beautiful it hurt to look at her, every inch of her remote and blocked off. Gone was the cheeky smile in those dark-blue eyes. Gone was any sense of familiarity. It felt like I'd lost a limb.

And I knew that I'd miscalculated. Badly.

I hadn't saved myself from potential heartbreak. I was already gone on this woman.

"She didn't eat my breakfast."

"What?" Brommy wrinkled his brow in confusion.

Shit. I'd said that out loud. I rubbed the aching spot in the center of my chest. I knew my heart was there. I could feel each pained beat. But it still felt cold and empty.

"Emma," I ground out. Hell, even saying her name hurt. "She refused breakfast."

Brommy sat a little straighter. "You're making the breakfasts here?"

An aggrieved snarl broke from my throat. "Who did you think was doing it?" The man had seen me bake. For fuck's sake, I'd baked for the guys all the time. There'd been a two-year period when they'd called me Cake, which had not been fun.

Brommy shrugged weakly. "I actually didn't think about it."

I experienced a moment's discomfort, wondering if it was pathetic that I'd been cooking and baking for everyone. I wouldn't have done it last year. Oh, I would still have baked; it relaxed me. But I wouldn't have made it my job to feed everyone day in and day out for every meal.

But now, it was something to keep my mind sharp and off things best ignored. Unfortunately, that did not work when it came to Emma. I thought of her every second I made her breakfast. Put all my remorse and hopes that she was all right into it.

And she'd sent it back untouched.

I rubbed my chest again. It was my own damn fault.

Brommy's lounge chair squeaked as he turned more my way. "Okay, let me get this straight. You're glaring into the deep end of the pool because you made breakfast for Emma, and she didn't eat it."

"No. That is *not* why."

"You're a shitty liar these days, Oz." He leaned back, stretching out and making himself comfortable. "You two hooked up at the wedding, huh?"

"What?" I snapped. Shit. I was *not* thinking about that. I could not think about Emma's soft skin, the shape of her mouth against mine. *No. Do not fucking think about it.* "How the hell did you come up with that?"

He gave a lazy shrug. "It's not a stretch. You've been panting after her; she clearly thought you were"—he made a face—"attractive. Weddings are romantic, I guess. At least it seems to make people horny."

"Jesus."

"And it was an overnighter. Come on, Oz." His eyes filled with humor. "It's me. I know you. You fucked her and—"

"Don't even go there, Brom. I didn't *fuck* her. All right." Damn it, I wanted to. I should have. *I am the stupidest man on earth.*

"Whatever you say." He shrugged again. "Yeah, maybe it's better to say that, if she's refusing your food now. Must have been . . . well, hell, it happens to all of us at some point."

"What happens?" I asked darkly.

His grin was wide and evil. "You know." He held up his index finger and then made it droop.

I stared at him. Hard. "Listen, shithead. I did not go limp. We did not have sex because . . ." Heat crawled up my neck. Why was I talking about this with Brommy? Because I didn't have anyone else. And for some reason, I needed to get things off my chest. I rolled my stiff shoulders. "No condoms."

He paused for a beat. "Ah. Unprepared. Rookie move, Ozzy boy."

"Being prepared implies that I was expecting some."

"You honestly didn't?" He sounded genuinely baffled.

I snorted with feeling. "Believe it or not, I was trying to keep my distance."

"Why the ever-loving donkey fuck would you want to keep your distance from Emma Maron?" He was near apoplectic now.

I ran a hand over my face and flopped my head back on the lounger. "I don't fucking know, Brom. Because she's not a one-night-stand type of woman?"

"No, she's not," he agreed heartily. "She's the 'Oh, thank Christ this one likes me. I'm gonna hold on and hope she never realizes what a stupid jackweed I am' type of woman."

"Thanks. And this coming from Mr. Never Commit." Brommy had tried to be supportive of my relationship with Cassandra, but he had been pretty adamant that it was a bad idea to propose.

"Hey, I never said never. If I find a girl that makes me smile in my darkest hours, I'm going to do my damnedest to keep her."

My chest caved in. Emma was the only person I'd ever met who could do that for me. The fact that Brommy obviously knew it was a testament to how willfully stubborn I'd been.

I'd spent my entire life either working to protect those I loved or living in pursuit of proving myself to be the best in my sport. I was a self-contained unit. I hadn't wanted it any other way. Because I hadn't known what I was missing. I hadn't known Emma.

I swallowed with difficulty. "I told her it was a mistake to start anything. That we were just messing around."

"Asshole." He said it with sympathy.

I grunted in agreement. "I need to go talk to her."

"She's not here." Sal's voice had us both jumping.

"Jesus," Brommy grumped. "How the hell do you move so silently?"

"Years of skulking." Sal took a seat on the end of the empty lounger next to me. "Better to eavesdrop that way."

"I love how he says that without shame," Brommy told me.

I was about to agree but then froze. "Wait. What do you mean she's not here?"

Sal picked at a nail. "She left. Early this afternoon."

"She left?" I sat up straight. Blood rushed in my ears, my heartbeat kicking into overdrive. "She left?"

"Repeating it won't make it less true," Sal pointed out helpfully.

"Sal."

"What?" He batted his lashes at me, and I swore to God I was two seconds away from tossing him into the pool.

He must have seen this, because he let out an exaggerated sigh. "She went to LA for the weekend to look at houses. Said the sooner she found one, the sooner she could get out of Amalie's hair."

"Earlier skulking expeditions get you that info?" Brommy asked.

"No. Amalie told me. We tell each other everything." Sal gave me a meaningful look.

I glared in return. But my heart wasn't in it. No, my heart was trying its best to beat its way out of my damn chest or crawl up into my throat. It couldn't seem to decide.

She wanted out of here. Because of me.

And why shouldn't she, dipshit? You told her you weren't interested in anything real.

"But it already is real."

Brommy and Sal looked at me with worry.

"What is?" Sal asked.

I rubbed my face. "Nothing." Wrenching out of my chair, I stood and rolled my neck, my mind racing ahead of the game, seeing the greater picture and all the play options. For once.

"Sal," I said. "You're going to put those sneaky skills to good use."

He leaned back and gave me a cool look. "Oh, am I?"

He wasn't fooling me. I knew the man, and he was all in.

"Yes. Pack a bag for LA. I'll pay for your room."

Chapter Twenty-Five

Emma

"All the fixtures are custom made by local artisans," Remington, my realtor, pointed out for the third time as we walked through the house.

I made an appropriate murmur, my heart not in it, and kept walking through the cold and lofty living room, my heels clicking hard on the poured-concrete floors.

"This place isn't you," Tate, my current real estate shopping buddy, said, not bothering to lower her voice. "It's too cold."

"Cold?" Remington's blond brows winged upward in protest. "Look at this light! You have the canal right outside your door. Do you know how rare it is to find a good house on the canal?"

We were in Venice, searching for homes here because Remington told me it was *the* place to be in LA. Maybe it was. But I couldn't get into the search. My head felt heavy, and my shoulders ached. I wanted a cool drink and a soft lounger to sprawl on.

And maybe indulge in a pretty little pastry that fills your mouth with its flavors and makes your heart flutter?

No. Not that.

Aggravated, I ran a hand through my hair, fingers dragging over my scalp in an attempt to work some blood back into my head. "Tate's right. This isn't me. But I'm beat. Let's call it a day."

Remington was not happy and shot daggers at Tate when he thought I wasn't looking. But Tate could take care of herself. She blew him a lazy kiss, and I bit back a laugh.

Tate was my oldest friend in Hollywood. We'd met as fresh-faced newbies at an audition for a cereal commercial. I'd been rejected because I was "too California blonde" despite being born and raised in Fairfax, Virginia, and too short, despite being one of the tallest actresses in the bunch. And my smile apparently looked like an invitation for sex. Tate had laughed her ass off about that. Until they'd told her she was too busty but asked if she'd consider dying her raven-black hair blonde.

We'd gone to lunch to complain and agreed that casting directors were the most nitpicky, clueless jackholes in the business. They weren't really; we'd eventually learn there were much worse players in this strange, messed-up business. But our bond had formed.

Now, Tate hooked her arm through mine as we strolled back into the hotel and were enveloped in the lush-green, kitschy banana-leaf wallpaper.

"You'll find something," she said, giving me a squeeze of support as we found the path through the garden.

"I know. I'm just tired." I unlocked the door to the extravagant bungalow I'd rented. I could have stayed in a simple room. I could have stayed with Tate. But I was licking my wounds by surrounding myself with a luxury that would have made young cash-poor me cringe in horror.

Tate dropped her purse on the side table, then flopped onto the couch with a sigh. "Hello, Marilyn," she said to the black-and-white photo of Marilyn Monroe. "We're home!"

I gave my own nod to Marilyn, then curled up on the other end of the couch.

"You want to call in for some cocktails?" Tate asked, eyeing me. "Or maybe go to the pool?"

No pools. I wasn't sure when I'd willingly go around one again, but not today.

"I was thinking about a nap." I kicked off my heels and wiggled my toes. When she didn't say anything, I glanced up and found Tate watching me with a dark frown.

"You okay? Is it the show?"

Tate was the only friend I'd told about getting the ax. Well, aside from Amalie, Tina, and Lucian. I pushed his name from my mind. Or tried to.

"I'm okay," I lied. "And it's not the show. Well, not really. I've settled down about those worries." Because a gruff and beautiful man held me in the dark and told me it was okay to mourn.

My chest tightened, and I turned away, staring blindly at Marilyn's sultry expression. Someone once told me that to be a star is to shine alone in the night sky. Always admired, always alone. I'd laughed that off. Why couldn't I have it all?

My vision blurred, and I pinched the bridge of my nose. "I'm just . . ."

A vibration at my feet cut me off as a text popped up on my phone. Given that I didn't want to break down and cry on Tate's shoulder, I pulled the phone from my purse.

Sal: I can't believe you went to LA without me!!

Smiling, I shook my head and tapped out my reply.

Who is this and how did you get this number?

There was a slight pause.

Sal: Evil Emma! And to think, I was going 2 tell U about the vintage 50s Dior ball gown in ice blue silk that I found. In YUR size!

He sent along a picture of the dress, and I sucked in a breath. It was gorgeous.

"Holy shit," exclaimed Tate, who was extremely nosy on the best of days and had leaned in to look over my shoulder. "Who is Sal, and if you don't want that dress, tell him I do."

I nudged her away with a laugh. "He's Amalie's assistant and dresser. He's a sweetheart and an expert at all things fashion." I'd told Tate all about staying with Amalie. I had not told her about Lucian. I couldn't. Not yet.

Just the thought of him now made my smile fade. I missed him. Damn it, I wasn't supposed to miss a man I hardly knew.

But I did know him. Not in length of time but in depth of character. I shook it off and answered Sal.

Forgive me, Sal! Or I'll never forgive myself! :)

Sal: You just want the dress.

Yes. But I assume you come w/the dress?

Sal: Is that innuendo, dear Emma?

I snorted.

Nice try, Sally.

Sal: :P I already bought the dress. It's yours.

I luv U, Sal!!!

I glanced at Tate. "I'm getting the dress."

"Bitch!" She pouted for a second, then poked me with her toe. "When do I get to meet him?"

Sal pinged another message before I could answer.

Sal: So, where are you staying? Please tell me it's fabulous. Let me live vicariously thru U.

You'll like this, then. Bungalow 1 at the Beverly Hills Hotel.

Sal: THE MARILYN!?! Without ME???

I laughed and showed Tate the text.

"Oh, I like this guy," she said.

"I do too." I liked everyone at Rosemont. A pang of something that felt alarmingly like homesickness went through me. I pulled in a breath and let it out slowly. I couldn't get attached.

Sal texted again.

Sal: Tell me you're going out on the town and having fun!

Ah. No. I might drag my butt down to the lounge for dinner but that's it.

Sal: Boooring!

That's me. Napping now!

I wondered briefly if he'd tease me about that, but he didn't.

Sal: Sleep well, fair Emma.

And it hurt. Because I wanted to hear those words from someone else. I wanted to talk to *him*. I just wanted . . . *him*.

"He's right. You are boring." Tate nudged me again with her toe, and I slapped it away. She made a noise of protest. "Let's go out."

"No." I put down my phone. "I can't. I . . ." My voice caught and died.

Tate's gaze sharpened. "Something is going on with you. Tell me."

It was on the tip of my tongue to deny it. But the words bubbled up without my permission. "Oh, where to begin?"

"At the beginning."

"I think we'll need drinks for that."

She was already headed for the minibar. "On it."

And so I spilled out my heart. But it didn't make me feel any better.

———

Eventually, Tate dragged me down to the lounge and we ended up on the patio, tucked in a private corner half hidden by potted ficus trees.

Tate ordered us a tray of oysters and two strong gimlets.

"What, no fruity drinks?" I teased.

"This is a gin-and-bear-it kind of night," Tate said with a straight face.

I made a fake gagging sound. "I hate your puns."

"You love them."

Our cocktails arrived. Tate shook her long hair back from her shoulders and took a dramatic breath. Surrounded by pink stucco and white wrought iron furniture, she looked a bit like a modern-day Rita Hayworth. "Here's to good drinks and a man-free night."

"Amen."

"Emma?"

We both froze at the sound of that familiar male voice. And my insides dropped.

"Oh, for fuck's sake," Tate uttered, glaring up at our intruder.

I didn't glare but put on my best "I am happy and perfectly fine" face. Because Greg, the cheating bent-dick bastard, was standing in front of me.

"You aren't sure?" I asked.

Greg's face scrunched up in confusion. "Aren't sure of what?"

"If I'm Emma."

He cocked his head. Greg had never been very good with any sort of verbal play. "Of course I know you're Emma."

"You phrased it like a question." It occurred to me just then that I'd teased Lucian in a similar manner when we'd first met, and he'd caught on right away. *Damn it, I will* not *pine for him.*

I glared at the jerk who'd tried to break my heart a month ago as he scratched the back of his neck, looking distinctly unnerved. Bumping into him was bound to happen. He played for the Rams, so unless he was at away games, he would be skulking about somewhere in the city. Of four million people. Damn it, why did I have to run into him?

"I was surprised." He squared his shoulders. He had nice ones—I'd give him that. "It's good to see you."

"I can't say the same."

Tate snorted into her gimlet. I shot her an amused look, then turned my attention back to Greg with a bland expression. I could be a grown-up. "Found a new place yet?"

I'd hired someone to move all my stuff from his house, but he'd sent a flurry of texts insisting that if I didn't live there with him anymore, he couldn't bear it either. My empathy was nil.

"No." His mouth quirked, and he looked at me with far too much fondness for comfort. "Can't seem to find anything that feels right."

"Right. Well." I lifted my glass. "Have a nice night."

See. Grown-up.

Now, fuck off, Greg.

He frowned. Not fucking off. "Are you here with anyone?"

"I'm sitting right next to her," Tate exclaimed in exasperation.

He shot her a brief glance, then focused on me, pulling out the charm. "Look, Emma. We need to talk."

I used to melt for that sweet, aw-shucks smile. It must have been the dimple. Greg had a great dimple. Just the one cheek. Add the caramel-brown hair and cornflower-blue eyes, and he came off as honest, kind. When he really was a big ol' lying, cheating . . .

Biting the inside of my lip, I regarded him coolly. Or at least I hoped I did. "Yeah, I'm not interested in having a talk. So . . ." I made a shooing motion.

"Come on, sweetheart. We lived together for a year. We can't just end things like this."

Like this? He'd ended things by sticking his dick inside another vagina. But whatever.

I really didn't want to get into this. Not in public, where God knew who might be taking pictures or recording. Not ever, really. Nothing he could say would make me want him. Even hearing his explanation would require too much effort.

Problem was he clearly wasn't taking no for an answer, which meant I had to get him out of here and tell him off in the privacy of my bungalow. Which would then be tainted with his presence. Damn it all.

"Save me some oysters," I told Tate with a sigh.

Her expression pinched. "You're not going to talk to this penis pimple, are you?"

"Penis pimple?" Greg put in with a scowl.

"You are all that and more," Tate snapped.

I rested my hand on her arm. "I want to do this in private."

Her gaze darted over my face, searching to see if I was really okay, and I squeezed her in reassurance. "I'll be right back."

"Okay. But if he gives you any grief . . ." She trailed off with a meaningful look at Greg, who rolled his eyes.

Collecting my purse, I got up and purposely stepped out of Greg's touching range. "Come on, pimple." I didn't wait for him but left with a graceful "I am in total control" stride.

"Listen, Emma—"

"Not a word," I cut in as we made our way along the secluded garden path toward my bungalow. "I'm not doing this until we're in total privacy."

"Fine."

The little dusk-pink Spanish-style bungalow was just off the path and had a wide terra-cotta-tiled stoop leading up to the front door. I was expecting that sight. I didn't expect Lucian Osmond to be standing there.

Bathed in the golden glow of the porch lights, he appeared surprised as well, as though he'd been caught out, but then I realized he was looking at Greg at my side.

Too shocked to process anything other than him at my door, wearing his customary jeans and a fine-knit olive sweater against the cool of the evening, I could only stand there gaping.

Then his gaze locked onto mine, and emotion sparked along my skin, hot and sharp. My heart swelled, flipped, and fluttered.

"Em."

God, his voice. Every time I heard it, my knees went a little weak. I sucked a breath. "You're here."

He didn't look away. "Yes."

"Luc Osmond?" Greg. I'd forgotten about him. "Oz?"

Lucian's mouth flattened. "Yep."

Greg brushed past me, striding up to Lucian. "Greg Summerland. You are a beast on the ice, man."

I shouldn't have compared the men, but I couldn't help it. They were both of a similar height and had a similar breadth of shoulders. Greg's build was a bit thicker about the torso, which I knew he preferred, given the amount of hits he faced each season. Lucian's body was leaner, his muscles cut with precision that I suspected came from constant physical work outside of hockey.

But it was more about the way they moved. Greg had a slow amble, as though he wanted to make sure everyone watched him. While Lucian possessed a fluid grace, a panther lying in wait. He could move with lightning quickness if he wanted, but most of the time he simply flowed. Swagger.

They faced each other, Greg with his expectant "Let's exchange compliments" look he got around fellow famous athletes, and Lucian with his grim reserve.

Greg extended his hand, but Lucian looked down at it like it was dirt. His wintergreen eyes moved up to meet Greg's, but he didn't attempt to shake his hand. Instead, he turned his attention to me. "Is this a bad time?"

I knew what he was asking. Did I want Greg here? Was I back with him?

A lump swelled in my throat. I missed him. It had been only a day, and I missed him. I was so screwed.

"Greg was just leaving."

Greg, who'd apparently forgotten I was there in the face of the great Luc Osmond, whipped back to me. "We were going to talk."

"You know what? I'm all out of talk right now." I inclined my head toward the path.

"Are you with Oz now?" he asked, incredulous. Then shook his head before I could answer. "I guess you have a type."

My back teeth met with a click. "Unless you mean *male*, Lucian isn't anything like you."

Lucian grunted. I knew him well enough now to understand that particular tone meant surprise. I couldn't look at him, though, not yet. I had to deal with an increasingly self-entitled ex.

"We're not doing this. Please go, Greg."

Given that Lucian was shooting a warning look that even Greg couldn't miss, and I wasn't budging, he let out a sigh. "Fine. I'll call you later."

"I wish you wouldn't."

He didn't answer, but he stopped by my side, bent, and gave my cheek a kiss before I could get away. "See you later, Emma."

I kept my gaze on Lucian, my heart thudding erratically against my chest. He stared right back, his expression tight and intent. I found myself moving forward.

As soon as I did, Lucian came down the stairs to meet me halfway. We stopped a foot away from each other. I caught the scent of his skin, burnt sugar and bittersweet chocolate; he'd been baking again. I could feel the warmth of his body. I wanted to press into it, soak it up.

I stayed still and searched his face. He gave nothing away, staring down at me with a solemn expression. When he spoke, his deep voice sounded rougher. "You okay with me being here right now? I could come back." He said it as though forcing the offer through his lips. But he said it. Lucian would never push me to do something I didn't want.

My smile was watery, weak, and fleeting. "I'm glad you're here. Greg was being a pest about wanting to talk, and I was trying to get rid of him as soon as possible."

Lucian let out a swift, audible breath. Only then did I notice he held a small white box in his hand. I knew those boxes. He'd brought along a pastry.

Hope warred with caution. I steeled myself for the worst and hoped for the best. "Would you like to come in?"

He hadn't yet taken his eyes from my face. "Yes."

The simple declaration had my heart flipping over in my chest. I merely nodded and made my way to the door, pretending that I wasn't shivering inside from nerves and need. I pulled out my phone and sent a quick text to Tate, then put it on silent before she had a chance to reply with a barrage of questions.

"My friend was waiting for me at the lounge," I explained, letting us in.

He frowned slightly. "You want to go back and meet her? I didn't exactly give you notice." So careful. Was he sorry he came?

"No. She lives close by." I walked into the bungalow. The house had been serviced, and the lamps had been left on in strategic places to give the space a soft romantic glow.

Lucian stopped in the center of the little living room, his wide shoulders tight, his stance on the balls of his feet like he might soon bolt. And it hit me how nervous he was. Oddly, it made me less so.

"You want a drink?"

"No." He glanced down at his hand and frowned, as though he was surprised to find himself holding the box. "This is for you."

He held it out, which meant I had to get closer.

"Thank you." My fingers felt numb as I reached for his offering. The box felt strangely light, which plucked at my curiosity, but I didn't open it. I set it down and met Lucian's troubled gaze instead.

"You had Sal find me, didn't you?" I asked as the thought popped into my head.

He understood me perfectly, and a small wry smile pulled at his expressive mouth. "I did."

"Just tell me one thing," I said with due seriousness. "Am I still getting that dress? Or do I have to kill both of you?"

Lucian's true smile broke free. "You're still getting the dress."

My answering grin spread like sunlight through my veins.

Lucian sucked in a sharp breath. "I missed that smile."

He was *not* going to make me cry. "It's only been a day."

"Has it?" He stepped closer.

"A half a day at best," I babbled, my heart beating frantically.

He kept coming, jade eyes warm but troubled. "It felt like a year."

"Lucian . . ."

He stopped within touching distance. Close enough that I had to tilt my head to meet his gaze. Remorse filled his. "I wanted to protect you. I wanted to protect me." His hand lifted and hovered, as though he wanted to touch my cheek but didn't yet dare. "But it was too late."

"Too late?" My mind had gone blank the moment he'd drawn near.

"Yeah," he rasped, his fingertip drifting along the edge of my temple. "For me, at least. I started hurting the second I let you go, and I haven't stopped."

My lids fluttered closed as the words washed over me. But I'd been burned by his rejection too hard to proceed without caution. "Is that why you came here?"

"I came to ask if you would consider being with me. For however long we have. Just be with me."

I swayed, wanting so badly to lean into him. "Despite the fact that our situations haven't changed?"

"Yes." He lowered his hand but didn't move away. "This is real to me. I'm not messing around. I like you. A lot. I want you so much it hurts. And that scared the shit out of me." He searched my face as his tone turned earnest. "It was so fast, so strong, I panicked, Em."

A soft pulse of feeling went through me. "You think I'm not scared? I just got out of a shitty relationship with Greg the penis pimple."

"Penis pimple?" he repeated, fighting a smile even though the air between us was still taut with uncertainty.

"Yes. And you just ended it with Cassandra the moron."

"I'll concede that Cassandra messed me up more than I'd thought. It's unsettling to realize someone was with me solely for the fame, and I didn't even notice or care." He winced a little. "Made me reassess all my interactions with women."

I didn't blame him for that. Greg had done a number on me as well. The worst thing about someone destroying your trust was that it became harder to give it to someone new.

"And yet you still want to try this?" I wasn't sure why I kept harping on it. I'd wanted to for so long. Part of me was yelling to shut the hell up. But I wanted him to be certain.

"Yes, Emma, I do."

A hiccup lifted my chest. I liked those words. So much. "Even though we might fail spectacularly?"

"Did you miss the part where I said I ache for you? That today felt like a year? Em . . . you're the first person who has made me smile since I retired. Even if I was still playing hockey, I'd want you. I am alive in a way I haven't been before. My world is brighter, more real, when you're in it. I was a fool to—"

I stepped into his space and wrapped my arms around his waist. "I missed you too. Today is already better now that you're here."

"Hell." He caught me up in a hug so tight I felt it in my bones. But I didn't care. His mouth pressed to the top of my head, and he breathed in before letting it out in a shuddering exhale. "Thank you."

"For what?" I asked against the snug warmth of his chest.

Long fingers threaded through my hair, and he eased me back to smile down at me. "For being you."

Then he kissed me. Soft, reverent, an apology. And it felt so good I lifted up on my toes, surging into the kiss. With a small grunt, he caught on fast, his head angling to kiss me deeper. Our tongues touched, a first taste. All our careful reserve melted, replaced by fraught, straining touches, licks, nips.

My body remembered just how much it loved Lucian's kiss, his taste, and kicked into hyperawareness, heat washing over me in a wave that had me moaning inside his mouth. Lucian fisted the loose folds at the back of my dress, his other big hand cupping my cheek, moving me where he wanted, taking long greedy pulls of my mouth.

"Tell me you have a damn condom this time," I pleaded against his lips.

He pulled back to meet my eyes. Hair rumpled, lips swollen, he appeared almost dazed. "I . . ."

"If you say no," I warned, stealing a quick, messy openmouthed kiss, "I might kill you."

A low chuckle rumbled in his chest, and suddenly he hauled me up, one arm under my butt, the other securing my shoulders. His grin was sweet and sultry. "I didn't want to appear presumptuous, but since death is on the line, yes, I have condoms."

I wrapped my legs around his waist. "Then take me to bed, Brick. It's been a long day."

"A year," he muttered, grinning and kissing my mouth as he hustled toward the bedroom. "Maybe more. Felt like forever, Em."

Yeah, it kind of did.

CHAPTER
TWENTY-SIX

Emma

I thought it would be fast, frantic. But as soon as we entered the cool quiet of the bedroom, Lucian set me down. His fierce gaze stayed on me as he toed off his shoes.

"Now yours," he said, voice deep and gruff.

I mirrored his actions, taking off my high-heeled sandals without looking away from him. A small smile curled at the edges of his lips as he reached behind his head and grabbed the collar of his sweater to pull it off. But when I moved to lift my top, he raised a hand to forestall me.

"No. I want to do that." He stepped up to me, stopping so close I could feel the warmth of his smooth skin. Fine dark hairs dusted his chest, flirted around the stiff tips of his little nipples.

Staring at the beautiful expanse of male strength, I found myself swaying toward him, the need to kiss, touch, stroke burning hot and pure through my limbs.

His gaze was a living thing, sliding like liquid silk along my sensitized skin. He breathed deep and steady, but the fluttering pulse at the base of his throat betrayed him. With infinite care, he ran the tips of his fingers along the ruffled edge of my shirt, back and forth, toying with fabric.

He watched the movements with a quiet absorption, as though he needed to witness what he was doing to me. His fingers slid underneath the top, and my breath hitched. Gaze flicking up to mine, he nearly smiled, the gesture halting as he found my nipple and rubbed in a lazy circle.

Heat coursed through me, so strong that my knees went weak. Whimpering, I grabbed his arm to steady myself.

"I've got you," he said, wrapping an arm around my waist.

But he didn't let up. His hand lightly kneaded my breast as his head dipped low. Soft lips coasted along the sensitive skin of my neck. He held me there, hand cupping the back of my neck as he pressed a lingering kiss to the tender hollow of my throat.

"How do you want it, Em? Slow and easy?" He tweaked my nipple. "Fast and hard?"

I leaned into him, pressed my lips to the solid curve of his shoulder. "I want it all. Everything."

Lucian grunted. "Good answer."

Our mouths met, the kiss urgent and all-encompassing. I felt it in my thighs, along the small of my back, in the throb between my legs. He kissed me like he meant it. Like it was all he'd ever wanted. And I kissed him back, loving the feel and taste of him. Loving that he was mine to kiss.

"I need you, Em." His fingers grasped my waist, clinging, his mouth molding to mine. "I need you."

With a deft move, he lifted my shirt up and off—my skirt followed— then captured my lips again as we stumbled toward the bed. Lucian sat on the edge of it with a grunt, his big hands grasping my hips to pull me between his thighs.

Lucian's gaze flared with heat as it slid to my bare breasts. Slowly, he trailed his fingers upward, his voice dropping low and rough. "It's probably wrong that I dream of these."

I huffed out a laugh, but it cut short as he leaned in and lightly kissed the tip of my nipple. My hands went into his hair, holding him there as he kissed me again and again, his mouth opening a little to barely suck. It was the worst sort of tease. The best.

Warm breath ghosted along my skin. "I dream of you every night, Em. Fevered dreams of wanting you." His big hand cupped my breast, plumping it up so he could lick it at his leisure.

My head went light, desire curling in wisps of heat through my belly. He kept me there, licking and sucking, tormenting my aching nipples. Each draw of his mouth tugged on something deep within my sex, made it throb, made my insides clench sweetly.

Slowly, his hands coasted down to my hips, tracing my panties before he tugged them down. He looked up at me, even as his hand eased between my thighs. Ice-green eyes burned bright. "I've never wanted anyone as much as I want you." The calloused tips of his fingers slid along my swollen, slick sex. "Now that I have you, I don't know where to start."

My lids fluttered, hands clutching at his shoulders as he rubbed back and forth. "Right there works for me."

His smile was sin and promise. "You like that, honey?"

"Yes."

He toyed with the entrance to my sex, pausing there to push just enough for me to feel it, to want it. "How about here?"

"There is . . ." My breath caught. He pushed in, long strong fingers filling me.

"Is what?" he murmured darkly, those talented fingers slowly fucking me, as though he had all the time in the world. The blunt end of his thumb found my puffy clit and circled it.

I whimpered again, falling against him, my arms wrapping around his neck. "So fucking good."

He made a noise, possessive and greedy, his mouth finding my nipple, his long fingers pushing up into me. "God, you're perfect. So perfect for me."

The slight curl of his fingers hit a spot, and that was it. I came in waves, shaking with it, heat swamping me. His eyes held mine as he coaxed me along, drawing my pleasure out.

With a groan that sounded almost pained, Lucian slid to the floor, his wide shoulders edging between my legs. He palmed my thighs in his big hands to hold me steady. And then, with an impatient grunt, he leaned in and kissed my throbbing clit. Kissed it like he kissed my mouth, greedy and deep, licking and sucking, nibbling with firm lips.

I cried out again, my knees so weak he had to hold me up. He ate me like dessert, lapping at my slit before thrusting his tongue inside me.

I couldn't take it. It was too much. I came again, writhing against his mouth.

"That's it," he said between frantic kisses. "That's it, Em. Work that sweet pussy on my mouth."

Oh, hell.

I crumpled, dislodging myself before falling onto his lap. I cupped the thick column of his nape and kissed him, drawing in his breath as he groaned and devoured me.

Lucian stood, taking me with him. We tumbled back onto the bed, and I wiggled to the side, my hands fumbling with his jeans, trying to draw them down. The hot length of his cock fell into my palm, and I held him firm, stroking the way I knew he liked.

"Fuck." His hips jerked. "Let me . . ."

His hands tangled with mine, and we worked to get his jeans off. Once they were free, I nearly flung them off the bed, but he caught them at the last second and wrenched a long packet of condoms from the pocket.

His smile was brief but wide and pleased, and I found myself laughing softly. He paused, his gaze darting over my face. "Fuck, you are so pretty, Em."

Simple words that struck deep within my heart. As soon as he rolled the condom over his thick length, I pulled him down to me, wanting to feel his strength and weight on me. Wanting to be surrounded by him.

The hot crown of his cock notched against my sex, and we both stopped, our gazes clashing.

"Em."

I knew what he meant. This felt different. This felt like more than sex. He didn't look away as he slowly pushed into me, all that hot *girth* making itself at home.

I moaned and spread my legs wider, working with him. He was big. And there. And it felt so good I could barely breathe through it all.

Lucian dipped his head, trembling with effort to go slow. "God. God. You feel . . ." He broke off with a tortured groan and a hard thrust, filling me completely.

I closed my eyes, my hands smoothing over his damp back. "So good, Lucian. So good."

That was all he needed. Moving like liquid, he rocked into me, kissing my mouth, whispering how much he needed this, how much he wanted me. I grew incandescent with it, heat licking through me in waves.

Lucian fucked like he did most everything, with perfect finesse and fierce determination. With swagger. Soon we were both panting, moving faster, reaching for that peak yet wanting to prolong it.

"I don't want it to end," he said against my mouth. But then he canted his hips, hitting that spot that lit me up and made me scream.

There was no more finesse, no more drawing it out. Just basic rutting, fucking each other like we might die and not get another chance. And when he came, I stared up at him, at those muscles straining, his wintergreen eyes gleaming in lust and surprise, as though he couldn't quite believe how good it was.

Neither could I. Because it had never been like this.

Chapter Twenty-Seven

Emma

"God, I needed that."

Lying against Lucian's damp chest, I felt his body clench in surprise just before a hearty laugh burst out of him, shaking the bed. I smiled against his skin and cuddled closer. For having such a hard body, he was wonderfully comfortable to hold.

Smiling wide, he turned until we were facing. His winter eyes were warm now, and his smile grew. "Oh, you did, huh?"

Unable to stop touching him, I trailed my fingers across the elegant line of his collarbone. "You sound surprised. Did you doubt your ability to please me, Brick?"

Quick as a flash, he captured my hand and nipped my fingertips. I yelped, even though it didn't hurt, and he grinned again. "If I had failed, I would have tried harder the next time."

I edged closer, and my breasts brushing against his chest sent a luxuriant shiver along my body. "Such selfless dedication."

Lucian's gaze grew slumberous as his hand slid over my shoulder to cup my neck. "Give it your all, or go home."

"Good motto." I traced the rise of his biceps. Lord, but the man had nice arms—muscled without being obnoxious.

He hummed in agreement. "Practice makes perfect and all that."

When I snickered, he pulled me completely against him. Skin to skin. His voice dipped a register. "I needed it too." Light but lingering kisses peppered my temple, my cheek. He was all around me, warm and firm, the scent of burnt sugar and musky sex.

I closed my eyes, wrapped my arm around his neck. My tongue flicked over the hard cap of his shoulder to take a tiny taste of his salty skin. Lucian shivered, hummed deep within his throat.

"Give me five minutes," he rasped, nuzzling my hair, "and we'll practice some more."

"Five minutes?" I teased, my voice slow like honey.

"Woman," he complained into the hollow of my throat, "you had me three times in a row. Give a man some rest."

I laughed, happiness bubbling within me. We were new lovers, but it felt as though we'd always been together. Not in the way of me wanting him—*that* felt so new and strong I wondered if I'd ever get enough of him to ease my thirst. But in how easy it was to be with him. How fun. I could not recall sex being fun. Feeling easy.

Maybe it was for other people. But I used to sink into my head and worry about how I looked, what I said. The true horror was I'd freaking *act* in bed. I hadn't been myself.

But with Lucian, I couldn't be anything but. Even if I wanted to, he'd notice. And he would draw me out of any shell I could hide behind.

Expression light, he nudged me onto my back and then rested his head in his hand as he lay at my side. His other hand settled gently between my breasts, as if to guard my heart. The action was so tender my chest constricted. He didn't seem to notice but studied me with a pleased expression. "You thirsty?"

I hadn't thought so until he asked. "I could go for some water."

The laugh lines around his eyes deepened. "I'll be right back." He kissed my mouth, then, with that effortless grace of movement, rolled over and got out of bed.

I settled back and watched him walk utterly naked across the room. Nude Lucian's swagger was a sight to behold, that insane butt flexing and squeezing with every step. Even the man's calves were stunning. A sight gone too quickly as he went into the bathroom to wash up.

As soon as he was done, he ambled off to the kitchen. I resettled myself in bed, fluffing bunched and scattered pillows and straightening the sheets that had somehow managed to become a long twist. The rattle of a tray announced Lucian's return. I flopped back against the pillows, breath short, and held up a hand.

"Slow down!" I pleaded. When he did, the dark wings of his brow lifting in amused confusion, I grinned. "Let me get a good look at you."

A flush started along his neck and crept up to his ear. But he complied, his gait loose hipped and rolling. "This slow enough?"

"I think I need to film it for posterity. I don't think I've ever appreciated a man's legs more."

That got a smile, though it seemed more of a "The woman is ridiculous, but I like it" one. "If you're good"—he set the tray on the side table—"I'll let you ride my thigh later."

That should not have made my sex clench with anticipatory heat so very hard. But it did.

Lucian looked me over. "Although I have to say you didn't do yourself any favors putting on that shirt."

"Was that bad?"

"Very," he said sternly. "You'll be taking it off soon, or no thigh ride for you."

"Yes, Lucian."

Lips twitching, he handed me a glass of cool water with a twist of lemon. I smiled at it.

"What?" He sat on the edge of the bed.

"You. Putting a lemon slice in the water." I took a sip.

"It makes it taste better," he grumbled, still a bit pink around the ears.

"It does." I drank some more, then handed it to him. "You're adorable."

He rolled his eyes and took a drink.

"You like taking care of people."

Lucian offered me more water. "I like taking care of you."

I took another long drink. "And I'm in true danger of letting you do it all the time. But it's more than that. You have this innate sense of seeing something ordinary and making it extraordinary."

"You're trying to embarrass me, aren't you?" He accepted the glass and drained it.

"No. I'm giving you a compliment."

Lucian set the glass down, a bemused expression playing over his face. "I have no idea how to handle those."

His honesty startled me. "You're fawned over by almost everyone you meet. Even dickhead Greg was sucking up to you."

Lucian ducked his head, shaking it a bit. "But I'm not that man anymore. Even when I was playing, that type of praise felt rote. It was more about my performance than who I was as a person."

Slowly I nodded. "When people tell me how much they love Princess Anya, I can't help thinking, 'But you're supposed to. That's my job.'"

"And yet if they complain or pick it apart, you can't help but think they're fools who don't appreciate talent when they see it." He said it with the dry humor of a man who'd lived it.

I laughed. "Yes, true. Although it sounds horrible when you say it out loud."

"Such is the strangeness of fame." He shook his head lightly again, then turned to the tray and picked up the white pastry box. "You haven't opened this."

"I was too nervous." I held my hand out for the box, and he gave it to me, his bemusement growing.

"I made *you* nervous? I was ready to get on my knees, Em."

My heart flipped over in my chest, and I covered the moment by fumbling with the string holding the box closed. It slipped free with a jerk, and the box, designed to open like a flower, revealed its gift.

A gasp escaped me. Nestled in a white cloud of spun sugar was a perfect little sphere-shaped gâteau covered in chocolate so dark and glossy it shone like midnight. But that wasn't what had my mouth falling open in awe.

Resting on the very top of the orb was a pink-and-gold butterfly made of sugar glass. The delicate wings were so fine and thin the light shone through them. It looked so real I half expected it to fly away.

"Lucian . . ."

"This is how I see you sometimes," he said in a low voice, eyes on the gâteau. "Beautiful and rare, something not to be contained but treasured."

My eyes misted over. He was killing me. I had been called *beautiful* before, but not quite this way. And yet I feared he saw me as fleeting. I didn't want to be a brief moment in his life. I couldn't bring myself to say it, though. Not with his gift in my hand.

"It's beautiful. Perfect." I looked up at him, afraid my whole heart was in my eyes. "I can't eat this!"

His brows snapped together. "Why not?"

"It's art. I can't go in like Godzilla and chomp it to smithereens."

Lucian choked on a laugh. "You really do have the wildest imagination. It's supposed to be eaten, Snoopy."

"Don't Snoopy me. I'm having a moment here."

Snorting, Lucian reached out and took the small cake from its nest. I would have mussed it or dropped the entire thing in my clumsiness. But his hands were rock steady, fingers deft as he plucked the butterfly off, put it back in the nest, then held the cake out to me. "Take a bite, Em."

I wanted to so badly my mouth watered, but I held back for a moment. "This is going to be a thing with you, isn't it? Feeding me, I mean."

His gaze went to my mouth. "Yes. I'm trying not to break down the reasons why. Only that it pleases me."

The words stroked between my breasts, sparking something deep within. Before Lucian, I had never tasted food with my whole soul. I'd gone through life observing it, mimicking it for entertainment. With him, every moment was one to be enjoyed, savored.

Eyes locked with his, I opened my mouth for him to feed me. His nostrils flared as he eased the sweet between my lips.

Bittersweet chocolate so dark and deep it was almost too sharp coated my tongue. Then I bit into the soft cake, releasing mellow creamy mousse. It wasn't chocolate—perhaps coffee or maybe caramel, the flavor elusive. But the combination of all that dark bitter bite with smooth cream made it something new, rich but not cloying.

I made a noise of satisfaction that had Lucian's gaze turning rapt. "Good?"

"Exquisite." I licked my lips. "More."

He sucked in a sharp breath. "Damn, I didn't think this through."

A glance down had me licking my lips again. He was hard. Gloriously so. Thick and pulsing. Raising a brow, I swiped my finger through the cream-filled cake, collecting a dollop. "You better take the last bite," I advised. "I'm going to be busy."

"What—"

I swirled the cream over the fat head of his cock and swallowed him down.

"Oh, fuck . . . oh . . ." A tortured groan ripped from his throat as he clenched the sheet with one hand, his head thrown back. "Em . . ."

He was beautiful. And delicious. And I savored him the way he deserved to be, slowly, thoroughly. Until he was whimpering my name, undone and panting.

Only later, when he'd fallen upon me—resting his head upon my upper chest, his arm wrapped around my waist like he needed to hold on in order to settle down—did the full interpretation of his dessert hit me. All that darkness swallowing up the light. A glossy beauty that wasn't made to last.

"I'm the butterfly. You are the cake."

Replete and limp, he turned his cheek more fully toward my breast, giving me a featherlight kiss. "Honey, to me, you're both."

But I wasn't convinced. And I didn't think he was either. But for now, it was enough.

CHAPTER
TWENTY-EIGHT

Emma

One convenience of the bungalow I'd rented was that it had a dining room that easily fit six. Since Tate hadn't stopped blowing up my phone for details, and Lucian admitted that Brommy and Sal had tagged along and were staying at the hotel as well, we invited them over for lunch, preferring the privacy of the room.

Though Tate and I could don big hats and sunglasses and often get away with not being photographed, I had no doubt that Lucian and Brommy together would instantly be noticed. The men were just too good looking not to cause a stir. And while I had no idea how big a hockey town LA truly was, enough people already had recognized Lucian for me to know they'd do it here too. Throw Sal, with his bold flash, into that mix, and we might as well have pointed a neon sign toward our party.

"Can I just say, thank God," Tate murmured to me as I poured her some champagne from the bar cart set up in the corner of the room. "I thought I might get a text saying you'd gotten back together with Greg."

"Ew." I wrinkled my nose. "I can't believe you thought that. Do you know me at all?"

She made a self-deprecating face. "I know, I know. But people do stupid things all the time." She glanced at Lucian, who, despite not cooking the meal, was setting up our plates with his typical fierce attention to detail. "That, over there, is the best choice I've seen you make outside of your career."

Heat suffused my cheeks, but I raised my own glass slightly, and we did a covert glass tap.

"Is this a private girl huddle, or can anyone join?" Sal asked, appearing at my side. He was wearing an authentic olive-green zoot suit with a cherry-red polka-dot tie. The outfit had so impressed Tate that, upon meeting him, she'd pressed a hand to her chest and exclaimed, "Be still my Chicana heart."

It had cemented an instant friendship.

I handed him a glass. "I don't know. Tell me more about this dress I'm getting first."

He had the grace to look sheepish. "I was a sneak, I know! And I wouldn't have done it for just anyone, but poor Luc looked so pathetic." He smirked at Lucian, whose head had jerked up on hearing his name, and he glanced our way. "Besides, he threatened to pound me into a Sal meat patty."

Lucian rolled his eyes. "There were no such threats."

"Maybe not verbal," Sal countered, taking the champagne bottle with him to the table. "But there were glares. We all know how potent your glares can be."

"He's got you there," I said with a grin, taking the seat Lucian held out for me.

Lucian grunted and sat next to me.

"Well, he looks damn content now." Brommy neatly slid into the seat between Tate and me. "Almost as though he's inwardly purring. I feel safe in the knowledge that I am leaving him in your capable hands, Emma."

"Sitting across the table won't prevent me from kicking your ass," Lucian drawled without heat. In truth, there was a lazy air about him now. He appeared a man content, his big body loose limbed and relaxed in his chair. It was a good look on him. Even better when his gaze met mine, and a hot knowledge of what we'd done last night and this morning simmered between us.

I want it again, his gaze said.

Heat swamped me.

Soon, mine said.

A small quirk of his brow. *Sooner than later, honey. Count on it.*

A sound of amusement ended our nonverbal eye communication, and I turned to find Brommy watching us with a sappy grin. "Just look at him." Brommy gestured expansively with his enormous hands. "Eye fucking and smiling like a teen who felt his first tit—" A bread roll hit his forehead dead center.

Lucian lowered his brow and gave Brommy a warning look. "Shut it, or the next one will be in your mouth."

Brommy laughed. "Just like the Oz of old." He wiped an imaginary tear but then threw up his hands in peace when Lucian growled. "Okay, okay, I'm shutting it."

I hid my smile by stabbing into my salad and taking a bite. Brommy was crude, but he wasn't wrong; Lucian did look happy. I'd done that— I'd made him smile with his eyes, made him laugh with ease. After a series of personal dejections and setbacks, that I could experience this little bit of happiness with someone who'd also suffered felt like liquid sunlight flowing through my veins.

Tate had been chatting with Sal, not really noticing us as he showed her images of outfits he'd picked up on his recent shopping trip.

"You have to take me with you the next time you go out," Tate demanded with a pout that I knew she practiced on unsuspecting men.

"Chica, we can go today if you want. Although I might have something for you already . . ." Sal flipped through his pictures. "Here."

Tate took the phone and squealed at the picture. "Want!"

Brommy, who'd been clearly trying to get her attention since he'd arrived, leaned over and glanced at the phone. "You'd look beautiful in that."

Tate glanced at him, and her red mouth quirked. "I'm not sleeping with you, so don't even try."

Brommy merely smiled. "I'd be disappointed if sleep was involved."

Tate did a double take, then laughed, truly amused. And I knew she was hooked. Which amazed me, because her usual inclination would be to verbally eviscerate him.

"Good Lord," I murmured to Lucian, dipping my head in close to his, mainly because he smelled good, and I wanted to be nearer. "That might have actually worked."

"You have no idea." His lips touched the shell of my ear and lingered. "Years, I had to witness this."

My mind went a bit hazy at that touch, the proximity of him. And I pulled in a breath, looking up to meet his gaze. As always, his eyes had the ability to make me weak. Make me want.

His attention focused on my mouth, and the wide expanse of his chest hitched. "Why did we invite everyone here again?"

"Because they were blowing up our phones, and we were being good friends."

"And we would have hunted you down eventually," Brommy put in loudly.

"He has the hearing of a bat," I whispered to Lucian, who chuckled.

"And the reflexes of a cat," Brommy added.

Lucian's hand whipped up and caught a bread roll midair. I yelped, jerking in my seat; he'd moved so fast. Lucian turned and gave Brommy a smug look. "Center beats cat."

And for one brilliant moment, I saw the full force of Oz, the great and powerful player who'd ruled his sport. He shone with it, confidence and cockiness oozing from his pores, until it occurred to him that he no longer played center. The realization crashing over him was painfully clear, from the way his expression suddenly blanked out to the tension visibly stiffening his spine.

I hurt for him. Because the agony exposed in the brief moment spoke of a man who didn't know who he was anymore. Unheeded and unwanted came the one piece of advice my mother had given me about men when I'd first started to notice them.

Don't try to pick up the pieces of the broken ones. You'll never be able to set them back to the way they were again.

Chapter Twenty-Nine

Emma

"You're squeezing it too hard."

"I am not. You're just nitpicking."

"It is not nitpicking when perfection is the goal. Hold it firmly; don't try to wring the life out of it, or it's going to splatter everywhere. And mind the tip."

"I can't believe you're already criticizing my technique. I just started."

"Snoop, you'll never learn if you can't take criticism."

With a huff, I set down the pastry bag and wiped my forehead with my forearm. "Tell me again, How is this relaxing?"

Lucian's white teeth flashed when he chuckled. He leaned a hip against the countertop and carefully tucked the strand of hair that had been tickling me back behind my ear. "I think one has to have a modicum of patience, honeybee."

"Patience," I muttered. "I haven't strangled you yet, have I? Telling me I'm squeezing too hard."

He grinned and dipped down to kiss my lips with affection. "In this case, yes. But if you want to give it a go on me—"

I poked his ticklish spot, and he skittered away with an actual deep male giggle that made me smile despite myself. "Don't you dare make innuendo. I'm grumpy."

He caught my wrist in a loose grip and raised my hand to his mouth. "You're wonderful." Holding my gaze, he sucked my finger into his warm mouth, the flat of his tongue stroking me.

Heat swelled between my legs, but it was the look in his eyes, all fond tenderness and affection, that had my insides fluttering. "You're forgiven."

Lucian's answering kiss was a little longer, a lot sweeter. I leaned into him, cake forgotten, my arms wrapping around his neck. I allowed myself to enjoy him, let go, and just feel.

Since returning home to Rosemont, we hadn't been taking it slow, per se, not when we couldn't keep our hands off each other for more than a few minutes. But we'd been cautious, each in our own way, guarding our hearts by making a point of not speaking too long or too deeply about emotions best kept to ourselves.

I told myself it was smart. But with each day spent in Lucian's company, it felt less like safety and more like a mistake not to say what I was feeling. I was an actress; I knew how to play a part. But I didn't want to do that with Lucian. The problem was I didn't know how to tear down the walls of caution we had between us.

It was easy to get distracted, especially when Lucian did things like lift me up and set me on the counter, spreading my thighs with quiet authority to step close and kiss me deeper.

"Man," a deep voice complained. "Not in the kitchen!"

We pulled apart to find Anton scowling at us in disgust.

"For God's sake, you cook food here, Luc."

Lucian kept his hand on my nape and snorted. "Keep interrupting me, and you can make your own meals."

"Hey, Anton," I said, content to stay in the circle of Lucian's arms, despite the side-eye his cousin was giving us.

Anton shook a reproachful finger. "And you, America's princess."

Lucian must have felt me tense, because his grip tightened just enough to convey support. But the damage had been done. My happy buzz flitted away, replaced by a heavy weight low in my belly.

I'd taken a night to read over the scripts sent my way. They were all wrong, all weak copies of my Princess Anya role or stale romantic comedies. I didn't have anything against a good romantic comedy, wit and verve, but the scripts I'd read didn't cut it. Nor did I want to be typecast. Frankly, I wanted something meaty, something to sink my teeth into. Something the polar opposite of Anya.

"With that sweetly beautiful face," my agent had said, "it's going to be tough to convince directors. They see you as a princess."

"I skewered no less than five men on *Dark Castle*," I'd snapped back. "I literally liquidated scores more. There was nothing sweet about it."

"And yet that's how they see you."

The whole thing left a sour taste in my mouth, and I turned to sneak a dollop of chocolate buttercream from the counter. Lucian looked on with quiet concern as I licked my finger. Usually, watching me suck my finger would have elicited a different response from him. But he knew me well enough to understand where my mind was going.

Under the curtain of my hair he stroked my skin, then turned to Anton. "Did you want something, or are you simply walking around trying to annoy people?"

I didn't miss the flicker of disappointment in Anton's eyes. Despite the apparent joy he took in needling Lucian, it bothered him to be so readily dismissed. Maybe even hurt. But it wasn't my place to play referee with them.

"Carlos told me you turned down the Raston fundraiser."

Lucian's eyes narrowed in warning. "I did."

"Who is Carlos?" I felt compelled to ask.

"Our agent." Anton reached over and grabbed an apple from the ceramic fruit basket on the opposite counter.

Frankly, it surprised me that they shared an agent, seeing how terribly they got along. But it also felt strange that I didn't know that. There wasn't any reason for me to, but I couldn't shake the feeling of being in the dark when it came to many aspects of Lucian's life.

Anton took a huge bite out of the apple and spoke between munching. "The Raston fundraiser is an annual event for charity that Ozzy boy has always participated in."

"Ant."

Lucian's sharp rebuke went unheeded.

"It raises an insane amount of cash for hungry children," Anton went on, speaking to me in a voice laced with admonishment. "Children who are invited to skate alongside their heroes like good old Luc here."

Lucian's hand slid from my neck as he stepped away and grabbed the dishrag from the sink. His shoulders worked beneath the fabric of his T-shirt as he methodically wiped down the countertop, going at it like the pristine surface needed a good polish. "As I told Carlos," he growled, swiping the same spot, "as I'm no longer playing, my presence would be superfluous."

"If it was superfluous," Anton pushed back, "you wouldn't have been invited."

"Frankly, I'm surprised I got an invite," Lucian said without looking up.

"Then you're not only stubborn but completely deluded. Fans love you. They want to see you."

"Go away, Ant."

Anton sighed and glanced at me, the thick wings of his brows so similar to Lucian's knotted. "Talk some sense into him, will you? Lord knows he won't listen to me, and those kids are more important than his bruised ego."

With that, he strode out of the kitchen, leaving me with a man intent on scrubbing a hole through marble.

"I think it's clean," I said with a nod at the counter.

Lucian paused, blinking slowly, then tossed the rag into the sink. He didn't turn my way. "Is this where you try to manage me, because I have to say I'm intrigued by what you think will work."

I huffed under my breath, delivering just enough snark to let him know he'd pissed me off. "An offensive player to the core, aren't you?"

He stiffened, and I winced, realizing that probably cut in ways I didn't want.

"Lucian," I said, softer, repentant. "I'm not here to manage you. I'm here to support you. If you'll let me."

He turned then, his expression mulish, and crossed his arms over his chest as he regarded me. "That work both ways?"

"Yes . . ." I frowned. "Why are you looking at me like I'm full of it?"

"That's not how I'm looking at you."

"Oh? Then explain that smirk, because I am armed with frosting and have been told I have a mean squeeze." I picked up the bag in demonstration. It got a half smile, which is what I'd been angling for. But it died quickly.

"You want to talk about the scripts you've been reading, Em?" His tone was quiet, but there was an underlining thread of accusation.

I set the bag down. "You think because I haven't talked about the crap material sent my way that you shouldn't talk to me about what happened with Anton just now."

Lucian leaned a hip against the counter. "It works both ways, doesn't it? You want me to open up—then why can't you?"

"Fine. I'll open up. I'm worried. I want to do more with my career than is being offered. I have to figure out how to do that when the powers that be hold all the cards. When I'm not with you, I think about that too much. My stomach aches at random times. And sometimes, in the dark of night, I try very hard not to freak out, because I know I'm so much better off than most people, and I shouldn't complain about being a famous actress who can't get her way. But I'm still scared and uncertain, and I hate it."

I stopped and let out a shaking breath. "Is that enough sharing for you?"

Lucian pushed away from the counter, the line of his mouth grim. He reached me in two steps and, before I could protest, pulled me close, wrapping me up in his arms. I sank against the broad wall of his chest with a shudder.

"I'm sorry," he rasped against my hair, his fingers clasping the back of my head firmly. "I hate that you feel that way."

I nodded and pressed my palm to his firm flesh.

He snuggled me closer, as though trying to eliminate any space between us. "No, I mean it. You shouldn't have to carry that load alone."

"Like you do?"

My soft whisper stilled him. Then he let out a breath. "Yeah, like I do."

I rubbed his chest. "That's the point, Brick. If we're trying to be together, we should be able to tell each other these things."

He huffed out a dark laugh. "Is that what this whole relationship thing is about?"

"So I'm told."

Lucian sighed and combed his fingers through my hair. "I didn't exaggerate when I said I was no good at this."

"No, you really didn't," I teased.

Lucian grunted. "Brat." He poked a ticklish spot, making me laugh and edge back enough to meet his gaze. His was fond but tired. "Cassandra wanted me to share my troubles. I tried in the beginning, but I found it easier not to."

"Why?"

"This is going to sound ridiculous, but she always agreed with me, even when I knew deep down that I was in the wrong." He shrugged, wincing. "I found I didn't want that type of support."

"Greg would tell me, 'Babe, stop complaining. You have it so easy compared to me.'"

Lucian scowled. "Fuckwit."

"Yes, he is." My smile ebbed. "I don't think I fully realized until just now how much that messed with my head."

He nodded, biting his bottom lip in contemplation. And for a minute neither of us spoke. We had so many walls, hidden ones and ones we'd shored up, as though under siege. He'd warned me he was an emotional wreck, but maybe I should have warned him too.

"I imagine going to that event, and all I can see is me standing there like a sad cautionary tale," he said with sudden frankness, his eyes bleak. "Look at poor Oz, can't play, cut down in his prime. Shake his hand, kids; give him a big hug of support."

"Oh, Lucian."

He held up his hands, warding me off, as his eyes grew shiny. "Standing there with the people I used to play with, compete against. Guys who still can play. And there I am, the one who has to walk away when it's over."

"So don't go. If it hurts you that much—"

"It hurts either way." He ran a hand over his face, grunting with a ragged sound. "I'm pathetic if I go. I'm pathetic if I stay home."

"You are *not* pathetic."

His smile was a bitter, twisted thing. "I keep telling myself that, but it doesn't take."

I ached for him, but he knew that. It was clear by the stiff way he held himself, eyeing me with a mix of caution and warning. I pressed my hand against the cool smoothness of the counter. "I didn't want to go to Macon and Delilah's wedding. I thought of all my friends and former coworkers looking at me with pity and . . ." I shuddered. "Pride is a fierce thing, isn't it?"

A stiff jerk of his chin was his only acknowledgment. His gaze moved off, away from me, and I knew he was trying to collect himself.

"But going took away all the what-ifs. I did it. It's over. Life changes, but they didn't pity me the way I thought they would."

Lucian slanted me a look from under the thick fringe of his lashes. "There's one key difference, honey."

"Which is?" I knew what it was, but I wanted him to say it. Because I wasn't going to be the woman who made everything easy for him.

"You still want to act."

"You don't want to—"

"Not in some exhibition. Not . . ." He took a breath, then let it out swiftly. "Hell, Em. I don't think I can handle getting on the ice again, knowing I can't go back to the sport."

The ice. He loved it with all his soul. I knew that. You only had to see him play to know it. The ice was a part of him, and it had been cut off without warning. I held his gaze, letting him see that I understood.

"If I told you I didn't know how to skate, would you teach me?"

He blinked, but a genuine smile of shock pulled at his mouth. "What?"

"Would you teach me?" I repeated. "For fun? Would you be willing to do that if I said I was a sad excuse for a skater?"

The smile tilted and grew. "Hell, you're good."

"Good?"

"Don't give me those innocent big blue eyes, Snoop." He touched the edge of my jaw. "You know exactly what you're doing, tempting me like that."

"Is it working?" I took his big rough hand in mine. "Will you skate with me, Lucian?"

"Damn it," he muttered, but he didn't look upset. His green eyes sparked with some unnamed emotion. "All right, honey. I'll take you skating. I'll try that much. For you."

CHAPTER THIRTY

Lucian

Ice had a scent, crisply metallic and pure. My love of that scent was so ingrained that anytime I caught a whiff of it, my heart rate would immediately kick up, and blood pumped through my veins with greater purpose. But a rink? That mix of ice and damp rubber, with a faint lingering of chlorine under it all? That was the scent of home. My religion.

Or it had been.

I caught a lungful of it as I led Emma into the main hall of the ice rink, and for the first time in my life, my insides lurched sickly, sweat blooming on my skin at the scent of ice. My heart rate kicked up, yes, but this wasn't the steady pulse of excitement. It threatened to pound that hurting organ right out of my chest.

My steps slowed to a painful halt, the space around me seeming to both close in and expand outward in a sickening sway. Emma's hand found mine, and she held on. Nothing more than that. Just stood by my side and held on. I grimaced, shaking and panting, my skin ice cold and fever hot.

I could only be thankful that we'd booked the place afterhours so we were alone. The thought of anyone else seeing me like this filled my mouth with a sour taste, and I swallowed convulsively.

"Let's sit down for a minute," Emma said, gently leading me along.

My clammy hand gripped her like an anchor even as shame swamped my system. I didn't want her seeing me this way either. But there was no help for it.

"I'll be . . . fine."

"I know you will." She eased me down onto a long wooden bench before sitting next to me, her hand never letting mine go.

Closing my eyes, I concentrated on breathing. In. Out. In. Out. I could do this. This was easy. A cakewalk. What the fuck did *cakewalk* even mean?

The thought clung to the edges of my mind like buttercream, and I focused on that instead. Of cakes and creams, gâteaux and tartes au citron. And slowly my racing heart slowed to an acceptable pace. After agonizing minutes, I could breathe without struggle.

"This pisses me off," I ground out.

Emma's thumb caressed my knuckles. "What does?"

I glanced over. She held my gaze with her steady blue eyes, a calm sea in the center of my storm. I forced myself to relax my grip on her. "Panicking over the simple sight of a rink. Places like this used to be my home. The embodiment of everything that was right in the world."

Everything I'd lost. I knew it. She knew it.

"When did you first learn to skate?"

Her softly spoken question startled me; I'd expected her to try to comfort me with platitudes. I turned toward the set of doors leading to the ice. "Seven. I wanted to fly." Longing and grief punched through me. "It was the closest I could come to it."

Shit. I *wasn't* going to cry. I wasn't going to do it. I blinked rapidly and breathed. *Just breathe, Oz.*

Emma pressed her cheek to my shoulder. "Let's fly, Lucian. Just you and me."

Fly. With her.

Heart clenching, I dipped my head and kissed the top of hers. "All right, honeybee. I'll take you flying."

Ordinarily, I could have laced up my skates with my eyes closed. Today, however, my fingers shook and fumbled with the strings as I thought of going out there. But I could deal. Emma wanted to skate.

Finishing up, I knelt at her feet, where she was putting on her skates. Unlike me, she had asked for a pair of figure skates.

"Let me see," I said, checking her lacings to make sure they were tight enough.

I redid one, giving her a look of reproach but tempering it with a small smile. Because she was damn cute with her white skates and a red wool beanie on her head.

"Better, Brick?" she asked, leaning down to watch.

I caught her sweet mouth with a kiss, lingering there because she tasted like heaven and felt even better. "Perfect, Snoop."

My hands smoothed up her thighs. She wore jeans in deference to the cold rink. I missed her floaty skirts and told her so.

Her eyes crinkled in amusement. "You just want to stick your hands under them."

"Guilty." I leaned in to nuzzle between her breasts, my hands snaking beneath her light sweater to find the silky skin of her belly. "Pretty sure I'm addicted."

She hummed in pleasure as I lightly kissed my way around her breasts. Her fingers carded through my hair, then gently halted my progress. When I looked up, she met my gaze with solemn eyes that told me all the stalling wasn't fooling her. "You ready now?"

No. "Yeah."

I stood, instantly feeling the change in my body, the added height of the skates, the way muscle memory adjusted to accommodate balancing on thin blades. Everything in me woke up. My focus narrowed onto Emma.

I held my hand out, and she took it, letting me haul her upright.

Smiling, she looked me over. "You're a veritable tree in those skates."

"You should have seen me in full gear."

Her lips twitched. "Man mountain, huh?"

"Pretty much." I held on to her hand firmly and glanced down at her feet. New skaters often let their ankles tilt, throwing them off balance and setting them up for an injury. But she held hers straight and strong. A good sign. "Let's do this."

The first blast of cooler air had me sucking in a breath as we made it to the ice. I meant to wait for Emma, take it slowly, but I stepped out onto the ice like a man let out of jail. Pure, pristine white stretched out before me, a perfect glide.

And I flew, the wind kissing my face, air filling my lungs. Racing along, I took a circuit around the rink, pivoting to run an old drill from high school days. My hands flexed with the need to feel my stick. I ached for that. Ached to drop a puck and play.

A wolf whistle pierced the air, and I caught sight of Emma clapping and cheering me on. She looked so damned impressed by some simple skating that I found myself showing off for her, going faster, weaving through imaginary defenders. Circling back around, I headed her way but stopped nice and easy, because I might have been a showboat, but I wasn't going to be the asshole who sprayed ice at a girl.

Cheeks pink, indigo eyes sparkling, she grinned wide. "You're beautiful."

"That's my line." I held out my hand. "Come on, then. Let's get you skating."

Over the years, I'd been involved with different charities and drives to teach kids hockey and skating basics. I enjoyed it immensely. Seeing a kid's eyes light up when they finally got the hang of it, watching their little bodies take to the ice, fed the kid in me who remembered what it was like to find something wonderful, something I could shape and control. I'd forgotten that.

Emma's teeth snagged her bottom lip, and she eyed me with clear hesitation. I knew that look too. She was nervous. Warmth spread through my chest, and I gave her an encouraging smile.

"We'll take it slow—" My words cut off abruptly as Emma shot onto the ice and took off. Just flew past me, all grace and flowing beauty.

Mouth gaping, I stood stunned as she raced along, doing figure eights. For a long moment, it didn't compute. Hadn't she said she couldn't skate? But there she was, gliding around like she was born to be on the ice. When she executed a jaunty camel spin, I burst out laughing. The little sneak had played me. She'd played me well and good.

I watched her move, golden hair trailing behind her like a banner, and it hit me hard, fast, and with utter completeness: I adored this woman. I was crazy for her.

I went out to meet her, keeping enough space so we wouldn't accidentally collide. She caught sight of me and flushed, gliding up to get close. We didn't stop but skated along with ease.

"Teach you to skate, huh?" I huffed out a light laugh.

She made a guilty face. "Technically, I said, *If* I couldn't skate, would you teach me?"

"Hmm . . ." I dragged the sound out, letting her squirm just a little. Mainly because I loved teasing her. She responded so beautifully to it.

"You mad?" she asked, slightly winded.

"Do I look mad, Snoopy?"

Her nose wrinkled cutely as she peered at me. "No . . . you look . . . weirdly smug."

Was that what she saw?

Grinning wide, I gave her a chance to skate a bit away; then I rushed her, scooping her up in my arms as she squealed in shock. Her thighs wrapped around my hips, and she clung to me. "Lucian!"

I kissed her forehead. "I've got you."

"You've got me; who's got you?" she quipped, relaxing a bit.

"Did you just quote super-campy seventies Superman to me?" I asked, chuckling.

"You started it." She held on a little tighter. "With your superhero body and whatnot."

"Whatnot?" I nuzzled her cheek, kissing my way along her soft skin as I took a lazy circuit around the rink.

"Skating with me in your arms like it's no big deal," she grumped while tilting her head enough to let me nip the edge of her jawline.

"You're light as a feather," I said. She snorted, and I kissed her again. "Tell me more about this superhero-body thing, though."

"Put me down, and I'll show you all my favorite highlights."

"Hold on," I instructed, then spun her around as she laughed and screeched. I set her down by the boards but kept my arms around her. "Where'd you learn to skate like that?"

Good to her word, her hands smoothed over my chest, stroking with appreciation. "There was a rink about two blocks from my house. I'd go there after school and take classes."

My hands found their way to the plump curve of her ass. "You have no idea how much it turns me on that you can skate."

"I have some idea." Her hips pressed against mine. "A pretty prominent clue there, Lucian."

"You are so getting some when we get home, Em."

She burst out laughing, her eyes sparking with humor. "I had no idea you were so easy."

"Yes, you did." I dipped my head and caught her mouth with mine, kissing her slow and deep, luxuriating in the warmth of her mouth against the relatively cold air. It swept over me that I was on the ice, enjoying myself. Happy. I was happy.

"Thank you," I said when we parted.

Her lips were slightly swollen and softly parted. "For what?"

"Bringing me here, getting me on the ice." I touched her cheek, brushing away an errant strand of her hair. "I didn't think I'd ever enjoy any aspect of skating again. But this is good. Necessary."

So was she. She had slid into my life at one of the worst possible times, and yet now that she was here, the thought of letting her go was unimaginable. Gratitude flooded me, and I rested my forehead against hers. As though she knew I was undone, she wound her arms around my waist and hugged me.

Before Emma, I didn't put much stock in hugging lovers. I hadn't seen the point of hugging unless it was a family member. I wasn't ashamed to admit I craved them from Emma. The press of her smaller curves against my larger frame made me want to cradle her with care. But the way she held me tight made *me* feel protected. And wasn't that a mindfuck?

I wrapped her up in my arms and grunted, wanting to tell her how much she meant to me but unable to form any actual words.

"I'll do the charity event," was what I ended up saying.

She kissed the center of my chest. "You're a good man, Lucian. And I'm proud of you."

I couldn't understand why she would be; all I'd done with my life was play hockey to the best of my ability, but I'd take her praise and hold it close. I didn't know how long we stood there; it felt so good I had no inclination to move. But eventually, she eased back.

"Come on then; let me see how fast you can go."

"You want me to show off for you, Em?"

"I do."

"Well then." I pushed off and did just that.

Chapter Thirty-One

Emma

The Raston fundraiser took place in Los Angeles, with a daytime skate and greet for the children and an evening dinner for all the donors. Lucian fell silent and tense on the drive down, but every so often, he'd reach out and rest his hand on my knee, as if to say he was still there with me.

I left him to his solitude, knowing that sometimes you had to work through some things yourself. If he needed me, I'd be here. By the time we arrived at the Staples Center, his leg bounced in an agitated rhythm as he scowled at the looming stadium.

"Hey," I said before we pulled up to the valet service, which was parking cars for other players.

Wintergreen eyes shadowed under severe brows looked my way. I wondered if he truly saw me in his disquiet. In deference to his beloved sport's rules, he wore a light-gray suit and ice-blue tie, which made him both devastatingly handsome and closed off.

"You got this." I touched his bouncing knee. "They love you."

Pale and pinched around the mouth, he stared at me, then blinked once. As if coming out of a trance, he took a long breath and gave me a tight smile. "I'm okay, Snoop."

I didn't think either of us was fooled, but he would be okay. I believed that much. I had to.

We went our separate ways once inside, Lucian instantly hailed and surrounded by his former teammates and fellow hockey players as I was ushered to a VIP section roped off for players' guests.

"Who are you here for?" asked a woman around my age with gorgeous raven hair that fell in a glossy sheet down her slim back. She looked familiar, but I couldn't place her.

"Lucian," I said, and she frowned, clearly not recognizing his name. "Luc Osmond."

Her expression cleared, and she smiled wide. "Oz is here? Really?"

"Yes."

"Oh my God, I'm so happy to hear that. We've really missed him, you know?"

Pride surged through me, and I found myself smiling back. Beaming, really. Because she was obviously excited, and Lucian was my man.

The woman stuck out her hand. "I'm May Chan. Drexel Harris is my husband."

We shook hands, when her name finally sank in. "Not the May Chan who owns Daisy Chain?"

"The very one."

I'd shopped at one of her vintage clothing stores a few times but had seen her only from afar. "I love your place. You have the best clothes."

May eyed my vintage 1940s A-line dress in dark-blue linen with little embroidered maroon butterflies on the bodice and grinned. "That's from Daisy Chain, isn't it?"

"It is."

"Another satisfied customer. Just what I love to see."

Our laughs cut short as the program began. The lights dimmed, and onto the ice came the hockey players, each of them escorted by a child on skates. It looked so damned cute, I found myself clapping and grinning wide. The players were announced in alphabetical order. As they neared Lucian's name, my insides clenched in anticipation.

The moment Lucian glided onto the ice, holding the hand of a little girl with a dark ponytail and a beaming smile, the stadium erupted into a ruckus of cheers. Goose pimples prickled over my skin.

He really did look like a man mountain in full gear, huge and eternal. His smile was the same tight one he'd given me before we'd parted, but as he continued to wave, and the crowd continued to holler and cheer, a real smile broke free—fleeting and shy—and my eyes burned with unshed tears.

"He looks good," May observed.

Of course he did. But it struck me that people might have assumed that Lucian had been diminished and sickly upon retirement. Is that what he feared they'd see when he came here? Either way, he was right in guessing that a lot of attention would be directed his way.

But he didn't show any tension as he took his place with the others, and they soon started a mock game, the guys working with the kids. I spotted Brommy and Anton on the ice, each of them helping out their own kid. But my eyes mainly stayed on Lucian. God, he was so good with the little girl he'd been paired with. Good with all of them.

He moved like he was born on the ice. And it broke my heart just a little bit more. I wanted to wrap him up and hold him close, this big strong man who'd been through so much in such short order.

"I can't believe he showed," said a woman behind me. I didn't turn but watched Lucian instead as her friend answered.

"I thought he couldn't skate."

I had no idea if they were talking about Lucian, but the chances were good, and my back went stiff, my ears homing in on their conversation.

"Well, he was an absolute mess when I left. Wouldn't even get out of bed."

"Oh, how sad. You poor thing."

My brow raised at that.

"I know. But it was for the best. He wasn't the man I thought he was, and I needed to move on."

"Such a shame. Ozzy would have been a legend."

"No more. Now he's just a . . ." An expansive breathy sigh stirred my hair. "A sideshow."

At that, I turned around. I couldn't help it. My hackles were up, and anger coiled in my belly. At my side, May stiffened too. Clearly she'd heard them as well.

Two women—one pale and blonde, one tanned and brunette—stood affecting tragic expressions. The blonde, who had to be Cassandra, was beautiful in the way of a catalog model: flawless but almost doll-like. It was uncharitable to liken her to a Barbie, but I wasn't feeling very generous at the moment.

Her big brown eyes locked onto me, and she gave me a bright smile. "Oh my God, are you Emma Maron?"

"I am." The words barely got past my locked jaw. I wanted to slap this woman. Which was a shock; I'd never wanted to raise a hand to anyone. Not even Greg when I'd found him cheating. But my hand twitched at my side.

Cassandra didn't seem to sense the danger and leaned closer. "I'm a huge fan of your show. Cassandra Lavlin. My fiancé is Adam Cashon." She looked at me expectantly.

"How nice." I wanted to turn away. I wanted to lay into her. I stood frozen.

She blinked, obviously expecting more. "And you're with?"

"Lucian Osmond."

It was fairly gratifying to watch the color leach from her face.

"Oh. I . . . ah . . . I know Luc . . . Lucian, that is."

"I know."

"You do?" She appeared pleased at this and glanced toward the ice. It didn't take any special talent to know she was looking at Lucian. *You don't deserve to set eyes on him.*

"Yes, his cousin Anton said Lucian had been engaged to a woman named Cassandra."

Her smile was a little less steady now, and she eyed me with wariness.

"How lucky for you to find another fiancé so soon."

May made a strangled noise of amusement, and Cassandra's friend glared.

"Uh . . ." Cassandra's nose wrinkled, and I knew she was trying to work out if I'd insulted her. "Thanks."

My answering smile was glacial. "I really should thank *you*."

"Thank me?" Confused brown eyes blinked rapidly.

"Yes. If you hadn't walked out on Lucian, I might not have met him. He's the best man I've ever known. So thank you."

At that, I turned my back on her. I could have said more, said worse, but she wasn't worth it. I moved to sit, but her hand on my arm stopped me. She'd stepped away from her friend and faced me on the stairs.

"Look, I know it sounded bad, what I was saying about Luc. But you should know hockey defines him. Without it, he's nothing more than a shell."

"You're wrong. He's so much more than that."

Her smile was tight and wary. "I hope for your sake that's true. Because the man I knew wasn't capable of loving anything more than the sport."

As though feeling my gaze, Lucian's head lifted, and his gaze collided with mine. Something light and sweet flashed in his eyes, and he smiled, giving me a wave. His smile dimmed when he clearly spotted Cassandra with me. I pushed a wide smile, but he didn't return it.

At my side, Cassandra took it all in. "Good luck with Luc."

She left then, heading for the boards. The program was over, and the players were meeting and greeting more fans and parents. My heels clicked on the concrete stairs as I descended, matching the pounding of my heart. I wanted to touch him, hear his voice, be close to him. I needed that.

Lucian skated up to meet me, beautiful man mountain that he was. He looked down at me from his great height with tenderness and affection, but his jaw was set in a hard line. "She bother you?"

He sounded as though he'd very much make an issue of it if I said yes. Lucian cared. He cared so much he rarely let anyone see it. But I saw him. I leaned in, resting my belly on the boards. "No, she doesn't bother me. Does she bother you?"

"No." His smile was tight, worried. "Not anymore."

I searched his face, wanting to reassure him, wanting him. "That woman did not deserve you."

Light filled his eyes with a quiet happiness. "We were poorly suited. I was meant for you."

"Kiss me."

Lucian's mouth twitched, but the tension left him. "There's a lot of press around, Snoop. You okay with being seen as mine?"

"That depends. Are you okay with being seen as *mine*?"

His gloved hand slipped behind my neck to cup my nape. "I'll wear a name tag declaring it if you want, honey." He kissed me, soft and deep and long.

I felt it in my belly, in the clench of my chest that filled with both longing and satisfaction. My hands found the bulky pads of his shoulders, and I clutched his jersey as I kissed him back. It wasn't until I heard a wolf whistle and Brommy's familiar voice catcalling us that I eased back.

Lucian smiled at me, a private look that promised more later.

"You were terrific," I said a little breathlessly, not willing to move away from him.

The corners of his mouth curled. "It was fun." He gave the back of my neck a squeeze. "Come on; I'll introduce you to everyone."

A long carpet had been placed on the ice for people to walk on and say hello. Lucian led me to a group of guys, all of them towering over me in their skates. I met Lucian's friends, the people who'd been such a huge part of his life.

It was clear that the guys loved and respected the hell out of him. They seemed to miss Lucian as much as Lucian missed them but were resigned to it. They'd all have to face the same someday.

A craggy, silver-haired man in his fifties came over to us.

"Em, this is Davis Rickman, my former coach. Rickman, this is . . ."

"Emma Maron. I watch your show religiously." Rickman shook my hand. "Pleasure to meet you."

Given that everyone here seemed to watch my show and felt the need to tell me, it was becoming a little easier to hear the praise. Whatever I did with the rest of my life, I'd entertained a good portion of people during my stint on *Dark Castle*. That was a reward in and of itself.

Rickman eyed Lucian. "You okay with the next half?"

Lucian might as well have been made of marble. "Of course."

The next half was a show of running drills, trick shots, and what I thought of as fancy skating. Watching Lucian speed around maneuvering the puck was sexy as hell.

God, he was beautiful when he skated. Joyous but also focused, that stern expression and ice-green eyes making for a combo that had many fans calling out and whistling in sheer lust. I was one of them. But then, I got to go home with him.

Lucky me.

"He's extraordinary, isn't he?"

I turned to find Rickman standing next to me. "Yes." But I wasn't talking about hockey.

I didn't like the way Rickman looked at Lucian, as though assessing every move he made. There was something covetous that rubbed me raw. "He was lucky to have a coach who knew to let him go."

Rickman turned my way, his eyes half hidden under bushy brows. "It was his choice. Not mine."

"You wanted him to stay?"

He shrugged. "Our hands were tied. But he's still the best player I've ever coached. Hockey smarts like you dream about."

I didn't know what to say to that and went back to clapping when Lucian whizzed by.

"Really is a pity," Rickman mused.

"He's alive," I snapped. "The pity would be if he died."

Flat blue eyes peered at me from a face set in stubborn if not sorrowful lines. "Some players would tell you they were better off that way than to have a career cut short."

Rage bubbled in my veins, but I managed to keep my tone cool. "Anyone who thinks that is a fool."

Rickman merely shrugged and went back to watching the players. "I'm not the one you need to convince."

Lucian

"So." Emma smiled up at me as she wrapped her arm around my waist, and we left the stadium.

"So," I repeated, biting back a grin. She was too adorable and felt perfectly right tucked up against me. Emma nudged my ribs, getting my ticklish spot, the evil woman.

I most definitely did not giggle. I grabbed her fiendish hand and pressed a kiss to her fingertips. "Did you have fun, Snoop?"

"Yes." She leaned her head on my shoulder, humming. "You were spectacular. A truly phenomenal player."

I'd been told that in so many different ways over the years that it had lost its meaning. But hearing the words fall from Emma's pretty mouth, her tone reverential and filled with awe, had nothing but pure pride swelling up in my chest. I wanted to crow, strut . . . pick her up, and spin her around for the joy of making her smile and laugh.

She'd gotten a small taste of who I'd been, me at my best. She'd witnessed fans cheering for me and cheered along with them, her eyes shining with pride. It made me want to put that look on her face every day of my life. I wanted her admiration, to make her proud all the time.

My chest ached with a sudden fierceness that had me pressing my hand to it. But she didn't notice. She was still chatting about all my "effortless skill," which was cute but made me feel like a sham.

Seeing her talk to Cassandra hadn't helped. The exchange hadn't looked friendly, and I could have guessed what Cass had said, but I didn't want to ask Emma. Mainly because I didn't want her to stop looking at me as though I was her hero.

I thought you were more than hockey, Oz. I see now that you weren't.

Annoyed that I even thought of Cassandra's last words to me, I shoved her into the back of my mind and caught Emma's hand.

A crowd waited on the edges of the roped-off area leading to the valet. Several players were signing autographs. As we drew near, shouts went out, calling my name. Emma waggled her golden brows. "Your public awaits."

"You mind?"

"Why would I mind? Fans deserve your time."

We headed their way, and I was quickly inundated with demands for autographs. But when I heard her name being called, I looked up.

Emma had been noticed. And all these die-hard hockey fans had swarmed. There was security nearby, and Emma didn't seem to be overwhelmed or nervous. On the contrary, her smile was gracious and beautiful as she signed autographs and posed for selfies.

"She really your girlfriend?"

The guy whose Osmond jersey I'd been signing glanced at Emma and then back to me, as though he couldn't quite believe it. Some days I couldn't either—not because of who she was to the world, but for the simple fact that there was no one I liked more than her.

"Yep. That's my girl."

"You lucky fucker." He was in his late teens, acne riddling the edges of his jaw, his body not yet filled in. I remembered those years. I didn't remember being so blunt, but I couldn't argue with his sentiment.

"More than you know." I handed him back his pen and jersey. I had intended to go over to Emma. But found I couldn't move. God, she glowed.

I now recognized how much of a hit her confidence had taken when she'd first arrived at Rosemont. She had always been beautiful, smart, and headstrong, but she hadn't radiated this level of self-assurance and happiness at first.

Rosemont had healed her.

I wanted to take some credit for her transformation as well. Without doubt, she'd brought me back to life, made me want to be a better man. But had I done something similar for her? I knew she liked being with me. But could I make her proud? Because after today, I would go back to Rosemont as a man without direction.

Her star was on the rise, while mine had fallen. A lump swelled in my throat as I stared at her. It was perhaps prophetic, or maybe a wish granted, that my phone buzzed with an incoming text from my agent, Carlos.

Something kicked hard and potent in the center of my chest. Rickman and my team's GM, Clark, wanted to meet.

Carlos: I'm not promising anything. But they have some interesting ideas that I think we should hear out.

I glanced up at Emma, still working the crowd, and my fingers tightened around my phone, a weird surge of fear and hope swirling within me. My fingers were steady as I responded:

I'll be there.

CHAPTER THIRTY-TWO

Emma

"Come with me." I took Lucian's hand and led him out onto the private patio of our bungalow. We'd been apart all day—Lucian in meetings, and me in meetings, then hanging out with Tate. I had so much to tell him; excitement and anticipation bubbled in my veins like freshly popped champagne. But that could wait. Here and now was our time.

The Marilyn Bungalow was booked, so Lucian had reserved us Bungalow 5, which had one particular feature I wanted to use. A pool.

He stopped at its edge, and a small smile played around the edges of his lips. "How did I know you'd eventually lead me out here?"

I toed off my sandals. "That's what you get when you torment innocent women with your late-night hot-body aquatics show."

He laughed, the sound rich and rumbling. Free. Lucian might not have been fully healed in mind and spirit, but he was slowly losing the tension that rode him and was starting to come out of his shell. I loved it.

"Hot body, huh?" Wintergreen eyes twinkled in the twilight.

"You know it, Brick. You're a walking inducement to sex. Temptation with swagger."

His nostrils flared, but his tone was smooth as cream. "You say the nicest things, Snoop."

"Mmm . . . now off with the clothes, honey pie."

Lucian's brow quirked, but he was far too distracted by me pulling my dress overhead to reply for a good moment. When he did, his voice had gone gruff. "You're stripping."

I grinned wide. "Observant tonight, aren't we?"

His lips twitched. "You really want to do this?"

I knew what he meant. High walls and greenery surrounded the pool on all sides, but it wasn't a private home. There was a chance we might be seen by some enterprising wall-climbing paparazzi. An admitted infinitesimal chance. But Lucian and I were both hyper-aware of our fame. Thing was, I didn't care anymore. If someone wanted to go to such lengths to try to embarrass me, there was nothing I could do about it. I wanted to live. I wanted to rejoice in life and just be.

I reached behind me and unhooked my bra.

Lucian let out a low groan when I tossed it aside. "Hell, Em. I don't think I'll ever not want you."

The intensity of his gaze felt like a velvet glove along my skin. "Good, because you're going to get me. A lot."

He grunted, the sound pleased and slightly predatory. A new pulse of heat went up my thighs and tightened my sex.

My fingers hooked on my panties, but I paused. "You're not stripping."

Lucian blinked, as if coming out of a fog, then shot me a wry look as he whipped off his shirt. Lord, but he was beautifully built, strong yet graceful, defined and tight. The olive tone of his skin took on shades of pale blue and grays in the dim of the evening. He held my gaze as his fingers fumbled with the button of his jeans. I grinned and slid my panties off.

"Fuck . . ." He blew out a hard breath, stalling, watching.

I laughed and slowly walked into the water, my breath catching a little at the sudden cool.

The first time Lucian had stripped for me, it had been a show. That much was clear now. This time, his clothes came off in a flash, flying onto a lounger in his haste. He gave me a narrow look as he walked up to the side and dropped into the water. But as soon as he swam near, I darted away.

"So it's like that, huh?" He gave me an arch look, laughter in his eyes. Then came after me.

I squealed, for the fun of it, and evaded. The pool wasn't very big or deep, and I wasn't really trying to get away. He caught me in under a minute, chuckling as he hauled me against the hard, warm length of his body. Laughing, I clung to his water-slicked shoulders and brushed a lock of wet hair off his brow.

"You caught me. Now what are you going to do with me?"

Humming, Lucian drifted us around. "I'm creating a mental list." His big hands slid down my back and cupped my butt, holding me against an impressive erection.

He chuckled again when I squirmed against him, biting my lip in lust and impatience. His mouth caught mine, and he softly suckled my abused lower lip. But he made no further move. He didn't need to. We both luxuriated in the simple act of holding on to each other, kissing slowly, thoroughly.

"I should have done this the first time we were in a pool together," he said against my lips, his hot and lazy.

I nuzzled his mouth. "Well, I tried to tempt you."

"Tried?" Lucian huffed out a laugh that ended up a self-deprecating groan. "I ended up fucking my hand all night and wishing it was you."

I wrapped my legs around his trim waist and wiggled, just enough for him to feel my slick sex against his hardness. He groaned again, his grip on my butt tightening. I bit his lower lip. "So did I."

"Fuck, Em . . ."

For long moments we drifted and kissed, murmuring words of need and encouragement. Lucian's shoulders hit the edge of the pool, and he held me close. Water spiked his long lashes, radiating them outward from pale-green eyes that weren't cold but filled with affection. "I shouldn't have resisted you. It was an exercise in failure."

"Resistance *is* futile."

Lucian laughed, slow and deep, but his expression remained thoughtful. "To think, we could have been doing this all along."

I peppered kisses over his cheek, his jaw, then stopped and smiled wide. "Well, there is something to be said for anticipation."

He touched my brow, wiping away a trickle of water, as his gaze searched my face. "God, Em, you look . . ."

"What?" I rasped, my heart thudding against the fragile wall of my chest.

"Happy," he said, his own smile blooming. "You look so happy."

"Because I am." I stared right back at him. "Because of you."

Lucian swallowed hard, his throat working. "I make you happy?"

"Of course you do." I cupped his damp cheek. "How could you not know that?"

He stared at me for a moment, then dipped his head and kissed me fiercely. It lit up my body, swooping through my belly, fluttering in my heart.

"Em . . ." His mouth chased and cherished. "You don't know . . . how could you know . . ." He trailed off, kissing my neck, my cheek, my mouth once more. "Everything was dark and empty until you came. No flavor. No joy."

He shuddered, resting his forehead against mine. "I'm just really glad I make you happy."

I held him close, our breaths mingling. "I live in a world of egos and make-believe. I thought fame was what I needed, that I'd be safe if I had it." Water lapped at our chests as I took in his face. "You're not safe, Lucian. But you're real. When I'm with you, I feel alive. I'm just me. And it took knowing you to understand that's the best thing any of us can be."

Night fell around us, the water tinkling as we stared at each other. Lucian's chest rose and fell as he held me, taking in my words. When he spoke, his voice seemed to come from the deepest part of him. "I don't know what I did to deserve you, Em. But I swear I'll do my damned best to make sure I earn the right to keep you."

Before I could tell him he'd already earned that right, he kissed me again and then promptly lifted us out of the water, heading for the bed.

———

Lucian

"God, you feel so good." Lying face to face, our bodies tangled up together as close as we could get, I pumped up into Emma's slick heat and groaned. Trembling, I cupped her flushed cheek and kissed her soft mouth. I loved her for hours, nice and slow, every inch of me aching for release, but drawing it out for as long as I could. We'd been at it all night and, now, in the hot sun of the morning.

"Lucian." She rocked with me, the tips of her breasts brushing my chest.

Grunting, I reached between us; found her sweet, swollen nipple; and tweaked it. The walls of her sex clenched in response, and she circled her hips on a moan. So fucking good.

So good I felt like I was flying.

Emma was in my arms, and all was right with the world. I couldn't pinpoint the exact moment that became my truth; maybe it had been from the moment we met. From the first, she made me smile, threw sunshine and air into my dark, closed-up world.

I needed her like I had needed the ice, like I needed food and water. I kissed her again, licked the plump curve of her lower lip. "Em. It's never been like this," I whispered. "Never like this."

Our gazes collided just as I hit a spot that had her coming around my dick, squeezing it so tightly I saw stars. I followed her with a long, ragged groan, pouring myself into her with tight, hard strokes.

Empty and replete, I pulled her impossibly closer with a sigh. For a long moment, we lay in perfect silence, content to just hold on to each other. Then she tilted her head to look up at me.

A sleepy but content smile lit her eyes. "You've reduced me to a boneless puddle."

I smoothed my hand over the silken curve of her cheek. "Let me do it again."

I was mostly serious. I didn't think I'd be able to move for a while. She'd wrecked me too.

With a dramatic groan she flopped back, then snuggled into the crook of my arm. "I need a long hot bath first. And coffee." She blinked up at me. "God, I would kill for one of your croissants right now."

I bit back a grin. As we were still at the hotel, that would have to wait. "It's gratifying to know you want me for my baked goods."

"And your dick too."

I choked on a laugh, then ducked my head to nuzzle her neck. "Saucy, Snoopy."

"Mmm." Her finger traced the whorls of hair on my chest. "I had a good conversation with my agent yesterday."

After the fundraiser, Emma had taken a meeting with her agent while I'd talked to Rickman and Clark. Neither of us had had the chance to discuss it with the other, as we'd basically gone at it like horny teens the second we were alone in our hotel room again. I couldn't say I was in a rush to tell her about my news; I knew it wasn't going to go over well. I concentrated on hers instead.

"What did your agent say?"

"There's a part. The director and producers both want me. It's a drama based on a huge bestselling thriller."

She told me the title, and I whistled low. "Who do they want you to play?"

"Beatrice."

I knew the book. Beatrice was the main protagonist, who was either slowly dissolving into madness or was actually being stalked by a killer; the audience wouldn't know until the end. If Emma pulled it off, she'd be a huge star.

"You can do this," I said with conviction.

She gripped my arm, holding on. "I know. I can feel it. This is my part."

I kissed her swift and soft. "Where is it being shot?"

"Here in LA for the most part. I think there are some scenes in Nevada as well." Her smile gentled. "I won't go far."

The promise had me pausing; the reality of our situation, of how I'd soon change it, crept back up to poke at my insides. I hadn't told her my news. I couldn't now. Not in the face of her happiness.

I pushed the thought away and concentrated on kissing her lips, light pecks that didn't need to lead anywhere but sent pulses of pleasure down my spine each time I touched her.

She made a noise of contentment, her fingers combing through my hair. "Oh, and there's something else."

"Something bigger than a kickass role in a potential blockbuster?"

"Well, not that good, but I think it's pretty great."

"Tell me, sweet Em."

She cuddled into me. "I want to take you somewhere. Will you come with me?"

"Not going to tell me where?"

"It's a surprise."

"Mysterious. I like it. I'll come." I tugged the comforter away, baring her to my gaze. "But you first."

After a long, thorough exchange, we both came.

CHAPTER
THIRTY-THREE

Lucian

The house was in Los Feliz where the road wound its way up into the hills toward Griffith Observatory. Hidden behind a private stucco gate, it was a Spanish revival–style estate from the 1920s. In a lot of ways, it was a smaller version of Rosemont, with its terra-cotta-shingled roof, white plaster walls, darkly arching doorways, and beamed ceilings. Roses clung to the walls and dotted the courtyard.

Our steps were quiet as she led me through a grand living room with a carved-stone fireplace, past a library paneled in oak, and into a light-filled kitchen with wide windows overlooking an oasis of a pool. Worn marble counters stretched cool and smooth under my palm. I surveyed the double-wall ovens and eight-burner stove. This was a chef's kitchen. And clearly the heart of a well-loved home.

"It's private," Emma was saying, walking to the arched double doors that opened to the outside. "And quiet."

"It has good light." My gaze roamed the kitchen, taking in the massive walk-in pantry and breakfast area. I had Jean Philipe's old farm table in storage. It would fit perfectly right here, glowing in the sunlight.

Glass-paned cabinets and shelves lined the far wall. More than enough room to hold platters, plates, cookware, crockery. I glanced up at Emma, feeling her stare.

She smiled shyly at me. "You like it."

"I do." Didn't explain the way my heart threatened to beat out of my chest.

"I'm buying it."

There it was. I'd expected it; why else would she bring me to see a house for sale? But the confirmation still hit with the force of a well-placed kick. "How many bedrooms?"

"Five." She didn't move from her spot in the sun.

"Kind of big for one person."

"Yes. But it feels good here. Like home." Her gaze didn't falter from mine.

Home. Hers. Away from mine. But did I really have a home? Rosemont was Amalie's. Yes, I'd always be welcome, and it had been my refuge. But was it home or a safe space to hide away from the world?

I ran my hand along the counter once more. Unlike so many counters in high-end California homes, this one was old. It had a history, its tale told through faint stains and the silky smoothness of the marble. It would be excellent for tempering chocolate, rolling out dough.

Home. The temptation of creating one with Emma burned in my gut like boiling sugar, sweet but painful. Because I couldn't do that. Not now, at least. "When are you moving?"

The floorboards creaked as she stepped a bit closer. "As soon as I can. Maybe two weeks."

I absorbed that. She was always supposed to go. And it wasn't that far from Rosemont. Why did it cut into me? Why did I feel cold along my skin, as though she were already gone?

Fuck. That hurt. She said I made her happy. I wanted to make her happy *and* proud.

"Lucian?"

"Yeah?" I tried to make it sound light, but the word came out terse.

Her expression was pained yet welcoming, as though she was trying to tell me something I kept missing. "Where do you really live?"

"What do you mean *where*? I live at Rosemont."

A little wrinkle formed between her brows. "You always lived there?"

"Of course not." I ran a hand along the back of my neck. "I had a condo in DC. A nice place in Georgetown, overlooking the Potomac. I sold it because I had no need for it anymore."

Did she think I was that bad off? Christ, I had been a star. I made over eighty million in my years of playing, with more coming in from endorsements. I was a wealthy man. Frankly, I probably made more than she did. Even without playing. Instantly, I felt like a dick for thinking that.

Maybe my scowl projected more of my thoughts than I realized, because she shook her head, as though apologizing. "It's just . . . we never talk about it. Your life. You stay in Rosemont like you're hiding away—"

"I'm not hiding away. I'm there because . . ." My throat constricted, and I made an aggrieved noise to clear it. "Mamie needs company."

Shit. It sounded utterly ridiculous. And we both knew it.

"That's it?" she asked softly, gently. "You're devoting the rest of your life to keeping Amalie company?"

My gut twisted, and I grunted, sliding my eyes from her, then getting pissed about that and glaring back defiantly. "She's my grandmother."

"I know. But what about your life?" She was closer now, facing me from the other side of the long kitchen island. "You're so young. You have so many options—"

"That's right," I cut in, feeling that old resentment, that old thwarted frustration build. "I do."

She paused, her brow knitting again. "You do," she repeated, unsure.

I puffed out a breath. "I didn't want to discuss it right now. But I talked to Rickman."

"Your old coach?"

I nodded. "Rickman, yes. And to Clark, the general manager of my team, as well as Jack Morison, the owner." My hands spread out onto the counter, pressing down to ground me. "If my doctors give me the all clear, and if I feel good about playing, they'll take me back."

It was as though all the air whooshed out of the room. Emma's mouth fell open, and she gaped at me in horror.

"They'll take you back?" She paled. "But you retired."

"We are all aware of that, Em."

"You retired," she said more forcefully, "because you were in danger of damaging your brain. Permanently."

"I know," I snapped. Then took a breath. "But I'm still in top shape. Being on the ice again . . . it felt good. I could still do this. I could just . . ."

"Just what? Fucking die?" She said it shrilly, then bit her lip like she was struggling to calm down.

"I'll be careful," I said, struggling, too, when all I wanted to do was shout. "I'll be very careful."

"Playing hockey. A full-contact sport." She snorted, making a face. "The very sport that got you into this position to begin with."

"Emma . . ."

"Don't Emma me." She waved a hand, as though she could bat her irritation away. "Don't . . . placate me!"

"Fine. I won't." I gripped the sides of the counter. "Then don't lecture me like I'm an ignorant kid."

"Then don't act like an ignorant kid," she retorted hotly. "Use that very great and very precious brain of yours. This is irrational—"

"Oh, for fuck's sake—"

"You used that brilliant brain when you retired. Use it again, damn it."

My teeth clacked together, and I ground them, unable to reply without yelling.

Energy crackled around Emma, lighting her eyes, drawing the lines of her body into sharp relief. She was beautiful, terrifying. "What about Delilah's offer? You love baking, creating desserts. You're an artist—"

"I'm a hockey player!" My shout echoed in the space and bounced back at me. "It's all I ever was or wanted to be!" The sound that tore from me was like a wounded animal's, shaming me, enraging me. I pounded a fist on the counter. "Don't lecture me on what I am when I have the chance to . . . to . . . fuck."

I turned away, my throat clogging. Panting, I set my hands on my hips and blinked rapidly to clear the burning prickle behind my lids.

Silence had a weight and coldness to it. I closed my eyes and took a breath. "I'm in the best shape of my life, Em. I can do this. I'll be careful now. I know what's at stake."

The words were as brittle as spun sugar. But she didn't smash through them like I expected. She didn't fight me. Her sigh was soft, a puff of air. I wouldn't have even heard it if I hadn't been so attuned to her response, waiting for the fight I wanted to have.

"You're never going to be happy with anything else, are you?" she said.

A ripple of *something* went through me, and all I could do was shake my head in negation. Closed off and shut down, the last thing I expected was for her arms to wrap around me from behind, for her to press against me and hold on tight.

I didn't expect it. But the second she did it, my body reacted with a full shudder, my heart kicking against the cage of my ribs. I cupped her slim forearms, rubbing her silky skin, needing that contact.

"I don't want to fight," she said.

I turned then, pulling her close. "I don't want to either."

We stood quietly, hugging in the kitchen that would soon be hers. I rested my cheek on her head, breathing in the scent of her hair, soaking up the warmth of her body. But too soon, Emma pulled away and tilted her head back. Her indigo gaze moved over my face.

"If you play for your old team, that means you're going back to DC."

The truth rippled out like a stone thrown into a pond. Again, she'd voiced something I hadn't wanted to. But it was out now. I let my arms slide from her, when all I wanted to do was hold tighter. "Nothing's set. This is just a tentative trial, but yes, if I play . . . DC is where I'd be based, but I'll travel all over."

"I know the drill." Her smile was wry and forced. "I'll be busy as well. Production starts soon. In fact, I have my first meeting next week. You know, to go run through some ideas, meet the cast, that sort of thing."

She stepped away, wandering around the kitchen. "This place needs a good farm table. Something like Amalie has in hers. Maybe a hanging rack for copper pots and pans over the island."

Emma babbling was not a good sign. A lump formed in my chest, growing in size as she talked about what she wanted to do to this place.

"The master bedroom has a partially enclosed balcony that over-looks the pool . . ." Her voice trailed off as she frowned. And I knew she was thinking about the balcony in her little house at Rosemont and the night she'd watched me swim naked.

Sorrow swamped me. This felt like a death. The end of us. I wanted to stop it. I *could*. All I had to do was say the right words. But they'd be a lie. I had to try, or I would forever be wondering if I had made the right decision. I'd never get out from under the loss. And I couldn't take any more loss in my life. Not right now.

"I don't want to lose you," I blurted out.

Emma glanced over at me, an uncomfortable expression drawing the lines of her face tight.

I stared back, imploring her to understand. "I just found you. But I can't walk away from this last chance. I want to feel like myself again, Em."

Her shoulders slumped on a sigh. "I know you do." She visibly swallowed. "I'm not going anywhere, Lucian."

But I was. And we both knew that it would take me away from her all the same.

CHAPTER THIRTY-FOUR

Emma

I wasn't numb. *Numb* implied a lack of feeling, and I felt everywhere. Horrible cramping feeling. I hadn't known it was possible to be so afraid for someone who was determined to ignore the danger they faced.

I glanced at Lucian's hard profile as he concentrated on the finishing touches of the seared-salmon lunch he was prepping. Lemony-yellow sunlight shone through the kitchen window and glinted off his inky hair. He appeared calm but not content.

Couldn't be helped. The ride back to Rosemont had been tense, each of us quiet and in our own corners. I'd hated every second of it. Somehow Lucian had become the central feature of my world, and it just wasn't a happy place when we were on the outs.

Not that either of us apparently wanted to admit we were in a prolonged fight. I was too good at pretending pain away, and so was he.

An awful solution, given that my anxiety and hurt ratcheted up every moment I kept my mouth shut. Now, a day later, we were making lunch for his family. Rather, Lucian was making it, and I kept him company in my customary perch at the kitchen bench.

A silent sigh rippled through me. I had hoped he would love the kitchen of the house I wanted to buy. I had hoped he'd see the possibility of turning that house into a home for the two of us. Which was just plain stupidity on my part. It was too soon to expect him to live with me. Not that I had gathered up the courage to even ask. We never spoke of love or forever. Why should I have expected anything?

But I had. I had built castles once again, picturing us in that smaller version of Rosemont. A place all our own. And he'd crushed it with one swoop. He was leaving.

It might have been easier to take if it wasn't for a career that could very likely kill him.

Grimacing, I looked away.

"It's ready." His deep voice sliced through the silence.

"I'll get the bread."

Stilted and not in the least bit genuine. That was how we talked now.

Swallowing convulsively, I grabbed the big breadbasket as he watched me with those cool-green eyes. I knew it upset him that I wasn't instantly on board with his plan. Just as I knew he honestly didn't want to hurt me. We were simply at an impasse.

Lucian carried the main dish, and we were met by Tina, who ran back for the iced tea.

"Well then," said Amalie with a clap of her bejeweled hands. "This looks lovely."

Sal moved aside a platter of ruby-ripe sliced tomatoes to make room for the fish. "I'm freaking starved."

"You're always starved," Lucian said dryly, earning a flick of Sal's neon-green manicured fingers.

"Now, where is Anton?" Amalie murmured, looking about the terrace, as though he might pop out of the shrubbery. But he walked through the kitchen doors, helping Tina with the drinks by carrying two bottles of wine.

I sat back and watched the way the Osmonds moved together, making everything just so, varying expressions of peace and expectation gracing their attractive faces. And at their center, stern and watchful Lucian directing them all.

Sadness warred with utter affection. For all of them. They were people who loved life, loved good food and good conversation. And they shared it with whoever needed those comforts.

After Sal poured her a glass of chardonnay, Amalie raised her glass with a gleam in her jade eyes as she looked at each of us. Lucian might have been the captain, but she was the queen.

"On trinque?"

Her grandchildren immediately answered as one. "À votre santé."

Sal and I repeated it and followed the ritual of clinking glasses with everyone. When Lucian turned to touch my glass, he held my gaze and murmured, *"À ta santé."*

My lids lowered, emotion filling me too hard and fast. And he knew it. His lips brushed my temple as he breathed my name. "Em."

I loved this man. And it was killing me.

When we pulled apart, I found Amalie smiling, pleased as punch. I blinked back tears and accepted the tomato plate Tina passed my way.

"So then," Amalie said. "Now that I have all my babies here, I have an announcement."

A ripple went around the table, and everyone but me seemed to brace themselves.

"I have decided I miss France. So"—she waved an elegant hand—"I am returning to Paris."

"You go to Paris every spring," Lucian said, his expression ever deadpan.

"Hush, you." She sniffed, as if offended, but we all knew she wasn't. "I am going to live in Paris permanently. My time here is over. New memories must be made."

The woman was seventy-five years old, and still she took life by the reins and guided it wherever she pleased. That was what I wanted: to have Amalie's fearlessness, her lust for life.

"Are you going to sell Rosemont?" Lucian couldn't quite hide the fear in his voice. I didn't blame him. This was his refuge and his childhood all rolled into one.

"Of course she's not," Tina said, with a slightly annoyed glance at him. "She's going to give it to you."

"Me?"

Anton snorted. "You act surprised."

Lucian's gaze narrowed and froze. "Because I am. I have no greater claim on this place than any of you."

"Oh, please. You're her favorite."

"If you're not, Ant, that's only because you're an ass—"

Amalie clapped her hands once. "Hush. All of you." She glared at each of them in turn. "Of course I am not selling, Lucian. How ridiculous. And you two. How dare you suggest I'd show that sort of favoritism?"

Tina winced. "Apologies, Mamie. It's only that Lucian lived here with you as a kid, and he's been fixing it up."

Anton simply grunted.

Amalie took a slow sip of her wine before continuing. "I will, of course, visit Rosemont now and then, but I am leaving the property to the four of you in equal partnership."

"Four?" Anton blinked in confusion.

Amalie quirked a brow. "You, Lucian, Tina, and Salvador."

Sal made a choking sound, his copper skin turning dark bronze. "Amalie . . . you . . . I . . ."

"You are like a grandson to me, my dear," she said with steel in her voice and kindness in her eyes. "And I shall not take no for an answer."

The threat that she'd fight any of her actual grandchildren who objected was also clear as a bell.

Sal sat back with a strangled gasp, now pasty and sweating.

Lucian flashed him a wide, amused smile. "Face it, Sallie—you're officially one of us now."

"Puta . . ."

Tina reached over to pat his hands. "Mamie is right. We love you, Sal."

Anton merely shrugged. "You're as much a part of Rosemont as Mamie is." He turned to his grandmother. "Thing is, Mamie, I can't be here to take care of this place. You might as well—"

She quelled him with a look. "Now then. I do not expect any of you to live here year-round, although, if that is your choice, you certainly may. Either way, there is a trust in place to take care of maintenance and the taxes."

Lucian and Anton exchanged a look. I knew Lucian well enough to understand that neither man would dip into those funds to pay for Rosemont. They were both wealthy enough to take care of the place themselves. As for Tina, I had no idea what she would do. But she immediately brightened.

"I'd like to live here." She turned to Lucian and Sal. "If that's okay with you two."

Lucian's eyes crinkled at the corners. "Sweetheart, you heard Mamie; it's as much your place as it is mine."

"Yeah, but you've been living here for a while. I don't want to step on your toes."

"You asking me?" Sal laughed faintly. "I'm still trying to pinch myself."

"Here, let me help." Lucian made as if to pinch Sal and was promptly swatted away. Lucian chuckled, but it quickly died down, and he shifted in his seat. "Thing is, I'm not going to be at Rosemont for a while."

"Oh?" Amalie sent a knowing glance my way, as if she'd been expecting this. I wanted to crawl under the table. She was oh-so wrong. "Do tell, Titou."

Lucian cleared his throat, took a sip of iced tea, then cleared his throat again. "I've been asked by the Caps to come in and see about playing for them again."

It was as if a bomb had gone off, and the table exploded.

"Are you fucking insane?"

"Luc, no!"

"Madre de dios."

"Non! Non, non, non!" Amalie emphasized each *no* with a smack to the table. Tears swarmed in her eyes. "You cannot, Titou. You cannot."

Lucian thrust his chin up and out in that dogged, determined way of his. "Mamie, I can."

Her eyes flashed. "Just because you *can* does not mean you should."

"Nothing is set in stone. They want to see how I do, and I'll get to see how I feel back on the ice."

"You promised me, Lucian." Her voice cracked at his name, and she glanced away.

"I know." Lucian's jaw worked. "But I have to do this for myself. Not for you or anyone else."

I cringed when they turned their outraged glances on me.

"Don't look at Emma like that," Lucian said in a hard tone. "She's got nothing to do with this."

That hurt more than I expected, and I ducked my head, my fingers twisting in the linen napkin on my lap.

"I will not be party to this," Amalie said, rising. Her voice shook as she glared at her stubborn, proud grandson. "I love you with all my heart, but I will not watch you destroy yourself."

She walked away, and I saw something crack in Lucian's eyes. But he didn't try to stop her. I understood then that Lucian would never beg for affection or understanding. He didn't know how.

CHAPTER THIRTY-FIVE

Lucian

My news went over about as well as I'd expected it to, which was to say spectacularly badly. Even after expecting the reaction I got, it hurt. My chest felt like it was caving in; my stomach twisted and burned.

One by one, they left me at the table, their bitter disappointment clear and cutting. All of them except Emma. She sat quietly at my side even now, her slim shoulders slumped.

"Well," I said. "That was some shit."

She didn't say anything for so long I thought she might have been ignoring me, but then she swallowed audibly and lifted her head. Her indigo eyes were filled with sorrow. "What did you expect?"

I flinched, hating her disappointment most of all. "About what I got."

She snorted eloquently but said no more.

I shifted in my seat to face her. "Just say it."

Some color found its way to her cheeks. Good. I wanted a fight.

"What do you want me to say, Lucian?"

"Anything. The truth."

"You don't want the truth."

I pushed back from the table. "I know you're all worried—"

"No," she cut in sharply. "We are terrified."

I took the hit and breathed deeply. She didn't understand. None of them did. "I want you to be proud of me."

"I am. In so many ways. You're smart, multitalented, dryly funny, and so very strong. You're a fighter, Lucian. I admire that so much in you."

"Then how can you not see that this is me fighting? I'm climbing back to the top."

Her hand gripped the edge of the table as she leaned in. "You're clinging on to an ideal. That isn't fighting. That's desperation."

She pitied me. That was worse than any anger she could have thrown my way. It clung to my skin, smothering me.

"Fucking hell," I ground out. "And you claim to know me? What do you know of loss? You came here to hide away after one small setback. You still have your career."

Emma stood with the dignity of a queen and stepped away from the table. "Nice. I see we're at the lashing-out segment of our argument."

"What do you expect me to do?" I shot back, desperation and anger making my words sharp and fast. "When you paint me as a coward?"

"I don't know." She waved an exasperated hand. "Maybe step back and really take a look at what you're doing. You were so brave to retire. Brave and strong—"

"It wasn't bravery. It was fear."

"Bravery is being afraid and still doing what needs to be done."

"Platitudes. Great."

Emma glared, her face flushing. But I pushed on.

"How can you not see? I'm doing this for us. I'm trying to be someone who can hold his head up and be fit to stand by your side."

It was as if I'd slapped her. She literally rocked back on her heels before standing straight. She took a moment to answer, and when she did, her voice was slow and steady.

"You seem to think a relationship is all about how much fame and recognition you can bring to the table. That isn't what I want. That was Cassandra. And I'm sorry she made you think that's all there is."

"That's not . . ." I trailed off because I didn't know if what she'd said was true. And it frustrated the hell out of me. I needed her. Just her. Not Cassandra, not anyone else. I thought Emma understood me on a soul-deep level. How could she not see how much I needed this chance?

"For better or worse," she said, cutting into my thoughts. "In sickness or in health. Isn't that how it's supposed to go?"

I couldn't meet her sad eyes. I wanted to shout. Inside I was breaking, crumbling along with her words.

"You once told me that I shined," she said. "And that nothing could change that. Not a loss of a role, not a setback. Why can't you see the same in yourself? Because you do, Lucian. You shine so bright—"

"That's what I'm trying to do, damn it! You told me I was hiding away at Rosemont. You were right. I'm trying to change that."

Panic crawled along the edges of my soul.

"Lucian . . . God. Why can't you see? I . . ." She lifted her hands, then dropped them, as if in defeat. "I don't know what to say anymore."

The finality of her tone chilled me to the core.

"So that's it? You're dumping me?"

They'd all left me. But she had stayed. I'd expected . . .

"No, Lucian. I'm not going to leave *you*. I'm telling you how I feel. That the idea of you doing this terrifies me and breaks my heart." She pressed her fist to her chest. "This is your choice. You decide where we go from here."

"Sounds an awful lot like an ultimatum to me, Em."

Logically, I knew she was right. About all of it. But my heart? My heart said I needed to try. I was supposed to follow my passion. Jean

Philipe had known. He'd warned me I wouldn't be content unless I did my best to keep what I loved close. He'd been right; I'd been broken when I left hockey. *If I could have that and Emma, I would be whole.*

Emma's soft voice drifted over the rift between us. "I'm not saying do this or else. I'm saying choose. Choose the life you want, but don't be surprised if the people who care for you can't stay and watch."

———

Emma

As soon as I was in the safety of the guesthouse, I leaned against the door and sobbed. Great wrenching sobs that wracked my body and made me heave. I stumbled into the bedroom, found a box of tissues, and curled up on the bed to cry some more.

The floodgates had lowered, and there was no stopping it. My soul ached; my heart cracked open. It fell in sharp shards to cut deep. I could feel myself bleeding on the inside, icy rivers of pain and regret.

He was going back to the sport that might kill him. Might destroy his mind.

I wanted to cling to him and beg that he stay out of this, stay safe. And I wanted to scream and kick him for his stubborn stupidity, his willful arrogance. Only I'd seen the desperation in his eyes, the pain. He was crumbling, too, and nothing I said or did would alter his course. He'd only dig in deeper and resent me even more for it.

He'd said he didn't want to lose me. But he'd already killed a significant portion of what we were. He didn't need to choose me over life—I would never ask that of him. But he chose to play Russian roulette with his life. How was I to watch that?

And that was the first lie that I'd told him. That I wasn't leaving him. Because I couldn't stay and watch this. I couldn't.

I loved him. Every inch of him. It was the purest, best feeling I'd ever experienced. And it was the worst. A terrifying free fall without a parachute.

The ground was rushing up at me now, the inevitable settling in with bone-numbing certainty. Someone once told me that as soon as your life becomes perfect, fate will find a way to mess it up. Fate had come calling, over and over again; that bitch had knocked my feet out from under me.

Another guttural sob tore from me, and I doubled over, wrapping my arms around my middle in an attempt to hold in the pain.

A warm hand grasped my shoulder, and I startled, blinking up to find Lucian hovering over me.

"Em . . ." His voice broke on my name as he looked me over. "Baby."

I wrenched away from him, horrified that he'd found me like this, not wanting him to see. But it was too late. He crawled into bed and gathered me close. "Em . . . don't—"

I covered my face with my hands.

Gently, he eased my wrists down. "Emma. Honey . . ."

"No." I didn't know what I was saying. Only that I wanted to hide.

"Yes. Look at me, Emma."

He ducked his head, met my gaze with his sorrowful one.

My lip trembled. "I just . . . I just . . ." I looked away, tears blinding me.

But he knew. Of course he knew. Lucian knew me on a level that no one else had managed to get to.

Holding my hands in his, he bent down and kissed me. I resisted for a breath, then gave in, surging up to meet him. His lips moved over mine, giving and comforting. He kissed me again. And again. Like penance. Like absolution.

One hand found its way to the back of my neck, holding me there. Gentling me. I let him take over, take me, slowly working the clothes off my aching body, stroking my raw skin with easy touches, as though he were mapping each curve to store in his memory.

He kissed me like it was his last taste and his first. And when he eventually pushed inside me, we both sighed, my lashes fluttering closed so I could just feel.

He made love to me in the cool, dim room, worshipping me with his body, his hands, his mouth, giving me everything. And when I couldn't take any more, when I begged for release, he eased me into it with quiet kisses, slow thrusts.

And he broke my heart all over again. Because I'd never been loved like this. Never been touched like I was both utterly precious and completely necessary.

I held him while he came in deep shudders that rolled through him. Lucian hugged me close, his breath unsteady and warm upon my skin. For a long moment, neither of us spoke, but when he finally did, it came out in a ragged whisper against my cheek.

"I'm sorry, Em. I'm so sorry."

He was sorry. But he wouldn't change his course. And now, neither could I.

CHAPTER THIRTY-SIX

Lucian

Everyone was pissed at me.

Mamie wouldn't look me in the eye. A few days after I'd told her I was going back to hockey, she'd taken Tina and Sal and gone to Paris for some "rest" and shopping.

Anton, of all people, had shaken his head and muttered about idiots. We hadn't spoken in weeks.

And now Brommy. He skated at my side, his jaw ticcing, eyes hard and focused. Ordinarily, he'd be cracking jokes, gliding around in circles until Rickman told him to get his fucking act together.

When I'd joined the team for an early practice session during training camp, you could have heard a pin drop for all the shock in the room. But most of the guys had quickly rallied, welcoming me back with open arms. I knew I was there only on a tentative basis. We'd play it by ear as my agent hashed out things with management.

Technically, I had one year left on my contract. There was a bunch of legal rambling, but the short of it was they could pick me up or drop me. I didn't think about that bit. I was on the ice again, suited up and feeling good. Physically, at least.

I glanced over at a sulking Brommy. "Just say whatever it is you're going to say, and get it over with."

Brommy glared at me. "All right. This is stupid. Fucking moronic. Shit, Oz, I thought you knew better."

Prickling heat crawled up my throat. "I know what I'm doing."

"Like ass you do." He shot ahead, traded a few slap shots with Linz, then met Hap at the goal to talk shit with him. We waited for Dilly, our offensive coach, and his assistants to call drills.

Grimly, I called for a puck, and an assistant tossed one over. Ignoring the rest of the field, I did my own thing, working through various patterns. But all too soon, Brommy was at my side again.

"What does Emma say about all this?"

Emma. Just her name had the power to slice me open.

She hadn't left me; I'd left her.

For two weeks we'd pretended that nothing had changed. We barely kept our hands off each other. There was something almost frantic about it, a desperation to get as close and as deep as possible during the time we had left to ourselves. She sassed and teased me, made me laugh every day. I fed her pastries and gâteaux, loving the way she moaned and devoured them like she often devoured me, with utter abandon and lusty glee.

But it was an illusion, and we both knew it. One that broke when she took me to the airport.

"I have to do this," I told her. "I don't want to spend the rest of my life wondering 'What if?'"

"I know." But her eyes were dead, her spirit already slipping away from me.

"This isn't goodbye, Em."

Her lips wobbled then. But she didn't cry. She hadn't cried since the night I'd found her curled up on her bed. Her smile was brittle, a stranger's. "Let's just call this *until we meet again*."

It had felt like death.

We still talked. But our calls were becoming less frequent. I was in DC, practicing and getting scanned, poked, and prodded every day. She was in LA, moving into her new house—that perfect house with a kitchen I ached to give a test run—and occupied with her own meetings and prep for her upcoming role.

Irked at Brommy, I scowled. "Don't bring Emma into this."

"Why not? She's your girl, isn't she?"

My fist tightened. "Fuck off, Brom."

He made a sound of annoyance, but I didn't care.

I missed her. I missed her with a strained yearning that had me looking around corners, hoping to catch a glimpse of her wide smile. I missed the feel of her warmth, the fresh sweet scent of her skin, the sound of her voice.

I ached for Emma.

This is hockey life; you're often away from the ones you love. Everyone on the team deals with it.

I don't want to deal. I'm tired. Fucking exhausted.

Without warning, the image of a kitchen flashed in my mind. Sunlight gleaming on the marble counters, the scent of baking bread in the air, and delicate red roses dancing along the edges of the windows, thrown wide open.

It wasn't Mamie's kitchen, I realized with a jolt. It was Emma's.

The kitchen that could be mine as well. It had been there in her eyes, that promise, the question she hadn't asked. Because I'd thrown a puck into the glass and shattered it all.

Grunting, I shook my head and focused on the now. My dream. My passion.

"I'm doing this," I said to Brommy. "You can either be part of it or not, but I'm back."

He bared his teeth, all but snarling at me.

"You got your grille fixed," I said.

That drew him up short, and he peered at me, as if I was totally clueless. "Yeah, Ozzy. I got my grille fixed. You know why? Because my dentist said the gap would start affecting the rest of my teeth. So I did the smart thing and fixed it."

"Subtle, Brom."

"I like to think so." He glared downfield, then sighed. "Fuck. Do what you want, Luc. Stupid as it is." He glanced at me with a slanted smile that held little humor. "I love you like a brother. So I'm going to worry about you like one. You got that?"

"Yeah, I got that." I gripped my stick. "Love you too, you big fucking bear."

Whistles blew, and we got down to business.

And it was awful.

"Oz, get your head out of your ass," Dilly shouted, red faced and likely straining something important.

I'd missed three passes, fumbled a shot. My game was off. Way off. I found myself thinking about flavor combinations instead of breakout patterns. Every time I got near the boards, a cold sweat broke out over my skin. I skated tense, waiting for a hit that never came. Because the guys were taking it easy with me.

It would get better, I told myself. But I was having a hard time believing that.

———

The next day was worse.

The press had gotten wind of my "interest" in returning. They swarmed like flies to fruit. Had I missed this? I couldn't fathom why as I dodged endless questions pelted my way and the incessant flash of cameras. Not for the first time, I missed the warm hum of the kitchen, the feel of a whisk in my hands, and the knowledge that I was in complete control.

In the privacy of a bathroom stall, I lost my breakfast, my hands shaking like autumn leaves. On the ice, I held back when I should have attacked. My mind kept drifting, wondering about Emma, worrying if she was eating all right, wanting to be with her.

This didn't feel like love or freedom. It felt like work. Worse. It felt like a farce. The end of the day was a relief.

"Hey, Drexel," I called to the forward as he exited the showers and headed for his locker across the way. "You going out tonight?"

Brommy was hooking up with a woman who'd been hanging around watching practice all week. I had similar offers, but I was still Emma's. I would always be hers. But that didn't mean I had to stay inside my hotel room all the time. Drexel and I used to hang out a lot after practice. We'd go to a bar, watch some sports, and talk shit.

He shook his damp head, scattering water droplets. "Can't. Gotta go home to Sarah and my little guy."

"That's right. You had a kid."

That was all it took for Drexel to show me multiple pics of his five-month-old, a chubby baby with ruddy skin and enormous brown eyes. I feigned interest, but on the inside, I ached.

Drexel left, and the locker room grew quiet. Everyone else had long gone home. My *home* was in California, likely swimming in a pool that stretched before a kitchen window where I could keep an eye on her while I kneaded dough or tempered chocolate.

No. *No.* My home was here. I'd made the choice. This was my life now. All I needed was time to get back into sync with everyone else.

I felt like vomiting again. I couldn't keep much down anymore. It was as though my insides were filled with sludge. Closing my eyes, I felt the various aches and pains that came with performing a sport at the top level. My thighs burned in protest and fucking screeched whenever I flexed them. My back killed me when I tried to straighten. But that sort of pain was expected. It was part of the life.

You don't have to hurt.

341

But who would I be?

You'd be hers. You'd be free. You'd be happy.

Blinking at the floor, I almost didn't hear the text when it came. Absently, I pulled my phone out of my bag and read it.

EmmaMine: I thought of you just now. The sun is shining through the kitchen windows and illuminating the countertop. I remembered that time at Rosemont when you were assembling those Earl Grey and lemon creme macarons, and the light hit your face just so. That fierce, stern face of yours, so wrapped up in the moment of making that perfect, delicate bite of pleasure that you barely blinked.

I swallowed convulsively as the next text came.

EmmaMine: It was art. It was love. You never admitted it, but I knew in that moment that you loved making people happy through your food. And I never told you how cared for I felt when eating your creations. How alive I felt. You woke me up, Lucian. Made me see that life was in the moment, not some distant dream.

The screen wavered in front of me, and I blinked hard, my chest aching so badly I couldn't breathe. She was right; it was love. But not just for the food. It was a labor of love. For her.

EmmaMine: Maybe I shouldn't be telling you this in a text. Maybe I'm just feeling melancholy. The days are long here, and work is . . . work.

Her texts stopped, and my heart thrummed, my fingers itching to respond. I couldn't move. Inside, I was splitting in two. I needed . . .

Another text pinged.

EmmaMine: I just wanted to say, whatever may come, knowing you, just as you were at Rosemont, was the best thing that has ever happened to me. You are a good man, Lucian. You always were.

My body went icy cold, then flushed burning hot.

When I thought of Emma now, it wasn't in visuals but in feeling. The satin softness of her skin, how I loved to stroke her, touch her just so I could assure myself she was real. I thought of the way she would kiss the spot at the crook of my neck and breathe me in like she was memorizing my scent. I heard the husky sound of her laugh in my ears and the way it always made me smile and sent hot lust licking over my skin. I thought of the way we could talk for hours and never run out of things to say. Of how she felt curled up against me in the smallest hours of the night, resting her hand over my heart like she'd protect it even in her dreams. And I'd pull her closer, aching with tenderness, knowing that I'd been given a gift.

Emma Mine. But she wasn't anymore.

I tried to hold it down, but I couldn't. My legs gave out from under me, and I crumpled. Curled up against the hard edge of the lockers, I cried as I hadn't done since I was a child. Every ugly, fearful feeling poured out of me in choking sobs, leaving me empty and alone on the damp floor.

Brommy found me a while later. "Aw, hell, Luc."

"Please don't say 'I told you so.'" I rested my head in my hands as he took a seat next to me.

"I won't say that." His shoulder pressed into mine. "All right, Oz?"

"Fuck you."

"So . . . no?"

A weak laugh escaped, and I ground the heels of my hands into my eye sockets. My head throbbed, a low-level pulse that I knew would grow into a full-on flare-up soon enough. "I'm so fucking stupid."

"Told you that weeks ago."

I glared at him balefully out of one eye. "I thought you weren't going to say 'I told you so'?"

"I don't believe I used those words." He grinned, but his gaze was sympathetic. "Talk to me, Oz."

"All this time, I thought if I just had hockey again . . ." I trailed off with a slight shake of my head.

Brommy nodded but didn't say anything. He didn't have to.

"I thought it defined me."

"I hope to God that the whole of my existence isn't reliant on hockey," Brommy said darkly but with a tinge of humor that made me smile tightly.

A wave of loneliness and longing rushed through me. "Emma tried to make me see it. She told me I was worthy without hockey. But I clung so tightly to this fucking illusion . . ." I ducked my head. "Fuck, Brom. I hurt her. I killed something good between us. And she . . ."

"She loves you."

The word struck through my heart and had me flinching.

We'd never said we loved each other. There were times I thought she might love me the way I loved her—all-encompassing, with my whole soul. But she'd never uttered the words. Then again, I hadn't either; it had been too raw, the wrong time, given that I was leaving her.

I left her. And she let me go, let me slip away. Because that was the choice I made. Not realizing that without her, life was nothing more than flat days and empty nights. I should have valued her over a dream that was nothing more than pride and fear. I needed to respond to her text. But what I had to say had to be done face to face.

I stood and rolled my shoulders to ease the tight ache in them. Oddly, my body felt lighter and easier than it had in weeks. Brommy wore a smug smile as he watched me.

"You gonna miss me, Brom?"

He laughed. "Naw. You aren't out of my life. You're just going home."

Home.

That was exactly where I was going.

CHAPTER THIRTY-SEVEN

Emma

Life was . . . fine. It was fine.

I had a career-making role, meaty and intense. A cast and crew that worked well together. I had a beautiful home that was all mine. It was perfect. Filled with light yet cozy and secure.

Technically, I had a boyfriend, whom I loved. Even if that boyfriend was in another city, off on a job that could . . . I sucked in a sharp breath and curled up on my bed.

I didn't want to think about Lucian. I would only end up crying. And I'd done enough of that.

It had been my intention to break things off with him. But I couldn't do it. Hockey was twined so tightly with his sense of identity that he was lost without it. Would I have done any differently if given a chance to get back an intrinsic part of myself? How could I hold that over his head?

I loved him. And if it meant letting him follow his dream, even if it left me behind, then that was what I would do. So I had let him go, holding back any pleas to make him stay. Whenever I was with him, I treasured the moments we had instead. But inside, I was crumbling.

Worse, he hadn't seemed to notice we were drifting apart. He hadn't responded to my texts. God, that hurt. I'd probably freaked him out. Or maybe even pissed him off.

Well, too fucking bad. Was it too much to expect a reply? Even if it was something as simple as a thank-you? I'd have settled for that. Shit. I didn't want to settle. For anything. *I shouldn't have to.* The painful truth was staring me in the face; I had to end it with him. I couldn't go on like this.

With a sigh, I sipped my wine and stared blankly at the Moorish-style ceiling that stretched overhead. It was really quite beautiful. And I couldn't enjoy any of it—not the house, not the role, not my life.

Night had fallen, the weather crisp, but not too cold to prevent me from leaving the double doors leading to my balcony open. In the distance, light reflecting off my pool created wavering blue shadows on the walls.

I closed my eyes and tried not to think of him. It didn't help that Édith Piaf began to sing about no regrets. Because I had oceans of regret when it came to Lucian. The music swelled and clutched at my throat with bittersweetness. Trumpets blaring in an insistent charge, strings soaring with hope.

My eyes flew open. I was hearing music, not imagining it. Lurching upward, I stumbled out of bed and flew to the balcony.

He stood at the far end of the pool, hands low on his hips in that arrogant stance of his, staring up at me in challenge. So much fucking swagger.

I should have been pissed. Yelled at him for his absence, his stubborn insistence, his silence.

Instead, a smile burst over me, tugging at my lips, lighting up my insides. For better or worse, this man would always light me up, make me feel alive. "You gonna stand there all night, Brick, or are you going to strip for me?"

His answering smile was pure and free. "I was kind of hoping you'd join me, Snoopy."

I pushed away from the balcony and dashed down the stairs, running to him. But as soon as I got within a few feet of him, I found myself halting, my skirt swaying around my knees.

We stared at each other in silence as Édith began to sing a jaunty "Milord."

Lucian's expression grew strained, a mix of regret and pained tenderness. It pierced my battered heart.

"You're here," I croaked. Why now, and for how long?

As though he'd heard my unvoiced questions, he gave me a small tentative smile. "I got your text."

"Funny, I didn't get a reply."

"Some things need answering in person."

My lips wobbled dangerously. Afraid I'd sob, I made do with nodding once.

Lucian's gaze softened. "I realized something, Em."

"Yeah?"

"Yeah." He took a step closer. "I realized I never told you . . ."

"What?" I whispered, my breath coming short.

"I love you."

They flowed over me, those words, sweet and warm. My heart skipped a beat, then started pounding. It was my turn to respond. I knew I should. But my mouth couldn't move.

Undaunted by my frozen state, he continued to speak, soft but insistent. "For a long time hockey was my love. Somewhere along the way, that love twisted and became more about my ego. About stats and fame. You were right; I thought it was what everyone valued about me. Even when they told me it wasn't."

He rubbed the back of his neck like it hurt. "I loved you, Em. Almost from the beginning. But I didn't love me."

"Lucian . . ."

"I don't regret going back." The corners of his wintergreen eyes creased in a pained expression. "I found clarity there. But I do regret leaving you."

The ground felt unsteady beneath my feet. I didn't know if he was here to stay or simply to reassure me that I was loved. Even if this was the end, he needed to understand a few things as well.

"I love you too, Lucian. So much."

He swayed, as though absorbing the words, and his smile grew. "I had hoped for that."

"How could you doubt it?" Even though I had doubted him too.

He took another step. "Because I've been pretty much a dumbass this whole time."

"Oh, I wouldn't say that . . ."

"I would." Lucian stopped right in front of me. "Em, I was lost. I thought everything that made me who I am had been taken from me."

"I know." I wanted to hold him, protect him, this big strong hurting man of mine.

But he didn't look hurt or lost right now. He looked at me with a new light in his eyes.

"I was wrong. Yes, I'd lost hockey. Yes, it fucking hurt. But I'm not that man anymore."

"Who are you, then?"

Lucian cupped my cheek with his warm hand and tilted my face up to his. "I'm Lucian, Brick, honey pie, the man who loves Emma, Snoopy, honeybee with all his heart. And I'm not going back. I'm staying right here."

A sob tore from me. He hauled me close and hugged me tight, his lips pressing against my hair. "I'll always love hockey, but it isn't what I want anymore."

Tears blurred my eyes, and my throat was thick, garbling my words. "What do you want?"

"You." He ducked his head and met my gaze. "I want to go to bed with you and wake up to you. To talk to you every day about everything and nothing. I want to bake in that kitchen, make you tempting treats, and watch your pretty face light up when you taste them."

He shook now, his hands combing through my hair. "I want to be the pastry chef at Delilah's restaurant or have a place of my own. Travel the world with you. To tell you how much I love you every fucking day of my life. I want . . . I want to come home, Em."

Laughing and crying, I stood on my toes and kissed him. And he kissed me right back, devouring my mouth with slow strokes. I melted against him, soaking up his warmth, the sugar-and-flour scent of his skin.

"I left you, Emma, without saying that you are everything to me. And I'll be sorry for that until my dying day—"

"Don't be. You came back."

"I had to. You're my heart and soul." His lips touched my cheek. "I'm not lost anymore, Em. You found me, and I'm never letting go."

Happiness bubbled and flowed between us, my heart molding itself back together and swelling with a sense of peace. Life was good. No, life was finally beginning. Threading my fingers through his silky hair, I leaned back and met his smiling eyes.

"Welcome home, Lucian."

EPILOGUE

Lucian

"Hold still."

Emma squirmed again, her lush lips curving in a smile as she gazed up at me coyly. "But it tickles."

My dick pulsed, sheer lust twisting my insides up in knots. But I kept my hands steady. "Almost there."

I piped another series of rosettes along the curve of her breast, heading for the pretty little pouting nipple, now deep pink and stiff. Her breath hitched, and I gave her a wicked smile. "Be good, or I won't lick it off."

"Liar. You can't wait." She was laid out on my bed, wearing nothing but the lemon-buttercream flowers and swirls I'd decorated her lovely body with.

"Guilty as charged." My mouth actually watered with the need to taste her, mix her flavors with my cream. Fuck up into the tight, silky-hot clasp of her body, where it felt like both home and the best pleasure I'd ever had in my life.

My hand shook a little as I circled her perky nipple, choosing to highlight rather than cover it. Emma bit her bottom lip, her lids lowering as she subtly arched into the tip of the pastry bag. Heat rippled through me, and I tossed the buttercream aside.

"Now, where to start?" I wanted it all at once. Every delectable inch of her. Always. All the time.

Impatient and aching, I stroked my shaft, keeping the hold light lest I blow now. Because nothing looked more delicious than Emma Maron spread out before me, smiling in that way that said she was all mine.

Happiness warred with lust, making for a heady cocktail in my veins. I had Emma right where I wanted her—with me. Everything else took a back seat to her and the way she watched me palm my dick, all greedy need and anticipation. It fueled my own.

"Lucian . . ."

"Yes, honeybee."

Her gaze narrowed. "I'm going to move."

"You wouldn't dare."

"Then you better come and eat me up."

I growled low in my throat and bent over her. The tip of my tongue touched down on her knee. Her creamy skin prickled as I slowly licked a path along her thigh.

She whimpered so sweetly.

I found her belly button and sucked.

"Shit," she said with a hiss of pleasure, her skin flushing rose. I grinned up the length of her body, then kissed her belly before tracing the fleur-de-lis on her hip. "Lucian . . ."

"Yes?" I nipped her waist.

She wiggled. "You know *what*."

Her dark tone had me chuckling. Her luscious cunny, all swollen and wet, waited half-hidden by the elaborate rose I'd piped just above it. I knew she wanted me there. She'd have to wait.

"I'm going to get you for this," she promised just above a rasp.

"I'm counting on it. Now hush, and let me do this, woman."

Her answering growl had me smiling again. I crawled over her body, holding myself over her on my hands and knees. She panted lightly, glaring up at me. But there was only impatient heat in those pretty eyes.

"Hello," I said, suppressing another chuckle.

"Asshole."

"Now there's a place I didn't cover. Maybe I should."

"Maybe you should—oh!" She gasped and bucked as I leaned down and lapped at her breast, flicking her nipple. God, she tasted good, sweet woman and creamy lemon. I sucked her deep into my mouth, loving the way she groaned and writhed.

Not letting go, I pulled back, tugging at her breast until her nipple freed with a decadent pop. Then moved on to her other breast, taking my time, nuzzling and licking until my lips were covered in cream, and she begged and whimpered for more.

A dollop of lemony confection slid down the plump curve of her pretty tit, and I chased it with my tongue, slurping it up, licking her nipple once more because I could. And then I did it again.

Her arm wound around my neck, urging me farther down. "Get messy with me, Lucian."

She was beautiful, flushed and fevered with her need.

"Yes, ma'am." I eased over her, my dick finding her waiting sex, and pushed into that perfect spot. We both groaned, our bodies sliding on slick buttercream. My mouth found hers, and she devoured me, her thighs clasping my hips, body working with mine.

I thrust deep and steady, reveling in the feel of her. It felt so good my body flared hot and cold and hot again. "I fucking love fucking you."

But that wasn't the only truth. I loved *her*.

I loved her so much I ached with it.

Pink lips parted, expression almost pained yet tender, she cupped my cheek as we moved together. "Lucian."

Just my name. Just her. All I ever needed.

I made love to Emma all night, tumbling and rolling about in bed, licking and sucking and laughing with her. We got so messy it took two showers just to get clean. Then we did it all again.

When the sun came up, we were on the floor, wrapped up in a comforter. Emma's hair stood out at odd angles, so adorably mussed that my heart flipped over at the sight. There were days I couldn't believe she was mine. But I'd never take her for granted.

Emma opened her eyes and instantly focused on me. A smile spread over her face, transforming it from beautiful to breathtaking. Because that look of love? It was all mine too. "Hey, you."

"I love you," I said in return. "Have I told you that lately?"

"Every day." She touched my temple. "And with every treat you set in front of me."

I'd been baking and creating nonstop lately—as soon as we'd moved into our new house, which we'd christened La Vie en Rose. Which really didn't fit for a house, but Emma had declared that she would always think of me when she heard that song. And since I thought of her when I heard that song—remembering the exact moment I stripped for her while it played, a part of me knowing even then that she would come to be my everything—the decision was made.

I'd been trying out dishes for Black Delilah, where I'd soon be chef de pâtissier for an excited Delilah. Turned out we worked well together. Since we were both headstrong and opinionated, it might have been a disaster. But I loved her creative vision, and true to her word, she gave me the freedom to express myself.

Emma was often on set now, playing the part of Beatrice in a role that would, without a doubt, make her a superstar. She came home exhausted every night. I would feed my girl and then tuck her up in bed and love her for as long as she'd let me.

Now, however, we were in danger of running late. With a grunt, I got up and winced. "Next time, we're staying on the bed."

"Hey, you were the one that rolled off of it." She stood as well and grimaced. "Okay, you're right. That was a monumentally bad idea."

"Let's take a hot shower, but then we have to hustle."

Today was Mamie's seventy-sixth birthday. After months in Paris, she had arrived back at Rosemont yesterday. We'd planned a family party for her on the terrace, and Emma and I needed to pack up the gâteau Saint-Honoré I'd made for her.

By the time we arrived at Rosemont, Tina and Sal were on the terrace putting the finishing touches on the table. Turned out they had decided to make Rosemont a bed-and-breakfast, but for people who needed refuge and healing. It would run from September to just before Christmas.

"Let me see," Tina said, reaching for the pastry box. Carefully, she took it to the kitchen and opened it up. "Ah, there it is. Hello, lovely. I will be introducing you to my belly shortly."

It was a simple gâteau with a *pâte feuilletée* base topped with a piping of vanilla *crème pâtissière* and ringed by caramel-covered pastry puffs filled with hazelnut *crème chiboust*. Emma called it my most creamiest of creamy desserts.

Sal smacked Tina's hand away from the box. "Stop talking dirty to it. You'll have your chance later."

"No one wants to hear that later either." Anton strolled in and cut his sister a reproachful look. "If you put me off the Saint-Honoré, I'll leave a toad in your bed later."

Tina's nose wrinkled. "What are we, twelve?"

"You two might as well be." I took the gâteau and put it in the walk-in wine fridge to keep cool.

"Like we don't know about the weird cream kink you and Emma have going," Tina said.

I glanced at Emma, and she lifted her hands. "Hey, I've never said a word. You know, about our kink."

Chuckling, I shook my head.

"You didn't have to say anything, love," Sal said. When I cut him a quelling look, he quirked a brow. "What? You two were loud in those early days."

"We still are." With that, I headed back outside and found Amalie waiting.

"Ah, mon ange." She kissed both my cheeks. "I have missed you."

"Missed you too, Mamie. You're looking well."

She waved me off with casual grace, then grasped my arm. "Have you asked her?"

"Not yet." Amalie had sent me the engagement ring Jean Philipe had given his bride. The deco cushion-cut diamond ring was just Emma's style, and it meant something to me. I wanted her to have a piece of my family's history.

"Soon, eh?" Amalie coaxed. Her grin was smug. "I knew you two belonged together. I just knew."

I rolled my eyes but then shook my head with a smile. "Yes, yes, you're very smart."

Emma came out just then, pausing in the doorway when she caught my gaze and smiling wide. The climbing roses that covered the wall momentarily framed her in a wash of crimson. A sense of peace flowed over me. Not for the first time and certainly not the last. Finally, I had found myself. With her.

And life was good.

SOME PASTRY TERMS

- Chef de pâtissier: pastry chef
- Gâteau: rich, elaborate sponge cake that can be molded into shapes, typically containing layers of crème, fruit, or nuts
- Pâtisserie(s): pastry/pastries
- Brioche(s): a soft, rich bread with a high egg and butter content
- Pain aux raisins: a flaky pastry filled with raisins and custard
- Chaussons aux pommes: French apple turnovers
- Pâte à choux: a light, buttery puff pastry dough
- Éclair: oblong dessert made of choux pastry filled with cream and topped with icing (often chocolate)
- Tarte au citron: lemon tart
- Macaron: a meringue-based confectionary sandwich filled with various flavored ganache, creams, or jams
- Croquembouche: a cone-shaped tower of confection created out of caramel-dipped, cream-filled pastry puffs and swathed in spun sugar threads, often served at French weddings or on special occasions
- Saint-Honoré: a dessert named for the patron saint of bakers and pastry chefs
- Pâte feuilletée: a light, flaky puff pastry
- Vanilla crème pâtissière: vanilla pastry cream

- Hazelnut crème chiboust: a pastry cream lightened with Italian meringue
- Paris-brest: a wheel-shaped dessert made of pâte à choux and filled with praline cream. Created in 1910 by chef Louis Durand to commemorate the Paris-Brest, a bicycle race.

ACKNOWLEDGMENTS

Many thanks to the talented team at Montlake, whose hard work keeps everything running smoothly. To my editor, Lauren Plude, for her thoughtful feedback and support; my books are so much better in your capable hands. And my agent, Kimberly Brower, who always has my back.

My gratitude to Amanda Bouchet and Adriana Anders for graciously looking over my French terms and phrases. Any mistakes there are my own.

And a special, huge thank-you to my Twitter friends and followers who, when I asked if I should write a story about a grumpy ex–hockey player who woos his heroine by baking her sweets, responded with an enthusiastic *yes*! This book wouldn't exist without you.

About the Author

Kristen Callihan is an author because there's nothing else she'd rather be. She has written *New York Times*, *Wall Street Journal*, and *USA Today* bestsellers. Her novels have garnered starred reviews from *Publishers Weekly* and *Library Journal*. Her debut book, *Firelight*, received *RT Magazine*'s Seal of Excellence and was named a best book of the year by *Library Journal*, Best Book of Spring 2012 by *Publishers Weekly*, and Best Romance Book of 2012 by ALA RUSA. When she's not writing, she's reading.